D0289283

THE
MOTHERS

THE
MOTHERS

A NOVEL

GENEVIEVE GANNON

wm

WILLIAM MORROW
An Imprint of HarperCollinsPublishers

This is a work of fiction. Names, characters, places, and incidents are products of the author's imagination or are used fictitiously and are not to be construed as real. Any resemblance to actual events, locales, organizations, or persons, living or dead, is entirely coincidental.

THE MOTHERS. Copyright © 2020 by Genevieve Gannon. All rights reserved. Printed in the United States of America. No part of this book may be used or reproduced in any manner whatsoever without written permission except in the case of brief quotations embodied in critical articles and reviews. For information, address HarperCollins Publishers, 195 Broadway, New York, NY 10007.

HarperCollins books may be purchased for educational, business, or sales promotional use. For information, please email the Special Markets Department at SPsales@harpercollins.com.

Originally published in Australia in 2020 by Allen & Unwin.

FIRST U.S. EDITION

Library of Congress Cataloging-in-Publication Data has been applied for.

ISBN 978-0-06-304206-3

21 22 23 24 25 LSC 10 9 8 7 6 5 4 3 2 1

For Vivi

PART ONE

One

IT WAS A PERFECT BABY, SLIPPERY AND PINK. ITS LEGS AND arms were tucked into its body and its head was bowed as if sleeping, or praying, like a tiny pious monk. Smooth and compact, shiny and hard, it seemed to be made of resin and sat on the sort of wooden display stand that might hold a Fabergé egg, or a football trophy. But it is a sort of trophy, isn't it? Grace thought, reaching out toward it.

"Oh!"

As soon as she made contact, the baby toppled off his wooden stand. His? Hers? Grace couldn't tell, but she sensed that knocking the model baby across the examination room shelf did not bode well for their appointment.

"What have you done?" Dan asked, his voice teasing.

"I'm so tense." She closed her eyes and took a deep breath. "Why doesn't it get easier?"

He took her hand in his bearish paw and squeezed it, giving three short pumps in place of a platitude about how everything would be fine. Grace tried to return the baby to its upright position in the display stand, but it was top-heavy and refused to stay in the base, which bore the label *Twenty-six weeks*.

She stared at the baby's face, which appeared peaceful and somehow wise. She could scarcely believe that a hot-blooded version of this creature could ever grow inside her, and for a moment she wanted to scoop up her handbag and pull Dan out the door before they caused themselves any more heartache born of false hope.

Her husband inched closer to her. "You're doing it again," he said, sweeping back the stray hairs that fell in pale wisps around her face.

"Sorry, what did you say?"

"I asked if you wanted me to book those cheap flights to Tokyo. You're staring at that baby like it leaked the final exam answers to your math students."

This is how they spoke to each other at the clinic: with careful, pointed cheer.

"You know I don't set exams anymore," she replied automatically.

Grace's brow creased as she focused on righting the baby, but its slick finish meant she couldn't get any purchase on the varnished stand. "I don't want to book anything while we're having treatment."

"We have to live our lives."

"I thought we were putting all our energy into this. I don't want to give up."

"I'm not giving up. I just think we need a holiday."

"What's keeping Doctor Li?" Grace asked, looking back to the closed office door.

A cable of tension stretched from the base of her skull all the way down her spine. She rolled her head back until she heard a satisfying crack. The motion gave her a sweeping view of the Empona consultation room—the bottles of hand sanitizer, the mauve and violet decor, the poster showing the cross-section of a woman's torso that looked like a piece of meat, eerily congruent with the disposable cover that had been pulled across the examination bed like butcher paper.

The door opened and Grace whipped her hands away from the broken baby model.

"Hello, Doctor," she said hastily.

"Hello, Ardens," Doctor Li replied. "I suppose you don't want me to say it's good to see you again," she said with a wry smile.

Despite the boxy skirt and prim, tightly buttoned shirt she wore under her white coat, Doctor Li looked breathtaking, as always. Before their first appointment Grace had thought Doctor Ashley Li could not possibly be as attractive as the photos of her in magazines, when in fact the pictures had scarcely done her justice. Were it not for her plain clothes and her purple rubber Fitbit, Doctor Li could be from the distant future when aesthetic imperfections, such as weak jaws and dry skin, had been bred out of the species altogether.

"How are you today?" she asked, pert and professional.

Dan straightened his back. "Excellent, Doctor, just excellent."

He always turned into a prize student in the presence of their doctor, as if he were expecting her to reward his good behavior by pulling out a vial of magical fluid with a secretive grin and the preamble, "I only give this to very special patients . . ."

Doctor Li walked purposefully across the room to the sink, where she squirted antibacterial gel into her palm and rubbed her hands together before seating herself at her desk.

"So," she said. "We're going to try again?"

"We should get a loyalty reward card," Dan said. "Every tenth round is free, right?"

Doctor Li opened the Ardens' file. "Let's hope it doesn't come to that."

"Doctor," Grace said, pulling a folded newspaper article from her handbag, "I wanted to know what you think about trying dehydroepiandrosterone." She pronounced the compound carefully. "I've been reading about a maverick fertility specialist in London. This article says he has the highest success rate in the country. Double the national average." She held out the clipping as evidence.

Doctor Li gave a reassuring smile. "Grace, I assure you, you're getting the very best care here. Everything that can be done will be done. Studies have not been able to demonstrate any real benefit to taking DHEA."

Grace silently refolded the article and returned it to her bag. Doctor Li was as compassionate as a patient could want, but every time she scuffed into the room in pastel-colored ballet flats to deliver bad news with her standard chaser "Sometimes it just takes time," Grace wanted to shake her and shout, "Easy for you to say!"

In three weeks she and Dan would celebrate their second wedding anniversary. The happy event had taken place within a year of their meeting on Grace's fortieth birthday, and it had given her a glimpse of the dream she had all but given up on: blanket forts in the lounge room; homemade Play-Doh cooked over the stove on a rainy afternoon; piggyback rides; fairy bread; and bedtime stories told with all the voices. These were things she had always wanted, but she feared she had missed the boat—until she met Dan. She looked at him now, her shrewd, caring, grizzly bear of a husband, and felt a surge of gratitude and love. She squeezed his knee and he rewarded her with a smile. Her heart lurched. He would make such a good father.

"As this is your sixth round of treatment, I feel I should take you through the statistics again," Doctor Li said.

"We know the odds," Grace said.

Doctor Li nodded and began tapping her keyboard. "I'm going to prescribe human growth hormones."

"What?!" Dan put a protective hand on Grace's back. "Like the performance enhancers athletes use?"

"They could help improve the quality of the eggs. We haven't used them before because we don't like to pump you full of too many drugs. But I think it's time we give HGH a go," Doctor Li said.

Grace forced a smile. At home with Dan, and out with her girlfriends, she was able to make light of her age—"You know the Chinese delicacy, the century egg? Well, let's just say my eggs would be highly prized in Shanghai," she'd joke while her friends dutifully tittered—but here, in this clinic, in front of the young specialist who was one part medical prodigy, one part *Vogue* model, Grace's sense of humor deserted her and she felt worn out and thin-skinned.

She swallowed. "You think these drugs will give us a better chance?"

"I believe so," Doctor Li said. "We'll start you on your FSH injections tonight and in a week you can come back for your first blood test."

"You do think it will work, don't you, Doctor? I mean, we're not wasting our time?" Grace asked, edging forward on her seat.

Doctor Li paused a moment. "At your age these things can be tricky, but we have the very best staff and equipment here. There's no medical reason you can't have a perfectly healthy pregnancy."

Grace exhaled and smiled. "Okay."

"So, I'll see you on the twenty-eighth, and you, Dan, will have to come in too to provide your specimen."

"Ah, the sweet ambience of the deposit room," Dan said. "Every time I get a whiff of bleach I get aroused."

Grace gave a tight grin, grateful for the attempt at levity.

Doctor Li tapped the end of her pen on her desk. "Right."

"Right," said Grace.

"Right," said Dan. "Once more unto the breach."

⁓

A light wind was blowing crisp autumn leaves along the footpath when Dan slung his arm around his wife's shoulder and steered her out of the Empona clinic. It had become routine for them to walk to and from their appointments. Parking was impossible—the clinic was ridiculously busy—and taking the backstreets home to Glebe gave them a chance to digest whatever the latest appointment had wrought. They strolled in companionable silence until Grace said: "Caroline Hawkins thinks it was a grape-skin extract that finally helped her get pregnant with Jamie."

She was forever venturing theories and half-baked hypotheses for Dan's consideration. Often they were things she had read on the internet and wanted to gauge how batty—or not—they sounded in the real world.

"I wouldn't be taking my cues from Caroline Hawkins," Dan said. "Didn't you say she paid two hundred dollars for a fertility crystal reading?"

"She's a doctor."

"She's a podiatrist."

"She's also a mother. Finally."

"To a very nice little boy, even though she made George

completely rearrange the bedroom to give it a feminine energy flow. The only time I'd ask Caroline's advice about anything would be if I had tinea."

Grace laughed softly. "I know, but maybe there's a placebo effect."

"You hate all that holistic, hippie, shaman stuff."

"The placebo effect is an established scientific phenomenon."

They strolled on for a few minutes before she said: "What about blood plasma transfusions? That doctor in London uses them. The one with the queues lining up around the corner."

"The one Doctor Li said was using unproven methods?"

"But if it's your own blood how could it hurt?"

He pulled her closer. "I wish I'd known when I was buying you that bracelet for Christmas that what you really wanted was blood and crushed-up grape skins," he said. "I'd have saved a fortune."

Grace smiled. The prospect of a new piece of reproduction artillery in the form of HGH had quelled her anxiety, and in its place was sunny optimism. She touched the milky opals set in the gold chain on her wrist.

"I'm sorry about those Tokyo flights. It's just that I think if I go I'll only resent the expense. I'll be thinking about how the money could be being put to better use. I'll be tetchy. We'll fight. I'll ruin it."

He kissed the top of her head. "Okay, but I want you to ask Doctor Li before taking anything she hasn't prescribed. That's what we're paying her for. We don't want something in the pills interfering with the treatment."

"She said most supplements are fine."

"She said most supplements are benign; that's not the same thing. We're going to have a long conversation with her before we commit to anything. Only supplements Doctor Li says are okay."

"You know I'm not going to do anything dangerous."

"Hmm."

"I read about this procedure where they scrape the inside of your uterus. It's supposed to make you more fertile."

"They *scrape* it?"

"With a little implement. They go up and sort of scratch away at the lining. Some studies say it doubles the chance of conception."

"Why does everything that helps conception sound like something they'd do to get you to talk in Guantánamo?"

"Or we could try the poppy seed oil again."

A year earlier—after round three failed—Grace's fallopian tubes had been flushed with iodized poppy seed oil. It was an old way of testing fertility that had been phased out as technology became more sophisticated. A researcher had recently published a paper suggesting women who underwent the procedure had a better chance of having a baby and so it was enjoying a forum-fueled revival.

Dan stopped walking and turned to face Grace, placing his hands on her shoulders.

"I'm serious, Grace. Nothing controversial. Nothing experimental or untested. No removing your ovaries and dipping them in maple syrup because some woman from Ottawa wrote a blog post about how it worked for her."

"All right." Her voice was small.

He murmured skeptically and continued walking. "I don't want you putting yourself at risk."

"We'll do everything right this time," she said. "No cheat days. No sneaky glasses of wine. My body is a temple. A child-friendly one that serves ice cream and pipes the *Frozen* soundtrack down my esophagus." She smiled. "I feel like we're getting closer. I trust Doctor Li and the team at Empona."

The Empona clinic had achieved an almost mythological status. Its founder, Roger Osmond, was a fertility pioneer the media had dubbed "the baby maker." Like Doctor Li, he had celebrity-grade good looks. He was all jaw and aristocratic cheekbones with a high brow crowned by a straw-colored bale of hair. Eager women spoke of the clinic with hushed reverence. According to various league tables—mostly compiled by bloggers from publicly available data—Empona was the best-performing clinic in the country.

"We'll get there," Dan said, taking her hand and swinging it.

"Yes," she replied with determination, "I believe we will."

Grace shuffled out of her shoes as soon as she entered their terraced house, the cool hallway a relief after the walk home.

"I'm going to have a shower," she said, kissing Dan's cheek.

"Do you need a hand?"

"Showering?"

"With the jab."

"Oh, no, it's okay."

"I'll get dinner on," he said. "I'm going to make a curry from scratch, using only organic vegetables and spices. Let's see if it fires up your insides."

"Sounds good," she called from the bathroom, pulling her dress off over her head.

Her shoulders tensed at the sound of a crash; he'd opened the cupboard of haphazardly stacked pots and pans.

"Sorry!"

She grinned as she listened to him bang around in the kitchen and rustle the cellophane spice packets he bought in bulk from a whole-foods store in Marrickville. Grace suspected Dan liked the process of buying the spices more than actually cooking with them. The warehouse displayed a rainbow of seasonings in old scrubbed wine barrels. He loved to browse the aisles, rubbing his hands together saying things like, "I feel like an apothecary of yore restocking my powdered newt and ground dragons' eggs."

The day they discovered the store, Dan had spent almost sixty dollars on spices whose pinnacle of achievement would be to funk up the pantry with a musty smell until Grace finally cleaned them out one empty, industrious afternoon. She had foreseen this when he'd purchased half a kilo of cardamom, but it was impossible to reproach him when he was so happy, and every now and then he would be seized by a fit of culinary enthusiasm that made the expeditions worthwhile.

Grace lined up her fresh cache of drugs on the bathroom bench, then peeled off her stockings and underwear and turned on the taps. She had made it a habit to shower before the hormone injections. The drum of water on her back helped her relax. She stepped out, dripping, onto the bath mat and opened her medicine cabinet in search of deodorant. Here we go, she thought. Day One. Again.

The shelves of her bathroom cabinet looked like they belonged to someone with a flourishing antiaging obsession. But unlike her friends, it was the aging of her insides rather than her deepening lines and crow's-feet that most occupied Grace's mind. Instead of employing salicylic acid and weighing up the merits of smearing caffeine onto her cheeks, she was squinting at the fine print on bottles of maca root and taking vitamins to thicken her uterine wall. From the aerial view she had of her stomach now it appeared thick enough, poking out beneath breasts whose nipples were slowly starting to point south. She examined her face, turning her head from side to side. There was a definite softening around the jawline. And her skin was slackening. She pinched her cheek and watched its surface crinkle.

This is why we have children, she thought darkly. To distract us from the ravages of time.

Yet, she worried about aging only insofar as she feared it was an outward sign of the gradual winding down of her ovaries. She had never been vain, though she knew she had always been considered pretty. Her skin was pale and clear and her cheeks high and flushed with a natural rosiness. These features were helped along by her long, swinging platinum hair, which she mostly wore pulled back in a ponytail. But her weight dragged down her self-esteem. Childhood teasing had lacerated her confidence. The common schoolyard scars might have healed over time were it not for the cruelty of an aunt Grace had overheard one afternoon.

"You should be relieved, Fiona," the aunt had told Grace's mother, "that your daughter is too heavy to ever be a target for predatory men."

Grace wasn't so big, not really—more voluptuous than anything. Doctor Li had reassured her, when she asked, that it shouldn't affect her fertility. Still, Grace had been taught to hate the excess kilos she carried. Even now she averted her eyes from the naked body in the mirror as she rubbed cocoa butter into her arms and chest before wrapping a towel around herself. Then, guiltily, she crouched and reached into the back of the cupboard under the basin, keeping her ears pricked in case she heard Dan's footsteps approach. She slid aside a box of soap and spare toothpaste and pushed her hand through the folds of old towels until her fingertips felt the dry cardboard of an airfreight envelope. It was stuffed with bubble wrap and had a hard glass heart. She dug inside the package until her fingers closed around the small bottle with a pipette's rubber stopper for a lid.

She unscrewed the top and squeezed the stopper so it emptied itself of air, then she drew in fluid the color of earwax. Grace brought it to her nose and sniffed. It was an indefinable aroma—chemical, but also organic, like rotten fruit that was starting to ferment.

She had placed the order through an obscure website late one night in a pique of desperation. The bottle had arrived alone and unmarked, like a prop from an espionage film. The instructions on the net said to add three drops to a glass of water in the morning and at night. Grace hadn't been able to bring herself to use it, yet she hadn't thrown it away either. The website, which mostly sold regulated medicines at massively discounted prices, promised an 80 percent success rate for women who were—in their words— "reproductively challenged."

While the package worked its way across the Pacific Ocean, Grace reassured herself that she would Google each of the ingredients and if any of them sounded even mildly nefarious, she would bin the whole potion. But the bottle was plain, with no hint of what was contained within. She rolled it in her palm. On the one hand, medical history was littered with accidental successes—during her teaching years she had lectured students about Alexander Fleming and his fortuitous penicillium spores, and Joseph Priestley whose recreational enjoyment of nitrous oxide gave the world anesthetic. On the other hand loomed the specter of armless thalidomide babies and uterine tissue dissolved by primitive abortifacients.

"Grace," Dan called. "Are you all right?"

With a jerk and a shiver, Grace shoved the package back between the towels. She focused on performing the now familiar series of injections and pill-popping, wincing as she always did when the needle punctured her skin. Her rump was tender and still tinged purple where the bruising from the last battery of injections had not yet healed.

When she opened the bathroom door she smelled spices heating in a pan. Dan appeared and pressed a stemmed glass into her hand. She furrowed her brow. "Wine?"

"Apple juice. From the health food store. Nothing but the best for our blastocyst. When that little guy is implanted your insides are going to be so nutrient rich he'll grow up to be Batman."

A hundred watts of guilt radiated through Grace's body, but she hid every one of them beneath a smile. "To baby Batman." She clinked her glass against Dan's, and as the chime of the toast rang out, Grace felt almost confident. Doctor Li had shut down her plan for DHEA but offered HGH in its place. Hope was not lost. Medical science had yet more tricks in its black bag, and she was comforted by the thought that if that ran out, there was always the little glass bottle, nestled between the towels, secretly waiting in her bathroom cupboard.

Two

THE PICKUP REARED UP, BOUNCING AS ITS NOSE SCRAPED the ramp that led into the shopping center car park. Priya Laghari steadied herself against the dash, her brown eyes flicking down to Nick's phone lying in the center console.

"There's one," she said, pointing to a free space in a back corner.

The car park was a grim place, rinsed of all color by the elements and marred by graffiti. Nick pulled into the damp corner spot that sunlight never reached.

"Back in a tick," he said as he climbed out.

Priya watched her husband jog up to the cash machine, her tongue pressed against her teeth in anticipation. She waited until he was punching in his PIN before inching forward and unclipping her seat belt. There was a cold, pointed stone in the pit of her belly. For a week now she felt like it had been wearing a hole in her stomach lining. Through the imaginary opening leaked a vague but very real sense of impending doom. The feeling never left her, yet she couldn't catch what was at its root, like grit in her eye that wouldn't wash away. Suspicion. It made her twitchy.

Her hand closed around Nick's phone. He had been sneaking

glances at it all day. He'd slide it up out of his pocket and run his eyes over the screen, then shove it back in a series of rapid movements, as if she wouldn't notice if he did it quickly.

Over the years she'd almost completely rid herself of the habit of going through his phone and she felt ashamed any time she slipped into her old ways. Snooping was a hangover from a rough patch during their first year of marriage when Priya discovered he had been sending flirtatious messages to women online. Under duress, he told their therapist he'd been briefly overwhelmed by the permanency of marriage. He said he felt he couldn't talk to anyone and so he'd acted out, seeking flirtations with glossy-lipped avatars and engaging in lewd texting with anonymous women who were eager to please and expected nothing in return.

It was a temporary panic, he insisted, and one she had thought they were well past. The counseling had worked, and seven years of marriage had slipped past.

Then, just last Thursday, as he'd gotten up from the couch to make microwave popcorn while Priya was selecting a movie, she'd idly picked up his phone to scroll through his photos. She swiped her thumb over the screen, but couldn't get access. It was now protected by a PIN.

That was all it took for a seed of doubt to drop into the pit of her stomach. Within moments it had sprouted tendrils of fear. She hadn't intended to look through his messages, but now that she couldn't, her suspicion was awoken. Her cheeks flushed with annoyance that left an aftertaste of fear in the back of her throat. She counseled herself not to jump to conclusions. She would simply crack the code and reassure herself she had nothing to fear. After all, they read each other's mail and shared a bed and a bank account. What could he possibly have to hide?

Frowning, she'd tapped in the first four-digit number that came to mind: 1203. Her birthday. Nothing. Then she tried his birthday. When that didn't work, the vague annoyance began to crystallize into something resembling alarm.

She considered a few more significant dates. His mother's birthday? Their anniversary? If she got the third guess wrong she'd be locked out and he would know she'd been snooping. She was frowning at the locked phone when she heard the microwave ping, followed by the sound of the waxed bag being torn open and the patter of the popcorn being poured into a bowl.

"Perfect every time," Nick announced from the kitchen. "Leave no kernel unpopped."

She put his phone facedown back on the table, then smiled as he entered the lounge room carrying a big, brimming bowl.

"You're the kernel king," she said, with fake cheer.

He crashed onto the couch, oblivious, and crammed a handful of popcorn into his mouth. "What are we watching? Not another art house snoozer, I hope."

"You loved that baroque architecture documentary we watched last week," she said, wounded.

"You're right," he replied, kissing her. "You make me a better, more cultured man."

"Hmm," she said, shrugging off his embrace.

Ever since then, she had become a lot more interested in his phone, and he, it had seemed, had become more protective of it. This was her first time alone with it in a week.

After checking Nick was still hunched over the cash machine, she hastily tapped more combinations into his phone. They were weird things, wild guesses, like 1717, his old football jersey number repeated, and 2626, the number of his favorite player. The digits vibrated, clearing the input field and denying her access. She made a third guess: 0709 was the date he'd picked up Jacker from the lost dogs' home. Success. The phone opened with a triumphant jingle.

Priya looked up. Nick still had his back to the car. She narrowed her eyes and homed in on the large blue checks of his flannel shirt, which she swore looked bulkier than usual. Nicholas Archer was a tall, hulking man—the type of man that women in their sixties would call a hunk. He ate birdlike servings of food and snacked on boiled eggs, which he bit into like apples, because he was vain and gained weight easily. His outfit of choice was an undershirt and an open shirt. Had he been working out? She tried to think of the last time she felt his shoulders. It had been a while.

Chewing her lip, she raced through his photo album. It was a chronicle of various houses he was working on. They progressed, like a flip-book, from timber skeleton to completed home. Next she went to his apps, looking for anything with a suspicious icon. Love hearts. Lightning bolts. Flames. Something that could signify a portal to connect with the opposite sex. His selection was harmless enough. Run tracker. Bureau of Meteorology. AFL. Sportsbet.

She opened his text messages. The last one was from her.

I've confirmed Dr. Carmichael for Sunday. 11am.

They'd been trying for more than a year to get in to see Doctor Carmichael at the Empona IVF clinic. A month ago they'd received a call: she had an opening in April, and now, just as Priya's anticipation was reaching a climax, here was a new threat to her happiness.

The other messages in Nick's inbox all looked innocent enough. One from his boss, Hector, relayed the details of a house in Wolli Creek that needed a granny flat. Lee Bridges from the football club wanted a lift to Thursday night's training session because his car was in the shop (*"Fucken fan belt!"*). She slid through more names, in search of women. Lorna. Lorna? Oh, that friend of his mother's who needed a door hung. Kim B. was Lee's wife; Priya clicked open that message just to be sure.

Thanks N. Lee will bring oranges. We got a new cooler too, so no need to borrow.

All aboveboard. Priya could see Nick plucking his banknotes from the machine and tucking them into his wallet. There were many more names. But he was coming now.

She was about to stash the device back in the car's console when she spied a hive-shaped icon made of yellow horizontal bars, and a label: *Bumble.* What the hell was Bumble? Fear was scratching at her insides, but she had to put the phone away.

It looked like a finance app. Maybe something to do with stocks.

The hexagonal interface filled her head with menacing memories of that day with the wasps back when their marriage was still new. The unpleasantness of the sexting was behind them, but there was still an undercurrent of tension. The experience had taxed their love, leaving it depleted. To combat it, they had thrown themselves into renovating their house. They shared a passion for the creative, hands-on work. It had been a warm spring day. The air was full of bugs and Nick had been tearing down the back wall to the thundering sound of Metallica. When he sunk the claw of his demolition bar into the timber, a lone insect had emerged from the cavity. One became two. Two became four.

Priya, in gardening gloves, her arms full of old wood, watched on but didn't register what was happening. Nick swung the pointy end of his bar into the wall again. As the metal sliced through the dried-out boards and crumbling plaster, more of the yellow-and-black drones appeared.

"Nick, be careful," Priya had called over the blare of the stereo.

His goggles were dusted with splinters and other particulate matter. "Nick! Is that a nest? Nick!"

He hacked at the wall again, this time ripping the nest right open. The angry, buzzing swarm spewed out.

"Shit." He dropped the iron bar. "Wasps."

One minute he'd been striding around the backyard looking every bit the hero of a beer commercial, the next he was being bundled into the back of an ambulance, shrunken and white. Priya was left to pace the fluorescent hospital waiting room for thirty minutes. When the doctor gave her the okay she burst into Nick's room and kissed him all over his face.

"I'm such an idiot." His voice was a frayed whisper.

"It was hard to see the nest."

"No, not that. Well . . . not only that. The messages—"

"Sh." She laid her head on his chest.

The near-tragedy brought them closer. Nick was off work for two weeks, weak and grateful for Priya's care. As he healed, they healed. And like the venom in Nick's system, the bitter hurt Priya had felt diminished and then disappeared. Months later, she stole a glance at his phone one last time to confirm the messaging really had stopped. It was clear. Her worry was subdued and she was reassured she could trust him again. Until last Thursday.

"Ready?" Nick said, clicking in his seat belt.

"Mm-hmm."

As he backed out of the car space she slid her phone from her bag and Googled the Bumble app. A voice in her head whispered: *Please not again.*

"What the eff?" Nick's tone made her jump.

"What?" She guiltily pulled her phone to her chest.

"Chewing gum," he growled, lifting his foot up. A string of gray goo stretched from the sole of his shoe to the pedal. "Hang on."

He wrenched on the hand brake and swung open his door, scraping the bottom of his boot against the asphalt and cursing quietly to himself. "They need to do something about this ghetto."

Behind them, a horn honked. "All right!" he shouted. "Some people," he grumbled as he got back in the car.

His focus once again on the road, Priya was free to peer at her phone. Bumble, as she feared, was a dating app. Not a stock-market monitor. Not a beekeeping advisory service, as some part of her subconscious had desperately suggested. Disappointment flooded her senses.

"Shit." Nick slammed on the brakes. They both jolted forward. Two teens on skateboards sailed across their path. "Hey!" Nick yelled. They laughed. One stuck up a finger. Nick flexed his own fingers, then gripped the wheel harder. "Sorry." He placed a hand on Priya's knee. "I'm on edge. I can't stop thinking about the appointment tomorrow."

Priya raised her hand to shield her eyes from the sinking sun. "I hate it here," she said, scowling at the grease spots and stray pieces of litter rotting in the gutters of the neglected mall. The ugliness was absolute.

Alongside the dirty white mouth of the shopping center was an advertisement for a new kind of cider. Shot on the beaches of Bondi, it urged drinkers to "kick back with a six-pack." It showed a panorama of sand, waves, and an ocean pool of rippling teal. The exported images felt a million miles from the Sydney Priya knew. The glittering harbor's sails and bridge were as foreign to her as they were to the tourists they attracted, with their walking sandals and their fanny packs, eating double-decker ice creams. She looked at the ad and wished she were there, with a scoop of strawberry melting into the fluffy white sphere of coconut. Nose rouged by the sun. The beachy smell of sunscreen in the air.

"Are you still cooking something for Mum's tonight?" Nick asked.

She looked at him and instinctively pulled her phone closer to her chest. "Yes. Why wouldn't I?"

"Didn't you say you needed pomegranate molasses? Should we stop?"

Pomegranate molasses was the secret ingredient of her famous chocolate mousse cake. The first time Nick took her home to his parents, tugging her gently by the hand as she trailed behind him, his mother, Kayla, had looked Priya over with barely concealed dislike. Priya had self-consciously rubbed her arm, feeling the woman's blue eyes on her dark skin. Dangling from her hand was a bag containing a Tupperware container, which she placed on the table. When she removed the lid to reveal a passionfruit sponge cake, Kayla had visibly brightened. Priya was still unable to enter the Archer household without a baked envoy to clear away resistance.

"No. Let's not. I can't face another shopping center," she said. The specialist store where she bought the molasses was on the other side of the freeway. "I have some left over from Easter."

"You're sure?"

"Let's just go home."

When Nick eased the car into the driveway, crunching the drifts of leaves that formed each autumn, Priya stayed strapped into her seat, staring straight ahead.

"Pri," he said as he unbuckled his seat belt and swung open the door, "are you coming?"

"No. I think . . . I think I'll go see Viv."

"What for? I thought you wanted to do this cake for tonight."

"I forgot I said I'd go over there."

She unclipped her buckle and climbed across to the driver's side, hovering over the gear stick and the console where the phone was still sitting.

"When will you be back?" Nick held the door open.

"Not sure." Her eyes involuntarily flicked down to his mobile. Without a word, he slowly leaned across her and picked it up.

"You'd better get going then." He stepped back, watching her. The silence pooled between them as he studied her face, his hand on the doorframe. "Say hello for me."

Priya nodded and started the engine.

"I thought you had the big dinner tonight."

Priya's sister, Vivian, opened the door, filling the porch with the blare of cartoons from deep in the house. "Avani!" Viv shouted over her shoulder. "I said to turn that television down."

"Dinner's not until later."

"Come in then. What's wrong? You look like something's wrong."

"Let's go to the kitchen."

Priya followed her sister down the hall, stepping over dolls and Lego bricks. Viv bent, collecting a lone sock and a bib as she went. Her house was narrow and cramped and filled with the smells of tamarind and talcum powder. Vivian's firstborn had arrived forty weeks to the day after she confided in Priya that she and Rajesh were trying to have a baby. When Avani was just seven months old Viv discovered she was pregnant again.

"That's what they call Irish twins," Rajesh had said at the clinic.

"Nope," the doctor said, smiling and pointing at the ultrasound.

"Just regular fraternal twins." Shanti and Shanaya were born six months later.

Viv took Priya into the kitchen and shut the door gently behind them. "Now, sit, tell me everything." She lifted her teapot from the drying rack and spooned in some loose-leaf tea.

"It's um—" Priya stopped as Avani pushed the door open and toddled into the kitchen.

"Hello, little one." Priya smiled.

When Avani saw Priya her dark eyes widened and she hurried on unstable legs to her aunt, her chubby arms outstretched. Priya lifted the little girl onto her lap, savoring the clean smell of baby shampoo. Avani made babyish noises—"lok" and "abuk," monosyllabic attempts at talking—as she touched Priya's earrings and lips, which were painted the color of a pink tropical flower. "Puc! Puc!" the little girl said. Priya laughed as Avani investigated her with her soft baby paws.

"She'll make a mess of you. Come here, bub." Viv took her daughter from Priya and used a tea towel to wipe the lipstick smudge from her hands. Avani resisted and tried to squirm away, but Viv outmaneuvered her. "So, tell me," she said, as she rubbed her child clean.

Priya took a mandarin from the fruit bowl and began peeling it. "I think Nick—"

She was interrupted by a baby's squeal.

"Shanti, how did you get in here?" Viv asked. One of the twins was in the kitchen doorway on all fours. "They've started crawling," she said. "I'm terrified." Viv slotted Avani into her high chair, then bent and picked up Shanti. "You said you think Nick . . ."

Priya lifted Avani out of her chair and held her close. "I think he's going back to his old ways." She paused and looked at the baby in her lap. She didn't want to say it out loud, that would make it real. She hugged Avani. "It's nothing," she said. "I'd better get out of your hair."

"Don't go. Tell me what it is." Viv put her hand on Priya's arm. "The tea's nearly ready. Stay."

"It's really not important," Priya said. "Don't worry. You've got your hands full and I'm going to be late. I'll call you tomorrow."

⁓

Nick's stereo was blasting AC/DC when Priya got home, so she retreated to her studio in the back of the house, where she put on some of her own music. As the opening notes of Rayella drifted into the room she filled her lungs with air, held it, and then exhaled. Nick had rigged up speakers in the four corners of the studio so Priya could be surrounded by song as she painted. He had also helped her discover the group she was now listening to.

"There's an opening act I think you'll really like," he'd said to convince her to join him at a concert. "Promise."

Priya had been skeptical, but she went along, and when the father-daughter group had proudly raised their instruments she was touched by their resonant, mournful voices. Nick's understanding of her musical tastes and the care and thought he had put into building her private sanctuary complicated her anger. She walked over to her phone and jabbed the stop button with her finger, cutting out the music and leaving her in silence.

The space had originally been intended as an extended dining area that would stretch into their large backyard. But when he had recovered from the wasp attack, Nick had instead built Priya a glass studio so that she had somewhere to paint and forget about her day job at the auction house.

He'd fashioned a desk out of a solid piece of timber recovered from a renovation site and installed a sink so Priya could clean her brushes. Glass jars with murky green necks stood along the windowsill. Priya burned incense to hide the smell of turpentine. She sat cross-legged on the floor, anxieties stewing in her stomach, until the rumble of his rock music stopped and Nick's voice sailed out from the main house.

"Pri, time to go."

Priya remained quiet through the Archer family dinner. They had agreed not to tell his family they had booked to see a fertility specialist—a decision for which she was now doubly grateful.

She grew steadily more apprehensive as she thought of the appointment. She needed to know just how bad things were before they saw the doctor. She longed for a baby, a cousin for her nieces, but she was terrified of what Nick was doing behind her back. She watched him take a swig of his beer, his second.

"What do you say, Priya? Can I rely on Nick?"

"Huh?" She snapped out of her trance.

Her brother-in-law Scotty described the new home sound system he had just bought. "Sure could use a hand hooking it up tomorrow."

In answer, Nick shoveled apple pie into his mouth, excavating the apple filling from the calorie-laden pastry crust. "I can't, Scotty, not tomorrow, sorry."

"Sure you can. It won't take long. There's some beer in it for you."

"What's so important that you can't spare an hour for the guy who helped you refinance your house?" Nick's sister, Mel, asked. Priya and Nick glanced at each other.

"I've got something going on."

"All day?"

"I'll clear, shall I?" Priya said, standing.

Nick followed her into the kitchen, carrying plates. "The appointment's not till eleven—maybe I should go over there first thing and help him out to avoid more questions."

"If that's what you want." Priya scraped leftovers into the bin.

"I really wanted tomorrow to be a day for us and our baby."

"It's up to you." She reached into the fridge, pulled out a can of full-strength beer, snapped it open, and passed it to him.

"Pri, I'm on the light beers. We've got the appointment in the morning."

"Sorry," she said. "One won't hurt."

⁓

Nick fell heavily to sleep not long after his head hit the pillow. Priya lay awake in the dark, staring at the green bars radiating from his alarm clock, waiting for the minutes to pass while Nick's breathing grew shallow.

Once she was sure he was in a deep slumber, she eased off the mattress, crept around to his side of the bed, and picked up his phone. It was tethered to the wall, charging. She typed in his code and fumbled, panicked, when it let out a melodic tingle as it granted her access. The room was filled with a bluish glow from the home screen, and Priya cupped her hand over it and hunted through the apps for the beehive.

As she searched she felt a flash of hope it had been deleted, or that she had been mistaken. But there it was: the wicked yellow hive, squatting on the screen, full of secrets. Her stomach somersaulted.

She took a breath and clicked. A string of faces appeared before her. All fair skinned. Mostly blond. Some were marked by a blue dot, indicating they had sent unanswered messages. She stabbed one icon at random. "Collette" had reached out to Nick. *Hi. I like your dog.*

What's his name? A winking face hovered next to the question mark.

He had not answered, or initiated the conversation. Nick grunted and stirred in his sleep. At the top of the screen was a picture of his grinning, carefree face. Bastard, Priya thought.

She touched more of the blue dots, opening messages women had sent. They said things like, *Hey cutie* and *Nice to meet you, Nick,* followed by a trail of love hearts. Priya was embarrassed by how forward the women were, but she could feel the knots in her chest loosen as she worked through them one by one and discovered Nick hadn't replied to any of their advances. Still, he had downloaded the app. And what if someone she knew came across him? The thought made her breathless with rage and shame.

The last message had been opened. It arrived about 4:45 that afternoon, while Priya had been in her studio, listening to Rayella and contemplating her apparently crumbling marriage. Nick hadn't replied. Feeling nauseated, she tapped the icon next to a blond named Megan.

Megan's face filled the phone in a column of little circles, alternating with Nick's face. It was a long conversation back and forth. Priya's eyes registered words, not sentences. They popped out at her: *Sexy. Breasts. Hard. Taste. Wet. Want.* Each like a dart hitting her in the chest. She scrolled through the exchange, her eyes bulging at the sickening flirtation unfolding before her. Her throat tightened. She threw down the phone in disgust. The name was burned onto her brain: *Megan. Megan. Megan.* After a moment, she picked the phone up off the carpet and flicked through the woman's profile.

Megan was thicker than Priya around the waist, with large cantaloupe breasts that were starting to sag. Priya had been spared that so far, at least. She was thirty-seven but looked younger. Her body and face were well preserved.

Megan was tanned, beachy and sun-kissed. Her blond hair was dry, like rope, and brittle from what looked like years of applying peroxide in a home bathroom. Priya imagined it would be crunchy to touch. Her hand self-consciously went to her own very long, very thick black hair, presently tamed in a plait. She didn't like the childish look but it was a necessity sometimes. As much as she loved her long hair, it got everywhere. She removed the elastic from the end and unwound the strands, letting them cloak her as she sat on the floor hugging her knees, trying to order her thoughts. In twelve hours they had their consultation with Doctor Carmichael to see if they were fit candidates for IVF.

A voice in her head was telling her the messages were just the beginning, and that he was cheating. Get out, it said. Get out. Get out. Get out.

~

Priya woke up alone. Nick had left for his run. She fanned her arm out across his side of the mattress and imagined what life would be like without him.

Her skull felt heavy. She groaned. Her sleep had been fitful and she had overslept; soon they would have to leave for the appointment. There was no question of canceling. There had been a gauntlet of tests to even get this far—screening for hep B, hep C, and HIV. The concept of IVF didn't sit well with her, but it had been two years since they had done away with contraception and they hadn't had so much as a pregnancy scare. Nick adored his nephews and Priya's sister's girls, and enthusiastically attended tea parties with their dolls and teddy bears. Angry tears filled Priya's eyes as she remembered seeing Nick sitting with Avani, his gigantic legs jutting over her table, a tiny plastic teacup pinched between his thumb and forefinger. As hard as it was for him to admit they might need help, he had been the one to suggest that they talk to a fertility specialist.

The waiting list for the Empona clinic in Alexandria was long, so they had put their names down, then had gone for an initial consultation at a clinic in Parramatta. There they filled out a whole forest's worth of consent forms and submitted their bodily fluids for testing. A softly spoken red-haired doctor told them they would need to undergo parental counseling before the process could begin.

"Counseling?" Priya had nearly stormed out. It was bad enough she had to suffer the ignominy of infertility, but now that she couldn't conceive naturally, her capacity to parent was being called into question.

"I'm sure it's standard procedure," Nick had soothed, eager to prove himself top dad material.

They attended a session of parental counseling and undertook one unsuccessful round of IVF. The clinic had the depressed air of an underfunded public health facility, and Priya was not surprised when the kindly redheaded physician told her the procedure had not been a success. Nick was genuinely shocked.

"This is why we have to go to that good clinic," he said in the car on the ride home. "This isn't the area to skimp."

So, that's what they were doing. They had an appointment at Empona and Nick had increased the number of casual laboring shifts he did for Hector on the weekends to help pay for it.

Priya jumped as she heard the back door slam.

"Pri?" Nick called out. "You ready? Time to make a baby!"

"In a minute," she said, her voice hard. She was no longer sure if she was ready. Their baby was being put at risk by his sleazy messages. And that was the cruelest betrayal of all.

Three

GRACE DROVE HER KNIFE INTO THE KIWIFRUIT AS SHE GAZED out the window of the boardinghouse's first-floor kitchen. Students were starting to file through the iron gates, and between the bare branches of the oaks that lined the street she saw a familiar car with tinted windows pull into the drop-off zone. The girls on the nature strip pricked up, like spaniels hearing a dog whistle. The Bentley belonged to soap-star-turned-network-darling Dominic Hawke and his makeup-artist wife who sent their two girls—aged five and seven—to Corella College.

Bonnie Collings, the boardinghouse's wiry cook, came into the kitchen carrying a tray of pastries.

"If they really didn't want a fuss he'd take those little girls around to the junior-school entrance," she said, joining Grace at the window.

Grace scrutinized the famous parents as they stepped, cashmere-clad, from the creamy leather insides of their car. The details of the conception, difficult pregnancy, and *miracle* birth of Hope Harper Hawke had been strung out across various glossy pages and one teary Sunday-night television special. Now here she was, happily running toward the school in a gingham pinafore with a little sister in tow.

The smaller one's hem nearly swept the ground, and their miniature Mary Janes made Grace's heart ache with longing.

Clusters of secondary-school girls moved toward the fence as Dominic followed his daughters to the gate, where he crouched to say goodbye. His wife stayed by the car, arms folded, cool behind sunglasses.

The plastic kettle snapped, bringing Grace back to reality. She halved another kiwifruit. Someone had told her kiwis were good for fertility and so she had taken to starting each day with two of the tangy fruits. She bit into the green flesh, wincing at its bitterness, as she watched the girls in blue uniforms fill the schoolyard.

"Surveying the enemy?" Bonnie asked, handing Grace a plum danish from the pile left over from the Year Nine parent night.

"Thanks." Grace bit into her pastry. "I'm surprised Mr. Lombardo didn't hide these in the staff room fridge."

"I liberated them," Bonnie said, winking and choosing an escargot for herself.

Outside, the students drifted toward their homerooms. As usual, the older girls dawdled, carrying hot chocolate in reusable silicone cups, trying to look casual as they strained desperately toward adulthood.

Slow down, Grace wanted to tell them, knowing they would roll their eyes at her if she did.

She put a hand to her belly. The Empona clinic had performed an embryo transfer nine days earlier and now she and Dan were in limbo while they waited to see if it had worked. Secretly, Grace felt something was different this time, though she tried to bury these thoughts. She had learned the hard way that hope and intuition were difficult to separate.

"I think you're wanted," Bonnie said, nodding out the window.

The Year Twelve math coordinator, Therese Swan, was running across the quadrangle to the boardinghouse.

"Grace!" Therese arrived at the door, breathless. "Will you watch my homeroom? I just got a call from Jake's school, he's had a seizure."

"Of course." Grace stood, dusting pastry flakes from her hands. "I'll take care of it."

"Thank you. Thank you so much." Therese's handbag bounced up and down off her hip as she hurried down the stairs and toward the staff car park.

"I hope everything's all right," Grace called after her.

"It must be so hard to have such a sick child," said Bonnie.

Grace murmured agreement but didn't voice the thought that flashed, unbidden, through her mind. *At least Therese has a child.* She was mortified that she was capable of thinking such things. She pulled on her jacket and set out for the Year Twelve building, hurrying to beat the bell.

Grace had joined Corella as a young teacher, but it had been years since she had stood in front of a class of her own. Her job now was to manage the boardinghouse, but she stepped in as an emergency teacher when needed.

"Seats, please, girls," Grace said as she entered Mrs. Swan's homeroom class, scattering gossip circles.

She took the roll, then the class captain read from the daily newsletter. Volleyball practice would be moved to the gym. All girls who wanted to audition for the school production of *Lysistrata* were to meet at the drama department at lunch. When the bell rang, one student hung back.

"Can I help you, Bridget?" Grace asked.

"I just wanted to tell you I'm looking forward to the bake-off, Mrs. Arden," Bridget said, bouncing on the balls of her feet. She was a boarder who had frizzy blond hair and a gummy smile like a cartoon sun: big and beaming. "I've got lots of ideas for things to make this week."

The prizes for Grace's weekly bake-off competition in the boardinghouse were simple: a week off bathroom-monitor duty and getting to pick the movie that played in the common room on Sunday night. Once the meals had been cooked, they were wrapped in foil, and Grace and the girls took the school's minibus to the Sydney City Mission where they served dinner—usually casseroles and pasta bakes—to homeless men and women.

"When I was home on the weekend I got some ingredients I'd like to experiment with. Some truffle oil and Gruyère." Bridget grinned again. Braces gave her smile an endearing awkwardness. "Mum brought them back for me from Switzerland in a special refrigerated bag."

"Truffle oil and Gruyère? For the bake-off?"

"Uh-huh." Bridget nodded. "Mum always lets me choose a present for her to bring back, and this time I wanted food."

This was partially the reason Grace had come up with the bake-off, to foster a social conscience in the girls and squash any prejudices they might feel toward those who lacked the good fortune to be sired by lawyers and suckled by surgeons.

"If we're going to cook for these men and women, there's no harm in making something really nice. Besides, I think they deserve a little truffle oil, don't you?" Bridget said.

Grace smiled, feeling a tug on her heartstrings.

"I think that's a very nice idea."

As Bridget skipped off to her first class, Grace suddenly felt a little weepy. The fertility hormones whooshing through her bloodstream, the sleeplessness, and the hope all sent her emotions into hyperdrive. She straightened her jacket and headed back to the boardinghouse, wishing she could bring home presents for a daughter of her own.

⁓

Climbing the stairs to her office, Grace detected a whiff of nutmeg: lingering evidence of a spiced latte consumed by one of the boarders. As she took a deep breath, inhaling the aroma, she couldn't help but wonder if her senses were sharpening as her body prepared for its biggest call to duty.

It would be four more days before she could reliably take a pregnancy test. She flipped open her calendar and drew a circle around the date. They were supposed to resist taking a home test—they should wait until the scheduled blood analysis at Empona—but Grace never could. She was, therefore, glad she would spend the night at the boardinghouse, and keep her mind occupied with the bake-off.

An hour after the last bell rang for the day, the boarders filed into the home-ec rooms for the bake-off and began unpacking the ingredients Bonnie had prepared. Grace walked from station to station, supervising.

"Catherine, those curls need to be tied back. We don't want to be serving hair pie. Annika, no handling hot pans with tea towels—where is your oven mitt?"

Bridget had brought in her imported ingredients, and as the cooking got under way she added them to the other students' dishes too. In her regulation Corella College apron, Bridget twirled from bench to bench, shaking truffle oil into risottos and grating expensive cheese onto lasagna. "Would you like some Gruyère for your risotto, Catherine? Stacey, truffles?"

"Truffles? For the bake-off?" Stacey Mannix said tartly.

"I thought it would be unfair to our guests if I didn't share," said Bridget.

"They're not our guests," Stacey replied.

"Of course they are," Grace said, smiling proudly at Bridget.

"I don't want anyone to miss out," said Bridget.

"I think it's a lovely idea," said Grace, nearly giddy with hormone-charged hope.

⁓

After the food was baked and wrapped, the group was joined by Mr. Bishop. It had taken Grace a year to get the school principal, Paul Lombardo, to sign off on the bake-off, and when he finally, begrudgingly did, one of the conditions was that the head of English had to accompany the group to the Sydney City Mission.

The girls squirmed and giggled as they took their seats and the minibus pulled out of the school gates. Laura Kelk yelled as a hot ceramic dish grazed her bare thigh.

"Girls, stop being silly, please." Grace clapped her hands. "We don't want any accidents."

"Do they seem worse than usual to you?" Mr. Bishop asked. "They're a bit keyed up."

"They're teenage girls," Grace said. "They're always like this."

The Sydney City Mission manager, Glen Thwaites, met them at their usual spot in the shadow of the freeway overpass, with trestle tables lit by gas lights. The April night was crisp, but there was something cozy and campfire-like about the yellow glow cast by the lamps. Grace unpacked the dishes and began distributing plastic serving spoons to the girls, who arranged themselves along the tables and peeled back the foil from their meals, unleashing the steamy aroma of meat and onions. A shuffling line of people grew quickly, drawn by the smell. Grace could detect the earthy note of Bridget's truffles. It made her salivate and stoked her wishful faith that her ability to identify the ingredient was further evidence that her body was changing. Preparing. Every one of her cells was humming with possibility. She rubbed her hands together.

"Good work, girls," she said, smiling and jostling between them. "Larger serves, please, Catherine. That's it, let's keep the line moving. You're doing well."

They were about halfway through their supply of food when a woman in a black tracksuit approached Grace with an empty plate. "Any more of that beef casserole?"

"Let me see; Stacey made the beef. Stacey?" Grace looked down the service line, her eyes seeking Stacey Mannix's blunt fringe. "Has anyone seen Stacey?"

Nobody answered. Grace folded her arms. "Well, who's on beef casserole?"

"It's here!" Laura Kelk pointed to the girl next to her. Bridget Hennessy was digging ground beef from the corners of a casserole dish with a serving spoon, too absorbed by her task to respond.

"Bridget, where's Stacey? Isn't this her dish?"

"What?" Bridget's head snapped up.

"Are you serving beef casserole?"

"My risotto ran out."

"Then where's Stacey?"

"Um." Bridget's eyes flicked from side to side. "I think she went to the toilet?"

"Who has she gone with? She didn't ask permission."

The girls were allowed to use the bathrooms in the nearby Travelodge, but they had to travel in pairs and they had to let Grace know they were going.

"She said she told Mr. Bishop."

Grace turned to her colleague. "John, did you give Stacey permission to go to the Travelodge?"

"Stacey Mannix? I haven't seen Stacey all night."

"Are you sure? She was on the bus."

Grace flipped open her folder to double-check her list of girls who had attended that night. A quick scan of the names confirmed Stacey had been on the bus when it left the school.

"Right." Grace slammed her folder shut. "Girls, put down your spoons, please. I need to do a head count." She could already tell there were fewer faces than there should have been and at a glance she could guess who was absent. "I'm sorry, everyone, this will just take a minute," she told the crowd.

The head count revealed she had correctly predicted the three culprits who had snuck off. Stacey Mannix, Lyndsey Hornery, and Annika Whitelaw were nowhere to be seen.

"Can anyone tell me where they are?" Grace asked, her hands on her hips. The students shuffled and looked at their shoes. "Anyone?"

Grace was not surprised her question was met with silence. The three fugitives were queen bees. Owners of Kate Spade handbags and wearers of Tiffany pendants, they were more sophisticated than their peers and, consequently, revered. If the other girls knew where they were, there was no way they would give them up.

"I'll check the Travelodge," Grace said, handing her folder to John Bishop. She pressed the button for the traffic lights impatiently, doubtful the girls would be there. The city-edge hotel's lobby was decorated with dusty fake flowers and had the antiseptic air of a nursing home. She ducked into the ladies', confirmed her suspicion, then hurried back to the students.

"I'm sorry, Glen, we're going to have to pack up early," she said, prompting a chorus of disappointment from the girls.

"Not to worry, Mrs. Arden, we're always grateful for your help."

"I'll leave this food with you and collect the dishes next week."

"I appreciate that."

Grace's concern for the girls was tempered with a heavy dose of annoyance. They had snuck off deliberately, jeopardizing not just her program but the meals of the people who relied on the bake-off for a feed.

"Shall we call Mr. Lombardo?" Mr. Bishop asked.

"Not if we can help it. Get the rest of the girls back on the bus, will you? I'll see if I can track down our truants."

As Mr. Bishop herded the girls back onto the bus, Grace charged to the nearby McDonald's, imagining the runaways squeezed into booths with some boys from Fullerton Grammar. When she pushed open the fast-food joint's door, she saw almost the exact scene she had imagined, but none of the students were from Corella.

Grace half-heartedly checked the toilets, then the deserted playground. She climbed up the plastic ladder in case the girls were sitting in the playhouse with their feet up on the walls, licking soft serves. But they weren't.

Next she checked the two-story KFC across the street. It was hot and loud inside, and smelled of salt and fryers. A grotty-looking man in fingerless gloves looked her slowly up and down as she entered. Two drunk teens in high-tops and singlets crashed into her on their way out. Grace's hands moved protectively to her belly.

"Holy shit," one snickered, as they hurried away.

The girls were nowhere to be seen.

When Grace stepped back out into the night annoyance gave way to fear. The rumble of heavy trucks on the freeway overpass was monstrous and the darkness of the car park made her shiver. As Grace hurried back toward the main road, her fingers curled around her keys, taking comfort from the long, jagged form of the boardinghouse master key. She was certain the girls had snuck off, but she couldn't deny her growing fear that something sinister had happened to them. What if they had been lured away by feckless guys in their twenties? Or worse, by sleazy older men who would offer to buy them a drink at a badly lit pub. Or worse still, an actual criminal. She thought of the girls, possibly terrified, possibly hurt, all because Grace had the trumped-up notion she was an inspirational teacher. She went back to check the McDonald's again. There were no teens left in the booths. Just a mess, and a stack of pink flyers. Grace picked one up.

Under-18s Dance Party. Kobuka Club. DJ Faustus and Liz Licker. No alcohol!

She swore under her breath. The address was just around the corner.

⁓

Gangs of girls in heavy eyeliner and tiny shorts leaned against the Kobuka Club next to guys tonguing bottles of Coca-Cola. The entrance was manned by a bored-looking woman chewing gum.

"Entry is ten dollars," she said when Grace approached.

"I'm a government liquor-license inspector," Grace replied in a flash of inspiration. She entered without pausing and felt a victorious surge of power when nobody stopped her.

The club was dark and crammed with bodies. Fake smoke filled Grace's lungs. Purple laser lights forced her to squint. As she pushed through hordes of teens, sticky drinks cascaded over her arms and onto her shoes. Grace felt prehistoric. The sensation was not helped by the tenderness in her lower abdomen, which had popped out, swollen, as if she'd swallowed a small helium balloon. She laid her hand across it, fearful of sharp elbows.

Someone trod on her foot in a spiky heel. Grace's yelp was drowned by the beat of house music. Her eyes watered. She directed her anger toward the missing students.

"Stacey! Lyndsey, are you in here? Annika?"

As she forced her way toward the bar she spotted a familiar flash of blue and burgundy. Two Corella College schoolbags were sitting under a table. Grace barged over, grabbed one by the strap and opened it. Inside she found blazers, pleated skirts, and socks tucked into shoes, as well as a bottle of Escada perfume and a pink leather makeup bag with a gold tassel and the initials *S.M.* embossed on it.

She looked up and saw Stacey, Lyndsey, and Annika clutching one another, watching her with bug-eyed panic. Stacey said something inaudible, then turned and tried to disappear into the crowd.

"Girls, don't even think about it!" Grace hollered. Her voice was swamped by the thrum of the music, but the students' escape attempt was foiled by the mass of bodies. Hemmed in by oblivious revelers, they couldn't get away. Grace hauled the bags over her shoulder and pointed to the door. The girls' shoulders sank and they slouched toward the exit.

"How could you be so irresponsible?" Grace said when they emerged from the club's smoky bowels into the cool night air. "How could you be so selfish?"

Annika and Lyndsey answered in sniffles. "Sorry, Mrs. Arden." They hugged themselves, trying to cover their exposed flesh.

"Are you going to tell our parents?" Annika asked.

"I haven't decided yet," Grace said honestly.

She debated her options as she marched the girls back to the bus. She could impose a punishment without involving the parents or Mr. Lombardo, who could use an episode like this as an excuse to shut down the bake-off. On the other hand, if she didn't report it and someone found out, the consequences could be even worse.

"Hurry up, the other girls are waiting. You ruined their night too. Not to mention the people who came for a meal."

Lyndsey started to cry but Stacey had a scowl on her face, which was made up with winged eyeliner and shimmery highlighter. Her lips were pressed into a pout and she looked bored and imperious.

"I don't know what you're looking so smug about, Miss Mannix," Grace said. "I've no doubt you were the ringleader of this little escapade."

"What are you going to do, ground me? We're not allowed out of that stupid school anyway."

Annika sniffed. "It's worse than prison," she said, wiping her eyes with the heel of her hand.

Grace pondered this. Another reason for the bake-off had been to get the girls out of the dorms. Looking at the young women before her—unsteady in high heels, like baby gazelles learning to walk—she realized how short she had fallen of her goal to provide a social outlet.

"Are you really going to let all of the parents know you can't keep control of your students, Mrs. Arden?" Stacey flicked her hair over her shoulder. "That we were roaming the streets just because you think you're Mother Teresa?"

Anger flashed in Grace's eyes. "So, you were banking on me covering for you?"

Stacey shrugged, a smile playing on her lips. "Good luck convincing the parents to let you take their precious daughters out again after this."

Any empathy Grace had felt evaporated. "I am so mad, I could just—"

She froze. Every impulse halted. A secret change was occurring. She felt a shift. A liquefying. *Oh no.* A new thought dominated her mind: *Please, no.*

"Mrs. Arden, are you okay?" Annika asked. Grace could feel the color leave her face as they reached the Sydney City Mission.

"That will be all, girls. Get on the bus, please," she managed. "Can you drive, Mr. Bishop?" She slid onto the passenger seat, wrapped her coat around herself and held it tight until they reached the school gates. The girls were mercifully quiet.

She could feel a familiar pain at the base of her spine. "Mr. Bishop, could you please do a head count and then send the girls to bed?" Grace said when the bus came to a stop.

"Are you all right?"

Her voice was grim. "I don't think so, no."

~

A sob caught in Grace's throat as she raced to her bathroom and slammed the door. She locked it then pulled down her stockings. There was blood everywhere. She went to her shower and turned on the taps as hard as they would go, filling the room with steam. She cleaned herself of the yolky red mess, staying under the stream until the water turned into needles of cold. She shivered as she felt the full force of what had just happened. It was like a fist to the face, a battering ram to the breastbone.

Mrs. O'Shea, the deputy boardinghouse mistress, was on call, but the journey home was more than Grace could face. Once she had scrubbed herself raw, she crawled into bed. She would spare

Dan the sleepless night. Besides, she thought, hugging herself, the breakfast routine would give her a reason to get up in the morning.

It was a gray dawn, the sky blotted out by a sheet of cloud. To Grace, the whole world was colorless. She sleepwalked through the morning and somehow made it to noon. After the lunch bell she called Dan. When she tried to speak his name she merely croaked down the line.

"Do you want me to pick you up?" he asked, understanding immediately.

"No, you were right. We can't stop living our lives. I just wanted you to know."

"Are you sure you're okay?"

"Yes. I'll see you at home tonight."

"Grace."

"Yes?"

"I love you."

She swallowed the lump in her throat. "I love you too."

By two in the afternoon she was in so much agony she had to call Mrs. O'Shea to come in early for her overnight shift.

When Grace got home the house was empty. She lay on the couch and stared at the TV. The sense that she had caused the transfer to fail weighed heavily on her soul. Her one job was to sustain and protect her baby, and she couldn't even do that. A tear trickled down her cheek and soaked into the couch cushion.

"Grace?" The familiar silhouette of Beth's curly hair appeared at the door. "Dan called me." Grace's oldest friend stood before her, holding up her spare key.

Grace sniffed and wiped her face.

"Oh, Grace." Beth wrapped her arms around Grace's hunched form. At her friend's gentle touch, Grace let herself sob openly, mourning all the failed transfers—the potential babies she had lost, which now numbered six.

"That's right, let it all out," Beth soothed. "Can I get you anything?"

Grace shook her head. Tucking herself into a fetal ball was the only way she could begin to alleviate the gnashing pain in her womb. She refused the blue pills she knew would dull the sharp edges. It seemed fitting that her physical suffering matched her emotional suffering. This was her penance. She had failed and she wanted to feel the pain bite into her soft insides.

"You know, in biblical times Egyptian women used linens similar to the products we use now," Beth said, picking loose blond strands from Grace's face. "In four thousand years we've barely advanced at all. If men had to deal with this they'd have invented some sort of space-style laser-equipped flying machine. You'd swallow it in pill form and a highly trained crew of miniaturized military men would zap away the uterus lining."

Grace smiled sadly. "Maybe it's a good thing men don't get them. Imagine PMS weaponized."

Beth laughed harder than the joke warranted. "You'll be okay," she said, nudging Grace's chin. "You're tough. How about I make you a stiff drink?"

"I really shouldn't."

"I think you get special dispensation after the day you've had." Beth marched to the kitchen with a take-charge expression on her face. Grace was relieved to relinquish her decision-making power to her.

When Beth returned she passed Grace a weak gin and tonic and pressed two pills into her hand. "Take those," she said firmly.

Grace obeyed and washed them down with a large gulp of gin. "I should be taking care of my body. But what's the point? I feel defective."

"You're *not* defective." Beth hopped onto the couch and tucked her feet up under herself. "And one drink won't kill you."

"Don't you have to get back to your chambers? Who's keeping the murderers off the streets?"

"I've taken the afternoon off. We never get to hang out anymore."

"Hang out?" Grace looked amused.

"Yes. Hang out. Now give me your hand. You're in desperate need of a manicure."

The next morning Grace woke feeling a little less raw. She was on night duty and so was free to spend the day doing all the things that made her feel good, like the forums advised. She bought a chocolate croissant at her favorite café and ate it as she read the paper in the sun, letting the warmth recharge her.

The sky was pink as she drove up the driveway that cut through the school's green lawns and parked her car. No matter how long she had been doing it, Grace could never get over the slightly topsy-turvy feeling of arriving at the boardinghouse after all the day students had left, and the stars were starting to come out.

The sinking sun cast a soft, gauzy light on the white columns of the convent. Sports practice was finishing, and girls in shorts and knee socks skipped toward the change rooms.

"Hello, Mrs. Arden," a little voice chirped.

It was Hope Harper Hawke. She was dressed in a hockey uniform and had a hooked stick resting on her shoulder.

"How was practice, Hope?" Grace asked.

"I scored a goal."

"Did you?" Grace bent down so she was level with the little girl. Hope had her famous father's eyes but her mother's coloring—hair like gingersnaps and freckles to match.

Grace knew it had taken Hope's parents eight rounds of IVF to conceive. If they had not persisted, this little creature would not exist. And yet she did exist, through sheer force of will. She wore pink sneakers that she no doubt picked out, and sported a Minnie Mouse Band-Aid on her knee from some unknown misadventure. "I missed sometimes too," Hope said.

"Never mind that," Grace said, smiling. "You're bound to miss sometimes. The trick is to keep trying."

Four

PRIYA TAPPED HER TEASPOON IMPATIENTLY ON THE TABLETOP, willing the waitress to leave. The girl had a trainee badge pinned to her shirt and was unsteady as she lowered the brimming glasses to the table. It wobbled as she set the lattes down, causing one of them to spill.

"Oops." Her face scrunched apologetically as she pulled a fistful of napkins from the dispenser and, in her haste, kicked the table leg, which sent more coffee sloshing onto the laminate surface.

"It's fine, it's fine," Viv said, dabbing at the milky puddle and waving her away.

"What's the reason for the category-five emergency coffee meeting?" their cousin Darsh asked.

Priya waited until the waitress was out of earshot before leaning forward and saying: "Nick's been messaging women again."

"What? No!" Viv said. "He can't be."

Priya squeezed her eyes shut. "He has a dating app on his phone. He's been chatting up women. One particular woman. Which is worse, I think."

"Tell us exactly what you found out," Darsh said, placing his soft hand over Priya's.

Priya dropped her gaze, her cheeks burning. "Her name's Megan. They've been writing to each other for weeks. Sexting."

Darsh winced. "Have they . . . met up?"

"I don't think so."

"That bastard," Viv spat. "Is she in Sydney?"

"What difference does it make?"

"Well, if she was in, say, Broome, we could be pretty sure he had no intention of ever meeting her. She's just a face on a screen. A cheap distraction. Like the first time," said Darsh.

"Does it make a difference?"

"I think so. I mean, he's done this before. But he stopped."

"And now he's started again." Priya pressed her fingertips to her eyelids. "I can't stop seeing the disgusting words they sent to each other. I feel sick thinking about them."

"What do you want to do?" Viv asked gently.

Priya shook her head sadly. "When this happened the first time I swore if he ever did it again I would leave him."

"Talk to him," Viv urged.

"What will that achieve? He won't tell the truth."

"As hard as this is to hear, I think if they're just texting, it's not as hopeless as you might imagine," Darsh said.

"Sexting, not texting. And these are only the messages I know about. What if it's been going on the whole time? You know what he used to be like."

"I'm angry for you," Viv said diplomatically. "Right now I could wring his neck. But don't jump to conclusions."

"Why are you defending him?"

"Nick has always been a flirt, but we know he loves you."

"Do we?" Priya arched her eyebrow.

"People do all sorts of things online they would never do in real life. You love him, don't you?" Darsh said, looking at her with big, sympathetic eyes.

Priya threw up her hands. "How can you love someone who makes you feel they could discard you at any minute? We're about to spend thousands on IVF. How could he do this?"

"How did the meeting with the specialist go?" Viv asked.

"We're waiting to get some test results. She said in the meantime we should keep trying." Priya shook her head. "Nick has filled my phone with apps to monitor my cycle and alert me to my most fertile times."

"So, he still wants to go through with it?"

"More than ever. Nick's desperate for children."

"And what about you?" Darsh asked.

"I want to have a child. I always have."

"You don't sound sure."

"I *am* sure! But now that he's done this, it changes things." Viv bit her lip.

"In that case, I can think of another app you need." Darsh picked up Priya's phone.

"What are you doing?"

"An experiment." His fingers flew across the screen for barely a minute and then he tapped it several times, causing it to jingle.

"What is that?" Priya said finally when Darsh slid her phone across the tabletop.

"It's your Bumble profile."

"What?"

"Your name is Rose. You're thirty-two. You love snowboarding. See, aren't you cute? That's you at Jindabyne. Now you can know for sure."

Priya looked at a blond in goggles with teeth brighter than the snowdrift backdrop. "Who is this?"

"It's just some stock photo."

"You can't do that." Priya's voice went up a pitch.

"It's not harming anyone. She probably lives in Sweden, or Iceland."

Priya stared at the picture. "No. I can't." She pushed the phone back across the table. "I'd be just as bad as he is."

Viv slid it back. "This is your marriage. You won't talk to him. How else can you know how bad it is?"

Priya stared at the profile. "It's entrapment."

"Not if you trust him," said Darsh. "If you trust him, I'll delete Rose and never mention it again. But if you have doubts . . ." Darsh nudged the phone closer to Priya's hand.

"I don't think this is how adults have relationships."

"He started it. If he wasn't messing around you wouldn't be in this spot."

"But he's not messing around. He's just—"

Viv raised a brow. "What?"

Priya picked up the phone. Darsh's idea was tempting. It was a noninvasive test, a way of peeking under the hood of her marriage to check what had gone wrong without having to completely write the whole thing off. She might get her hands burned, but it was better than the engine blowing up when they were flying down the freeway with a baby in the back seat.

"I'll think about it," she said.

"Here comes the lady of the house," Stavros called as Priya pulled into the driveway. She had always liked their friendly, talkative neighbor, who waved from his position at the back of Nick's pickup. Nick was standing on the bed, gesturing to Stav and instructing him on how they could maneuver a bulky item cloaked in the wool blankets he kept in the cab for transporting delicate pieces.

Jacker barked a hello and Priya gave the excited mutt a scratch behind the ears in reply.

Nick squatted and began to heave the shrouded cargo toward Stavros, who had his feet firmly planted and his knees bent.

"What's that?" Priya asked.

"It's your new tub," Stavros said proudly, as if he had made it himself.

"I salvaged it from that ramshackle Victorian in Woollahra," Nick said, straining. "I know you've always wanted one." He stopped a moment to lift the corner of one of the blankets to reveal an old bath with lion's feet. "It needs a clean but that's no trouble. Plenty of CLR in the shed."

"You do all right with this weekend work," Stavros said. "Half of your house fell off the back of a truck."

It was true. Their brick three-bedder was embellished with found objects from Nick's side job. He had sourced and restored ceiling roses, cornices, and stained glass, which he then grafted onto their home. A slab of black granite became the surface of a kitchen island. He had rescued cabinet doors, stripped them, punched out the plywood and replaced it with glass. Hector paid him an hourly rate to lend his strong back and builder's know-how. The cash was good, but as far as Priya was concerned, the loot was better.

"You got it? It's heavy," Nick said to Stavros. Jacker circled and occasionally barked, supervising the work.

"Do you need a hand, Stav?" Priya asked, wary of the angle the tub was coming off the back of the pickup.

"We're all right."

"I don't want you injuring yourself," Nick said to Priya.

Nick's muscles bulged as the two men carried the bath across the front yard. The sight reminded Priya of his Bumble profile photo, and her emotions flip-flopped. He may have messaged those women, but he wasn't salvaging antique bathtubs for them. His face shiny with sweat, Nick looked handsome and happy, and Priya felt a pulse of possessive desire. He was grinning at her with such high-voltage pride she couldn't stop herself from smiling back.

She tightened her grip on her handbag, thinking guiltily of the Bumble profile on her phone.

"Do you want to stay for dinner, Stav?" she asked. "I'm doing a coconut duck curry. There'll be plenty to go around."

Nick whistled. "Priya's duck is pretty hard to pass up."

"Thank you, Priya, but no. You have yourself a good night. And hey, enjoy the tub. Imagine bathing little Nicky Junior in that," Stavros said.

"Yes," Priya said with a smile. "Imagine."

You told him? she mouthed to Nick when Stavros's back was turned. Nick shrugged, a grin on his face.

"Don't be too hard on him, Priya," Stavros called out. "He's just excited to become a dad."

⌒

Around one in the morning Priya woke with a jolt to a trill of ascending notes cutting through the quiet. Her phone was telling her that now was the optimum time for conception. The fertility app was illustrated with a silhouette of a baby the color of alfalfa sprouts crawling inside a black square. A cartoon curl sprang from his head. It was flashing, demanding that she have sex with her husband so that a real baby might come to life. Of all the apps he'd downloaded, this was Nick's favorite.

"Look at the cute little sprog," he had said when the graphic had materialized on her phone.

Priya had confided her intimate biological details to the app, and it had generated a calendar for conception. She preferred to trust her body's own rhythms, but as Viv had sagely said, even psychics have to look both ways before they cross the street.

The alarm trilled again. It was a pleasant, almost celestial sound. Like a doorbell at a center for born-again Christians. She looked at Nick's placid face. The alarm didn't penetrate his heavy slumber. For as long as Priya had known Nick he had gone to bed at precisely ten and woken up at five and not a second before.

She stopped the alarm, shuffled onto her side, and tentatively laid her palm across his chest, testing how it made her feel. The room was silent. Across the expanse of his prone body she could see his phone sitting treacherously on the bedside table. It was next to a bottle of Fertilipill—bullet-sized pellets Doctor Carmichael had recommended Nick take. Priya stared at his phone, willing it to share its secrets. Had he replied to Megan? The thought made her stomach contract painfully. Her eyes flicked back to her husband's peaceful face. She leaned across his body and stretched her hand toward the device. Nick stirred and swallowed as her breasts brushed against him, but she pressed on. Her legs scissored open across his body. Nick's thighs were like ballasts. The ridges of his stomach muscles were unyielding beneath her weight. Carnal hunger stirred against her will. Her body was awakening. Goose bumps shot up on her spine and along her arms. The ovulation alarm on her phone tingled again, urging her to slide down her husband's boxer shorts.

But she had another mission. She picked up his device and quickly tapped in the security code. She scrolled across to the beehive app, glancing down nervously again at Nick. She felt sure the hammering of her heart would wake him.

She called up Megan's face. The sight doused Priya's arousal. She took a deep breath and opened the conversation. Megan's tarty responses sat there, unanswered. Priya exhaled with relief and quickly closed the app before her eyes could alight on the previous messages Nick had sent. He stirred again, giving off a contented sigh as if he knew she had been comforted. Priya replaced Nick's phone, rolled over, and tried to get back to sleep.

Five

GRACE STEPPED PAST CRATES OF NAPA CABBAGE, DAIKON, and bunches of baby bok choy and checked the handwritten address on the card Caroline had given her. Chinatown was filled with hawkers clutching laminated menus, trying to entice her inside for yifu noodles or sea whelk soup. Diesel fumes and the smell of roasting duck fat greased the air. She turned down a laneway, hoping it wouldn't be another dead end amid the network of tiny alleys she had been searching all afternoon.

She slipped into a narrow store that displayed assorted shriveled ephemera, the fifth such shop she had entered that day. She squeezed between glass cases that held desiccated animal parts, and past shelves stacked with boxes stamped with foreign scripts, until she reached the proprietor. A tendril of smoke uncoiled from the tip of an incense stick. She gave him her best smile and asked, "I don't suppose you have any royal jelly?"

The old man nodded and shuffled to a back room. Grace knew the pure form was difficult to source. She clasped her hands together, hopeful.

Since their first round of IVF failed, Grace had been taking the capsule form of royal jelly—a secretion bees feed to the larvae that grow to be queens—but the only thing that really worked, Caroline had said, were the vials of pure jelly, not available at the local chemist.

"It tastes like burned plastic but it's supposed to be awfully effective," Caroline said. "One woman I know tried for years to conceive, only to find herself pregnant with twins two months after starting a daily regimen of the pure stuff."

Grace, like so many women struggling to conceive, was devoted to a religion of miracle cures. Secondhand tales of success formed the bedrock of her beliefs. If something worked for just one woman it became lore, these urban fertility myths passed around by desperate women like old Italian nuns clicking their rosaries. *Hail Mary, full of grace, the Lord is with thee. Samantha Bricker got pregnant taking royal jelly, please let it happen for me.*

When the shop owner returned with a large plastic container of capsules, Grace tried not to let her smile falter. "Thank you, no, I need the jelly," she said. "The pure jelly?"

He shook his head, and she backed out onto the street, defeated. She needed to be at school soon for her night shift.

"Damn," she said, looking at the time as she ran to catch her bus.

⁓

Grace's desk phone was ringing when she entered her office, its red light flashing. She had three missed calls.

"Hello?"

"Grace, can you see me please." It was a statement rather than a request. Paul Lombardo sounded like an undertaker.

"Right away?"

"Right away."

She arrived in the principal's office to find her boss standing behind his desk looking agitated. Gray sweat rings were visible under his arms.

"Ah, Grace." He gestured toward a chair. He was a mousy man with a pointed chin. "Mr. Bishop said there was a mishap at the bake-off."

Grace silently cursed. After her failed cycle, she had forgotten to report what had happened. "Yes. That is, we sorted it out."

"Grace, three of the girls went missing. Why didn't you tell me about this?" His voice was stern.

"Oh, Paul, I meant to." He twitched, annoyed—she suspected— at her use of his first name.

Teachers at Corella addressed the principal as Mr. Lombardo, but Grace was not a teacher and many of her interactions with Paul Lombardo happened late at night or early in the morning, in a state of emergency or circumstances that were otherwise delicate. In these dimly lit interactions, a whispered "Paul" and "Grace" had become the norm.

"Mrs. Arden," he said, with emphasis. "When did you plan on informing me about this?"

"I was going to email you."

"Why not on the night, while they were gone? You didn't think to call me?"

"It was after hours. I found them straightaway. They snuck off to a party."

"Mr. Bishop said you were gone for forty minutes, and that he and the other girls were sitting in a cold school bus on a dark street waiting for you."

Grace nodded, dismayed at what she feared was coming. "Right."

"We have policies."

"Yes."

"Procedures."

"I know."

"They're there for a reason. I am shocked at you, Grace, truly shocked."

He employed this exact turn of phrase with students, and Grace bristled at being spoken to like a teenage girl who'd snuck off campus during class time.

Paul Lombardo was shaking his head. "Grace, this is a serious infraction."

"I'm sorry, Paul."

"If something had happened . . . If the parents found out nothing was done about it—"

"I've disciplined the girls."

"The girls?!" His cheeks flushed red. "If something happens to one of our students, I assure you, Mrs. Arden, the parents aren't going to blame the girls. The parents aren't going to *sue* the girls."

"Right. Of course. Again, I'm sorry, Paul. It was a momentary lapse."

"This is not what parents who enroll their daughters in an institution like Corella expect."

As he muttered about responsibility and diligence, memories of her horrific night flashed through her mind: the blood, the fear, the white-hot pain that had followed her into her dreams and stabbed her stomach while she slept. Nobody at the school knew she was going through IVF. She wanted to shout, *Don't you understand that every day I'm being put through an emotional meat mincer?* But she would sooner die than let her private pain taint her professional life. Instead she sat silently before Paul Lombardo with clasped hands, penitent, knowing that contrition was the only thing that would appease him.

Paul was pacing the room, sliding his hand through his hair. "Truancy is serious, but we have a duty to protect our students, in particular the boarders whose parents trust us as guardians." He paused. "I'm afraid I'm going to have to suspend the bake-off."

"What?!" Grace wanted to protest further but she sensed now was not the time.

"We're going to have to review whether the benefits of running the program outweigh the . . . risks."

"It's a good program, Paul. The girls love it," she said.

"Are you sure it's not the opportunity to sneak away that they love?"

"It's the first time it has happened. If you could only see what they've achieved—"

Mr. Lombardo cut her off. "It's not the actions of the girls that's the problem, it was the school's failure to prevent them. Grace, they're teenagers."

She wiped her clammy palms on her skirt. When she spoke again her voice was calm. "When will a decision be made on the program?"

"I'll let you know." He took a seat and leaned back. "Grace, you know I think you're an excellent boardinghouse mistress. But this could have gone badly. Very badly. You should have called me immediately. If the parents knew about this, it wouldn't just be your program they'd be wanting to review."

"Yes, Mr. Lombardo."

Grace stood to leave. She was at the door when the principal called out again. "Grace." She stopped and turned.

"Yes?"

He furrowed his brow. "Is everything all right?"

"Of course, Paul." She gave a firm nod.

"Okay. You had better get back to work."

Back at the boardinghouse, Grace broke up a squabble over who owned a half-empty bottle of perfume, then went to the kitchen to lay out some gingerbread she had bought for the girls.

"Hello, Mrs. Arden. What's that?" Bridget Hennessy entered, carrying a calico bag.

"A treat for after dinner," Grace said. "But only for girls who have done their trigonometry homework. Doesn't Mr. Park's class have a big test tomorrow?"

Bridget sighed as she placed her swag on the countertop. Her blond waves were swept off her face by a white elastic headband. "I hate trigonometry. I wish we could do the bake-off every night."

Grace felt a pang of guilt.

"Next time can we do something a bit more exciting than the same old casseroles?" Bridget asked.

"I don't think there will be a next time," Grace said. "Mr. Lombardo has canceled the bake-off."

"What?" Bridget's eyes welled up. "When will it start again?"

"I'm not sure."

"It's because Stacey and the others snuck off, isn't it? It's so unfair," Bridget said hotly. "Why should the rest of us be punished because of what those other girls did? They're such . . . such . . . bitches."

"Bridget, language."

"It's true," Bridget said. "Do they think they're the only ones who hate being cooped up at night? And now they've spoiled the one cool thing we had to look forward to."

Grace offered Bridget a piece of gingerbread, inwardly pleased at the *one cool thing* comment. "Graduation will be here faster than you think. Have you put any more thought into your university preferences?"

"I feel like I should put down things like engineering or law. If you can get into those courses you should do it, right?"

"If that's what you want. You seem hesitant."

Corella College had an unspoken policy of nudging the girls toward blue-ribbon courses and top-tier universities. It wanted acceptance rates that would look good on prospectuses and marketing material. Grace disagreed with the policy. She believed the girls would have the best chance for success if they pursued something they were passionate about.

"I want to be a chef," Bridget said. "But Dad says I have to do something more serious."

Bridget pulled open her drawstring bag and took out a tin, an egg, and some spices. She poured milk from the fridge into a saucepan, which she put onto a hot plate, then added chocolate and nutmeg.

"There's a class at the Cordon Bleu in Rozelle every Saturday morning." Bridget's face lit up. "I can pay for it with my pocket money but Dad would never let me go. I heard him tell Mum my cooking was a fad."

Bridget strained her mixture into a jug and poured two glasses and passed one to Grace. It tasted surprisingly good—rich and spicy.

"If you explain to him how serious you are he might consider letting you do the course," Grace said.

"No, he won't."

"Bridget, I'm sure if you appeal to his sense of reason, he will realize it's your choice."

Bridget hung her head. "Mrs. Arden, there must be something

you can do. Please. You have no idea what it's like to be told you can't have the one thing you want most in the world."

⁓

The next night, Grace sat at her dining room table drafting a letter that implored the parents to support the bake-off. She promoted the program as something that could increase the girls' chances of getting sought-after jobs. It would look good on their résumés, she argued, and elevate them above their peers.

"What's this?" Dan asked, stooping to kiss the top of her head when he arrived home.

"Paul might cancel the bake-off. I'm writing to the parents of boarders, appealing to their mercantile sensibilities."

"They can't cancel it! It's a great program. Probably the most worthwhile thing they do at that school."

"It wasn't exactly popular," she murmured.

"The parents can't all be so shortsighted."

Grace sighed. "No. But like anything, there's a line of resistance and the hostile minority are the most vocal. A few parents were against the program from the start."

She stabbed at the keyboard savagely, reminding the parents that the bake-off was merely cooking and charity, and it was voluntary at that. *The girls are free to join in, or not,* she typed.

"I've got something that might cheer you up."

"Oh yes?"

Dan rummaged in his work satchel and pulled out a red-and-white box. The lettering was in Chinese and it was illustrated with gold bees.

"Royal jelly?" Grace's face broke into a smile. "How did you find it?"

"A good reporter can find anything."

"The perks of being married to a journalist," Grace said.

She slid her fingernail underneath the seal and flipped open the lid. From inside she plucked a plastic vial. She opened it, brought it cautiously to her nose, and sniffed. "Pew, Caroline was right."

"Let me have a whiff." Dan leaned toward it. "Oof. It's a bit ripe."

"I'll get a spoon." Grace disappeared into the kitchen, returning a moment later. She squeezed some jelly onto the spoon, closed her eyes, and put it in her mouth. "Argh!"

"Is it bad?"

"Ooh, yes, it's bad. Ugh. Ack. Oh, that must mean it's good for you, right?"

"I know something else that might be good for you."

"Mm?" Grace was studying the back of the royal jelly container.

"There's a press junket on the Gold Coast. They're putting me up. You should come. It could be our last hurrah if that jelly does the trick."

Grace felt a twinge of annoyance. "Why do you have to talk about parenthood like it will be the end of our lives?"

He laid his hands on her shoulders and said gently: "We can still enjoy ourselves while we're waiting for it to happen for us."

"I'm just so scared we're going to miss our chance," she said.

"I know you are, but this is exactly why we need a holiday. All this stress can't be good for you."

Grace looked at his pleading eyes. Dan was indefatigably positive. In her peripheral vision she could see the squeezed-out tube of royal jelly, and she felt her throat tighten. An accusation was forming: he had bought the jelly only to bribe her into saying yes to the holiday. But before she spat the words at him she took a breath and thought of everything else he did for her. It was, she suspected, just the hormones making her defensive.

"Perhaps a holiday in the sun is a good idea." She pursed her lips. "They say vitamin D helps conception."

Dan laughed. "That's the spirit."

That night, they made love. And not because an ovulation calendar said they had to.

~

It was with a renewed optimism that Grace floated to school the next day. She covered Therese Swan's homeroom class again and asked Bridget Hennessy to read the morning's announcements. When the bell rang the girls collected their books and headed to their first class.

"Well read, Bridget," Grace said. "How did things go with your father?"

"Why would you care?" Bridget replied, shouldering past the other students.

"Bridget," Grace called her back, surprised.

The student halted. Her shoulders rose and fell as she huffed and turned, but she wouldn't look Grace in the eye. A scowl crossed her face.

"What's wrong?" Grace asked. Bridget's bottom lip trembled. Grace softened her voice. "Bridget, if something's troubling you, it always helps to tell someone."

"But you're the one who gave me the bad advice in the first place," she blurted.

"What?" Grace felt a pang of alarm. Calmly, she said: "Tell me what happened."

"I-told-my-father-about-wanting-to-be-a-chef-and-he-said-no-daughter-of-mine's-going-to-work-as-a-common-cook-if-she-wants-to-remain-a-part-of-this-family." The words rushed out of Bridget and culminated in a torrent of tears.

"Oh dear," said Grace, rankled by the man's callousness. She passed the box of tissues on the desk to Bridget. "I'm sure he didn't mean it."

Bridget blubbered loudly. "He did. He said he didn't spend a hundred thousand dollars on tuition just so I could make pasta for people who had actually done something worthwhile with their lives."

"Maybe you just surprised him," Grace said, keeping her voice low and soothing.

"Dad says I have to do medicine or law. He said if I say the word 'cooking' one more time he'll pull me out of Corella and enroll me in the public school down the road where those boys got arrested for making homemade bombs."

"Well," said Grace, "let's not lose hope yet. In the meantime, I'll talk to Ms. Collings about letting you practice in the kitchen here."

"Really?"

"I don't see why not. But you have to do it during your free time. No cooking during study hour."

"Of course, yes. Thank you, Mrs. Arden."

"Now off to chemistry or you'll be late. Scoot!"

⁓

On Saturday, Grace and Dan returned to the world of stirrups and speculums. The Empona waiting room was busy, as always, and packed with aspiring parents seated two by two staring with fixed determination at magazines in their hands. The air was charged with apprehension. Grace's eyes skated over the couples. One pair looked much older than her and Dan, which gave her a guilty sense of comfort. She reasoned, if the doctors had told this couple they had hope, her odds must be even better. The woman's hair was permed. Her partner's sea captain's beard was neat and white. His whalebone corduroys spoke of tastes formed long ago.

In the far corner, beneath a mute flat-screen TV, was a pair still tuned in to the younger generation. The woman had a blunt fringe, mulberry-painted lips, and shiny plastic arrow earrings. Grace could see from the fluttering of her lashes that she too was assessing the other patients and probably feeling grateful she wasn't as old as Grace and Dan. Grace tried to ignore the latent envy stirring in her blood. The woman with the arrow earrings had years of possibility ahead of her, and though they might be filled with disappointment and tears, her window of opportunity was open far wider than Grace's.

Grace's nose twitched with the prickly tingle that meant she might be about to cry. This was yet another side effect: her hormone treatment ushered in the full gamut of emotions at the slightest provocation. Telstra ads reduced her cheeks to riverbeds. Sentimental movies left her openly sobbing.

"Mr. and Mrs. Arden," the receptionist called. "Please go through."

The small act of standing and walking toward the office where their hopes had been raised then dashed so many times already was enough to make Grace tremble.

~

After the appointment, Dan and Grace stopped at the supermarket. Grace was staring, dazed, at a crate of spinach when a voice snapped her back to reality.

"Folate?" asked the woman, as she reached for a bunch of the leafy vegetable and placed it in her own basket.

"Excuse me?" Grace looked at her, her mind still blank. Then she realized: it was the woman with the mulberry lips and the arrow earrings. Up close she was even younger than Grace had first thought.

"I eat it raw, for all the good it does me," the woman said. She clocked Grace's confusion. "You were just in Empona, weren't you?"

"Oh, yes, sorry. Just a bit dazed."

The woman's eyebrows knitted together. "Bad news?"

"Not yet. Just bracing myself, you know. Mentally. We had a transfer today."

"It's brutal, isn't it? This is my third go."

"Seventh for me."

The younger woman's face was a collage of pity and empathy. Looking closely, Grace saw the fringe hid a rash of pimples across her forehead. "I had a friend who got pregnant first time. It seemed so easy," the woman said. She gave a quick shrug. "I'm doing everything I can, but I feel like I'm trying to start an engine that's missing a spark plug. Doctor Osmond suggested some new pills but I keep thinking he's just throwing darts in the dark. If they really did work surely he would have prescribed them up front."

"Doctor Osmond is your doctor?" Grace asked. She loved Doctor Li, but the name Roger Osmond evoked the messiah's halo and a heavenly hum. Li was the standout prodigy, but Osmond was the grand master. "Do you mind if I ask you the name of the new supplement?"

The woman dug into her handbag and pulled out a plastic bottle. "They say it's a sort of embryo glue, to help the embryos stick to the uterus wall. At least, that's the layman's pitch. I'm sure the reality is more complicated."

"Glue?" Grace read the label, frowning, irritated that Doctor Li hadn't told her about it. "Mind if I take a photo?"

"Of course not." The woman held up the bottle and Grace snapped it with her phone camera. "They taste like grass clippings and fish heads, but in my madness I've convinced myself that that just means they're the real deal."

"That's familiar logic," said Grace. "Thanks for the photo. And good luck."

"Thanks." The young woman paused before walking away. "Good luck to you too."

Grace nodded and smiled. She put two bunches of spinach into her trolley and wheeled it to the checkout. As she was waiting in line she pulled out her phone and texted the photo of the pills to Doctor Li with the question: *If we have to do another transfer, can we try this?*

Six

NICK ALWAYS SPRANG OUT OF BED LIKE A WIND-UP TOY AND slid on his shorts and a T-shirt while Priya was still in the grips of her dreams. Sometimes she would stir at the sound of him bouncing around looking for his Nikes, but usually she would sleep through it. He would run seven kilometers each morning, and it was only when he returned that Priya would drag herself to the kitchen to blindly boil the water for the first of her daily caffeine transfusions. Nick never drank coffee.

"Running is nature's stimulant," he'd say, hopping from foot to foot, his skin lacquered with sweat. He'd kiss her forehead then dive into the downstairs bathroom to shower.

This was one of the many ways they differed. His energy drained away during the day, and by nine each evening he would be fading, just as Priya's synapses were beginning to fire. Her mind was at its brightest when the stars were. Most of her paintings were completed by lamplight, with the companionable moon watching through the glass ceiling of her studio.

This morning she lowered two English muffins into the toaster and cracked an egg into the frying pan. When the hiss of the shower stopped, she yelled out to Nick.

"Don't forget the appointment with the urologist."

"Uh-huh," he called from the bathroom.

"Nick." She went to the bathroom and leaned against the door-frame, her arms folded, an eggy spatula in her hand. "You won't forget."

He was staring intently at the mirror as he dabbed wax in his hair and tweaked the ends. "Would you let me?" He smiled and followed the comment with a wink.

Priya looked into his eyes in the mirror. "Don't worry," he said, walking over to her and trailing a hand through her hair. "Everything will be fine."

Priya looked away. Her insides felt like they were tearing them-selves apart. This was the Nick he presented to her—considerate, faithful, loving. But then there was the Nick she had discovered for herself—secretive, untrustworthy, and, worst of all, seemingly unable to be satisfied with her alone.

"Just nervous, I guess. All those needles . . ."

"Are you okay?"

"Uh-huh."

He nodded, satisfied. "It's not really fair," he said, upbeat again. "You have to be pricked and pinned and pumped full of drugs when all that happens to me is they give me a stack of porn and tell me to make nice with Mr. Hand."

He may have been joking, but she could hear the vulnerability in his voice. He punched one fisted hand into the other, trying to work out the nervous energy.

"You'll do great," she said.

"When we get back perhaps we can road test the new tub. You know, to relax."

He'd installed it the weekend before and then they'd both scrubbed it until it shone. It was deep and perfect for soaking.

"Maybe." Priya contemplated the confusing symbol of his devotion to her.

A phone call came from the urologist's office three days later confirming that Nick Archer was more virile than a pack of oxen. Figures, thought Priya.

Hurricane Nick. That's what the girls used to call him. When Nick and Priya first met at the technical college where he was learning construction and she was completing a certificate of art restoration, he would blow around the campus like a force of nature, sweeping other students up in his excitement.

"Girls!" He'd run past Priya's table where she was eating lunch with her friends, their books spread out so they could gape at the colors of Paul Gauguin or whichever artist they were in love with that week. "Come to the track. We're running a relay to raise money for the uni games. Students versus faculty."

Priya had never met anyone like him. He laughed easily and often, throwing his head back with glee. He was so sure of himself, but not in a way that made others feel small. He was always friendly, always inclusive.

"Girls!" He'd jog past, a box of napkins under his arm. "Come to the courtyard outside the science labs. We're having a sausage sizzle to help pay for an atomic microscope. What about you, Priya?" He slowed to an on-the-spot jog, then winked. She sat up straight as if she'd been bitten.

The next month it was, "Girls! I'm running for student council. Vote one Nick Archer!"

"Not much can stop Nick Archer when he sets his mind to something," one of his cronies said, passing her a button with Nick's face on it. He'd won the election by a landslide.

Priya was in her office at the auction house answering a few final emails before leaving for the Empona clinic when she found herself opening her Bumble app and looking at Rose. Tousled and carefree Rose. Priya slid across to the panel of bachelors lining up for the beauty queen's consideration. They seemed so distant. So unreal. She could message any of them now, and what would it mean? She wouldn't hear their voices, or feel the warmth of their skin. She wondered if Darsh was right. Were a few text messages really that bad?

She thought of the antique bath Nick had salvaged. They'd spent a morning on their knees, cleaning up the clawed feet with toothbrushes and a solution of baking powder and ammonia. Priya admired the detail of the paws and the swirls of the beast's fur forged in iron. After, Nick had told her she had to christen it, and tossed her a bottle of fancy bubble bath. As the water gushed into the porcelain tub, she sat on the edge and trailed her fingers across the wall tiles he had laid. In the face of so much good, how big a sin was the flirtation, really?

Her phone exploded to life. Nick.

"Hello?"

"Pri. Don't be mad."

She stiffened. "That's never a promising start to a conversation."

"I know. But Hector just asked me if I could lend a hand this afternoon on a mansion in Rose Bay."

"This afternoon? Nick—"

"I know, the Empona appointment, but he's really in a bind. He said he'd pay me double time. And you don't really need me for this part, right? I mean, I want to be there with you. But it's nearly a thousand bucks for half a day's work."

Priya bit her lip. The thought of Nick not coming to the appointment made her suspicious and fearful. But on the other hand, Empona's services did not come cheap.

"You're right. We could use the money."

"I'll only go if you're sure."

"I'm sure."

"Okay. I'll see you tonight. Think fertile thoughts."

As Priya walked to her car she wondered if he really was going to a building site, and she couldn't deny her disappointment and doubt. She picked up her phone and felt its weight, contemplating Rose. Then she tossed it onto the passenger seat and put the key in the ignition. It would be hard for him to explain if the thousand dollars didn't materialize.

Twenty minutes later Priya was stalled on the M5 and worried she was going to miss her appointment. She needed a chai tea. And a massage. And a positive pregnancy result. And to discover Bumble had been installed on Nick's phone as a prank, by a mate, without his knowledge. "C'mon," she muttered, craning her neck as she tried to see how far the congestion stretched.

The tedium whipped up her worst fears. It made her fingers itch for her phone, and the app that held the key to discovering just how rotten her marriage really was.

Rose had become like a demon that haunted her. A voice in her head. Priya would slip her phone from her pocket and hunch over the profile. She was Gollum hoarding her own private precious that was sucking her life force. A junkie with a secret.

Activating Darsh's Bumble plan wasn't as easy as merely striking up an online conversation with Nick. She had to find him. He had to choose her. That is, he had to choose Rose. Every time Priya flicked open the app she feared she would see confirmation he was still on it, still fishing. She was yet to come across him and the suspense was a torment.

When she finally arrived, the Empona waiting room was crowded, as usual, with couples. None of them looked up as Priya entered. At least you have each other, she thought bitterly. She checked in with the receptionist then took a seat and picked up a magazine, determined to ignore the phone in her pocket.

Of course she couldn't, and soon she was opening the app and letting the wave of nausea roll over her. Priya took it all in: Rose's peachy skin, her tumescent lips, her hand raking slippery locks away from her face. Light bouncing off the snow gave the effect of a studio shoot. It lit up Rose's face and lent a brilliance to her smile.

Rose was exactly the sort of girl Priya thought Nick would go for. A snow bunny. A bikini babe. A woman who could work behind a bar and earn twice her salary in tips, leaning forward as she pulled down on the beer tap, her breasts squeezed together as the glass filled with ale.

Priya clicked on the "Profile edit" icon to see if she could change the name of her avatar. Rose felt inauthentic. The woman in this picture's name should be hip, with an edge. Kit, or Quinn. Something androgynous, fun, and flirty.

But the name setting was fixed.

She found herself once again sliding through the brawny beach shots and the photos of the preening men looking for love. Their teeth were bared, smiling, and their arms were crossed, with their hands tucked under their pecs to pump them up.

Priya broke away from the screen for a moment and realized the couple nearest to her were staring at her: a woman in a fertility clinic waiting room swiping through a dating app.

"It's my sister's phone," she said, half apologetic, then gave a silky fake laugh. The couple returned painted-on smiles with raised eyebrows. Priya was about to banish the device to her handbag when she saw something that made her stomach seize. The next suitor on Rose's Bumble account: Nick.

Seeing his face was like the sharp drop on a zero-gravity ride. The floor had just fallen away and now her guts were in her skull. Priya put her hand to her forehead. She knew she shouldn't torture herself but she couldn't stop looking at the pictures he'd selected for his profile. The first was a shot she had never seen before. It was taken on a building site and he was hauling something large that was out of frame. His face was shiny with sweat, like it was when she first saw him each morning after his run. He had a come-and-get-it smile. Oh God, she thought, what if that's what he was doing each morning, not running at all but fucking Jenny McAlister at the end of their street, in the dirt among her azaleas? She slid to the next photo. In this one he looked swarthy. Dark stubble had grown through. The photo was a few years old, taken at a beach wedding. In the next frame he was wrestling with Jacker, who was going crazy. She remembered that day. It was at a barbecue at Stav's, and Jacker had just been sprayed with a hose. Photo number four was another jolt. She had taken it when they were in Surfers Paradise. Nick was biting lasciviously into an ice cream. At the time she had squealed because she couldn't bear the feel of anything frozen against her teeth. He'd sunk his incisors into the scoop just to make her squirm. Priya had held up the camera, laughing, so she wouldn't have to look. Bastard, she thought. Filthy, lying bastard. The pain was deep and visceral. Her stomach churned.

She ran to the corner of the waiting room and vomited into a mauve rubbish bin. The other patients looked on with a blend of revulsion and envy—perhaps assuming it was pregnancy nausea.

She tore tissues from a box on the magazine table. As she was dabbing her mouth the receptionist called her name. Priya sat a moment, her phone in her hand. Her husband was smiling back at her, his essential details below. *Nick, 36, builder.*

"Mrs. Archer?" the receptionist said again. Priya had to go. But there was a crucial decision to be made. She held her breath and swiped right on Nick. She waited for one airless second to see if her device would show they were a match. It was silent.

"Mrs. Archer?"

"Yes," Priya said. "Coming."

She dropped her phone into her bag and walked into the examination room.

Doctor Carmichael was reading her iPad when Priya entered the room.

"Mrs. Archer, welcome," she said, standing and shaking Priya's hand.

"My husband can't make it today," Priya said.

"That's not a problem. I have your results. Everything seems fine except—"

"Except?"

"We found a small cyst."

"What?"

Priya had been so distracted by the whole Nick-and-Rose heartache she had forgotten to mentally prepare herself for the results of the tests she had undergone.

"Is it dangerous?" When Doctor Carmichael said *cyst* Priya heard *cancer*. She imagined a hard little fist of black-and-blue cells punching its way through her reproductive organs.

"It's completely benign. But it's right on your ovary. I think you should have it removed before we begin any fertility treatment."

"Surgery?" Priya felt momentarily dizzy. After the morning she had had, this was too much. She cursed her husband. Why wasn't Nick here for this? She swallowed. Her mouth was as dry as paper.

The doctor gave a curt nod. "I think it's best. It's a simple procedure," she added. "The fertility treatment might not be as effective otherwise. Truly," Doctor Carmichael said, gently patting Priya's hand, "it's nothing to worry about. Just a slight delay."

⁓

When Priya emerged from the consulting room she had a text message from Nick. *How did it go? All okay? Will be home late. I've got to drive to Penrith to get something. Will bring back dinner.*

She checked to see if Rose's Bumble account had registered a match with Nick. It hadn't.

She thought about the cyst lurking, nefarious, in her belly. She had thought she couldn't sink any lower than throwing up in the consultation waiting room, but her appointment with Doctor Carmichael had knocked her down a few more pegs. Everything was coming apart.

The drive home was lonely. She turned on the radio, but the mindless chatter just made her want to scream. Priya was desperate to unburden herself.

"Many women go on to have perfectly normal pregnancies after something like this," Doctor Carmichael had said.

This was what life would be like without Nick. She would have nobody to talk to, nobody to confide in. They had been together so long she didn't know anything else. Despite everything, she needed him.

When she arrived home his pickup was parked out front. She was hit by waves of anger, relief, gratitude, and fatigue. His boots were flopped by the back door, their tongues hanging out and their laces lying across the tiles as if they too were exhausted after a day's hard labor. Nick was in his chair with a beer in hand. Priya was reassured to see his hair was dulled by dust.

"I'm shattered. How'd you go?" he said, standing and kissing her. She could tell this wasn't his first beer, and in a split-second decision a lie escaped her lips.

"It was all fine," she said airily.

"Really?" He beamed. "Are you sure? You look awful," he said. "Not awful, just a little strung out." He touched her cheek and guided her to the couch. "Are you sure everything is okay? What did the doctor say?"

"Oh." She looked up into his face. His brow was creased with worry. This concerned face was different from the cocksure one she had seen on Bumble earlier that day. Confusion descended. She put her hand to her brow. The photo of him at the beach was three years old. The shot taken on the building site was one she had never seen. How old had those messages he had shared with Megan been? Did she check the date?

She wanted to tell him the truth, but uncertainty held her back. She had felt so alone leaving the clinic after scheduling her surgery, with nobody to confide her fears to, to comfort her, or to simply hold her hand. Yet Nick's Bumble profile was a sign that perhaps she couldn't trust him and shouldn't rely on him. That she may have to get used to the idea of facing life alone. "They want to do more tests," she said, her voice quavering.

"But nothing to worry about yet?"

Priya blinked back tears. "No." She offered a brittle smile. "Nothing to worry about yet."

He pulled her to his chest and held her. "You had me scared for a moment there." He stroked the back of her head. "Stay here, I'll get dinner."

She heard him open and close the oven and distribute food onto plates. He served it on the coffee table, and after a few bites she began to feel her strength restored.

"Nick—" The question was on her lips, in her mouth, right there, waiting to be released. *Are you cheating on me?* She didn't speak.

"What is it?" he asked, his face earnest and warm.

Instead of answering she crawled into the space next to him, taking shelter from her worries. She was too tired to fight.

He laid his arm over her and she gave herself permission to feel comforted by him. After the blow she had received in the doctor's office, she needed something sound and reassuring. With his strong arms, Nick pulled her closer until she was on his lap. Their bodies slotted together, a familiar position.

After a moment Nick said: "We've had a bad run, haven't we?"

Priya's anger at his betrayal stirred. She tried to quiet it, but it lived in her, like a beast, only half tame. She could control it sometimes by willing herself into a state of calm. But often, it disobeyed. The creature did not like the way Nick spoke about their bad run as if it had nothing to do with him. He was the one who had socked Priya's heart, boxing it for sport. A hard right jab of secrecy, an uppercut of sleaze. He hadn't endured half the misery she had.

She closed her eyes and tried to visualize a future in which she was happy again: a future with a baby, and Nick, a devoted father. Nick stroked Priya's hair and her back, murmuring comforting words.

"We'll get through it," he said, subduing the animal inside her with his strong fingers.

He smelled of plaster dust. Beneath that odor she could detect his skin and his hair. It was the perfume of her only love and her happiest days. Of honeymoon mornings and late nights in the tiny student apartment they had shared when she had been accepted into university. He had worked lovingly and uncomplainingly to support them while she studied. They'd been so happy. The memories had been forgotten lately as distance gaped between them. But with his touch and compassion, it felt like her husband was returning to her. He kissed her temple, and she felt his lips brush her cheek. She turned her head, and his breath entered the whorls of her ear. He leaned closer and kissed its inner chamber, then again, more firmly. Her mouth broke open and he kissed this too, like a man with a craving. Priya couldn't stop herself from kissing him back. She swiveled her hips, sinking onto him. She parted one leg and slid down so that his body was moored in the delta between her legs.

He bucked. It had been so long since they had made love spontaneously and joyously. The coupling recently had been regimented and purposeful. Nick ripped his shirt off and tugged his T-shirt free from his pants. He was breathing heavily now and Priya knew nothing would stop what was about to happen. She could not order her thoughts. Nick was removing her clothes and the air hitting her body stoked her arousal. He stood and turned her onto her back. He hovered a moment, waiting. He was watching her, seeking permission. Priya reached for him and pulled him into her. He gave a shout and a shudder, then kissed her breathlessly, desperately. She kissed him back and felt the familiar rhythm of her husband. He moved with self-assuredness, innately understanding what she wanted. Memories came to her, floating like fireflies carried by a breeze. They were beacons reminding her of the first time their bodies had crashed together, and what a revelation it had been for her. Nick was nothing like the timid, bookish boys she had known, with their over-wet lips and impatient hurtling toward the end.

Once twenty-two-year-old Priya had given in to Nick after a post-exams party, everything had changed. She wasn't tossed aside by the hurricane and discarded in the wake of spent passion, as she had feared. He had come back to her, again and again. They had been in love, wildly so. They had been together for eight years when their first year of marriage brought the pain of his first indiscretion, but they had come through it stronger. It was the silent nothingness that resulted from their attempts to conceive that had seemed to stifle things. She could see it now. Disappointment had leaked into their marriage like poisonous gas, quietly shutting it down. As Priya clung to Nick, one half of her brain glowed in ecstasy, another part, almost outside her body, remained rational. She could fight for him. She could take on those blank, blond strangers who offered themselves up online like day-old bread. The question she couldn't answer was, if she was going to spend the rest of their lives worrying he was sneaking around behind her back, was he worth fighting for?

Seven

GRACE NEVER CEASED TO BE AMAZED BY HER BODY'S ENDLESS capacity to work itself up into a frenzy. She had taken dozens of pregnancy tests in her lifetime and every single time, as she tore the sticks from their cardboard boxes, her palms grew sweaty and her pulse started galloping off like a stallion after a shot had been fired. Today was no different.

Grace willed her hands to not shake as she unbuttoned her jeans. She had spent years visiting friends to celebrate their babies, years waking up early on a Saturday to purchase flowers and onesies. Years putting on a brave face to coo and gush at showers, in birthing suites, at first birthdays, and then, inevitably, back at the same house for another baby shower. She did the test, placed the stick on the edge of the basin, washed her hands, and set her alarm for three minutes. She paced the hallway, vibrating between abject fear and fervent prayer, thinking surely she had paid her dues. Surely it was her turn.

Her timer pinged and she hurried into the bathroom. A single blue line stared at her, like the slash on a roadblock sign, denying her. She squeezed her eyes shut and swallowed a sob, let the shock rush over her and its residue corrode her. It was not her turn. It felt like it would never be her turn.

As Grace poured a slug of gin into a glass then twisted in some lime, a familiar sadness descended. A tiresome blankness.

She had been prepared to fail the first time. She had felt herself passing through the stages of grief. Denial. Anger. Bargaining. Depression. And, finally, acceptance. She ticked them off like items on a to-do list. The first transfer, she felt, was no more likely to result in a pregnancy than the initial consultation. There was no logic to this other than the instinct for self-preservation.

But now, after the seventh time, she sat at their oversized table—purchased with the unspoken agreement that it would be needed for family dinners, homework, and constructing model solar systems—and drank.

"Have you seen my universal adapter?" Dan asked as he carried his suit bag into the dining room. His face fell when he saw Grace's fingers curled around her glass like a security blanket.

"Did you take a—"

"Yes."

He was silent a moment.

"Do you want me to pull out of the trip?"

"What? No, no, of course not."

Dan was due to fly out to a press junket in L.A.

"Are you mad that I did the test without telling you?" she asked.

"Of course not." He kissed the top of her forehead. She still had to go into Empona for the blood test, and the only thing to be thankful for in this moment was that she was relieved of the sickening, knife-in-the-stomach anticipation.

"Are you sure you're not mad?" she said. "You seem . . . something."

"Why would I be mad? I have to finish packing."

She poured herself another drink, then she ransacked the fridge until she found a small wheel of Camembert they'd had since Easter. She had been avoiding soft cheese, along with shellfish and alcohol, so Dan had refrained in solidarity.

She peeled the foil off the cheese and scooped some quince jelly from a jar. These were the luxuries her friends with children claimed they would trade their youngest for. "All I eat is Bega slices these days," Rochelle had said one night when she and Grace shared a cheese plate after a rare night out together at the theater. It was a hollow complaint. The Camembert tasted like fatty failure to Grace. What were cheese and sloe berries to a downy-cheeked babe?

She returned to the fridge, knowing there were some muscatels in syrup somewhere. If she was going to wallow, she was going to go all out.

That was another thing she could be grateful for. She and Dan both earned a good salary, which meant they were spared the financial anguish many infertile couples faced. She glumly ate another gooey piece of Camembert, then pushed the plate away, feeling queasy.

"Dan," she called. "Come and have some cheese before I eat any more. It's going to make me sick . . . Dan?"

When she got no answer she climbed the stairs to their bedroom. "Dan?" It was empty.

She heard a rustle in the study, so she pushed open the door. Papers were flapping by the window, which was propped open with a lead glass paperweight.

"Dan?"

She stopped outside the room neither of them went into. The

door was kept closed. It was a waste of space but they couldn't bear
to do anything with it. Even in the short term. Even though it meant
Dan's mountain bike had become a permanent fixture in the dining
room and Grace's clarinet kept company with the ironing board in
the laundry. The walls were white except for a small patchwork of
colors where they had tested out squares of chalky pink and sailor
blue. A pine dressing table sat against one wall with a few scattered
items on top: a pile of folded, knitted baby jackets, a teddy bear,
a bottle of No Tears baby shampoo that Grace had put aside almost
two years ago thinking they would need it someday. Under a veil
of dust, it looked like a shrine. She inched the door open, her heart
starting to thump. "Dan?"

It was empty.

She returned to the dining room, where she heard movement
coming from the kitchen.

Dan was in the pantry. The light was off and he was cloaked
in darkness. His back was to her and his shoulders were shaking.
His face was in his hands as he sobbed silently. Grace stepped back,
feeling she had trespassed on a private moment. The lonely figure
broke the pieces of her heart into smaller fragments. She couldn't
leave him there in the dark, among the cornflakes and bags of rice.
She stepped toward him and entwined her arms with his. He tensed
at her touch, but then relaxed. He let out an anguished noise. She
wrapped her arms around his chest and pressed her body to his.

"Sh, it's okay," she said, then tenderly kissed the back of his neck.

He clasped her hands and continued to sob.

"Come out of here," she said, guiding him from the pantry and
walking him to their bed. She eased him onto the mattress then lay
down beside him, tucking his head under her chin and stroking his
hair as he shook with silent grief.

Dan took a cab to the airport in the morning. "I'll be back in time for the blood test," he said, kissing the end of her nose.

"I can't bear the thought of going through the whole routine at Empona."

"It's two days away. Maybe it was a false negative."

"Don't even think it," she said. "That's the point of taking the test early. To guard against hope."

The house was cold without Dan. Grace made microwave mac 'n' cheese for dinner and ate it from a mug. There was a gaping hole in the middle of the week, which had been previously occupied by the bake-off. Mr. Lombardo had shut the program down for good, citing parents' concerns after news of the nightclub incident had trickled out. Grace felt like she had failed Bridget. The young student had taken full advantage of the kitchen practice time Grace had arranged for her, and Grace strongly believed that if Bridget wanted to explore her passion for cooking, she should have every opportunity to do so. At least there was something she could do about that, Grace thought, picking up her phone.

The Saturday morning peace was broken by the blare of Grace's alarm. She slammed it off and swung her legs out of bed. Dan's flight was due in at two in the afternoon. She would pick him up from the airport then drive straight to Empona for the test that would confirm what she already knew. But that wasn't her focus now.

She dressed quickly and was soon on the road to Corella. When she pulled into the driveway Bridget Hennessy was standing at the door to the boardinghouse, as planned, in casual clothes. She bounced on the balls of her feet with excitement as Grace's car came to a stop. By her side was her calico bag.

"Hop in," Grace called.

"Thank you, thank you, thank you, Mrs. Arden," Bridget said as she fastened her seat belt.

"Now remember, if anyone asks, I approved your request to attend a lecture series at Sydney University," Grace said. "We don't want this getting back to your father."

Bridget nodded her head in fierce agreement.

Grace had little doubt as to exactly which parents had been so vehement that the bake-off be shut down. "Okay," she said. "Are you all belted in? Good. Let's go."

She set her GPS for the Cordon Bleu culinary school in Rozelle.

***

Six hours later Doctor Li confirmed what they already knew. The latest attempt hadn't taken.

"I'm so sorry, Grace, Dan," she said.

Grace expelled a long gust of air. "I never thought we'd have to do it eight times."

"Well, we have a couple of options after the last collection," Doctor Li said.

The young physician had done her job well on the latest retrieval. With her skilled and steady hand, she had removed nine eggs. When it had come time to implant them, five had been viable. They still had four left on ice, three blastocysts and one strong-looking morula—an embryo not quite as developed as a blastocyst but still good enough to transfer.

"Could we just talk about the genetic test results again?" Grace said. "We're still a bit confused. I know we have three viable embryos but the fourth isn't as strong?"

Doctor Li nodded. "Essentially, the test returned a possible error. They can't rule out there being a problem, but they also don't know for sure that there is."

"If we don't implant it, we could be wasting a perfectly good embryo, but we'll only see if there is an error if we implant it."

"That's right."

"And testing it again could damage it?" Grace asked.

"Yes. My recommendation would be that since you have three other viable embryos, we should not transfer the embryo with the potential problem. Not yet, at least."

"But what does it mean?" Grace asked.

"We can't say for sure. There could be an abnormality with part of one of the chromosomes. It appears as a deletion. It's unclear if the deletion is an accurate representation of an abnormal chromosome or a misrepresentation of a healthy chromosome. That is to say, we don't know if the error is in the embryo or the test."

"So it could be fine?"

Doctor Li nodded. "She could be fine."

"It's a girl?" Grace asked, a smile appearing on her face.

"Yes, this embryo is female. But as I said, I don't recommend implanting it now. You have three normal embryos and, if you agree, I'd like to transfer them all."

"What, all three at once?"

"It's not something I like to do, but given your age, Grace, I think it's our best shot."

"Three," Dan echoed.

"What are the chances that all three will take?" Grace asked.

"Honestly, very little, which is why I think we should try."

"What about two?" Dan asked. "What are the odds of two taking, and we end up with twins?"

The idea of two babies appealed to Grace. It would mean the one baby they wished for would get a sibling after all. She knew there was no chance of it happening otherwise.

"I don't think you're likely to end up with twins," Doctor Li said, extinguishing Grace's burgeoning fantasy of matching jumpsuits.

"Doctor Li," she said. "I have to ask, if we put three embryos in, what are our chances of getting even one to take?"

"With three, I think you have a fighting chance."

Grace smiled, with hope in her heart.

"You don't have to make a decision today. But we'll book you in for a transfer date. Go home and talk it over. You can decide between now and then."

A knowing look passed between Dan and Grace. "If you think this is our best chance," Dan said, "then we don't have to think about it."

Eight

SIX A.M. FROST COVERED THE YARD, TURNING IT AS WHITE
as if someone had sprayed the grass with fake snow. It was a rare
sight in June, even in Western Sydney, which experienced an entirely
different climate from the subtropical east. It had already been the
coldest June on record and it was only going to get colder, the TV
weather reporter had said. But inside her house, Priya was starting
to sweat. She pulled off her jumper and turned down the dial on
the heater.

She laid an old bedsheet in the passageway to protect the floor-
boards, then lifted Nick's desk onto it and dragged it out to the
studio, where she jammed it up against the wall. The old desk
joined Nick's barbells, kettle weights, and toolbox, which were neatly
stacked in a pile, the product of her morning's work. She returned
to the second bedroom to pick up a few stray items.

They had decided they would lay carpet in the second bedroom,
so she didn't bother putting more sheets down. Priya went out to
the shed and fetched a tin of paint and a knife. Jacker followed as
she brought them into the second bedroom, wagging his tail and
licking his chops.

"It's not food, you silly thing." She laughed as she dug the blade under the lid and prized it open.

Dollops of paint the color of a springtime sky splattered onto the wood as she dunked her roller into the tray, liberally coating it. She painted the ceiling, and when it was dry she brought in the ladder and hand-painted fluffy white clouds and golden stars. She worked all day, painting a fat sun in one corner and a sleeping moon in another. She added cherubs riding shooting stars like rodeo cowboys. Next, she mixed white into the blue to lighten it and painted Saraswati, the Hindu goddess of music, riding her swan and playing a vina. In another corner she depicted Krishna with a flute in his hands. Next to him she painted another pink cherub. In the Archer sky, Judeo-Christian references mixed with Hindu deities. Priya imagined lying on her back with a squirming toddler in her arms, pointing out the gods. She did not adhere to her parents' faith, but she wanted her child to be aware of it. She realized, sadly, if she didn't teach him—or her—nobody would.

Once Priya had finished the mural she began to sketch a jungle scene on the white walls. She was adding color to a giraffe when she heard the door slam, followed by the sound of Nick kicking his boots off by the door.

"How's my patient?" he called. "Why are you out of bed?" He folded his arms when he came into the room and found Priya working. "You didn't move all of that stuff by yourself?"

"Nick, I'm fine."

"You just had surgery."

"It was a minor procedure. Besides, Stav helped," she lied.

Nick's face broke into a smile. "That looks fantastic," he said, walking around the room and appraising her work. He rested a hand on her shoulder. "Are you sure you're okay?"

"I promise."

Doctor Carmichael had performed a quick, clean laparoscopic cystectomy and excised a lump the size of a peppercorn. Priya was prescribed anti-inflammatories and a few days of bed rest. "We'll make an appointment for ten days from now and see how you're healing. All going well we can start you on the treatment," the doctor had said.

Nick was treating Priya like a queen. Jacker was giddy to have someone home during the day, and when Nick arrived at night, the three of them would cuddle up on the couch under a blanket to watch a film. She was beginning to believe things would turn out okay.

"Come on," he said. "Time for a rest. I'll heat up some lasagna. You sit down, put your feet up."

As she dropped her paintbrush into its pail of water and stood up straight, she felt a slight ache in her back and a tightness around her abdomen.

"Here we go," Nick said, taking her by the hand into the lounge room. A few minutes later he brought in two steaming plates. He was bending down to arrange them on the coffee table when there came a tingle from his back pocket. It cut through their domestic scene like lightning. Priya's heart was slammed by the sharp-edged memory of all the intimate communications she had seen. "What was that?" she asked. It was a noise she'd never heard from his phone.

"Erm, an email, I think," he said. "Hang on a tick." He disappeared into the kitchen again. When he came back carrying the cutlery he had forgotten she was standing and was halfway into her jacket.

"What's happening?" he asked.

"It's Wednesday. I'm going to go to class."

"But we're about to eat dinner."

"I'll heat it up when I get back." She couldn't meet his eyes as one word played again and again in her mind. *Megan. Megan. Megan.*

"Are you sure?" he asked, uneasy.

"Uh-huh." She hooked her handbag over her shoulder, wincing a little as an ache radiated at the base of her spine. "I think it will be good for me. I need to get out of the house. Use my brain."

"You spent all day painting."

"Drawing relaxes me." She picked the car keys up from the sideboard.

Nick's eyes followed her, unconvinced. "Okay," he said cautiously. "I'll see you later, I guess."

⁓

When Priya arrived at the Fairfield Art Factory she dropped a ten-dollar note into a jar in exchange for access to the open bottles of wine and a cushion on the floor with a view of the naked woman who had hung herself over the edge of a chair like a discarded overcoat.

"That pose is a bit personal," her friend Husani whispered, nodding at the model as Priya settled herself next to him. He was holding a piece of charcoal delicately between his fingers, which were blackened around the nail bed and tips. He kept his head down, trying to copy the model without looking directly at her.

Priya smiled. "Don't be embarrassed. It's art," she said, and drew a thick black line that mimicked the curve of the woman's torso. Out, in, out. "Damn, proportions are off." She softened the line, smudging it with her finger.

"Change," their instructor, Suzette, called. "A horizontal pose this time, I think."

The model contorted her body into a new shape. Priya turned the page of her sketchbook.

Husani leaned toward her. "When are you going to come and see my art?"

"I see your art every week."

"Not this. My real work. It's crying out for a professional critique."

Husani had just completed a fine-arts degree, and though Priya didn't know exactly how old he was, she figured he couldn't have been more than twenty-two.

"I don't specialize in contemporary art," she said.

"Art is art. You know what's good and what isn't."

He was always needling her to come to his house. Maybe he imagined her job at the auction house came with useful connections and hoped she'd introduce him to the right people.

"We'll see. I have a lot on this week," Priya said. "We acquired a Blackman."

He gave a low whistle. "Niiice. How much will that go for, then?"

"Why, are you looking to buy?"

"Just getting a feel for the market." He tossed his head back to flick the curls from his eyes. His movements were languid, almost floppy, as if his actions were controlled by marionette strings, not muscles.

"Maybe I can come on Sunday afternoon. Though I don't know how my husband would feel about me spending an evening at the home of a young artist."

Husani's eyes glimmered, proud to be considered a threat. Priya threw a nub of charcoal at him. She imagined he wouldn't look so bold if he saw the colossus she was married to.

"Yesss." He pumped his fist with comic emphasis and Priya, despite herself, laughed, pleased that the class had succeeded in taking her mind off the messages in her husband's phone. If only for a few moments.

~

Priya had lingered after class, talking to Husani and Suzette, so Nick was in bed when she got home.

"You're back," he said sleepily when she entered the room after showering away the day's paint and dust. As she got into the bed he wrapped his arm around her waist and pulled her to him. He was on his side, forming a human fortification for Priya to lean against.

"Good class?"

"Mm-hmm." She felt a moment of remorse for running out on him so suddenly and remembered, with a rush of guilt, the mild flirtation she had enjoyed with Husani and how harmless it was. She pictured Nick alone, on the couch, wondering what had caused her to leave. Then the imaginary Nick picked up his phone and the taunting returned. *Megan. Megan. Megan.* Priya licked her lips and laid her palm on his chest, trying to summon some faith in her husband. The familiar bedtime smell of him, soap and freshly laundered pajamas, helped. "How was your day?"

"We found a concealed fireplace at the house over the bridge," he said, moving onto his back and talking with his hands as he described pulling down some hastily thrown-up drywall. "Original grate and everything. It had these beautiful pea-green tiles. I was thinking I could build a fireplace into our front room. Imagine it in winter—a crackling open flame, the smell of burning wood."

He was staring at the ceiling, drawing the picture with his

hand, and Priya knew he could see it. He looked at her, on her back, passive and still.

"What do you think?"

"Sounds wonderful."

"We could toast marshmallows over our very own open fire." He slid his hand over her belly and let it linger there.

Priya remained motionless. She was envisioning the scene, but with not quite as much optimism as Nick.

"How are you feeling?" he asked.

"I feel okay."

"And you're seeing the doctor on Monday?"

"Eight a.m."

"I'll take the morning off work."

"You don't have to."

"I want to."

He slid his hand across her nightdress. It was forest-green silk that she hardly wore because it had to be dry-cleaned. Who dry-cleans their nighties? she'd thought as she'd fished it out of a half-off bin during the Boxing Day sales. But feeling the fluid fabric between her fingertips had been irresistible.

"The doctor really seems to know what she's doing, doesn't she? Did you notice when we were leaving, the car in her reserved car space? Mercedes. Customized paint. That lemon yellow's not my taste, but it's a good sign. You don't get a Mercedes from being a useless doctor."

"I'm sure she's very competent," Priya said.

He stroked the fabric again. "You left so suddenly tonight," he said, bringing his face close to hers. She felt his weight shift as he leaned into her. "Is something wrong?"

Priya's heart started to thump. This was her chance to clear the air before they committed themselves to something irreversible. Now that the cyst had been removed, there was nothing stopping it. Soon she would begin to alter her body with hormones. If they succeeded, there would be another person who could be hurt if their marriage failed.

She wanted to ask him about the beep his phone made before she ran out. She knew the sounds of his phone, but even her own phone sometimes trembled with an odd notification from a little-used app.

The discovery of Bumble, and of Megan, had shoved her onto a dangerous precipice. She realized in that moment in the dark that she was afraid to find out how bad it was. She feared that the truth could force her into a position where she could not in good conscience go through with IVF. And then what? No Nick and no baby.

Her silk gown was working its magic on him now, and as his excitement built, his touch loosened her resolve. The memory of their recent passionate night was fresh in her mind.

"Nick," she began, intending to tell him she was tired, as she had so many nights this year. But he covered her mouth with his own, kissing her. "The other night was great," he murmured, kissing her again.

She squeezed her eyes shut and tried to find the will to push him off. But her arms refused to obey. When she opened her eyes she saw the man who loved nothing more than to smash through brick walls with a sledgehammer to the beat of Metallica turned up full bore, but who also cared deeply about authentic filigree tap enamel. He was flirtatious, but it was a manifestation of his flaws, his insecurities, and an inextricable part of his personality. It was just one thread of what made him who he was, but it was woven into the fiber of his being. There was no way to cut it out or remove it.

It would always be there. If she and Nick broke up, and he started seeing someone new, that woman would have to deal with this strand of his personality too. The new woman would get wonderful, happy, energetic hurricane Nick, but she would get the threat of infidelity too. And Priya had always known this.

At their engagement party, he'd been on the dance floor with Eliza Gray, holding her hand and touching her waist as they performed a poor man's cha-cha, twirling and zipping to Billy Joel. Priya had worn a sari, and she could see the way her aunts and uncles, in their lehengas and kurtas, were looking from her to Eliza, to Eliza's legs, to Nick.

Viv, noticing this, had cut in. "Nick, I think Priya needs reinforcements. She's fighting off a gang of judgmental relatives."

"After this song!" he'd called without missing a beat. Viv had taken his hand and dragged him to the front of the room for the speeches. Priya, the dutiful bride-to-be, had smiled with a veneer of happiness, but inside her chest felt like it was caving in and she was fearful of how many more times in her life she would be made to feel this way.

In their bed now she felt that same collapsing feeling. "No, Nick," she said, and pushed him off.

He lay on his back, rubbing his brow. "Priya, what's going on?" His voice was taut with frustration.

"I'm not in the mood."

"You're never in the mood. No wonder we can't get pregnant."

She sat up. "Are you saying it's my fault?"

"No, just—" He was exasperated. "Certain things need to happen if you want to have a baby."

"I've just had an operation. You were hurting me."

She was lying and they both knew it.

"You said you were fine. You spent all day moving furniture."

"And now I'm sore."

He rolled off the bed and disappeared downstairs.

"Nick," she called. "Nick!" The sound of the television drifted upstairs.

When Priya woke up the next morning, her phone was glowing yellow. Rose's Bumble profile was strobing with excitement, and a message: *You have a new match!*

~

Monday morning. The day of the appointment. Priya pulled out her phone and contemplated Rose. She rubbed her thumb back and forth over the screen, agitated.

She and Nick had barely spoken since their fight, and Rose hadn't spoken to Nick either. He'd slept on the couch. Priya was still in bed when she heard him return from his run. When he came into the bedroom, pulling off his T-shirt, she was staring at his face on her phone screen via Rose's Bumble profile.

He paused when he saw her, then kept walking. She could feel irritation radiating off him. She clenched her jaw in righteous anger. When he came out of the en suite she was still in bed.

"Are you going to get ready for the doctor?" he asked.

"Of course I am," she shot back.

"You're just staring at your phone."

She gritted her teeth. Anger gave her the courage she needed to confront him. "You know how mesmerizing these devices can be." Her voice was icy.

"What?"

"You know what I mean." She narrowed her eyes at him.

"I don't know what you're talking about." He turned his back and pulled on a T-shirt.

Priya leaped out of bed. "Your phone, Nick. I saw the messages on your phone."

"I—" He was trapped. She could see him calculating his next move.

"Megan!" she yelled, to short-circuit any more lies. "I saw your disgusting, sleazy messages to Megan. You're cheating on me."

His eyes widened in shock and alarm.

"Look . . ." His voice faltered. "Is—is that what all this has been about?"

"What do you mean, 'Is this what all this has been about?' Like it's nothing. We've been trying to get pregnant for years, and you're cheating on me!"

As she heard the words aloud she felt the full horror of them.

Nick was rubbing his face. "It's not like that. They're just messages."

"Just messages?" She snatched his phone off the dressing table. She scrolled, searching until she found it, then started to read from the app: *At night in bed I dream about your perfect breasts.* At night? At night! When you're lying next to me? ME who, sorry, doesn't feel like fulfilling your every desire because I've just had an operation to help conceive your child."

"I don't care about her, she's just a face on a screen."

"Tits on a screen!"

"It's not like that. She's not real. I just wanted something uncomplicated."

"What?!" Her rage was explosive. Priya felt like her soul might split through her skin.

"It's been stressful. I just needed a little release."

Priya squeezed her eyes shut. Her voice was deathly quiet. "Can you hear the words coming out of your mouth? I mean, can you actually hear yourself, Nick?"

"I know," he pleaded. "I know it sounds fucked up. But I'm telling the truth. The whole infertility thing has really thrown me. I'm stressed because I'm worried about you. Please believe me."

"Oh, *you're* stressed? *You're* worried about how your body's going to change, are you? *You're* worried that there's something wrong with you, because my tests came back perfect!"

She could feel tears building up inside her, like the tide rushing in. She didn't want to cry, but she couldn't hold it back. She tried to breathe. To regain some control. But the messages were flashing before her eyes. *Sexy. Breasts. Hard. Taste. Wet. Want.* She had memorized them, like a playground rhyme. Eenie. Meenie. Miney. Moe. Catch a cheater by his toe. She was looking at her coward of a husband who was desperately trying to convince her not to believe what she had seen with her own eyes, and what her brain had absorbed, against her will, and forced her to replay over and over again. In traffic. In the lift at work. On the examination bed, while her legs were spread open so strangers could prod and poke her soft, sensitive folds with cold metal instruments.

"Nothing happened. We just talked," he said quietly as her tears began to flow. "Pri." His voice was soft, pleading. "Pri, come here. I never meant for you to see those."

"And that makes it okay?"

She threw the phone at him. He turned away from the projectile and it struck him on the back, making a satisfying *thwack* before clattering to the floor. Nick followed it, falling to his knees.

"Pri, please." He shuffled to her. He put his arms around her waist and rested his head against her belly. Priya became rigid, but didn't pull away.

"I love you so much. And I want us to have a family together. You've got to believe me."

She removed herself from his embrace and sat heavily on the bed. "How can I?" And when he didn't answer, she added: "I think we should cancel the appointment."

"What? No!"

"No? Nick! You've been writing to other women."

"That's got nothing to do with this. We've waited months to see Doctor Carmichael. Please, can we just go?"

"How can we commit to a child when I can't trust you?"

He ran a hand through his hair.

"Sometimes—" he began. "Sometimes when I've been feeling, I don't know, lonely, I've found myself talking to strangers online. Not for sex or anything, just—I don't know. They flirt with me and it makes me feel better about not being able to get you pregnant."

Priya closed her eyes. "You don't get to use that as an excuse. Like, you've failed me so now I have to feel sorry for you."

"I know, but it's true. You were never supposed to find out." His voice quavered. She looked at him and saw tears in his eyes.

When she spoke, her voice had softened. "How do you think it makes me feel? I can't get pregnant and you're off sniffing around other women." Tears were rolling down her cheeks, but with the pain came relief. These accusations had been festering inside her. Expelling them was cathartic.

"It wasn't meant to be—I didn't mean—it was never like that."

"What was it like?!"

"I don't know." He threw up his hands. "I know it's shitty.

But it seemed harmless and it made me feel better. I thought if I could deal with it online I wouldn't have to trouble you with it."

"Why don't you talk to me if you feel lonely? Do you think you're the only one who feels alone?"

"I try, but you never seem to want to talk anymore. You didn't tell me you feel lonely. You just went cold on me."

"That's because I know you're talking to other women."

"Pri, I'm so, so sorry you saw that. But believe me, there's nothing to it. It's like pornography, but not. With this, the person talks back. They respond."

She twisted her body away, not wanting to think about it. "I don't want to know."

"I'm just trying to explain it. You have to believe me. I hardly ever do it. And I would never, ever meet up with one of these people in real life. I mean, what kind of person goes on to a dating app just to have text sex with some stranger?"

"You do it," she mumbled bitterly.

"*You* would never do it. That's what I love about you." He shuffled toward her. "You're so good, Pri." He climbed up her body, kissing her stomach, chest, and neck as he rose to his feet. "You're so smart and so good. It was a stupid crutch that didn't mean anything. Please, let's just go to see the doctor. You've had surgery; don't you want to know everything's okay? Let's not ruin this chance. Let's not let me being an idiot derail everything we've ever wanted."

She sniffed. "Okay. I won't cancel. But I'd like to go alone."

He let his head fall forward. "If that's what you want. But please promise me you will go."

All the way to the clinic she heard her phone vibrate as it received entreaties from Nick. *I'm sorry. You were never meant to see. Please believe me. I feel awful for hurting you.* Mixed in with a smattering of *I love you*s.

When she parked at Empona she felt rooted to her seat. Walking through the clinic's doors would be another step down the path she shouldn't take with an unfaithful husband. She wanted to believe what he was telling her, but she knew it might be foolish to do so.

She watched a couple walk up the ramp to the automatic doors, their arms around each other, their faces full of guarded hope. Priya took a deep, shuddering breath. She couldn't go any further without being certain. She opened the Bumble app on her phone and went into Rose's profile. She found Nick's smiling face and clicked on the conversation bubble. *Hey,* she typed. *What's up, cutie?* Then she stepped out of her car and slammed the door behind her.

Nine

A TRIPLE-EMBRYO TRANSFER SOUNDED LIKE AN EVENT THAT called for a grandstand theater, with trays of silver surgical equipment glinting under stadium lights and a team of surgeons in green gloves and masks. It was seismic. Three! But Grace was taken into the same small surgery where she'd had all her previous attempts, passing through the airlocked clean room to change into a paper gown and a pointless paper shower cap that was too small to hold her long blond hair. She giggled as she snapped it into place, on account of the Valium that Dan had encouraged her to take. Then she sailed, detached, into the surgery, where she settled herself onto the chair and tried to stop her gown from rucking up. Doctor Li tapped Grace's knee and her legs swung open like saloon doors. She slotted her ankles into the stirrups.

An embryologist Grace didn't recognize was at the workstation. Nurses rushed in and out. Grace lay back and looked at the ceiling, enjoying the way the Valium dulled her feelings.

Somewhere in the room three potential humans were sitting in a petri dish. Three almost-souls who would be pushed through a catheter, to float in the soft pink tissue inside her, and hopefully latch onto the rough red walls. The tiny specks should be welcomed by an environment that was thick and marshy, if her profusion of medications had done their job.

"How are you feeling?" Doctor Li asked.

"Good. Ready."

The image of her uterus beamed on to a small monitor looked oddly empty. She was so used to seeing ultrasound images of babies—at barbecues, retrieved from handbags, stuck to fridges. The black abyss on the screen resembled something else entirely.

Dan crouched so his face was close to Grace. "Can you believe that's where our baby's going to be?" He pointed to the monitor. "I have a really good feeling about this."

Amid the excitement she thought of their other embryo—the morula with the possible abnormality, their little girl all alone in their allotment of the Empona freezer. Early in the process, Grace and Dan had agreed they would donate any unused fertilized eggs to science. But now, with her three potential babies waiting and ready not far from her, Grace wondered if maybe they should keep the fourth embryo for a try later. Give her a chance.

Doctor Li approached. "Okay, Grace, here we go."

⁓

"Do we need takeaway?" Dan asked in the car home.

"No, we're fully stocked." Grace had ensured they had supplies for her confinement. "Is it terrible that a small part of me is glad to have an excuse to stay in bed all day?"

Dan laughed. He had brought the television upstairs so Grace could watch Netflix in bed, and he had set up a temporary nurse's station by clearing the bar cart of its bottles and wheeling it into the bedroom. It was stocked with snacks, painkillers, water, orange juice, and magazines.

"Is there anything else you need?" Dan asked.

"No, thank you." She kissed him as he fussed over her blanket. "Unless you have some embryo glue."

She said it in the half-joking way she used when she wanted to broach a thought she didn't entirely trust to see how he reacted to it.

"We could ask one of the nurses about it," he said.

They had already had this discussion. Grace had argued that if Doctor Osmond had given it to his patient, the worst thing that could happen would be that the glue would have no effect, but in the end they had decided that Doctor Li was treating them, and they shouldn't mess with her regimen.

"No, you're right. I trust Doctor Li."

"Would you settle for some honeycomb ice cream?"

"Ooh, yes, please."

"I'll run down to the supermarket and get some."

As soon as Dan was out of the house, Grace's mind began to roam. Her thoughts still had the quality of being wrapped in tissue paper, owing to the Valium. She mentally cataloged the plastic bottles and pill blister packs in her overflowing bathroom cupboard to be sure they had done everything they could to help the three little embryos. There was one thing she hadn't tried that might help.

Grace threw back the blanket, crept into the bathroom, and knelt before the vanity unit. She felt around in the old towels until she found what she was looking for. She pulled out the cardboard airfreight envelope and withdrew the little glass bottle.

She removed the stopper and held the dropper up to the light, asking herself: Do I dare?

The obvious answer was no. She did not know what was inside the bottle, and with the stopper removed the peculiar scent of chemicals and old fruit was filling the air and irritating her nose.

Still. Her subconscious nagged. She had read so many blogs and customer reviews gushing about this elixir—half a dozen at least. She'd followed the thread of their online IDs and verified the women making these claims were in fact real people. One of them even had a public Facebook page, filled with photos of a little girl with hazel eyes and pinchable cheeks. People wouldn't make up the claims, Grace told herself. They wouldn't be so cruel. She had seen it spoken about in enough forums, mentioned by enough women, for her common sense to falter.

She had read and reread the instructions from the website so many times she knew them by heart, and now she mouthed the words as she filled a glass with water and squeezed in three drops. The brown fluid dispersed quickly. It was such a small amount. It couldn't possibly be harmful, she reasoned.

She sniffed the water and wished she had an old-fashioned poison taster. As the image of the medieval servant choking filled her mind's eye she thought: So what if it is poison? If she couldn't get pregnant, what did she have to look forward to? Shuffling around her house in Ugg boots, her weekends filled with the birthday parties and graduations of other people's children. The future seemed so shapeless without offspring to fill it, just her and Dan adrift in a middle-aged hinterland.

She picked up the glass and stared at it. Sydney's drinking water was full of chemicals, anyway. What were a few more? Her hand hovered, holding the glass before her.

On a more rational level, she thought that, if it were dangerous, she would have heard. This was a product whose name was whispered across internet sites the world over. If it were dangerous the site that sold it would have been shut down. A journalist would have uncovered it. The online store also sold acetaminophen and Viagra.

Surely huge multinational pharmaceutical companies wouldn't allow their products to sit on the same virtual shelves as poison.

But still, as she cautiously lifted the glass to her mouth, her mind raced. Was this madness? The water smelled normal. She dipped her tongue in, like a cat. It tasted like water. She took a small, cautious sip. The moment she swallowed, sanity returned. She jerked the glass away and looked up at her face in the bathroom mirror. Her reflection was pale, stricken.

Are you insane? she wanted to ask it. *You've just had three embryos transferred to your uterus and you're drinking something you ordered off the internet? A month ago you wouldn't even allow yourself cheese.*

She tipped the water down the drain then emptied out the pipette and the tiny glass bottle. She washed her hands vigorously with soap and brushed her teeth, spitting and gargling and then repeating the process. She lowered her head and let the tap run over her tongue. She scoured her taste buds with her toothbrush then threw the brush in the bin along with the bottle and its packaging, then emptied the entire contents into the outside bin.

"Stupid," she said to herself as she hurried back into the house. "Stupid. Stupid. Stupid."

Ten

"I SAID I WAS SORRY," NICK SAID. "WHAT WILL IT TAKE FOR you to believe me? I'll do counseling, I'll do therapy, anything."

"We've been through counseling before," Priya said, exhausted.

"And it worked."

"It appears it didn't."

"So, what? You're just going to give up?"

They had been repeating the same fight over and over, exhuming all the old grievances they thought were long laid to rest, filling their days with undead resentment. And despite the knockdown, drag-out fights sparked by the smallest things, there had been no real conversation about their future.

"How could I put my body through that knowing any minute you might—" She broke off.

"What? Leave?"

He was angry. Insulted. Priya went quiet, knowing she had gone too far. But she was angry too. He was forcing her to argue against starting IVF when he was the reason they couldn't go ahead. She wanted a baby, more than anything. But she also wanted to know that baby would have a stable, happy life.

They fell asleep in their clothes.

After Nick got up the next morning, Priya lay curled up in the duvet, listening to the morning news. It was almost eight when she heard Nick leave and was able to drag herself out of bed. She would be late for work.

When she went downstairs Jacker was at his bowl, wagging his tail happily as he lapped up the egg on his dog chow. Nick liked to give Jacker an egg to keep his coat shiny. Priya looked at the happy, scruffy dog and gave him a scratch. How many times had she watched Nick crouch beside Jacker's bowl and crack an egg over his food, with a loving pat and a "There you go, buddy"?

The thought gave her hope for their future. She took her phone from her pocket and sent him a message: *Okay. Six weeks of counseling. Then we'll see.*

When she got home that night Nick was in the kitchen, slicing carrots into matchsticks. He had the makings of a green curry spread out on the counter.

"That smells good," she said politely. It was one of three dishes in his repertoire, along with Guinness pot pie and lasagna.

He gave her a kiss on the cheek, hesitating as he lowered his face to hers. In turn she offered a forced smile.

"I got something," he said, sheepish. "To help." His eyes stayed cast down as he took something from his pocket. "A bloke from work gave it to me."

He handed Priya a business card. It was creased from when he'd sat on it and warm from being close to his body.

"Said she saved his marriage."

Priya read the card: *Clementine Crosley. Marriage Counselor. Dip Psych B.S. Ph.D.*

Nick slid a hand through his hair. "She's pricey. But worth it. I suppose it's like IVF. You've got to pay for a full and proper service."

"I'll call tomorrow and make an appointment," Priya said, pleased he was trying.

⁓

The counselor, when they saw her, did a good job of drawing out their emotions.

"If I'm cold it's because I'm sad. Not because I don't love you," Priya said. She was sitting upright on a chaise longue in a tasteful office.

"You're always checking up on me," Nick said. "I feel like you want to catch me out."

"I don't *want* to catch you out. I don't *want* you to be doing anything I could catch you out at."

Their hour was nearly up and it felt like they were going in circles. Nick folded his arms and scowled at the bag squatting at Priya's feet. "And there's nothing in your phone you wouldn't want me to see?"

Priya shifted her bag with her foot so that it was behind her ankles. "You know there isn't," she said, looking out the window so he couldn't meet her eyes.

She still had Rose. She'd laid the bait for him. A simple *Hey. What's up, cutie?* And he hadn't answered. She had followed up with another message a few days later, just to be sure. She'd felt guilty the whole time, but also like it was a necessary step.

Cute puppy. He looks kind of like the border collie we had when I was growing up. What's his name? And what breed is he? Looks like there's some boxer in there.

Nick loved to speculate on Jacker's origins. He was on the smaller side, with short tan fur. Stavros liked to tease that maybe he had some poodle in him. "Or some bichon frise."

"No way," Nick would say, wounded.

She knew all his weaknesses, all his desires. She also knew what she was doing was wrong, but she wanted their baby and she had to be sure.

"I think today has been really productive," their counselor, Clementine, said. When she stood to shake their hands and see them out Priya noticed she had the beginnings of a baby bump. She was struck by a bolt of envy and felt her smile slip as she said goodbye.

"Thank you very much, Doctor Crosley," Nick had said, laying his left hand over Doctor Crosley's right as he shook it, smiling. Priya noticed him encase the woman's slender fingers, and her envy was joined by a twist of jealous mistrust. She was glad when they stepped out into the car park and she could draw fresh air into her lungs. Her head was swimming with conflicting thoughts and feelings.

"That went well, I thought," Nick said. "I mean, we started to get some things out in the open."

It was true. Priya felt like she'd been cracked open. She felt exposed and a bit bruised, but also lighter.

"We could pick up some fish and chips then finish painting the mural in the baby's room," Nick said.

"I think it's a bit early for that, don't you?"

"It'll be a good activity. Like when we renovated the house the first time around."

"I was going to go to my art class."

"Priya." His face fell. "We have to work on this."

"Nick, we are. We will. But this is my one thing that I really look forward to."

"If we're going to fix this maybe you should put us ahead of your project."

"I didn't see you volunteering to paint when you had football training," she countered. "This class is important to me."

"Okay." He threw up his hands like a martyr. "You go. I'll paint. I'll stay inside the lines you drew."

Priya felt guilty. "How about we do it on Saturday?" she said. "Make a day of it."

Nick grunted. "I'll make a start tonight."

⁓

Priya drove to the Fairfield Art Factory, where she poured some cheap wine into a tumbler and sat cross-legged on a cushion on the floor next to Husani.

"How'd the Blackman sale go?" he asked.

"The what? Oh, the painting. Um. Record bid. Nine hundred thousand."

Husani gave a low whistle. "That's why I always wanted to be an artist. So, tell me, when are you coming to look at my work?"

"Sorry, Husani, I've had a lot on my mind—"

Priya broke off as the model stepped into the room. It was someone new tonight. She dropped her kimono to the floor to reveal large breasts. Her dry blond hair looked like straw. Priya kept her head down and made the woman's feet the focus of her drawing, but she couldn't stop another image flashing into her mind. *Megan. Megan. Megan.* This model was younger than Megan, and looked nothing like her in the face. But the hair and the figure gave an overall impression of the woman in Nick's phone. Priya hadn't had the opportunity to check if he was still talking to her. She sat grinding her teeth as she tried to sketch, thinking: Nick ruins everything. She wanted desperately for things between them to be better. But she also felt like he was acting as if they were equally to blame for this crisis in their lives. Her hand wouldn't stay steady, and her lines were all over the page. She only got through two poses before she put down her graphite stick and told Husani she had to go.

"Are you coming next week?" he asked.

"I'm not sure I'll be able to make it next week. I'll text you. I'm really sorry, Husani. I know I said I'd come and look at your work. It's just a bad time right now."

"Hey, it's okay. I didn't mean to hassle you."

On the way to her car she pulled out her phone. It stopped her in her tracks. Her Bumble app had a blue spot on it. Her thumb hovered over it, afraid. She stood in the car park, clicked on her husband's message to Rose and read it in the dark: *That's my buddy Jacker. Man's best friend. We're a package deal.* And a smiley face. A disgusting, cheesy smiley face.

Her hands were trembling. She stood in the dark, staring at the screen. She couldn't move until she had dealt with this. She tapped in a response. *Oh. You come with baggage?*

A reply had arrived by the time she reached her car.

Cute baggage.

Priya momentarily considered deleting the app. Forget about it, and close her mind to what Nick was doing online. Stay married, have a baby. Try not to think about it. But instead of backing away, she plunged in further.

Are you single?

The minute she sent the words she wished them back. She could see the bouncing dots that meant he was typing. They bounced. She waited. A response appeared: *; p.* And then: *I told you I was a package deal.*

Enraged, she typed more: *I assume you are single, since you're on here. So, your buddy Jacker is your one true love? What do you love about him?*

He's so playful.

He didn't deny being single. She read over the messages, imagining her husband alone and bored on the couch. Had he written anything unforgivable? Not yet. Her phone trilled: *Are you playful, Rose?*

Anger flared in Priya's chest. She wanted to tell Nick she knew who he was. She wanted to scare and shame him. But that wouldn't give her the answers she needed. Instead she typed, *I can be playful,* and inserted a winking emoji.

The car was cold, illuminated only by the gray light of her phone's screen as she sat, staring at the conversation panel. It cast an unfeeling glow. Nick didn't respond.

She turned on the engine, pumped up the heater, and headed back to their house. As she made her way up the brick path she and Nick had laid by hand, she checked the device one last time. There was a reply: *What games do you like to play, Rose with the sexy smile?*

Instead of going into the main house, Priya snuck around the back to the studio and pulled an old canvas down from the stack on top of the wardrobe. She dropped a sheet over his weights and flicked on her stereo. She squeezed shiny slugs of vermilion, white, and royal blue onto a palette and sat down to paint. Feeling the oils glide beneath her brush comforted her. She had betrayed him too, she knew. Tricked him and trapped him, but he had forced her.

When she picked up her phone an hour later there were two texts from Nick—*Where are you?* and *It's late, are you at Viv's?*—two missed calls, and, finally, mail for Rose. *So, tell me, Rose, are you a cat or a dog person?* Priya angrily punched in a response.

Dog, definitely.

You sound very sure of yourself. I love Jacker. I love all dogs. But I also love pussy.

Priya threw the phone aside, ran to her sink, and vomited.

~

Jacker found her the next morning on a nest made from cushions. He wedged his muscly body up against hers for warmth and was soon snoring. Her paints had dried on the palette.

She got up, unfolded her stiff joints, and took the palette to the sink to clean it.

There was a blue dot on her screen. *What do you say, Rose? What are you down for?*

I'm down for anything, she shot back. Her mood had turned from sad to furious. She had to push it to see how far he would go. *When can I see you?*

The dots appeared and then a message: *This weekend?*

She felt like her chest had been cleaved open.

She shook Jacker from the blanket. The beast looked startled, then hurt. "I'm sorry, Jacker," she said, scratching behind his ears. "It's not your fault your master is a deadbeat."

Saturday afternoon, she typed. *Two o'clock. Do you know the Exeter?*

A message buzzed in. *Perfect.*

~

On Saturday, Viv put her arm around Priya as they stood a block from the Exeter.

"Are you sure you want to do this?" she said.

Priya looked at her sister imploringly. "This is the last thing I want to do. What I want to do is paint our nursery with my faithful husband." A tear rolled down each cheek. "I feel so guilty. So angry and so guilty." She swiped her face with her sleeve. That morning she'd told Nick she was catching up with Viv. He'd said he was going to watch the game at the pub. "Do you think I'm a bad person?"

"No," Viv said emphatically, squeezing her shoulder. "If he shows up you're a smart person. It just feels so final."

"I feel like I'm about to commit a crime. But I need to know."

Viv nodded. "Okay, let's go." She looped her arm through Priya's as they entered the pub and made their way upstairs. Not long after they sat, a waiter appeared, but Priya barely heard what Viv ordered as her eyes darted around the bar downstairs. A football game was playing on the flat-screen TVs mounted on the walls. She trained her eyes on the front door.

"There he is," Viv said, jolting to life. Nick was exiting the men's bathroom, wiping his hands on the seat of his jeans. Priya flew out of her chair and whipped off her sunglasses.

"What are you doing?" Viv hissed, grabbing her wrist.

"I'm going to kill him." Priya's voice was high. Shocked. "I can't believe he actually showed up."

"Let's see what he does," Viv said.

"I can't look," Priya said, sinking into her chair and holding a hand up to her eyes.

"He's not doing anything."

"Of course he's not doing anything, his girlfriend is a figment of our imagination. Oh God," Priya said. "Why did I do this? Why?"

In the back of her mind was her upcoming appointment with Doctor Carmichael. She wanted to be spending her day preparing for a baby, not staking out her spouse in a pub.

Viv grabbed Priya's hand and held it tightly. Together they

watched Nick stroll around the room as casually as if he were taking in a garden show. Waiters delivered plates the size of hubcaps covered in chips and chicken schnitzels smeared with parmigiana sauce and capped with oily cheese. Priya stiffened as she saw Nick walk with purpose toward a booth.

"What?" Viv swiveled to see better. His target was a blond in a blue baseball cap sitting in a banquette reading the menu.

Nick sidled up and tapped her shoulder. She looked up and Nick shot the blond his million-dollar smile as he spoke. She was responsive, but shook her head. He nodded and took a step back. He swung around to take in a view of the room and checked his watch. It was ten past two. He took a seat at the bar and signaled to the barman that he wanted a beer. They watched as he pulled out his phone and played with it, turned to look at the door, then went back to drumming on the bar.

"The bastard's nervous," said Viv.

"I can't bear this, let's go," Priya said.

"We can't. He'll see us."

Something crucial must have happened in the football game, because the group of men erupted into a roar. Nick looked up; his eyes zipped around the bar until they locked onto Priya, glaring at him from the balcony. He did a double-take, then squinted. Her long black hair was tucked away in a ponytail under a Rabbitohs cap. *His* Rabbitohs cap.

"He's seen us," said Viv.

He jumped off his stool and made for their direction at the same time Priya leaped from her seat and barreled down the spiral staircase. She pushed past him, thumping into his left shoulder so that he snapped back, shocked by the force.

"Priya!" he said, alarmed. "What are you doing here?"

She turned, fire in her eyes. "What am I doing here? What are *you* doing here?" She took a step toward him and punched his huge chest. "What are you doing here, Nick?" Her voice rose. She hit him again, and again, pummeling his barrel chest with her delicate hands.

"I—I just came to watch the game."

"Liar! You came here to meet her."

"Her? What her? There is no her."

"Rose! You came here to meet Rose. Down-for-anything Rose."

His eyes widened. "Wha— How?"

"*I'm* Rose."

Nick's face went white. "You set me up?"

"You forced me," she howled, and hit him again. Her fists bounced harmlessly off his chest. "How could you do this?" she cried, her blows landing without effect as her last burst of energy left her. "We're trying to have a baby and you're sneaking around with internet sluts."

Nick held his hands up. "Priya." He seemed barely able to process what was happening. He gripped her wrists to still her hands. "Stop it, will you? Don't you see how messed up this is?"

"You messed it up!"

Viv stepped between them, breaking contact. "Priya, come on." She turned to Nick. "Stay away," she said savagely, her finger held up in warning, her eyes wild. "Just stay away, Nick."

"Viv, c'mon," Nick appealed. "I'm sorry."

Nick threw his hands over his head as Priya ran for the door.

Viv caught up to her sister in the street and wrenched the car keys from her hands. Priya was panting, her face twisted in agony. Her mouth was a slash of pain.

"I'll drive," Viv said, opening the passenger door and helping Priya in.

"Get me out of here," Priya said between gasps. "Get me away from him."

"We'll go to my place. You can stay with us," Viv said, starting the engine. "I'll send Rajesh around to get some clothes."

Priya's phone rang. Nick. She stabbed her thumb over the reject button. "Why did I do this?" she asked.

"Because you had to," said Viv.

Eleven

GRACE WAS ALREADY AWAKE WHEN THE BIRDS STARTED chirping at five o'clock on the morning of her forty-fourth birthday. *Forty-four,* she mouthed to herself, testing out the feel of the words. Another F-word drifted into her mind.

The three embryos had failed. They were all Grade A and—Grace and Dan had learned—all boys. Specialists had sent in a battalion of three strong soldiers and not one of them had survived in her hostile womb.

Grace had filled the day with activities so she wouldn't have a moment to dwell on what options remained. She wasn't ready to face it. And so she had organized breakfast with her mother, morning tea with some of the Corella staff at the Vaucluse House tearooms, and lunch looking out over the harbor high above the Palisades. And in the evening, a themed dinner party for eight. But the sun was barely up and already she could feel a black shadow creeping across her heart.

She had made an afternoon appointment to have her hair set in hot rollers for the party, but after considering, she stole out of bed and left a message with the little salon on Bridge Road to cancel. The hours in the chair would afford too much time to contemplate a milestone that was—she felt—hollow. It had been two weeks since the three embryos had failed and Grace couldn't stop blaming herself. That brown bottle. The drops in the water. She was dogged by the thought that this time it really was her fault, and she hated herself for it.

Before meeting her mother she drove to Corella to find Bridget waiting for her as usual. Grace shuffled into the passenger seat and stuck the learner plates to the windshield while Bridget made her way to the car. They had decided, after Grace had been chauffeuring Bridget to her cooking class for a few weeks, that it was a good opportunity for Bridget to practice for her driving test.

"Hello, Bridget."

The girl was all smiles. "Happy birthday, Mrs. Arden." She held out a cake box tied with ribbon.

"Is this for me?"

"It's for your dinner party tonight."

"Shall I open it now?"

"Yes, please." Bridget looked ready to burst with pride.

Inside the box was a chocolate layer cake with *Happy Birthday* expertly piped across the middle.

"Bridget, this is wonderful. The decoration is so intricate. How did you manage it?"

"Ms. Collings helped. I wanted to do something to thank you. I wouldn't be able to do anything like that if it wasn't for you."

"I'm really touched," Grace said. "Thank you very much."

She leaned across the seat and hugged her.

After she had seen Bridget off to class Grace called the hairdressing salon and told them she would come in for her appointment after all.

Nine hours later Grace walked into the house with her hair high-lighted and set in a chignon, her arms weighed down with gifts and Bridget's cake box.

Dan whistled appreciatively. "Look at you."

"It was a surprisingly good day, in the end," Grace said. "Look what Bridget made for tonight." She popped the lid off the cake box.

"That's your kindness coming back to you," he said.

Grace tilted her head. "I can hardly take credit for Bridget's thoughtfulness. She's always been a very sweet girl. It's sad to think she'll be leaving Corella soon."

"You can still be friends."

"It's never the same."

"My Year Eleven English teacher, Mr. Dobson, taught me every-thing I know. He had a heart attack two years after I graduated. I still think about him from time to time. I like to think, if he were alive, we'd drink whiskey together and discuss the state of modern media."

"I'm sure you would. Do you need a hand with anything in here?" The kitchen was a hive of activity. Pots were boiling. Pastries were baking.

"I most certainly do not. Shoo, go pamper yourself, this is my department."

"I want to help," she said, dipping her finger into a jug of sauce and tasting it.

"You need to shower."

"How about this: we cook together, then we shower together."

Dan smiled. "Deal."

They took their time in the shower. Grace had to tilt away from the spray so that she wouldn't upset her hair. Afterward she changed into a black flapper dress and elbow-length gloves. Her costume was more 1920s than 1930s, but when she saw it in a vintage shop on King Street, it had been too late to change the theme. If pressed, she would say she was a thirties gal who was behind the times.

Dan sat next to her on the end of the bed and held out a present. "I thought this might go with your ensemble."

She smiled at him. "Thank you." Grace tore off the paper and eased open the jewelry box. "Dan," she breathed, taking in the soft glow of a pearl necklace.

"It's vintage. I had it cleaned so it looks new. Let me help you." He slipped the pearls around her neck.

The clasp—which sat at the front—was inlaid with tiny diamonds.

"It's perfect."

Dan had spared no expense for the party. He had set up the bar cart with cocktails in the lounge room, and arranged hors d'oeuvres of caviar blinis, pâté on melba toast, and pork pigs tucked into crispy pastry blankets. Noël Coward played in the corner. Their friends—Beth and her husband, Grant, Kent and Melody Caruthers, and Rochelle and Brian—all arrived in quick succession. Caroline was unable to come because her son, Jamie, had a fever, and for this Grace was relieved. She didn't want Caroline filling her head with more methods and tricks that had worked for friends of friends.

Caroline had her own podiatry practice, and while her scientific mind seemed at odds with her enthusiasm for alternative treatments such as feng shui and numerology, she delivered them with the authoritative doctor's confidence that Grace found hard to resist. She was glad to be spared the argument for the night.

"Unusual theme," Kent said, accepting a Dark 'n' Stormy from Dan. "Well executed, though."

"We thought the thirties was a neglected era. Everybody loves nineteen-twenties flapper parties, then they seem to skip straight to nineteen-fifties *Mad Men,*" Dan said.

"I enjoyed the challenge," Melody said. She wore a mid-calf dress with puffed sleeves in a blue floral pattern. Her blond hair was expertly curled and pinned. "It's called a Victory Roll," she said.

"The reason nobody throws thirties parties is because the nineteen-thirties was the era of the Depression," Brian said. "Should we read something into that, Gracie? Are you feeling down and drab as you get another year older?"

"Not at all." Grace touched her pearls self-consciously.

"I don't know what you're so cocky about, Brian, you'll be forty-seven in December," Beth shot back.

Brian was wearing spats and had penciled on an eyeliner mustache. Rochelle laughed. She had dug up a real fur muff, which she now didn't seem to know what to do with. "It was my grandmother's," she said, plopping it on her lap as she sat on the couch.

"So, you've come as fascism," Kent observed, looking pleased with himself.

"I'd never buy real fur, of course, but it does feel lovely." Rochelle stroked it like a cat.

"You look marvelous, Beth," Dan said, handing her a Tom Collins in a tall glass.

"I'm Ginger Rogers." Beth kicked up her foot for effect. She was wearing a red kerchief knotted around her neck and a white sailor's hat. "From *Follow the Fleet.*"

"So you are," said Dan. "I thought you were joining the navy to head to Pearl Harbor."

"We had the hat," she said, slipping it off her head and spinning it around on her index finger. "So I built a costume around it."

"I wish I'd thought to model myself on a thirties film star," Rochelle said. "Without my muff I just look like a sort of communist train conductor." She patted the fur idly.

"Well then, you must keep your muff out where we can all see it," Kent said.

"Kent!" Melody whacked her husband's belly, causing him to eject an *oof* sound.

They all laughed. Even Grace found herself smiling, but before she could say anything more, the oven timer screeched.

"That would be the dinner gong," Dan said, standing. "Follow me through to the dining room, please."

They settled themselves around the candlelit table and Beth gave an account of the most recent case she had been working on—a twenty-one-year-old man who had committed a "thrill kill" in regional New South Wales, executing an elderly couple in their home apparently for no reason.

"Most murderers aren't that remarkable. They just got caught up in drugs, or they have deep psychological disturbances. Of the hundreds of people I've defended, I'd say only a handful of them have been purely evil."

"His poor parents," Melody said, visibly shivering.

"I don't know how sorry I feel for the parents," Brian said. "They're the ones who unleashed the little sadist on the world. I'd be investigating what it was they did wrong that messed him up so badly."

"The parents had probably spent twenty years trying everything they could to help him," Melody said. "Maybe he had some sort of personality disorder."

"No," Beth said. "He didn't have any recognizable disorder."

"God, it chills you to the bone, doesn't it?" said Rochelle.

"I think we all know that once they're born there are very hard limits to how much control we have over them," Melody said.

"But we can change their lives for the better," Dan said. "The cake we will eat later comes to us courtesy of one of Grace's students who will no doubt grow up to become one of the country's most renowned chefs, thanks to Grace's efforts. Her father is forcing her to study law or medicine, but Grace has been secretly driving her to culinary classes each Saturday."

"Well done you," said Kent. "You can still be hugely influential in young people's lives even if you don't have any children of your own."

For a moment the only noise was the chink of cutlery on china.

"Still, IVF doctors can do wonders, can't they," Grant said. Dan and Grace looked at each other.

"Oh, are you still doing that?" said Melody. "You hadn't mentioned it. We thought you'd decided not to . . ." She trailed off.

"What's the success rate?" Brian asked.

"It's pretty good, isn't it?" said Rochelle, hopeful.

"Actually, no," said Grace. "Now that I'm forty-four I've got a less than two percent chance of conceiving."

Doctor Li had also told them that if Grace was determined to continue down the IVF pathway, they should consider moving to donor eggs or a donor embryo.

"What?" said Grant. "That's outrageous. The way people write about it, you'd think you were guaranteed a baby. Famous women forever seem to be carting little bundles home from the hospital even though they're in their late forties and early fifties."

"It's all a bit Wild Wild West, isn't it?" Brian said. "Who regulates these places?"

"You could never know," said Grant.

"That's not exactly true," Grace said, thinking of the conscientious Doctor Li.

"Who's for red?" Dan asked, producing a bottle of Barossa Shiraz. "This is a nice little drop we first tasted on our honeymoon."

"I wish we had time for winery tours," Brian said. "But between work and the kids it's hard to get away."

"Dan takes photos of the wine labels," Grace said. "We loved this and didn't want to forget it."

"That's a smart idea," said Beth.

As Dan went around the table, pouring, Rochelle's hand moved to her wineglass, covering it. There was a pause. Grace met her gaze. Rochelle's eyes welled up as a silent understanding passed between the two women. Grace concentrated on keeping her face still. Rochelle already had two children and she was forever saying what a handful they were. She had had two difficult pregnancies in quick succession, and she was exhausted. Certainly she hadn't been planning another baby, as far as Grace knew.

"We didn't want to say anything until I was further along," Rochelle said quietly.

"When are you due?" Grace asked.

"I'm sixteen weeks but I'm high risk because of my age."

Brian leaned forward and took a piece of bread from the plate in the middle of the table and began buttering it. "That's what got us into this situation in the first place. I didn't think there'd be much risk we'd get pregnant again. We probably weren't as careful as we could have been." Everyone felt the thump of Rochelle kicking her husband under the table.

"I think I'll have more wine," Grace said, holding her glass up to Dan, her voice high and tight.

As he poured she cleared her throat, then spoke again. This

time her voice was steady. "A toast." She raised her glass. "Here's to the children in our lives, and the new one about to join us. Sons, daughters, nieces, nephews, students. Whatever form they take. They keep us young, and given the number of candles on the cake that's in our fridge, I'm thankful there is about to be one more."

"Well said." Dan raised his glass as Rochelle clapped.

"Here's to you, Gracie," Beth said. "The classiest dame there ever was."

"Cheers!" came the chorus. "Happy birthday."

Grace smiled at her friends. Dan kissed her cheek and she turned into him, clasping his back to hide her hand going to her eye to wipe away a tear.

Bridget's cake was demolished and six bottles of wine were drained before two a.m. when the last guests said their goodbyes. With the house empty, Grace began to clear the table.

"Let me do that," Dan said.

"I can manage," she said.

"It's your birthday." He took the grimy dish from her hand.

"You cooked all day." She snatched it back.

He stood back and watched her roughly fill the dishwasher racks with crockery.

As she tried to jam in one last plate there was a crack. Grace held up her grandmother's good china, which was now two jagged halves. She pressed the pieces together, feeling a surge of anger then a rush of misery. Hopelessness covered her like a lead cloak. "Oh," she sobbed, overwhelmed.

"Are you okay?" Dan asked.

She wanted to say so many things—that she was annoyed with

herself, angry and sick to death of her own weak will that stopped her from feeling anything but pure excitement for her friend—but she held back her fears; she had burdened Dan for too long. She took a breath and tried to overcome the emotions coursing through her. "Yes. I'm sorry," she said. Her hand went to the string of pearls around her neck. "Thank you for everything you did today. I couldn't have asked for more. I'm really"—her voice faltered—"very lucky."

"I've been thinking," he said, rubbing her shoulder. "What do you say we get a dog? A little spaniel or something to keep us company."

"That's . . . that's a great idea. I love spaniels."

"Me too. I don't know why we never thought of it before. I suppose I thought it was something that would come after kids. A Christmas puppy for them to play with."

Grace smiled sadly. "And now if we wait until we have children to get a dog we may never have either."

Silence fell again.

"We still have one more embryo," Dan said quietly.

She bit her thumbnail.

"Doctor Li said there's a chance she's okay," he added, still cautious.

"I almost wish she hadn't told us," she said. "If your child is born and there are complications, you just deal with it. But asking us to make the conscious decision to give life to a child who might always suffer seems like too big a task to place on two people's shoulders."

"I'm not scared to raise a disabled child."

"I'm not either. I just think, if we choose this one, are we condemning her to a short and painful existence, when a donor egg would give her a stronger body?"

"It's impossible to know." Neither of them spoke for a moment. Dan touched his wife's arm. "Do you want to do another round?"

"I don't think another round of retrievals is an option."

He nodded.

She looked at her hands. "If we used a donor egg I'd feel guilty about abandoning our last frozen embryo."

"Maybe the possible exclusion means it won't take. I mean, none of the others have."

"Who knows what it could mean? She might need full-time care. She might not need any special assistance at all. She could be perfectly healthy."

"And even if she isn't, she's still our little girl."

"Yes, she's ours. What kind of parents would we be if we abandoned her?"

"So, what are you thinking?"

"I'm imagining her in that cold refrigerator in Alexandria waiting for her chance." Grace had tears in her eyes. "I think . . . I think I want to give her a chance."

Dan broke into a smile. "Me too." He hugged her. "Let's do it. Let's go get our girl."

Twelve

NICK AND PRIYA STARED AT EACH OTHER FROM OPPOSITE ends of their dining table like old foes, while a neckless man in a shiny blue suit opened a glossy portfolio and laid out a series of pricing structures his real estate agency offered.

"I recommend going for this package," the agent, Brett, said as he tapped the second-most expensive option with a silver pen. "A lot of young families are slowly starting to look west, but we need to entice them with a high-impact campaign. Spend money to make money and all that. We'll do print. Online. And a digital street sign. They have these nifty features now where we can embed an LED screen into the sign to give a three-sixty-degree view of the interior."

"I've seen those in Paddington and Darlington," Nick said. "Surely you're not recommending something like that around here? It would be stolen in sixty seconds."

Brett looked dubious. "It was just a suggestion. Right," he said, with a salesman's gusto. "Let's take a look through the place before we get down to brass tacks."

"You've seen the front," Nick said, as they walked through to the entrance hall. He gestured to the original master bedroom.

"That's the guest room. I added another story with a new master bedroom and an en suite."

He took Brett up the winding stairs. Priya stayed in the hallway and tried to block out Nick's description of all the features she had carefully chosen and he had lovingly installed. A young couple had come by earlier to pick up their marital bed. Nick had told Priya she could have it, but she said she had nowhere to put it.

"Besides," she reasoned, "we should sell it and split the money."

She wouldn't have minded if Nick kept it if she could be sure he wasn't going to invite Barbie doll internet women into it. It had sold on Gumtree in less than an hour. Mattress and all. Priya threw in the blue linen bedding free of charge, knowing she'd never be able to sleep soundly in it again.

"We'll have to hire some furniture," Brett said. Priya listened as he explained to Nick that furnished houses fetched a better price. "Also, it'll cover the discoloration in the paint."

When they had shifted the bed they had discovered a perfect headboard-shaped outline on the wall. The bedroom Nick had built had large windows on all sides that bathed the room in light during the day, and the sun had leached the color from the yellow walls. Where the bed had rested was a dark shadow in the original buttery cream, protected, as if from a nuclear blast.

The men thumped down the stairs.

"Next?" asked Brett.

Priya's and Nick's eyes went to the second downstairs bedroom.

"Another bedroom?" Brett charged toward it.

"We don't need to look in there," Priya said.

At the same time Nick said: "It's the same as the other one."

Brett had already opened the door and stepped inside. The

jungle scene had been completed. Amid the palm trees were laughing monkeys, a smiling elephant.

"Hmm," Brett said, his enthusiasm dipping for the first time since he crossed their threshold. "I'd recommend painting over this."

Priya's lip trembled. Nick took Brett's arm by the elbow and guided him out of the room. "Let me show you what I did with the kitchen."

There was no prenup, and only one shared asset. The house would be sold at auction. There was a small amount owing on the mortgage; the remaining profit would be divided fifty-fifty, less the agency fees.

The tour complete, Brett pressed them for a decision. Nick was staring at the brochure with his hand over his mouth. His eyes were tired.

"What do you think?"

Priya shrugged. "I just want it sold."

"We don't have to hurry," Nick said. "You can live here. I'll move out."

"No," she said. "I want a clean break."

"Ah, do you folks need a moment?" Brett asked.

"We'll take this package," Priya said, tapping the one Brett had suggested. Nick nodded but didn't speak.

"Okay." Brett retrieved the silver pen from his pocket and clicked it open. "If you just sign here and here, we'll get things moving."

Nick took the pen. He looked up at Priya, the nib hovering over the page. "We don't have to rush into anything," he said.

"Nick." She closed her eyes.

"This is our home. We could rent it out, see how things go."

"I've spent fifteen years seeing how it goes."

Nick flinched. "Lucky you were on your guard," he grumbled.

She heard the scratch as he scribbled his signature. When she opened her eyes it was done. She signed her name alongside her husband's.

"Okay, folks." Brett slid the brochures into his briefcase. "You can relax now. Leave it all to us."

Nick shook his hand. Priya turned away so he wouldn't see the distress on her face.

～

When Priya returned to her sister's place the house was silent. There was a note on the side table: *Hope it went okay. There's leftover masala in the fridge xox.* Priya put the bowl in the microwave and retreated to the couch while it heated, her feet tucked up underneath herself.

She had to shift to find a comfortable position. Her backside was tender. She was secretly taking hormones Doctor Carmichael had prescribed. Priya had stormed into the decision to sell the house, but she couldn't bring herself to sever the IVF process they had begun. She had thought that once they did the transfer there would be no turning back, but what she had discovered was she was already past the point of no return. In her imagination, the baby already existed, conceived in their minds, now waiting for biology to catch up.

If it was a girl, they had decided they would name her Isabelle after Nick's maternal grandmother. If it was a boy, he would be Sadavir, for Priya's maternal grandfather. Isa and Sadavir were too real to abandon.

In a few days she had an appointment booked to retrieve her eggs, which she had decided to freeze. She was thirty-seven and about to be single again and reasoned it was good insurance. It would be a while before she would be ready to even think about dating. Then it would take time to find the right person. If and when they were ready to discuss pregnancy she'd be . . . what? Forty, at the least. But her eggs would be thirty-seven.

Vivian padded out from her bedroom, rubbing her eyes. "How was it?"

Priya shrugged. "It wasn't fun, that's for sure."

"Did he try to get you back?" she asked.

"No. But he tried to stop me selling the house."

"It's very fast."

"Why wait?" Priya said.

Viv bit her lip. "How are you feeling?"

Priya sighed and shrugged. "Empty." She stabbed a chunk of curry with her fork.

"I saw this in the bathroom bin," Viv said, taking an empty vial and alcohol swab sachet from her dressing-gown pocket. "You're still doing the treatment?"

Priya swallowed the curry and nodded. "I couldn't back out. We've come so far. I thought this time next year I could have a baby . . . and now it's all gone. Not just the baby, but Nick, the house. Everything. And now, maybe I'll never get the chance to be a mother."

"But . . ." Viv struggled to find the right words. "You and Nick have broken up. What are you planning?"

"Freezing my eggs," Priya said.

"P-ya!" Avani called.

"How did you get out of bed?" Priya asked the little girl standing in the doorway. "You naughty little rabbit," she said as Avani motored across the room and threw herself at her aunt, hugging and clambering onto her lap.

Priya stroked the girl's curls and kissed her head. "I just want to keep my options open," she said.

⁓

A few days later, Priya walked up the ramp to Empona with a headful of questions and a heart whirring like a hummingbird.

"There's been a change of plans," she explained to Doctor Carmichael.

"Has something happened?" The physician looked immediately concerned.

"Nick and I split up."

Doctor Carmichael tilted her head sympathetically. "I'm sorry to hear that."

"But I still want to have a baby. I want to be a mother now. I'm ready. Nick and I . . . we were planning . . . that is to say, I've been ready for years. I was hoping you could tell me about using donor sperm."

"Priya." The doctor removed her glasses. "I find myself in an unusual position. It is not my job to counsel you. But the split is very fresh—are you sure this is how you want to proceed?"

"Yes, Doctor Carmichael, I'm sure."

"Having trouble conceiving is stressful. A lot of couples separate then reconcile. Maybe if you wait—"

"The split had nothing to do with infertility," Priya said quickly.

"Okay then." Doctor Carmichael held Priya's eyes for a moment, then the professional briskness returned. "In that case, let's look at options."

"I thought it would be good to find an Indian father. So the baby looks like me."

"Well, you can use a local donor of Indian heritage, or you can use an international donor."

"I understand."

"And there are additional fees."

"Of course."

Doctor Carmichael spun around on her chair and pulled some documents from her filing cabinet.

"These outline the costs." She passed them to Priya. "The good news is the donors are all vetted. Given your history, I would recommend we proceed straight to IVF. We'll retrieve your eggs today as planned and freeze them. Then I'll give you some information to take home and consider."

Twenty minutes later Priya was in the surgery with her legs in the stirrups.

"Your follicles look good." Doctor Carmichael smiled. "We'll see you after your nap."

When Priya woke the doctor was smiling. "We got six," she said. The number was written on the back of Priya's hand in black marker. "Six is very good. Go home and rest, and when you're ready, you and I can talk more about donors and your baby."

Thirteen

"WE'VE THOUGHT A LOT ABOUT THIS," DAN TOLD DOCTOR LI. "We won't abandon her just because she might have an abnormality."

"We'll love her no matter what," Grace said.

"I understand," Doctor Li said. "We'll need you to sign some fresh consent forms."

"Of course," Dan said.

"Would you like to see one of our counselors before we go through with the transfer?"

"I think that would be a good idea, but we know what we're doing, Doctor. We want this."

"Of course you do," Doctor Li said. "And I wish you the best of luck." She handed them a printout. "Take this to Doris and she'll book you in for the procedure."

The waiting room was crowded with couples, all looking a little on edge. Grace rested her head against Dan's shoulder. The transfer might fail, like all the others had, but at least they weren't sitting around. "What a madhouse," she said.

As the receptionist was showing them what to sign, Doctor Li joined them at the front desk.

"Doris, can you please arrange the earliest possible appointment for the Ardens."

The receptionist clucked her tongue as she clacked the keys and read her computer screen. "The surgery's busier than a bricklayer in Baghdad."

"See if you can work your magic," Doctor Li said. "Grace and Dan have waited long enough."

Fourteen

"HE'S HANDSOME," DARSH SAID.

"I don't care that he's handsome; I just care that he has no history of diabetes or heart disease."

"You should put that on your dating profile when you're ready to get back out there."

Priya gave a hollow laugh.

His name was Braj. He was a twenty-eight-year-old dentist from Bangalore, not far from where Priya's family originally came from, and thanks to the skillful hand of Doctor Carmichael, his sperm and Priya's ova had created three healthy blastocysts.

Because Priya had chosen a sperm that had already been donated she didn't have to wait the usual three-month quarantine period. It was screened and clean and ready to go. Avani, Shanti, and Shanaya all had the flu, so Priya had asked her cousin to come to the clinic with her, to hold her hand and help her home.

"Are you sure you don't want to shift one region over?" Darsh asked in a hushed voice as they sat in the waiting room. "You don't want to find out he's your cousin. You know those IVF horror stories that crop up every few years. 'I married my brother.' 'My mother is my sister.' And so forth."

"There are more than a billion people in India, I think the chance the person I chose to be my donor is somehow related to us is microscopic."

Empona's receptionist, Doris, called Priya's name. "Mrs. Archer? Mrs. Priya Archer?"

Priya flinched. "Hopefully that's the most painful part of the procedure," she said. Darsh squeezed her arm.

She walked through to the surgery and soon she was in the chair. Even though she wished it was a partner who was by her side, she was grateful to have Darsh there.

As if sensing what she was thinking, he put his arms around his cousin and gave her a kiss on the cheek. "We'll all stick by you," he said. "You won't be doing it alone."

"Thanks, Darsh. That means a lot." She drew a deep breath. "It's all happening so quickly, but now that I'm not preoccupied with Nick, I know this is the right decision."

"Are you ready, Mrs. Archer?" the embryologist asked.

"It's Laghari," Priya said. "Archer was my married name."

Doctor Carmichael came toward her with a long, fine tube. "We're putting two in, as discussed," she confirmed.

Priya nodded.

"Here we go," Doctor Carmichael said.

Priya felt her heart starting to pound. For the first time in a long time she felt like she had something to look forward to.

Fifteen

THE WINTER SKY WAS SQUALLY. GRACE HAD OPENED ALL THE windows to let in fresh air after she and Dan had spent almost two weeks hibernating inside, hoping with everything they had that this last transfer had worked. The wind was sucking the curtains out the windows, making them dance like ghosts. As Grace pulled them in and drew down the sash, she spied their neighbor Mrs. Goss's spinning weather vane. The cinematic portent of change made the hairs stand up on the back of her neck.

It's too early, she thought, touching her belly. And yet, she had an irrepressible urge to do a test.

She guzzled a liter of water, then opened her bathroom cupboard. On the shelf was a leftover pregnancy test at the ready. Her bladder was full, but when she sat down and tried to pee on the stick, she found she couldn't. Her body was clamping up as if protecting her. It was once again betraying her. She took a deep breath and tried to conquer her fear.

This one little girl was their last chance. Everything was hanging on their morula. But how could she survive when three strong boys had fallen?

But then, Grace reasoned, hadn't she been awfully tired lately?

And hadn't she had an acute hankering for vanilla ice cream? She had always had a sweet tooth, but this was no slight fancy; she craved it physically, like an addict lusts for a hit of heroin. At eleven thirty the night before she had pulled her jacket on over her pajamas and driven to the nearby 7-Eleven to buy a liter of French vanilla. She took a plastic spoon from the coffee station and started eating it in the car, sliding the spoon across the top of the tub and filling her mouth with creamy perfection. Half an hour later she was sitting at her dining table chasing the last milky puddles around the bottom of the plastic container. And afterward, she wanted nothing more than a long, bumpy, briny pickle. There were none in the house, and so she ate a handful of salted cashews and returned to bed. But as she lay in the dark, trying to sleep, the thought of the pickle took hold. She fantasized about feeling it snap between her teeth, slimy, salty, and sharp. It was all she could think about until she threw on her jacket for a second time, grabbed her car keys, drove to the supermarket, and bought a half-kilo jar, which she opened in the car park, licking her fingers as she devoured pickle after pickle. The cravings offered dangerous hope and had her heart in a stranglehold.

She felt the release and had to dive between her legs with the plastic test to make sure she caught the stream. And then it was done. The second the test made contact the chemical reaction began. Her nerves fizzed.

Grace did up her pants and looked at her watch. It had been nine seconds. She washed her hands and set the test on the bathroom countertop. She couldn't bear to watch it. She stepped into the hall and closed the door. For three minutes she paced up and down, mimicking expectant fathers waiting outside 1950s hospital delivery rooms.

When the time came to look she walked into the lounge room where Dan was reading, unaware.

"I took a test and it's ready," she announced.

He lowered his tablet. "And?"

"And I haven't looked yet."

He leaped off the couch. "Well, come on," he said. Having borne witness to the French vanilla expedition and, an hour later, the great pickle quest, Dan couldn't help but draw conclusions of his own.

"It's in the bathroom."

They hurried upstairs, anticipation building with each footfall. Dan put his hand on the doorknob. "Ready?"

"Yes, let's get it over with."

They opened the door and walked toward the counter. When she looked at the test she could hardly believe her eyes.

"Dan!" She held up the stick, revealing two little bars. "We're pregnant. We're pregnant!"

⌒

The next hour was a flurry of phone calls. They called Beth, then Grace's mother, Fiona, who was so happy she cried. "Oh, thank heavens." They called Dan's parents, who were equally ecstatic.

"No more, we have to wait," Grace said.

"How are we going to bear the waiting?"

She took Dan by the hand and led him into the untouched room. She lifted the teddy bear off the dressing table and swept the dust from the top with the sleeve of her shirt. "I still can't believe it," she said. "Our little morula. She's going to be fine, I can just tell. She's the strongest of the bunch. Stronger than three perfect boys. She's going to be a hell-raiser."

As the weeks passed, Grace became hyperaware of her belly. She was unable to stop caressing it, soothing herself that it would come to no harm. She had nightmares of waking up with an empty womb, her belly's contents scooped out while she slept. But she had good dreams too: sweet, fuzzy-tipped adventures with roly-poly babies. Caroline recommended an app that charted the baby's growth and helped Grace prepare for each stage.

Your baby is the size of a pumpkin seed.

Your baby is the size of an olive.

She would talk to the creature she was carrying inside her. Not out loud, generally, but in her mind. When she was alone, she would whisper.

"See that, little girl, that's a Labrador."

"Smell that? It's jasmine. That means spring is coming."

"That noise is an ice cream truck. I bet you'll love ice cream, my little one."

At work, she transformed into the most patient, serene person on staff. As the days began to pile up, her pants and skirts grew tight. The skin of her belly became taut. She hugged Bridget Hennessy goodbye after graduation and told her the good news.

"Oh, Mrs. Arden, that's so exciting."

"Promise me you'll let me know how you go in your exams," Grace said.

"I promise. Send me pictures of your baby when she's born!"

Your baby is the size of a plum.

Your baby is the size of a peach.

Grace didn't mind the nausea. She embraced each reassuring heave. The first kick filled her with such delight she thought she would never be happier. The baby seemed to enjoy music; Grace would turn up the stereo to try to coax a wriggle or a kick out of her little seahorse. Driving put her to sleep.

Your baby is the size of a pear.

Your baby is the size of a mango.

Dan would read the newspaper to Grace's bump. "'Man Survives Seven-Story Fall.' What do you think of that, little Petri?"

Somewhere along the line, the baby girl had been assigned the nickname Petri on account of the dish where her life began. Speculation on her personality and preferences became a favorite topic of conversation.

"I wonder if Petri will like coriander," Dan said.

"Maybe not at first. But she'll develop a taste for it. Petri will have a sophisticated palate."

She became a proxy for making a case against Grace's and Dan's dislikes.

"Petri won't like jazz. You'd better turn that down."

"Or perhaps it just means I have to listen to it as much as I can before Petri arrives."

Dan, upon seeing Grace cutting pineapple—which he couldn't stand—for an upside-down cake, declared, "I don't think Petri likes pineapple."

"I think she does," Grace said, smoothing a palm over her bump.

"It's awfully sugary," Dan said. "Too much sugar can't be good for growing Petris."

Grace pursed her lips, then boxed up the pieces of pineapple in Tupperware and took it next door to Mrs. Goss.

As she grew, Petri ruled over their home like a queen.

Grace returned to her yogi-style state of disciplined eating. Cheese and salmon were expunged from the fridge. Booze was not allowed in the house. She even threw out a bottle of vanilla essence because it contained alcohol. The nausea faded. Everything was on track. Grace's skin glowed. Her breasts felt like cement cantaloupes. Her hair became thicker, more lustrous.

"You look like a goddess," Dan said, marveling at it one night.

Grace felt happier and more content than she could ever remember.

There was a host of tests. Because Grace was over forty, precautions were advised. But everything seemed fine. All the results came back clear. Doctor Li recommended an obstetrician in Camperdown— Doctor Torres—who would see them through the pregnancy. Doctor Torres's waiting room was full of round women and had a box of toys to occupy small children. To Grace, it felt like a milestone. From here on, everything would be as with a normal pregnancy.

They both liked Doctor Torres. She was a little older than Doctor Li. A mother herself, she had a relaxed manner.

Doctor Torres squirted the cold gel on Grace's stomach then slid the wand over it.

"Does it look like everything is . . . okay?" Grace asked.

"It looks like everything is fine," the doctor said. "We've got a nice strong heartbeat."

Dan and Grace clung happily to each other.

"Do you want to know the sex?" Doctor Torres asked gaily.

"Oh, we know the sex," Dan said. "We did IVF."

"Ah. No surprises here, then. See the spine? He's got his back to us. Come on, little fellow, turn around."

They could see the spine stretch and move. "He's an active little guy," Doctor Torres said.

"It's a girl," said Grace.

"Oh, she is? Let's see if we can get another angle on our little miss. Come on, little girl." She moved the device over Grace's belly. "Here she is. Oh look! Oh!" Doctor Torres exclaimed, surprised.

"What?" Grace jolted.

"What is it?" Dan's voice shot with alarm.

"Oh, it's nothing bad. But I think the lab may have made a mistake. Look."

They squinted at the screen.

"Look there." The doctor pointed. "Can you see?"

They both leaned toward the monitor.

"It's a boy," Doctor Torres said.

"A boy?"

"We were told the embryo was a girl."

"See for yourself." She wiggled a finger at the blurry creature tucked into the white snow of Grace's uterus.

"Huh," said Dan. "Are you sure?"

"Quite sure."

"But how?" said Grace. "I mean, I'm happy. I'm just confused."

Doctor Torres shrugged. "Clinics make mistakes. It happens more often than you would think."

Sixteen

PRIYA STARED AT THE SINGLE BLUE LINE ON THE PLASTIC stick and felt a flood of sadness tempered with relief. She was able to embrace the doubt that had been fluttering in the back of her mind, like a moth butting itself against a windowpane: insistent but easy to ignore. The symbol was a dash. A minus symbol. *You are minus one baby,* it told her.

She wanted a child, desperately, but she wanted a child with Nick. Or rather, an as yet unknown partner. When she pictured motherhood, so many of the images were of a rambunctious toddler trailing after his big strong dad. The vision was Sadavir, curly-haired and chubby-cheeked, playing in the dirt with a plastic spade as Nick spread fertilizer over the crop of carrots, or mowing his Tonka truck across the back lawn as Nick restaked the tomatoes. Or little Isa, whom Nick would let stand on his feet while they danced at a wedding. Her grin, toothy. Her eyes, Archer blue.

Priya didn't have that lawn anymore. The garden bed was up for sale. There would be no weddings. She pulled a blanket around her shoulders and curled into a ball in her sister's armchair to contemplate this new reality. A secret fear she kept locked away in a hidden corner of her mind was this: if she fell pregnant to a stranger, there would be no reviving things with Nick; they would be over forever. But she couldn't dwell on that. The only way was forward.

She would have to go in for an official blood test, and when Doctor Carmichael learned of the failed transfer she would ask Priya if she wanted to try again. Priya bit her nails as she thought of it, her movements fidgety and tense. She couldn't commit to an answer.

It had been one thing when she was doing it with Nick. Creating a family with her husband. All their hope and sadness was shared. His disappointment had been a balm for the hurt she felt over the sleazy messages. He wanted this with her, that much she knew. A thought struck her. Would he want to have a baby with Megan? She couldn't bear to imagine it.

Priya stood up, struck by an urge to see her house. He had been living there but had promised to be gone in time for the house to be prepared for the auction. She picked up her phone and dialed.

"Priya?" His voice was in her ear after one ring.

"Nick. I was going to go over to the house before the cleaners come in." She had to steady her voice. "One last look around, you know."

"And you wanted to know if I'd be there?"

"Well, I won't come if you haven't left."

"I have. We're renting in Chippendale for now."

Priya's heart stopped. *We?*

"We being me and Jacker, that is," he rushed to explain.

"Oh. Well, lucky Jacker."

"Nah, he hates it. There's no yard. At least, not one big enough to satisfy him. Is there, boy?"

Envy bit again. Priya missed Jacker.

"And you definitely won't be there tonight?"

"Nah, we've got an event for—"

"Okay, I don't need to know!" She was terrified of being ambushed by a Megan story. In her mind, the blond was with Nick constantly. Priya imagined she had ropey hair, a sandpaper tongue, smoker's breath.

"Right. Sorry, right. I'm still in the process of moving everything, but I won't be there tonight."

"In that case I'll head around."

"It's all yours."

She had thought about taking a souvenir, perhaps an ornamental knob from one of the cupboards. Something to remember the place by. But when she stepped into their old hallway, it felt different. Without their shared furniture, it was as if the house had died. The bedrooms were unfamiliar. The kitchen seemed off-balance without the granite-top kitchen island that Nick had sold. She climbed the spiral staircase to their old bedroom.

The upstairs bathroom was the only place that felt the same, with its lion-claw bathtub. She gave the iron foot a half-hearted kick. She opened the door to the mirrored cabinet. It had been cleared out, except for the few things Priya had left behind. An ancient pot of lip balm. Half a tube of hand cream. She poked around the drawers and under the basin for other personal items she might have overlooked. In the corner was the old wicker laundry basket they had had since before they were married. The bottom half was a rash of mold from years of soaking up steam. She scooped it up, planning to squash it into the bin. She wanted to break its flimsy slats and feel it crack and crunch.

Between the clothes basket and the wall she spotted a scrap of fabric she didn't recognize—pink-and-purple synthetic lace. Priya bent closer and realized with horror it was a pair of women's underpants. Twisted. Used. She jerked upright and let out a cry of disgust.

She dropped the basket and hurried down the stairs and out the front door, not stopping to take a souvenir. As she ran down the path, she realized the last thing she wanted was to be reminded of her former life and everything she had lost.

⁓

The sky was a perfect, unblemished blue for the auction.

"This should bring out a crowd," said Viv as they parked across the street from the house.

"I still can't believe he had a woman in our home," said Priya, staring at her soon-to-be-former front door.

"Would Nick do that?" Viv asked. When Priya frowned at her she threw up her hands in a show of innocence. "Sorry!"

In the few months Priya had been living at her sister's house they had had more than a few fights over Viv being too soft on Nick.

Viv undid her seat belt and squeezed Priya's forearm. "Can you imagine living the rest of your life in fear he's cheating on you? You did the right thing."

"I know."

"Are you nervous?"

"I'm quite sad about the house, really. We worked so hard on it. I loved the leadlight glass we put in the kitchen."

The advertising photos had come out spectacularly. Shot with a wide lens, the house appeared spacious and airy.

"It was such a beautiful place," Priya said, holding one of the glossy brochures Brett had given her as she stared past her sister to the house.

"They're bad memories you don't need," Viv said.

Prices in the area were on the rise as city land values climbed and Sydney's populace continued its inexorable march west. The local council had announced funding for a neighborhood renewal program, and the coats of paint and graffiti removal were already making a visible difference to the community hubs. Brett had commented that these factors would all help drive up the price.

"Good," Priya had said at the time. "I'm going to need every cent I can get."

They watched the first trickle of potential buyers arrive for the final inspection at nine thirty before the auction started at ten. Then the numbers steadily built as batches of people arrived in twos and fours.

"What if we don't sell it?" Priya said in a moment of panic. "Would one of us have to move back in? Will Nick take it and shift that woman into our home?"

"It will sell," Viv said. "Look at these hordes."

Nick's truck pulled up. Priya sank into the car seat as she watched him step out alone and scan the crowd. He walked up the pathway and was invited into his own home by a young woman in a red blazer and an overblown smile. Brett jogged to the stoop and shook Nick's hand.

"You don't want one last look?" Viv asked.

Priya shook her head and crossed her arms over her chest. She scowled at the house, as if it were the veranda that had betrayed her, the pitched roof that had cheated.

"Come on," said Viv. "Let's get a spot. It's nearly time."

A large crowd had gathered by the time the auctioneer stepped up to the front gate.

"This is a lovely home. Custom renovated with a modern master bedroom and en suite," he began before counting off its many charms.

Nobody moved. Not even a twitch.

"Perhaps we over-capitalized," Priya said, chewing her nail.

Someone offered $510,000, and the man in gray responded with $520,000. This back and forth went on until it started to slow toward seven hundred. When they hit the mark and the auctioneer announced that the house was on the market, it was like someone suddenly lit a fire under the street.

Priya could feel tension rise in the crowd. Her eyes darted from face to face. They landed on Nick. He had his fist to his mouth and was staring straight at her. He raised his eyebrows ever so slightly. Priya looked away, the memory of pink-and-purple polyester flashing into her mind.

The two bidders continued to duke it out up into the high nine hundreds.

Priya watched the other contenders. The person she considered to be third in the running had gone quiet. He was speaking on the phone, his eyes down, nodding.

"One million."

Viv gasped and squeezed Priya's hand. It didn't stop there. The price kept climbing and climbing.

The auctioneer's face was growing red with excitement. He was a showman, a ringmaster, spitting and launching his fist into the air, trying to shake more money from the crowd.

"Are we all done? Are we all out?" he called, the contract poised about his head. "Sold!" He dropped it into his palm with a smack and the crowd let out a sigh and a cry. The buyer shouted, his supporters slapped his back and cheered. A woman in a striped dress threw her arms around him, and he hugged her, lifting her off the ground.

Priya watched the celebration, feeling empty. There was a finality to it that hit her with a dull thud. The house was gone. It was over. There was a vague relief too, though. Because she wouldn't be destitute, or dependent on her sister. The sale had given her options. Freedom. She now had almost half a million dollars free and clear.

Seventeen

THE BAG HAD BEEN PACKED FOR WEEKS AND WAS WAITING by the door like a faithful dog. Routes to the hospital were mapped out and emergency plans were in place. In the end, the careful preparation went to waste, because Grace's labor started when they were already at the hospital.

She and Dan were visiting Carla—a woman from their neonatal class—who had just had her first child. At forty-four, she was also an IVF mother, and she and Grace had bonded, sharing fears and advice.

Grace handed Carla's husband, Roy, a maroon box containing biscotti and was given a swaddled pink baby in exchange.

"He looks so much like Roy," Dan said.

"Little Maverick," his mother cooed. Grace and Dan avoided each other's eyes, lest Maverick's parents detect their opinion of the name.

"Here, Grace, sit down." Roy ushered her to a chair in the corner of the room. Grace moved slowly these days. She was thirty-eight weeks and it was an abundance of caution, as well as an abundance of belly, that caused her to tread carefully. As she lowered herself into the seat she felt an almighty cramp.

"Oof," she said, keeling forward. "Dan, you take Maverick, will you." Another bolt of pain hit her as she held up the baby. "Ah-ohh."

"Are you okay?"

"Yes, ah, but you'd better take him." She passed the baby over. A switchblade sliced through her abdomen. "Ow, I'm not okay, I'm not okay," she said, gripping the chair's arms.

Roy and Dan gathered around Grace, helping her to the door, while Carla, who now had Maverick in her arms, craned her neck. "Is it happening? It's happening, isn't it?" she said, pressing her call button.

"He's early," Dan said.

"Oh God, he's still in breech," said Grace, clutching her belly. Doctor Torres had warned they might have to try to turn him if he didn't turn on his own.

"It's okay, Grace," Dan said as a nurse hurried into the room. "We're in good hands."

The labor progressed quickly. The pain was otherworldly. All Grace could think was that this was the final test. She had sworn she would do anything for a baby, and the universe was making her prove it. She only had to survive a few more contractions and she would have her baby. She bore down and breathed and pushed. Soon the pain ebbed away and the room came back into focus.

And there he was, being held up by the doctor, shaking and purple and utterly perfect. He was slick and covered in blood and vernix, screaming his little heart out. She could see his gums and his tonsils. His eyes were squeezed shut as he howled and his hair was plastered flat and wet against his head. He was taken out of her sight for a moment.

"Where is he?"

"They're wrapping him and cutting the cord."

Grace shuffled up onto her elbows, eager to see him. It had gone quiet.

"Is he okay?"

The blessed cry once again filled the room, an irrepressible confirmation of his existence. Dan was shaking her arm and kissing her face.

"You did it. You did it, Gracie. You were magnificent."

"Can I see him? Where is he?"

"They'll bring him back soon. He's a big boy. Listen to those lungs."

"I can't believe he's here."

"You were so strong." Dan kissed Grace's sweaty head. "I love you so much."

"I still can't believe it. I want to see him."

"He wants to see you too." The midwife brought the bundle toward them. "Listen," she said. "He's crying for his mother."

"I can't believe he's finally here." Grace wanted to cry too. She wanted to cry with joy.

⁓

And then, blinding love. Ten thousand suns' worth. The world shrank to their hospital room, filled with a galaxy of adoration. Grace felt she would live forever because nothing could kill her love for this little boy. It would burn long after she was dead and had become dust. His eyelashes were a marvel. His fingernails, finer than the Louvre's rarest treasure. His lips, a Botticelli dream. His dimples, the reason people believed in heaven. They named him Samuel Benjamin Arden. Sam.

"Look at that hair," said a nurse. "I can see he gets that from you, Dad. It's like a shock of bear fur."

"Who does he look like?" Grace asked.

Dan, on the bed next to her, squeezed her shoulder. "I can't say."

Sam lay against Grace's chest. Dan grazed his fingers through the boy's fine black hair. Neither of them spoke. They were both looking at the baby, and something was coming into focus. As they processed his features, his arrival, something else became apparent. His face was covered with the waxy substance that protects babies in utero, but there was no mistaking it. His eyes were brown. His skin was dark. His hair was black. There was no biological sense to what they were seeing.

⌒

None of the hospital staff remarked on Sam's appearance. The only words that passed nurse Janette's lips were compliments.

"He's so teeny," she gushed over Grace's shoulder.

In the early stages of labor, there had been talk of the arduous road to conception. Grace assumed they thought she and Dan had used a donor egg.

"We'll give him a bath so you can have a break, Mumma. Dad, do you want to help?" Janette asked.

"Of course," Dan said. Grace made a little noise as Janette lifted Sam out of her arms.

"We'll get him all nice and clean for you." She swept him away with Dan following closely.

Grace watched Sam go, missing him already, but also wondering: How long had he been out of her sight after the birth? She was exhausted and couldn't think straight. The voice in the back of her head was insistent: he was her son. But he didn't look like her. Or like Dan. Something, somewhere, had happened.

⁓

When Sam was clean and back where he belonged, in Grace's arms, Janette asked if she was ready to try breastfeeding.

"Yes, please."

Grace knew it could be tricky and frustrating, but he latched on straightaway.

"There now, you're a natural," Janette said.

Grace felt a flutter of pride, but she was mesmerized by her son, and her breasts. They were so pale, with veins close to the surface, they almost looked blue. She had never noticed before how very white they were.

Dan stroked Sam's cheek and laughed. "He's only a few minutes old. How does he know how to do that?"

Their son suckled hungrily.

"That's genius material there," Janette said, with pride.

"He gets that from his mum," said Dan.

⁓

When the doctor returned, Grace thought he might say something, but he just smiled and asked routine questions. She looked at Dan, who cleared his throat. "Doctor," he said, hesitant. "We were wondering if you would be able to explain why our boy looks different from us. His coloring is, well, it's not like anything in either of our families."

"Hmm." The doctor frowned. "You were an IVF couple?"

"Yes, but he's biologically ours."

If the doctor was surprised he didn't show it. He frowned and stepped closer to Grace, who was cradling Sam, and leaned in, peering at their boy like a specimen. "How are you doing there, little chap?" He looked up. "He's both of yours?"

Dan and Grace nodded.

"No donor sperm?"

They shook their heads.

The doctor grunted. He pressed his pen to his mouth and regarded Sam for a moment.

"Well, well . . ." His eyes darted from Grace to Dan to Sam and back again.

Grace sensed what he was thinking. "It's not that," she said. "He's definitely Dan's."

Dan looked at the floor. "Grace, nobody is suggesting—"

"There's no way he's not Dan's," she said. "Besides, even if I had . . . if . . . I mean, I'm the one who had the fertility problems."

The doctor sucked in a breath. "Well, it's rare, but this has been known to happen. Sometimes recessive racial features reemerge. Dormant genes, or perhaps a chromosomal aberration of some sort."

"An aberration?"

"Yes, a chromosomal aberration."

"Is it possible that something happened in the IVF process?"

"I don't quite follow."

"Because of the way the baby was conceived."

He frowned again. "I don't know about that. But . . . there have been cases of IVF clinics implanting the wrong embryo."

"What?" Grace sat up.

"A handful of cases around the world. But those sorts of things are incredibly rare. It's more likely one of you has a great-aunt or -uncle who had a darker skin tone."

All eyes fell on Sam, sleeping in his mother's arms. Grace's blond hair was twisted up on the top of her head. Strands of it hung down around her face and neck, like trickles of platinum. "I've got a pretty tangled genealogy," Dan ventured. "Scottish. Maltese. Lebanese. Italian."

"That must be it," the doctor said. "Somewhere in there, there's a gene that's popped up in your little boy here."

Grace exhaled. "So, that's it, then?"

"I couldn't say for sure. If you're worried—"

"No!" Grace interrupted. "We're not worried at all. We just wanted your opinion."

She looked down at her son, sleeping peacefully. "I'm glad there's nothing wrong."

~

They moved to the family suite—a double room cheaply decorated in inoffensive, unisex yellow. As if displeased with his new home, Sam wailed and wailed. Grace paced the room with him, swaying gently trying to get him to quiet.

"What are we going to do?" Dan whispered.

"Do? What do you mean, do?"

"Grace, there's obviously been a mix-up of some sort."

"That's not what the doctor said."

"There's nobody in my family that looks like Sam, and I know there's certainly no one in yours."

He paced, walking from the bedroom door to the dressing table and back again, clenching and unclenching his fist. "What if he's not our son?"

"How can you say that? Of course he's our son!"

"I don't mean it like that. I mean, what if there's another couple's genetic material? Mr. and Mrs. Smith—or Singh—with all their medical history. With grandparents. What if they try to take him back?"

"That's insane."

"Is it?"

"Dan, you're scaring me." Grace was still swaying, though less gently. "They won't try to take him because they'll never find out." Her voice was taut. She finally had her baby. After years of longing and painful treatments, she had him in her arms, and even now, something was trying to threaten that.

"Grace, please."

"What?" she snapped. "What do you want from me?"

Dan raked a hand through his hair. "I just think we should discuss this. What if the clinic discovers they made an error?"

Her eyes filled with tears. Dan was breathing life into the conclusion she had toyed with. She had tried to block it out but his words made it real.

"They wouldn't," she sobbed. "They can't take him. Why are you saying these things?"

"We should at least speak to someone, that's all I'm saying."

"Who are we going to speak to?"

"A lawyer, a family lawyer. We need to know our rights."

"I gave birth to him. You were there, holding my hand. You saw them cut his umbilical cord. That makes him our son. He's a part of us."

"If there is another set of parents, that means they want a baby too. What if they somehow find out they have a son living in Glebe?"

"They wouldn't!"

"We don't know that, Grace." He took her hand and guided her to the mirror in the corner of the room. They stood in front of it, a trio, finally. Her hair fell over her shoulders, bright blond. Dan's hair was dark, but it was brown, not black. His eyes matched hers, a common pale blue.

Sam's hair was jet black, his irises like two pieces of perfectly round onyx. His skin was a faultless brown. Grace pressed her lips to him and kissed his cheek, which had formed inside her, loved and wanted and nurtured for thirty-eight weeks.

Dan tickled Sam's clenched fist with his finger until the baby curled his fingers around Dan's and held tight. The difference in tones was stark. Like chalk and chocolate.

"Grace," Dan said. "If something went wrong, if there's been a mix-up, we have to be prepared. People are going to notice. This won't just go away."

PART TWO

Eighteen

DOCTOR ASHLEY LI'S PATIENTS WERE LOOKING AT HER WITH wet-eyed hope, their fingers entwined, knuckles white. There was a dull ache beneath her breastbone that was empathy but also disappointment. She regularly had to explain to desperate parents-to-be that something had gone wrong, and it never got easier. The first time she had to break the news to someone that the procedure had failed, she found herself stammering and apologizing profusely. On that first day, Ashley was still a stranger to failure and so overcome with guilt and anguish, she had cried. She and the would-be mother had held each other until the patient had pulled away, betrayed, and said: "I don't know what *you're* so upset about."

Today, this day, the man's face was red by the time she finished explaining what had happened. Tears spilled from his eyes. "You're a cheat!"

Ashley trained her gaze on the floor.

"Martin," his wife said, "it's not Doctor Li's fault."

"I understand you're upset, Mr. Crawford," Ashley said. "It's a tricky process. Sometimes this happens."

Martin Crawford kept his mouth shut. He was holding back gulps, choking and fizzing, as if he had swallowed a small explosive and wanted to contain the blast.

In these situations, it was best to use clinical language and stay detached, Ashley had discovered. That didn't mean being unkind. Just professional. She picked up the box of tissues on her desk and passed it to Martin. Today's failure was the worst kind. More had been lost than an ovum or embryo. She had had to explain that the eight-week-old baby that had been growing in Leslie Crawford—which they had already started affectionately referring to as "little bean," and for whom a grandmother had started knitting booties—had not survived. It was their third miscarriage.

"We knew this could happen," Leslie said gently to her husband, whose shoulders were heaving as he sobbed noisily.

Leslie Crawford had first presented at the clinic a year ago with irregular periods and an unshakable desire for a child of her own. Tests confirmed what she had already sensed: she wasn't ovulating. When Ashley delivered this crushing news, she also offered a solution: they could import donor eggs from the World Egg Bank. This was what the Crawfords had eagerly done, ordering a batch of seven.

"Promise we won't end up with half a dozen mouths to feed, heh-heh," Martin had said, in a more optimistic mood at the time. But as was so often the case with this delicate operation, there were casualties. Three had failed to thaw. Four had been fertilized and, of those, two had been fit for implantation.

"Two is a solid number," Ashley had reassured them, coaching them through every step of the way. She was fond of the Crawfords, Martin with his nervous jokes and Leslie with her determined pragmatism.

One of the embryos had attached, and at seven weeks Leslie's progress had looked promising. The ultrasound showed a small kidney-shaped blur in her uterus. As Ashley smoothed the wand over Leslie's still-flat belly the machine amplified the thrashing heartbeat.

It came through like a broadcast from underwater, mighty and clear, and they had all laughed, delighted and surprised by the volume. "It's so strong," Martin said. "He'll be a footballer."

"*She'll* be a footballer," Leslie countered.

But the following week Leslie Crawford had noticed spotting and called the clinic, concerned. The receptionist had told her to come in on Friday—three days hence—for a checkup.

"If the bleeding gets worse go immediately to the emergency department."

The next morning Leslie was rushed to the hospital with pain so acute she thought she might faint. It subsided and the hospital sent her home. At her follow-up appointment with Doctor Li, the ultrasound confirmed what they'd all feared. The baby had not survived.

Ashley opened her drawer to retrieve the business card of her preferred grief counselor. "I want you to take care of each other through this difficult time. And when you're ready, we can try again."

"Oh yes, it's all so easy. Just do it again. How many more times are you going to take our money?" Martin Crawford spat. "Where does it end?"

"Martin! We knew this was a possibility."

"It's okay, Mrs. Crawford. If I were in Mr. Crawford's shoes I daresay I'd be feeling the same way."

Ashley's empathy took the heat out of Martin's rage. He took a deep shuddering breath and let his face fall into his hands.

"I'm sorry," he said.

"I want you to know we're doing everything we can to help you bring a baby into the world. The fact you were able to get pregnant is a very good sign. But"—and here she paused for emphasis—"it was not a good sign that we were not able to detect a heartbeat at five weeks."

Martin Crawford lifted his crumpled face. "There was a heart-beat. We heard it."

Doctor Li tapped at her computer, entering details into the couple's record.

"Of course," she said calmly, her eyes on the computer screen, "our policy with Egg Bank procedures is that if a heartbeat is detected at five weeks the transfer is deemed a success. If it fails after that the whole process must begin again. But since no heartbeat was detected, *as I see it says on your file,* you are entitled to another round free of charge."

The Crawfords looked at her.

"Yes, well." Martin nodded, his eyes shining with tears. "Thank you, Doctor," he said. "I'm so sorry about"—he blubbered a little—"about my outburst. It's just, we've been trying for so long. We were so excited. Already started picking out names."

"I understand."

"Thank you, Doctor Li," Leslie said.

"You're a good woman, Doctor Li," Martin said, holding her hand between both of his. "Everything we read about you is true."

"That's kind of you to say, Mr. Crawford."

After the Crawfords left, some of the day's burden lifted from Ashley's shoulders. Patient outbursts were part of the job, but they never got easier. Ashley preferred it when they yelled. She could calm them then. Tears were harder to stop.

She had never been good at navigating social interactions. As a student, parties terrified her, and since she spent most nights in the company of *Kumar and Clark's Cases in Clinical Medicine* and *Berek and Novak's Gynecology,* she had never had much chance to become more confident through practice.

As she made notes in the Crawfords' file an email arrived from her boss, Roger Osmond. *Dinner at my place? Nine?*

Doctor Ashley Li smiled and leaned back in her chair. It was an ergonomic thing that tilted obligingly. As she composed her reply she noticed Leslie had left her office lanyard sitting on her desk.

"Oh, Mrs. Crawford," she called, leaping up off her chair.

She hurried down the passageway through to the reception area, where she spotted Leslie and Martin paying Doris.

Ashley held up the plastic card. She was about to call out to the Crawfords when her gaze fell on a dark-haired woman, alone, in the corner of the waiting room reading a battered paperback. The young woman looked up at the commotion of Ashley rushing into the room, and Ashley felt a jolt of electricity. The woman had straight black hair and Asian features, but light, stony eyes. Their eyes met for a moment before she turned her attention back to her book. Ashley shivered, as happened from time to time when she encountered someone—usually a woman, but not always—who resembled her. A person who made her think: Could you be my half sibling? It was like a ghost blowing icy breath on the back of her neck. She had never known her father, and these occasional encounters left her with a vague sense of loss.

"Doctor Li?"

"Yes?" Leslie Crawford was standing right in front of Ashley. "Oh, Mrs. Crawford, Mr. Crawford. You left your security pass on my desk." Ashley held up the plastic card.

"Oh dear." Leslie laughed. "How careless. Please don't take this as an indication of the sort of parent I'm going to make. Thank you," she said, sliding it into her bag.

Ashley said goodbye to the Crawfords again and, with a final glace at her doppelgänger, she returned to her office.

Nineteen

THE WIND CHILLED THE BACK OF PRIYA'S NECK AS SHE hurried along the beachfront. She laid her palm across the bare skin, still unaccustomed to her short hair. She had spontaneously cut it the day she moved to Coogee. New life, new look, she thought, as the kitchen scissors sheared through her plaits before they tumbled into the sink. The thrill was brief. What remained of her hair stuck out like bottle-brush bristles. She had tidied it as best she could and placed the two plaits into a snap-lock bag to post to a charity that made wigs for children with cancer.

She walked along Coogee's main street, planning to spend the afternoon paddling her feet in the glassy rock pools. Under her new white dress was a new red one-piece, and she was wearing stiff leather slides purchased on a whim the day before. Old Priya never made impulsive purchases. New Priya could do what she wanted.

Crowds had descended on the foreshore in colored droves. Zinc-nosed men in sunglasses stood with their hands on their hips. Women in broad hats chased toddlers in rash vests. Children and couples played amid the lapping waves, and Priya's good mood shifted. She retreated to the beach's grass fringe, where she settled herself and opened her book.

Coogee was not quite the fabled Bondi, but it was as close as she could afford, and far enough away from her old life to offer a semblance of a fresh start. Following her separation from Nick the landscape of her life had changed. She tried IVF again after her first round didn't work. When a second attempt failed too, the blow was heavy. She found herself sitting up late at night once her nieces were asleep, drinking vodka straight, alone, and finally judged it would be best to cash in her long-service leave, take a few months off work, collect her thoughts, and figure out what to do next.

"You need to start fresh," Darsh had told her over dinner one night. "Come live by the beach."

Viv encouraged Priya to move too. "It will be good for you. And we'll visit all the time. Promise. It will give us an excuse to come to the seaside."

Priya had moved and she still hadn't had a single visit. She was lonely. She felt it keenly.

A high-pitched squeal broke the calm. A little boy was rolling around on a picnic blanket near his mother. Nine months old, Priya guessed. He was chewing on a plastic ring with tiny milk teeth. Behind him was the plate-glass side of a bus stop. Priya caught sight of her own silhouette: a stranger in sunglasses with a choppy pixie cut. She was putting on a brave face, but she couldn't even convince herself she was anything other than a lost soul. Losing Nick had hurt, but losing the chance to have a family with him broke her heart.

She patted down her wayward hair and scanned the grassy verge for another corner where there weren't so many children and smiling families. She considered retreating to her balcony, which she had fashioned into an alfresco studio to make use of the strong northern light. She had produced more paintings in a month in Coogee than she had all year. That, at least, was something to be proud of. And even though she often had to rescue winged creatures from the sticky surface of her canvases, the balcony gave her an empowering, room-of-one's-own sense of independence. She packed away her book and brushed the grass seeds from her legs.

On the way home she stopped at the grocery store, where she loaded up with milk, oranges, coconut water, bay leaves, butter, and eggs. The price tags—five dollars for a packet of bay leaves—made her miss the Lebanese nut shop near her old house where she could buy any spice she could imagine, as well as freshly baked za'atar and tubs of labneh, with loose change. The closest thing to that in Coogee was a grease-splattered kebab shop that mostly serviced late-night clientele.

As she stepped out into the sunshine she rummaged in her bag and realized something was missing. Keys, she thought. *Where are my keys?* She found a patch of grass and emptied out her bag, hunting for the bunch of keys she knew wasn't there. Annoyed at her carelessness, she pulled out her phone and searched for the number of a locksmith as she trudged up the hill to her apartment.

Trent from 24-Hour Locks said he would be there in an hour. The security light flicked on with a *bink!* and moths gathered to hover around it.

Priya's consolation was that she had an excuse not to see Rajesh's friend Morgan. She clicked into her text messages. *I'm really sorry, Morgan. I'm locked out of my flat. Do you mind if we do it another time? I'm waiting for a locksmith,* she typed to the number Rajesh had given her.

She got a reply immediately: *I'm sorry to hear that. Do you want to have a coffee while you wait? I'm not far from Coogee.*

My clothes are wet from the beach, she lied, hoping to be rid of him.

He buzzed back straightaway, refusing to take the hint. *How about we postpone until nine tonight? That will give you a chance to clean up, then we can meet for a nightcap?*

Priya didn't want to see him, but she knew that saying no would only delay the inevitable. When Rajesh had given her Morgan's number, he and Viv had made her promise she would go out with him just once.

"He's a great guy but he doesn't know many people in Sydney," Rajesh had said.

Morgan had recently transferred from Melbourne, and Rajesh had presented it as a favor. Would Priya meet his friend who was new to the area and make him feel welcome? It was a poorly disguised setup, but one she couldn't get out of without seeming rude.

Okay, I'll meet you at nine, Priya wrote. She sat in the fading light, watching bugs land on her shins, and tried to empty her mind.

It was dark by the time the locksmith arrived.

"Sorry, busy day," he said as he emerged from the branches that crowded the pathway up to Priya's apartment block. He had broad shoulders and was wearing his cap pulled low over a shaved head. Dark tattoos peeked out from the collar and cuffs of his uniform like a black undershirt.

"That's okay, it's up here," Priya said, taking him into the stairwell.

The building was a brick, 1930s block filled with the smells of other people's dinner. Of Gravox gravy and steamed vegetables. Frying onions and roasting meat. The sounds of TV shows drifted into the hall. As she climbed the stairs, with the man's heavy footfalls close behind her, Priya chatted idly about how she had just moved to the area.

He set his toolbox down on the landing outside her door. Seven slow minutes later the lock clicked and he pushed open Priya's front door.

"What a relief," she said. "Let's get some light."

"Those hinges could use an oil," he told her, following her with his toolbox as she slipped inside.

"It's fine, really, you don't have to," she said, backing into the apartment.

"I'll just give it a quick spray. Part of the service." He took a can of lubricant from his metal case and shook it.

Priya searched for the remote control to switch on her living-room light. She blindly felt the top of the coffee table, then stuck her hand between the couch cushions, wishing the owner had just put in a regular light switch.

The locksmith sprayed the door hinges, swinging the door to test them.

"It's fine, really. You don't have to bother," she said, patting the top of her television cabinet hoping to locate the block of plastic.

"No point doing it if I'm not going to do it right," he said, filling the air with the hiss and fumes of the aerosol lubricant again. "That should do it." He shut the door all the way so that they were in complete darkness. Priya took a step backward into the kitchen and flicked on that light. It shone a triangle of yellow into the lounge room, leaving the locksmith concealed by shadow. All she could see of him was his steel-capped boots and the sharp corner of his metal toolbox.

Her heart rate quickened. She flexed her fingers and told herself not to be paranoid, she had nothing to fear.

"Good as new," the locksmith said, his voice coming closer. "Is this what you were looking for?" He picked up the remote from her key table and clicked on the light.

"Yes, thanks," she said, pulling her credit card from her wallet. She paid him and opened the door.

"You have yourself a good night," he said with a smile.

"Thanks," Priya said a little too loudly, trying to hide her nerves.

After she carefully clicked the door shut behind him, Priya wiped her sweaty palms on her dress. Living alone had bequeathed her with a new jitteriness. The western suburbs were as rough as guts but at least there she had Nick, and her sister down the road. In Coogee, she was utterly alone, surrounded by miles of ocean and rich, unfeeling strangers.

Priya sat on her couch wishing she hadn't said yes to meeting Morgan. She longed to phone Viv but knew the household would be in the middle of the raucous dinner-bath-bed routine.

Her Coogee rental wasn't what she had hoped for but she had attempted to make it homely. The walls were crowded with paintings and prints she had collected and mounted in two-dollar frames from IKEA. The centerpiece was a reproduction of a very old Indian painting of a young couple in a garden. It was slightly gauche, but it had belonged to her mother, Dyuti. The palette reminded her of the way Dyuti would hum at the stove while Priya and Viv did their homework at the kitchen table.

She must have drifted off, because the next thing she knew she was waking up sideways on the couch. She sat bolt upright, disoriented. Her phone was flashing with a message from Darsh. *Let's go out!*

Where are you? she texted back.

Coogee Pavilion. Come!

I can't, she typed. *I have a date.*

She felt momentarily grateful to Morgan for giving her an excuse not to face the dewy, nubile patrons of the Coogee Pavilion.

Call me tomorrow with details!

She slid off the couch and went into her bedroom to find

something to wear. Now that he had saved her from ritual humiliation, she felt Morgan deserved a little effort.

⁓

"Do you want kids?" Morgan asked, as he dribbled miso soup down the front of his shirt.

Priya forced a smile. A pregnancy inquisition was the last thing she needed.

"Maybe," she said, cutting her noodles with the edge of her spoon. "So, town planning. How did you get into that?"

"It's a funny story, actually," Morgan said, spearing a piece of sushi as he launched into the tale. When he finished he picked up a tempura prawn. "I don't know about the sushi," he said. "It looks a little fishy."

Priya smiled, feeling a little bad that his attempts at humor were being wasted on her.

"So," he said, forging on in the face of her polite silence. "You work at an auction house. How did you get into that?"

She managed a smile as she spoke of her love for her work. "I wanted to be an artist, but patrons are a little thin on the ground, so I had to look for a more realistic goal. The auction house lets me work with beautiful art every day and I still do some of my own stuff at night."

"I'd like to see it sometime."

Priya put a piece of sashimi into her mouth. He was a nice man. And once, Priya might even have found him attractive. But he was no Nick Archer, and she ended the night after their plates were cleared. She walked home feeling restless. She was miserable and she couldn't imagine anything could cure her of it. Living in the idyllic suburb of Coogee made it worse. As she made her way to her apartment past groups of comfortable, happy people, she only felt lonelier, and longed for her bed. She clicked on the light in her tiny flat and opened the window to disperse some of the stale air. In six steps she was in her pokey bathroom. She removed her eye makeup and brushed her teeth. Her arms felt like lead.

Her bedroom was a bare place with cheap venetian blinds that didn't completely block out the streetlights. Here she couldn't help but think of Megan and Nick, and wonder if they were together. She could almost feel them, next to each other, and she found for the first time she understood the appeal of a warm body, even if you didn't love the person it belonged to.

She wondered if Nick pulled Megan into the nook under his arm the way he had with her, their legs twisted together like vines, his arms hugging her body. Did he sleep in the same way with a new person, or did they have their own position? She let the thought burn in her chest for a minute then picked up her phone and cycled through her contacts list. Nick. Husani. Morgan. Nick. It had been nineteen days since their last contact. He'd written to say that if she was ever missing Jacker and wanted to see him, all she had to do was say the word.

You could take him for a walk sometime. I know I'd miss him like crazy if I were you.

She hadn't replied. It had upset her too much. But now, looking at the message, her lack of response seemed churlish. Cold, even. She felt she should explain to Nick why she hadn't written back. But it was almost midnight. She didn't want him to think she was messaging because she was in bed, lonely, on a Saturday night. She turned her phone off and tried to sleep, promising herself she would find the nerve to respond to him in the morning.

Twenty

SAM LOVED TO BLOW RASPBERRIES. HE HAD A SYMPHONIC range, each as distinct as an orchestral instrument. Some strummed. Some tooted. Some hummed. Grace had nicknames for them all. There was the Bugle. There was the Horse Whinny. Her favorite was a half-gulp, half-sigh she thought of as the Harried Businessman. He would part his lips, suck in a breath of air, and make a noise: "A-humph."

"A-humph." Grace liked to repeat it back to him, leaning over his bassinet, where he lay now, being gently bounced by her foot. "A-humph," he said. In raptures, in love, she copied it. "A-humph." It was their own call-and-response. "A-humph!"

"He's like a tiny gentleman worn out from his demanding routine of kicking his legs and yawning," she said to Dan.

"He is." He came, smiling, to her side to watch their baby, who was flapping his arms and looking at them with wide-eyed curiosity.

"A-humph," said Sam.

Grace laughed and touched the baby's nose, then his stomach, delighting as his eyes crossed then uncrossed, following her finger.

"He knows we're talking about him."

"Of course he knows."

"He's so perfect."

She was tired, of course. To her bones. Her nipples were cracked and sore, and she felt in constant need of a shower. Her hair was lank and thin. Her mobility was restricted by the long seam of stitches the obstetrician had put in. There was a tautness, and a constant fear of ripping, that slowed her movements.

But nothing mattered when she held her baby in her arms. When she cuddled him she felt restored. And she needed to do this often, not just out of love, but because there was something gnawing away at her insides: the corrosive knowledge of what she believed could be true, and the fear someone else would discover it. A voice whispered from the corner of her subconscious: *There has been a mistake.* Mostly she was able to push it back into the depths of her mind. But when her guard was down she found herself scrutinizing her little boy's face for evidence he belonged to her and her husband, desperately trying to identify something that linked him to her or to Dan. His rounded nose, for example. Most babies were born with a button nose, and she searched Sam's for signs of the particular stubbiness that made Dan's nose his own.

"He looks like you, don't you think?" she said, as they sat on the couch, watching Sam in his bassinet. Sam watched them watching. "A-humph!"

"If he does, let's hope he grows out of it."

A joke. *I should laugh,* she thought. Instead she nudged her husband and tried to play along with his valiant attempt at jocularity. "You're not so bad."

He nudged her back.

They had been fighting more than usual. The skirmishes were not about anything substantial. They skirted around the elephant in the room and conducted proxy wars over empty milk cartons in the fridge and forgotten promises to replace the dead lightbulb.

"I'm sorry I've been so difficult," she said.

"New mother's prerogative."

"No, this isn't normal new-mother stuff. I know you're scared too, and I've been acting like you're not."

He held her close and stroked her back.

"Does that mean you're ready to get some professional advice?"

Her body went rigid. "Dan. That's not what I meant."

"I know it feels like by seeing a lawyer and asking questions we're admitting something could be wrong. But the facts won't change just because we ignore them. We should prepare ourselves. It's reckless not to."

"Why is it reckless?" This sentence burst out of her. Sam was startled and began to cry. "Oh, I'm sorry, little boy." She leaned down and picked him up. "Sh."

"I can see him, Dan," she said. "I know he looks different to us. But he's our son."

"This is not about whether we love him—"

"You're just going to stir up trouble," she said, holding the baby to her, sliding her hand down the curvature of his back.

"What if the clinic used the wrong sperm, or the wrong egg? What if another couple had an embryo transfer on the same day as us, and we got their baby instead?" Whenever he said such things he lowered his voice, as if their house were bugged.

"So what!" Grace said. "That doesn't mean he's their son. *I* gave birth to him. *I* felt him grow inside of me. From a speck to a being who would kick and punch like he couldn't wait to get out."

A familiar thought flashed through her mind. What if their embryo had been implanted in another couple? She dismissed it almost as soon as it landed. But the thought left a trail, like comet dust. The implication was clear. That couple could have another, unknown baby—their little girl, their Petri. A complicated barrage of anger and envy filled her chest. It was like a bad nineties melodrama or a glossy magazine cover. "*Switched Before Birth!*" What if that's what had happened? Would some medical or ethical authority demand a straight swap? Her heart rebelled against the idea and she pulled her son closer. Sam was the one she had nurtured. Sam was the one she loved.

"How would the couple even know this had happened? We didn't."

"What if an Indian couple gave birth to a baby with your blond hair? Don't you think they'd investigate it?"

During her pregnancy, Grace had dreamed of a little blond baby, just like her. Petri's hair would grow long and be worn in pigtails that Grace would tie with velvet bows. But that dream was no match for the giggling, raspberry-blowing, dimple-kneed baby Sam. "A-humph!"

"Maybe they're thinking the exact same thing I am. Maybe they just want to be left alone with their blond baby." She stood quickly, her joints cracking. "I have to get out of this house," she said. "I need air." She had been sealed inside with her thoughts for too long.

"Grace."

"What do you say we go for a walk?" Grace said to Sam.

"Grace!"

She carried her son upstairs and changed him. Before slipping on his socks she couldn't resist lifting his left foot and play-chomping the tiny fleshy pebbles on the end.

"Yom. Nom-nom-nom," she said, trying to coax out a laugh. Sam squirmed on his changing table and kicked his legs.

"Are you ready for an outing?"

She helped him up into a sitting position and pulled down the jumper Fiona had knitted for him—one of the many gifts she had given her only grandson. Before Fiona came to the hospital Grace and Dan had had an urgent, hushed discussion about how to raise the subject of Sam's appearance. Fiona had thrown open the door before they'd agreed on anything.

"Oh!" Fiona had said, popping up like a jack-in-the-box after leaning over Grace to see Sam for the first time. But when Grace had passed the bundle to her mother, Fiona had been enraptured. Grace witnessed the birth of a love so unconditional, and so unquestioning, it made her ache. Soon Fiona was cooing and jiggling Sam, and Grace had felt an immense sense of comfort, and a flicker of hope that maybe everything would be okay after all.

But strangers were a different matter, she thought, as she laid Sam's shade cloth across his stroller. Since Sam was born she had ventured out with him no more than half a dozen times. She was wary of the lingering looks and could never tell if they were admiring her baby, or pausing to wonder what the Nordic-looking woman was doing with an Indian baby. The world was full of diverse families and she was sure nobody would be rude enough to ask. But she felt like there were prying eyes and double-takes lurking around every corner.

"So, you're going out?" Dan said when Grace appeared in the hallway with the stroller.

She nodded, defiant and fearful in equal measure. "I can't stay in this house another second."

Dan leaned forward and pulled Sam's shade cloth down farther. "Don't be gone long."

"He's covered up," she said. "I'm just going to the market."

Dan put his fist to his mouth. Grace shot him a sharp look. He sighed and retreated to the dining room. Grace stepped onto the porch, relishing the kiss of sunlight on her face. "We'll be back later," she called. "Don't worry. Everything will be fine."

The Glebe markets were full of human bowerbirds combing through secondhand leather jackets and handmade soy candles. Visiting the markets used to be Grace and Dan's favorite way to spend a Saturday morning. They would stroll with a coffee in hand, then sit on the grass while musicians played. Grace's mouth watered as she imagined eating a gözleme with lemon off a paper plate while she and Sam enjoyed the fresh air. She had been subsisting on toast and muesli bars for too long.

The market was set up in a primary school on Glebe Point Road and it was difficult to navigate the stroller along the narrow paths between the stalls. She had forgotten how crowded it could get on a sunny day. The dirt thoroughfares were rutted and crammed with shoppers. Grace slowly picked her way toward the food carts, stopping every couple of meters to bend over and make sure Sam's shade cloth was firmly in place.

In the distance she saw a mop of blond curls and panicked, thinking it was Caroline. Beth had met Sam, without probing her friend, but Grace had kept him away from Rochelle, Melody, and Caroline. At first her girlfriends had been concerned. Then suspicious. And, finally, offended. Every time a woman Grace's age fell into her field of vision her heart jerked in alarm.

We just want to know everything's okay, Caroline had texted a few days earlier. *The first few months are hard. Let us help you.*

Melody lives in Randwick, Grace told herself. Caroline is across the bridge in Mosman. They won't be at the Glebe markets. Still. People milled around, slowing her progress, and she began to turn the stroller around. Another woman with a stroller was coming her way and Grace had to wait to let her pass. The two mothers smiled at each other, their knowing eye rolls a salute of weary solidarity.

As Grace waited her eyes drifted across the crowd. Cut-off jeans were back in fashion, apparently.

And then she saw her. Grace blinked, thinking her eyes were playing tricks on her. The woman was carrying a basket and hanging off the arm of an older blond man. He looked familiar. There was a rakish, Robert Redford quality to his looks. The beautiful woman with large, saucerlike sunglasses and black flowing hair was unmistakable. It was Doctor Li.

Panicking, Grace tried to back away, but there were people clogged up behind her, poring over a bakery stand. To her right a leather-goods stall blocked her in. Doctor Li and the blond man turned. Grace slid her sunglasses down over her eyes. Too late. Doctor Li spotted her. She lifted her hand in greeting.

There was no avoiding it now.

"Hello, Grace." Doctor Li waved as she threaded her way through the crowd.

Grace bent and tugged at Sam's shade cloth, ensuring his privacy was complete—it was becoming a compulsion.

"Hello, Doctor Li," she said.

The blond man followed. His hands were sunk in the pockets of his leisure jacket, a satisfied but not unpleasant smile on his face. "Roger, this is Grace Arden. She and her husband, Dan, were patients at Empona," Doctor Li said.

"Hello." The man reached out and shook Grace's hand. "Looks like you left a satisfied customer," he added, crouching down to Sam's level.

"Yes," Grace said, reflexively jerking the stroller back toward herself.

"Grace, Roger founded Empona," Doctor Li said.

"Oh, you're Roger Osmond?"

"That's right. Pleasure to meet you."

"I—how—thank you," Grace managed. Her thoughts were jumbled. "Thank you so much," she said again. She looked from

Doctor Li to Doctor Osmond, hanging close to each other. These were the people who were responsible for Sam, Grace thought. They were also responsible for her current predicament.

"And this little bundle is—?" Doctor Li inclined her head toward the stroller.

"Sam."

"Samantha Arden, what a perfect name," Doctor Li said.

"It's Samuel," Grace replied automatically, then wished she could take it back. She thought she could see the question form on Doctor Li's lips, but the woman didn't say anything.

The couple stared at Grace, waiting to be properly introduced to the baby they helped create. "I'm sorry, he's sleeping at the moment," Grace said.

She knew in normal circumstances this would be no excuse not to draw open the covering and show off her son, so she offered an explanation: "I'd let you have a look but he's been awfully colicky lately and I've only just got him to sleep."

"Why did you bring him to the market?" Doctor Li asked.

"Ashley," Doctor Osmond said. "You've never had a newborn. I imagine poor Grace here has been under house arrest for as long as she can remember."

Grace smiled gratefully. "Yes, that's right," she said quickly. "I thought, while he's taking a nap, I'll get some much-needed fresh air."

"How long were you with us before little Sam arrived?" Doctor Osmond asked.

"It took eight rounds."

"Eight? You and Doctor Li are practically old friends."

"It felt like a lot at the time, but now that he's here, it seems like very little work for such a huge miracle."

"That's what I like to hear," Doctor Osmond said with a broad smile. He had movie-star teeth and a cleft chin that wouldn't have looked out of place on a Roman statue.

Grace forced a smile. She knew she was not playing the role of the lucky mother to their satisfaction. The whole scene was unfolding like the stiff first read-through of a bad script.

"He's just the light of my life," she said, in an impersonation of contentment.

"It's a funny thing," Doctor Li said. "We're fertility specialists but our clinic is only concerned with conception. Sometimes couples get pregnant and we never hear from them again."

"We like to keep track of everyone, but the parents of newborns aren't the best at returning nonessential phone calls," Doctor Osmond said, smiling.

Grace longed to be able to lift Sam out of his stroller and listen to them praise his beautiful face and intelligent eyes, but she couldn't. Least of all with these people.

"You must bring him by the clinic for a visit when he's feeling better," Doctor Li said.

Grace studied the woman's face for signs of contrition or remorse—anything that might indicate she had an inkling of what had happened. She seemed normal. Warmer than usual, if anything, proud to have performed her duty for a satisfied patient.

Grace made a noncommittal *mm* sound, then started backing up her stroller. "I'd better get him home. It was lovely to see you, Doctor Li. Nice to meet you, Doctor Osmond."

Sam began to cry. Grace leaned down as she turned the stroller away. "Sh, be a good boy," she whispered. She turned right and crossed the square of sparse grass, determined to get Sam away from the curious gazes of Doctor Li and Doctor Osmond as quickly as possible.

Twenty-One

"DON'T YOU THINK IT WAS STRANGE THE WAY GRACE ARDEN didn't want to show off her baby?" Ashley Li rubbed lotion into her hands while Roger sat propped up in bed reading from his iPad. "Roger?"

"Her baby was sleeping." He didn't look up.

"Since when has that ever stopped a proud mother?"

There had been something disconcerting about the evasive way her former patient had behaved at the market but Ashley couldn't put her finger on it. It was more than new-parent fatigue. Reading people had never been her forte, but in this case, she knew something was wrong.

"She said he had been sick."

"It was so odd." Ashley returned the tube of cream to its spot on Roger's dressing table, then picked up her hairbrush. She owned two of almost everything now. One set of possessions lived at Roger's town house and the other stayed at her apartment gathering dust.

"Don't let it worry you," he said. "She was probably just worn out."

Ashley nodded, wanting to accept the wisdom of her older partner, as she so often did, but in truth she was a little hurt. She and the Ardens had worked so hard for that pregnancy. When the blood test had positively confirmed the three home tests Grace had taken, they had hugged. Over the following months, as Grace had moved on to a different doctor, she had sent regular updates: a snap of the 3-D ultrasound, photos of the growing bump, and a joyous shot of a nursery, decorated and ready with a note saying, *We owe everything to you.* Then just as the baby was due, the communication ceased.

Ashley had not been offended or concerned. She expected that once the tyranny of the first few months receded, a photo of a six-month-old Arden baby would pop up in her phone, with a beaming face covered in mashed banana.

But when they ran into each other at the market, Grace had seemed off-kilter, withdrawn.

"I hope they're coping okay," Ashley said. She wanted babies for all of her patients, but Dan and Grace were one pair she had really been rooting for.

"She's a new mother with a baby who has colic. She could probably hardly remember her own name," Roger said. "Now, come to bed."

"It was just so odd," Ashley said again, biting her thumbnail. There had been something secretive about Grace. Furtive, almost guilty. It was the type of thing you'd expect to see in a case of domestic violence—the red eyes, the hidden baby. But Dan would never do that to Grace. Ashley didn't know much about people, but she knew that for sure.

"Perhaps she has postnatal depression," Ashley said. "She'd poured all her effort into the pregnancy, and now it has left her feeling depleted."

"That's not part of our job."

"She's my patient."

"The maternal and child health-care service will be taking good care of her." Ashley climbed into bed next to Roger. "I'm sure she's fine," he said, kissing her forehead. "She seemed like any other new mother to me. You've got to learn not to get so attached."

Roger flicked off his bedside light and rolled over. Ashley lay on her back looking at the ceiling and replaying the scene at the market over and over. Maybe there was no baby and Grace had just been pushing an empty stroller. Maybe something had gone badly wrong late in the pregnancy and it had driven Grace over the edge. They were all wild theories, none of which fit what she knew about the vulnerable but ultimately very cheerful woman.

Ashley was still awake at midnight when, out of nowhere, a forgotten detail dropped into her mind: the exclusion in the genetic-test result. A possible abnormality. Ashley sat up.

"That must be it," she said into the silence. She felt momentary relief at having solved the puzzle before her heart ached at the realization. The poor baby, she thought. The poor Ardens. They had been so keen to have a baby no matter what, but it seemed something had happened that had sucked the life right out of Grace.

She crept out of bed and into the lounge room where her iPad was charging on the coffee table. She picked it up and Googled *Grace Arden*.

She had never looked up a patient on social media before. She hadn't the slightest inclination to go trawling through their personal lives. But now she was concerned. Did Grace and Dan have a strong network of friends? Were their families supporting them? Had Grace recently signed up to some sort of support group for parents of children with special needs or, worse, a terminal prognosis?

Ashley toggled quickly through Google search results. None gave her answers. She refined the search. *Grace Arden Sydney*. She found a LinkedIn page and a few references to Grace's work at Corella College. Her fingers flew across the keypad as she typed different search terms. *Grace Arden, Dan Arden*. A new set of options appeared, including a link to Dan's Facebook page.

"That's it," Ashley said, as she delved into his page.

There were a few photos. One of Grace and Dan painting a nursery. Another of Grace with a round belly and a pink face. Scrolling down, Ashley found a post thanking a cousin who sent a gift from England. Paddington Bear had arrived safely, Dan reported. An ultrasound image announcing the impending arrival of baby Arden had a smattering of messages attached to it. There was a birth notice: a black-and-white photo of two tiny feet clad in booties. The caption read, *Welcome Samuel Benjamin Arden, born 5 May 2016*. There was a flood of congratulations. Then nothing. It was less than Ashley expected, but it confirmed the IVF transfer had resulted in a baby.

She clicked on the photo of the booties, copied it, and zoomed in. The tiny feet encased in wool revealed nothing. Ashley leaned back, contemplating the evidence. The absence of photos was strange and seemed to confirm what she had concluded: the baby suffered from some sort of genetic abnormality. Ashley put a hand to her chest. She felt wretched. The diagnosis must be crushing for Grace and Dan to be so secretive about it. Images flashed into her mind of babies with congenital disorders, and she wished that Grace had opened up to her. She might have, at the very least, been able to provide a referral to a trusted specialist.

She went to the kitchen for a glass of water to try to still her churning stomach. Was she to blame? Had she helped bring to life a child who would know only pain and suffering in its short existence? No, she told herself. It had been Grace and Dan's choice; and besides, they had not been certain of the abnormality. She shut off her iPad and went back to bed. She told herself she bore no more responsibility than a doctor who helped deliver unwell babies in the nineteenth century, when a devastating condition could not be predicted. So why did she feel so uneasy?

⁓

Roger had left for the clinic when Ashley woke the next morning. The bedroom smelled faintly of his aftershave. Ashley had a rostered day off but Roger and Doctor Carmichael were seeing patients. As soon as the clock struck eight she picked up the phone and dialed reception.

"Hello, Doris, it's Ashley. I was wondering if you could check something for me."

"Can I put you on hold a minute, Doctor Li? I've got two other calls coming through."

"Yes, that's fine."

As she listened to the Mozart hold music, she idly plugged Grace's, Dan's, and Sam's names into Google's news search engine. A birth notice had been placed in the *Sydney Morning Herald*.

Grace and Dan Arden are thrilled to announce . . . There was no more detail than a name.

"Yes, Doctor Li, what can I do for you?"

"About ten months ago I had my last appointment with Mr. and Mrs. Arden. The mother's name is Grace. I was wondering if we had a record of a live birth."

"Let me see. Arden, Arden. It doesn't appear so."

"Hmm."

"Oh, no, hang on a minute. I was looking at the wrong entry. We do have a live birth for Arden. Fifth of May. It was a little boy. 3.1 kilos. They named him Samuel."

"Any notes about problems? Complications?"

"No, just the date, weight, and name. That's all the information I have."

"Does it say which hospital he was born in?"

"I only have the details I gave you, Doctor Li."

"Thank you, Doris. I'll see you on Monday."

Haunted by Grace's drawn face, Ashley went back on to Facebook. This time she searched Grace's page. Her privacy settings were locked down, presumably so students couldn't snoop through her personal life. But there was one photo Ashley could see: Grace cradling a bundle. The image was black and white. Ashley could just make out a baby. He had Dan's dark hair. Grace was smiling. There was something unusual about the smile, though. Was it restraint, or just fatigue? Ashley had seen hundreds of photos of mothers and newborns and none of them looked like this. Or was she just imagining it? Like a Rorschach test, where what you see reflects your own view of their world.

Ashley leaned closer to the iPad and focused on the baby's face. It was an out-of-focus smudge. There was nothing visibly wrong with him.

"What is going on?" she said.

Twenty-Two

IT WAS A GRAY, IDLE SATURDAY MORNING WHEN PRIYA FOUND herself flicking through her phone and opening her NetBank app. The money from the sale of the house was mostly untouched and all those zeroes made her nervous, sitting in an account she could access every day through an ATM, as if the pile of bills could just blow away.

Thoughts of the house prompted thoughts of Nick, and she found herself wondering if Megan was with him, her acrylic nails digging into his arm as she fantasized out loud about what they could spend the money on. In a flash of jealousy, Priya threw her phone aside. She'd had a restless night, plagued by worry. As she'd tossed and turned, panic overcame her—she'd missed her chance. Her isolation exacerbated her fears. No longer did she end her workday cooking with Nick and tossing scraps to Jacker, while they talked idly about the family they assumed they'd have. Dinnertime sounds in her shabby flat were limited to the *clack-clack* of her knife on the chopping board, when she bothered to cook. She'd gotten out of the habit, instead buying premade salads from Coles Supermarket. She'd peel away the glassine lid and eat them standing up in the kitchen. She could eat filet mignon every night if she wanted, she thought glumly, looking again at her bank balance. There was no need to save. All the money in the world couldn't buy what she needed. But she had been formulating a plan.

She picked up the phone again and called her cousin.

"Darsh, are you free for a catch-up? There's something I want to ask you."

"Sounds ominous."

"I hope not. Can you come now?"

She suggested Gelatissimo in the heart of Coogee beach, thinking an ice creamery in June was the perfect setting for a delicate revelation and private conversation. She chose a table up the back and ordered two chocolate sundaes.

Darsh walked through the door a minute later. He'd shaved his head, and a pale blue scarf hung around his neck. "What's going on?" he asked, accepting his ice cream suspiciously.

Priya leaned forward. "I've been thinking. I need your help. You have a lot of gay friends, right?"

"You know I do."

"And some of them are couples with kids?"

"A few." He raised a perfect brow, intrigued.

"I was hoping you could tell me what they did to have children. You know, the processes they went through."

"Oh." Darsh blew out a puff of breath. "Now there's a can of complicated worms. Let me think. Kai and Lewis opted for surrogacy. They went through a clinic in Thailand."

"Isn't that illegal?"

"Very. And it's not even an option anymore; Thailand has closed its doors to foreigners. India too. But there are other countries where it's available to Australians. Canada. Ukraine. The U.S." He counted them off on his fingers. "I assume this isn't a hypothetical question."

"I've been thinking about doing another round of IVF, but I'm reluctant. I don't think it will work for me."

Darsh tilted his head sympathetically. "I'm sure that's not true."

"Going through it alone is hell. If I'm going to be a single parent, maybe it's better if my body doesn't have to go through the pregnancy. One less thing to try to recover from while I'm raising a newborn alone."

"I'd be happy to put you in touch with any of my friends you wanted to speak to."

"I know it's not going to be easy," she said. "But I really want this. I think about it constantly. It's keeping me up at night."

Gelatissimo was a bad choice. The place was filled with children. Priya watched them hopping up and down in front of the ice cream freezer trying to pick just one flavor. A father hoisted a little girl with pigtails onto his hip so she could see the full range of options.

"Pink!" the girl declared.

"That's blood orange, sweetie. Are you sure you wouldn't prefer chocolate? Or caramel?"

"Pink!" she said again.

Priya's smile faltered. She wanted a child, but really, she wanted a family. Darsh placed his hand on her knee. "I say this from a place of absolute love, but do you really want to be a single mother? How will you work?"

Priya idly stirred her melting ice cream. "My office is actually really great when it comes to flexibility for parents. I've got that lump sum from the house."

"I just wish you didn't have to do it alone."

"I don't have any alternative."

Darsh looked Priya in the eye. "I like Nick. I always did."

"Darsh!"

"If you'd never seen those messages, where would your life be now?"

"Don't, please." She held up her hand.

"Really, though. If you and Nick were together and you never knew those messages existed, what would be so bad about that?"

"I'd be living with someone who was lying to my face and sneaking around behind my back."

"You don't know what he would have done."

"I saw enough at the Exeter to know he can't be trusted."

"But he didn't *actually* cheat."

"He was with that woman. That—that Megan. I found her cheap, dirty underwear in my house. Do you know what that felt like?"

"That was after you separated. Priya, you can't hold that against him. He was fucking miserable, so he banged some woman who was there while his heart was broken."

Priya snorted but the thought of Nick's broken heart softened her a little.

"Forgive me, dear cousin," Darsh continued, pointing his spoon at Priya. "But you dumped him and sold the house he'd spent years building."

"I didn't do it for fun!" Priya reared up, indignant. "And we built that house together. I lost it too. Now he's shacked up with his internet floozy and I'm out here in Coogee in a musty old flat with a stupid haircut!" She tugged the short strands of hair, on the verge of tears.

"He's not with her."

"What?"

"He's not with her. He slept with her once. The fact that you happened to see her underwear in the bathroom is the world's worst coincidence."

"You've been talking to Nick?" Priya's shock made the question come out like an accusation.

Darsh shrugged and dug into his sundae. "He called me. He was desperate. Like I said, I always liked him. You know that when the family excommunicated me he always used to take me out for beers. We talk a lot, actually."

"I can't believe this. Why didn't you tell me?"

"I didn't want to upset you. Besides, we mostly just talk about sports. He was my cousin too. That doesn't just go away."

Priya lapsed into silence.

"You know I cheated on Lukas," Darsh said. Lukas, Darsh's elfin, Danish first love, was one of the things that cleaved Darsh and his family apart.

"What?" Priya was stunned.

"Very occasionally and very discreetly. It didn't come close to meaning I didn't love him."

"That's different."

"Oh, gay relationships are different?"

"Don't do that. And yes, if you want to know, I think in this case it was. When you and Lukas got together you were both sleeping with other people all over town. Your relationship had a completely different dynamic."

"But then we decided to commit. I'm not proud of what I did. I'm only telling you so you can know what it's like being inside the head of a person who did the cheating. And I can tell you now, if Lukas had taken me back, there's no way I'd risk that again."

"You and Nick aren't the same person."

"You're right. Nick and I aren't the same. Nick never crossed that line while there was a chance he could still be with you."

Priya was silent.

"Get down off your pedestal, Priya Laghari. Nobody's perfect."

"What are you saying, Darsh—you think I should go back to him and play happy families?"

"I'm merely pointing out that while you're trying to come up with a way to build a family without a man, there's a very sorry, very good one still desperate to do it with you." He shrugged. "What you're considering is complicated and hard and will completely change your life. I just think talking to the person who wanted to do it with you is something worth exploring."

~

True to his word, Darsh arranged for Priya to meet his friends Jordan and Leroy, who had had their son via surrogate in Thailand. After exchanging a few emails—*To ensure you're not a member of the federal police*, Jordan joked—they invited Priya to brunch at their fashionable home in Maroubra, where they served up quiche and horror stories from their five years of trying to conceive.

"We had two surrogates whose transfers failed before we got our son," Leroy said. "We spent five months in India holed up in a Marriott with dodgy electricity and still came away empty-handed."

"We know a couple whose surrogate changed her mind at seven months. Nothing you can do in that case. It's their prerogative."

"It sounds like such an ordeal."

"It's not easy. Five years of heartbreak. It put a strain on us, that's for sure."

"But it was worth it?"

They were sitting on the patio, overlooking the landscaped backyard. A plastic ride-on fire truck, a trike, and a swing set sat on the grass.

"Of course it was worth it. But you're best off knowing the facts going in."

"Get yourself a good lawyer."

"If you've got the money, go to America, where they have surrogacy agencies."

"Avoid Mexico; the word is they treat the women terribly."

"And Cambodia; it's completely unregulated there."

"Don't even think about starting the process unless you've got a hundred grand put aside."

"At least!"

When she left, clutching a list of names and numbers, Priya's head was spinning. But she felt now she had a road map. The money she had earned from the house gave her a range of options. She still hadn't decided on a course of action but she felt she was getting closer.

She took the scenic route home along the coast. When she came over the crest of the hill she had a perfect view of the Coogee inlet. A canary-colored strip of sand divided the promenade from the water, and beyond the yellow lay the boundless blue, flashing silver where the waves caught the sun. She slid her sunglasses down over her eyes and imagined herself at the beach with a toddler wearing a floppy hat, a miniature bathing suit, and flip-flops half the size of Priya's hand.

The buildings around her new neighborhood were old but well preserved. They were the color of milkshakes: strawberry, banana, and peppermint. She took in the view and the sea air and wished she didn't feel so desolate. In Coogee, it seemed she only saw people who looked like her behind counters in shops or driving cabs, except for the wealthy whose conspicuous jewelry deflected judgmental stares like Wonder Woman's bracelets. These women looked like Priya, only with blow-waves and floaty silk chiffon dresses. She didn't fit in with them either.

Her chest tightened and she realized she couldn't spend another Saturday alone in Coogee, among the tanned and happy people who wore their swimsuits to lunch. She turned onto the main road and headed west.

When Priya reached Viv's house they were making kinna-thappam—steamed rice pudding—the way Viv and Priya used to with their mother.

The girls were far too young to help but Viv liked to envelope them in the ritual. Avani played with dough, sucking it until it melted all over her fingers in a sticky, viscous mess, while the twins watched from their high chairs. There was basmati rice everywhere.

Priya gave each of the girls a loving squeeze. With her and Viv's parents now dead, she worried that their heritage was retreating. Rajesh's parents would arrive for dinner at Viv's house with their arms full of dosas and homemade salted mango. Having married Nick, Priya had no one in her life to reinforce the traditions she'd spent her teen years trying to escape but now appreciated as a key part of her identity.

That was why she had sought an Indian donor, and why she had been deeply disappointed when Leroy told her that India had closed its doors to foreigners seeking surrogates. If India had been an option she would have traveled there without hesitation. She could have stayed for an extended visit, caring for her baby full-time and raising him in his ancestral land. She could have reached out to her mother's extended family in Kerala. She very much liked the idea of being about to introduce Dyuti's grandson to her cousins and aunts and uncles, to hear their stories about her and to tell them what she remembered of her mother.

Priya helped her sister transfer the porridge-like mixture into the steamer, all the while avoiding eye contact.

"What's wrong?" Viv finally said.

Priya bit her lip. "Do you think I made a mistake with Nick?"

"Where is this coming from?"

Priya shrugged. "Darsh told me he's not with that Megan woman. He's single."

Viv spoke gently. "You do remember that day at the Exeter?"

"I've had two hundred days worse than that since then."

"Have you been talking to him?"

"Just occasional messages about the dog."

"Do you want to work on it? Or do you just want a baby?"

Priya dumped the dirty bowl into the sink and blasted it with water. "You say 'just want a baby' like it's a small thing."

Viv tilted her head. "You know what I mean. When Nick was messaging that woman you were so miserable. I don't want you to have to go through that again."

"Viv," Priya said, "I want to be a mother."

They looked at the twins, who had fallen asleep in their high chairs. They were a matching set, already inseparable. Viv and Priya had been like that once. Even after they both married, the intimate sorority remained intact. But once Avani came along, things changed. Even in the womb, the little tadpole squirmed between the two sisters and Viv began a journey that Priya didn't—and perhaps couldn't—follow. Priya had always thought they would raise their kids together, but Viv had entered motherhood alone, and things weren't quite the same.

Priya looked at her nieces and thought that if she had a child of her own, she would never be alone again.

After the kinnathappam was cooked and eaten, Priya lingered in her sister's company. They washed the dishes, then Priya helped with bath time.

"Do you want to stay over? I'll make up the couch," Viv said after the girls had been put to bed.

"No, I'd better face the music, or rather, the silence," Priya said. "Besides, battling Sunday traffic to Coogee would take up most of the morning." She tiptoed into the girls' room and kissed them good night.

When she got home she propped her laptop up on her knees and opened the NSW Department of Family and Community Services web page and searched for advice on adoption. It explained that each country had its own rules, and that prospective parents had to file individual applications, which was time-consuming and costly. You could not begin the adoption process while undergoing IVF, it warned. Priya's shoulders sank. This rule meant she had to choose one or the other, and the wait on adoption meant if it fell through, it could be too late to give IVF another go. She scrolled through the fact sheets on the website, which announced the typical wait time for families who adopt a child from overseas was five years, "but it can be much longer."

"Five years," she whispered. All the options she had thought she had when she and Nick realized they were having trouble conceiving—IVF, surrogacy, adoption—suddenly didn't seem realistic at all. She stared at the screen, watching her dream of a family begin to fade, and quietly began to sob.

Twenty-Three

A TENSE SILENCE HUNG OVER THE KITCHEN, BROKEN SPO-
radically by the sounds of breakfast: the scrape of a butter knife
on toast, the clatter of a cup on a saucer, and the ping of a spoon
following it. Sam was feeding, and the radio was off. It had been ten
long minutes since Dan had announced he had made an appointment
with a lawyer.

Grace still hadn't responded. Their son was latched to her breast,
and she was admiring the soft down on his cheeks as he suckled
hungrily, making darling, perfect noises of contentment. His eyes
were gently closed, his lashes fluttering ever so slightly. She stroked his
cheek with her index finger, trying to hold back the tears gathering
in her eyes.

"Grace?"

She picked up her piece of toast and bit into it.

"The lawyer sounded very good," Dan said beseechingly. "He's
done a lot of work in the medical malpractice space. Remember
the class action about the prosthetic knees that wouldn't hold their
shape? He was the lead guy on that."

A tear rolled down Grace's cheek. "Sam's not a prosthetic,"
she said.

"Grace."

"He's not some foreign item that can be removed, readjusted, or sent back to its maker and replaced with a more natural-fitting model." Her voice wobbled.

"This lawyer said there shouldn't be anything to worry about. Wouldn't it help you sleep at night to know we've got a professional looking out for us?"

Grace looked up at him. Her glassy eyes sharpened. "You told him?"

"I didn't say anything specific. I asked some general questions about rightful parents. Donor laws, IVF, and that sort of thing."

Every word felt like he was prodding an open wound with a salted knife. The worst of it was that he'd done it without her say-so. She was losing her teammate. He was supposed to be on her side, but he no longer considered her judgment sound. She watched him chewing his crust and felt the sting of betrayal.

Though perhaps he was right, she thought, scratching the back of her neck. There were moments, late at night, when she felt positively unhinged. She was so tired that her nightmares bled into her waking hours and she had trouble distinguishing them from reality. Sleep came to her in ragged snatches. When she had first started nursing Sam she dreamed her breasts were riddled with malignant lumps; the next day she had to keep pressing her palms to her chest to reassure herself the tumors weren't real and that she wasn't pumping their boy full of poison. The only thing she could trust was her instinct to protect Sam. She found her voice: "What if they take him from us, Dan? What if they take away our son?"

"That's why I called a lawyer," Dan said, his voice cracking. "To guard against it if they try." He stood, sighed, rubbed his chin then his eyes, and went to the kettle to make another cup of coffee. It was his third day without shaving and he looked as strung out as Grace felt. "I got an email from my aunt in Queensland."

"Oh?" These days she spoke almost exclusively in a tone of detached melancholy.

"She said Sam was very beautiful."

"He is. Aren't you?" Grace looked down at Sam, who had fallen asleep at her breast. Milk leaked onto her shirt. She dabbed it with her sleeve.

"She saw his photo on Facebook. Grace, I thought we agreed on this. Can we just cool it with the social media until we know our rights?"

"People will be suspicious if we don't post photos. What kind of parents don't post photos of their newborn?"

"It's too risky."

"It was black and white. Nobody would have been able to tell. I'm not stupid. It was just one picture. Everyone kept asking me why there are no photos. I did it to stop the questions."

Tears began to roll down Grace's cheeks. Dan filled a cup with hot chocolate and brought it over to her. He laid his hand across the back of her neck and gave it a reassuring squeeze.

"I know. I know. It's unfair."

"Maybe we should move away."

"What do you mean?"

"Move to Broome. Or New Zealand. Just get away. A fresh start where nobody knows us."

"Like fugitives? You're talking like someone who thinks we have something to hide."

"I want to be able to show him to the world. We waited so long for our baby. But now it feels like we don't really have him. Like he could be snatched away. And I'm just going crazy cooped up in this house all day with no visitors and there's no end in sight. My girlfriends are mad at me. I'm too scared to go to mothers' group. Where will it end, Dan? What's going to happen?"

Twenty-Four

THE FIRST THING ASHLEY DID WHEN SHE GOT TO WORK ON
Monday was pull up the Ardens' file. She didn't know what she
was looking for, but in any case, there was nothing to be found.
Everything was in order. The baby had been born and nobody
had made any comment about abnormalities. Only one thing was
strange: the morula had been identified as female, but the Empona
birth record showed that the baby was male. Grace had told her
so herself. The lab must have made a mistake. Ashley made a note
to raise this with Roger. Occasional clerical errors were inevitable
but should be minimized where possible. In a way she was almost
pleased. She'd been fighting for more staff for months, and this was
a clear example of why they were needed.

Still. The mystery gnawed at her. No mother hid her child from
the world. Maybe she really was tired. Maybe he really was sick. But
that didn't seem reason enough to be so secretive.

Ashley opened Grace's Facebook page and stared at the one
solitary black-and-white photo. She had half a mind to call Grace,
but she had to know what she was dealing with first. She didn't want
to upset her former patient unnecessarily. She thought about the
day at the market again and wondered: Had there been a shadow of

reproach in Grace's conduct? Did Grace blame Ashley for whatever
had happened?

"Doctor Li," Doris buzzed her, "your eight a.m. is here."

"Thank you, Doris."

Doctor Li closed Grace Arden's Facebook page and opened her
first patient file for the day.

That night Ashley set her phone to private and called Roger's home
number. He was the only person she knew who maintained a land-
line. The ring sounded old-fashioned and far away. It was eight
o'clock. The phone rang out. Ashley sighed. He wasn't home. She
turned on *Midsomer Murders* to kill time and then dialed again
at nine.

"Hello?" he answered.

She hung up and raced out her front door. She drove toward
Empona, the busy city streets fraying her nerves. The clinic had
expanded and moved to larger, more modern premises, and she just
wanted to get there, find what she needed, and get out. She felt like
a criminal.

Empona's new home, a Gothic Elizabeth Street building, was
shrouded in darkness. Ashley swiped her security pass against the
censor and was granted admission. The cavernous lobby was dark.
She turned on the flashlight on her mobile phone and opened the
door to the fire stairs. As Ashley climbed, her footsteps echoed
loudly on the polished concrete steps. She was short of breath and
sweating when she reached the fifth floor.

As she pushed open the heavy fire-exit door the familiar scent
of pear and lilac hit her. All was dark and still. Machines hummed.
Ashley went to Doris's neat desk and, feeling like an intruder, began

to paw through her neatly arranged paperwork. The various forms were in uniform stacks, like a paper city. The only personal item was a framed photo of Doris's grandsons at Disneyland.

A noise made Ashley jump. The door to the stairwell swung open. The reception area filled with light.

It was their technician, Dale. "So," he said, "what are we looking for?"

Ashley had offered him two hundred dollars to come in and help her figure out what had gone wrong with Grace and Dan's genetic test. They weren't doing anything wrong, she had stressed, but she wanted him to keep their investigation a secret for now.

"Honestly?" she said. "I don't know." She put her hands on her hips like a small-town cop with a mystery on her beat. She was acting on instinct.

"Okay," said Dale. "Why are we looking?" He flicked on a switch so the overhead lights came on. Ashley cowered under their glare.

"You'll look more suspicious if they catch you sneaking around here in the dark," he told her.

"I'm just worried about a former patient," she said.

She took him through the story. While she spoke, Dale logged in to Doris's computer and examined the Ardens' record.

"I've stared at this a million times. The test went out and came back fine," she said.

"But it says here the embryo is female," he said, looking at the documents.

"I know. Someone ticked the wrong box somewhere."

Dale opened the schedule on Doris's computer, navigating back through the calendar to the previous August.

"Let's see who was working the day of the transfer . . . Whoa, busy day."

"Every day is a busy day."

"Yeah, but this is one for the record books." The calendar was a checkerboard of tightly packed appointments.

"It was right in the middle of that hellish flu season," Ashley said.

They leaned toward the screen. Then Ashley saw it. The appointment before the Ardens': Archer.

A cold terror clawed at Ashley's stomach as the germ of a horrifying theory formed. With a shaking hand, she grabbed the mouse and zoomed in on the entries. Two transfers, Archer and Arden, at 9:15 a.m. and 9:45 a.m. in the same surgery, with the same embryologist.

Arden. Archer. To speak the names, they sounded quite different. But written, the shape of them was very similar. Only a few pen strokes distinguished them and at a glance they looked interchangeable, particularly if the person reading them was in a hurry. Under stress. They were also near each other in the alphabet. If, say, two items were being stored alphabetically, as records and samples were at Empona, there was a high chance the Arden and Archer items would be near each other.

"It can't be," she said.

But she knew it could be. She had read about this before. In New York in 1999. In Leeds in 2002. And Singapore just a few years ago. There had been an Italian case too. And they were just the ones she knew off the top of her head.

She remembered the abstract from a risk-minimization seminar she had attended on human error and the case of Baby K.

There is an error in approximately one in every 200,000 ART cases, it had read. The most extreme of these was when an embryo was implanted in the wrong mother.

It was only a hunch, but the pieces were clicking together. Grace's evasiveness. The busy clinic. The overworked embryologist. The system with poor oversight. She recalled how easy it had been for her to alter the Crawfords' records so they could have a second round of eggs from the World Egg Bank. Ashley's hunch gained strength. At university, their lecturer had taken them through a cautionary case study of a woman from Michigan who had learned at thirty-two weeks that the baby she was carrying was the biological child of another couple, and that she would have to give it up once it was born. But what if the child had already been born? What was the statute of limitations on correcting a mistake like that? A week? A month? A year?

Cold sweat was pooling under Ashley's arms. The answer lay in the storage freezer, but she was scared to look. Grace and Dan were her patients. If there had been a mix-up with the sperm, or the egg, or the embryo, it was her responsibility. Dale laid his hand on her shoulder.

"Let's go check out the freezer."

She nodded. Soon they were moving down the white corridor toward the storage facility. Dale opened the door.

"Do you want to do it, or should I?"

Ashley grabbed hold of the top of the storage container and pulled it open. She read each of the labels. The name *Archer* jumped out at her. The one next to theirs held a straw marked *Arden*. She slowly removed it. It contained a frozen morula. Female. There was a code: *Possible exclusion*. The Ardens' embryo had never been used. The child Grace had given birth to could not possibly be her own. Someone had made a terrible mistake, and for a second, Doctor Ashley Li thought her heart had actually stopped.

Ashley sat on the floor massaging her temples, trying to picture the day of the botched transfer, but almost a year had passed. She had no more chance of remembering the events of September 5 than of July 13 or November 7. But when she focused on the last time she had seen Grace and Dan Arden in the clinic, there was something—a muddy memory, just out of reach. She concentrated on it. There had been an error with their paperwork. Doris had called her into the reception area right before the transfer. Ashley tried to recall the details, but her instincts told her that the paperwork wasn't the problem.

Once she was in the transfer room, Ashley would have been given the catheter already loaded. She didn't want to shift blame, but the simple fact was that it was the embryologist's work. She tried to picture who was on staff that day, but she had done so many transfers with the Ardens it was difficult to say. She didn't want to avoid taking responsibility. She didn't want anyone to be responsible. This was a nightmare.

"I bet nothing like this has ever happened before," Dale said. "Whoa. We're going to be on the news."

"No! Dale, just . . . let me think." Ashley's stomach twisted as the implications sank in.

"What's there to think about? This is, like, medical malpractice. I mean, this is a serious breach of our duty of care."

"And what if we report it, what then? This couple has their baby taken away from them."

Dale opened his mouth to argue, but stopped himself. "I didn't think of that. But somewhere out there is the baby's real mother."

"What's a real mother, Dale?" she snapped. "Somewhere out there I have a real father who has never bothered to learn my name."

Dale blinked, startled. When he spoke, his voice was gentle. "But,

Ashley, this is a completely separate set of circumstances. This child has parents out there who—given they were doing IVF—probably want him."

"I need to think. If the Ardens' morula is still in our storage container, whose baby did Grace give birth to?"

"It has to be that other couple," Dale said. "The Archers."

"We don't know that for sure. It could be anyone's."

Ashley returned to Doris's desk, with Dale on her heels. She scrolled back through the daily logs until she found the record for Priya Archer.

She opened Priya's file. Had she had a successful pregnancy? Ashley's mind was bounding ahead. If the Ardens had the Archers' baby, and the Archers had their own baby, then maybe . . . maybe it wasn't so bad. How many embryos had the Archers had on ice? She knew she was grasping desperately. Sam was the Archers' child. They would want their son. But it seemed easier if they had one of their own . . . She clicked open the file. Priya had not had a successful transfer.

There was a note. Priya had started treatment with her husband, Nick, but in the end had used donor sperm. The husband was no longer in the picture. She was of Indian heritage and sought an Indian donor.

"Oh my God," Ashley said as the black-and-white image of the baby flashed in her mind.

Grace knew. Grace knew she had someone else's child and she hadn't said anything. That's why she was so secretive at the market. It explained why there were no photos of Sam online.

"That's why she was acting so strangely," Ashley said, hardly able to believe it.

She reread the notes on the Ardens' case over and over, searching for a clue she had missed, some proof she had got it all wrong. But deep down she knew that she was not wrong.

Dale was watching her. "What are you going to do?"

"I don't know." She bit her thumbnail. "What do you think?"

"This is above my pay grade."

"I suppose we have to report it to the Health Complaints Commissioner."

"And Doctor Osmond?"

"He'll need to be told." The thought turned her blood cold. Roger would want to know who had been treating the patients. He would want to know who had threatened his reputation and endangered the clinic. He would explode.

"Come on," she said, shutting down Doris's computer. "It's late. There's nothing we can do tonight."

Dale nodded. Before they left she stopped and grabbed his arm. "Dale, promise me you won't breathe a word of this to anyone until I've figured out the best way forward."

"You think I want to cause *more* trouble?"

"Dale."

"Okay, I swear. Not a word."

⁓

Ashley went straight to Roger's office the next morning, and in clear and clinical language laid out everything she had discovered. He was holding a pen in his hand, clicking it as he listened. The clicking grew faster as he learned the facts, in-out-in-out.

"Does anyone else know?"

She thought of Dale. "No."

"And you say it was just a hunch that made you investigate this? Nobody has complained?"

"You saw the way Grace Arden was acting. I was worried about her. I thought maybe the genetic testing had missed something. I wanted to help."

"Do the biological parents have any idea?"

"You're the first person I've told."

He leaned back in his chair. His pen clicking slowed. In. Out. In. Out.

"Well, if we have a healthy baby, and happy parents, with no complaints, I don't really see that there's any role for us to play."

Ashley's jaw dropped. "You can't be serious, Roger."

"What are you suggesting—that we take the baby from his mother and father and give him to a woman who doesn't even know he exists?"

"No, but don't you think she deserves to know?"

"To what end? The family is happy. The biological mother has moved on with her life. What possible purpose would be served by dredging up the error?"

She looked at Roger as if seeing him for the first time. Their relationship had always been uneven—she the younger woman, still finding her feet, he the lauded miracle worker. But now the light of his halo was flickering. "How can you be so calm about this?"

"I'm not calm at all. But it's done now." His voice had a steely quality Ashley had never heard before.

"We have to tell them," she said. "We have to call the mothers."

"Has a complaint been filed?" he said slowly, each word deliberate and loaded.

Ashley glared at him across his large mahogany desk. "No."

"Then we'll review how this happened and look at what can be done to ensure it doesn't happen again."

"What about the child?"

"He stays with his birth parents. If nobody is upset, nothing needs to be done."

"The biological mother isn't upset because she doesn't know."

"Ashley!" He slammed his hand on his desk. "There will be an internal investigation. We will deal with it at a clinical level and leave the family in peace. Now drop it."

Ashley was speechless. All she could do was stare at the man she had shared a bed with for the past year and wonder how she could have been so wrong about him.

"You just want to protect your reputation," she said finally.

"I'm not going to tear apart a family!" he boomed.

"What about the family that will be destroyed by this secret?"

He got to his feet. "This is *my* clinic. *I'm* the director. I'm *your* employer. Don't you forget that. The decision is not yours to make."

The young doctor stared at him, defiant. "It's not yours either."

"Do you really want to rip a two-month-old boy from the arms of a mother and father who love him dearly?"

Ashley wanted to argue, but found she couldn't. He had her there. No matter how sure she was that it was right that the child should know his biological parents, the thought that he might be taken from Grace and Dan was too cruel to bear. She imagined the little boy, thrust into the arms of strangers, wondering what had happened to the only mother and father he had ever known.

She turned and exited Roger's office without a word.

⁓

On the other hand, a mistake had been made, and Grace and Dan had concealed it. She thought of the child. Not as he was now, but aged five, aged nine, aged twelve. She thought of his eighteenth birthday, and the years he would spend not knowing where he came from. Ashley had been inexorably shaped by the fact she had never known her own father. Sometimes when she stared at her reflection long enough she could no longer see herself; she just became a collection of parts that didn't make sense. It was a confusing and lonely feeling. But there was one key difference between her situation and that of baby Sam. Her own father had abandoned her mother before Ashley had been born. He had no interest in her and his absence had haunted her her whole life.

She knew what she had to do.

Twenty-Five

THE CALL THAT WOULD CHANGE EVERYTHING CAME AT ONE minute past eight in the morning. Priya was on a bus to work when the Empona clinic's number flashed up on her phone. The familiar digits brought the memories of past calls rushing back: nail-biting fear and failed tests. She ignored the ringing. Five minutes later it started again. The caller wasn't going to give up. With a ripple of irritation, Priya accepted the call.

"Yes?"

"Hello, I'm calling for Priya Laghari."

Priya's throat tightened. The tone of the voice on the phone put her on her guard. The woman sounded nervous—no, scared. She sounded scared. "This is Priya speaking."

"Ms. Laghari. My name is Ashley Li, I'm calling about the Empona clinic. I need to speak with you urgently."

"What is it?"

"Not on the phone."

"I'm sorry but I can hardly hear you."

"I said it can't be on the phone. I need to discuss something delicate with you."

Priya pulled her diary from her bag and flipped it open. "I can come in on Tuesday or Wednesday evening."

"No!" There was a pause. When the woman spoke again her voice was even softer than before. "Not at the clinic. I'll come to you. What part of town are you in?"

"What's going on?"

"Please. I will explain everything in person."

They agreed to meet at a little French café in Coogee at five that afternoon. The woman had insisted it be somewhere quiet. Nine hours later Priya found herself ensconced in white linen and dark wood, facing a beautiful doctor who had just said the most extraordinary thing.

"I don't understand what you're telling me," Priya said slowly.

The woman—Doctor Li, she said her name was—leaned across the table, keeping her body low. She was wearing dark Jackie O glasses, but even so Priya could tell she had the kind of beauty that men start wars over. It only added to the unreality of what she was hearing, as if this woman were a spirit who had stolen into the human realm to reveal an unimaginable truth hidden from mortals.

"Something happened at the clinic. An error. A terrible, unintentional error. Your embryo was somehow implanted in another woman's uterus and it resulted in a viable pregnancy." She paused. Priya waited. "And a live birth."

Priya's eyes grew wide. "You mean a baby?"

"Yes."

"Is it still . . ."

"Alive? Yes. From what I can tell he's perfectly fine."

"A boy?"

"Yes."

Priya felt light-headed. She understood what the woman was saying, but the words weren't having any effect.

"When did this happen? How?"

"I don't understand fully myself, but when I made the discovery, I felt compelled to tell you as soon as possible."

Priya found herself short of breath. "I have a son?"

"Technically, yes."

"I have a son."

"I wouldn't have told you if I didn't have good cause."

"Why are you telling me at all? He must be, what, living with this other couple." She could hear her own heartbeat and see the tremble in her fingers as she reached for the milk jug next to her tea. She looked up at the woman. "How do you know this?"

The woman lifted her chin. "I'm a doctor at the clinic. Or . . . I was."

A faded memory clicked into place; Priya had seen this woman before. That's why she had butterflies when the doctor had entered the café. It wasn't the sort of face you forget. Asian angles combined with an English-rose complexion. Priya looked up sharply. "Was it you?" She couldn't believe how calm she sounded, how rational her line of questioning.

"I don't believe so. I—we haven't figured out how it happened. But I don't believe the error was mine. The place is . . . well, it's understaffed. An incredible number of couples come to Empona for treatment. It appears the embryologist was at fault. But . . . I can't say for sure."

"I can't believe this," Priya breathed. The little boy she had dreamed of was real and living somewhere in Sydney. *Sadavir. My Sadavir.* She had been hoping and praying for him so much it almost felt as if she had willed him into being.

She reached for her tea and took a sip, but tasted nothing. She needed something normal to bring her back down to earth. She had not yet absorbed the force of the news, and for now she was only able to contemplate it as if it were an abstract math problem or a science question: If a human ovum is fertilized and placed in the uterus of another woman who carries the baby to term, who is the rightful parent of the child?

Another thought struck her: Nick's sperm. Harvested. Labeled. Frozen. It was never supposed to have been used. But maybe it had.

"Exactly when did this happen?" she asked.

"The error occurred last September. The baby was born in May. He's two months old now."

A picture was filling Priya's mind—an infant, chubby and smelling of talc, with her eyes and her father's nose and dimples from no-one-knows-where and, maybe, Nick's smile. But no, Empona never created an embryo from Nick's sperm. They'd only got that far at the Parramatta clinic. A pang of disappointment jabbed Priya right in her gut. She had a son, but he wasn't Nick's. Why did that hurt? It was all too much.

"What should I do?"

"I can't answer that."

"What normally happens in these situations? Has this ever happened before?"

"I'd suggest finding a good medical-negligence lawyer. They'll be able to advise you."

"I feel like I'm dreaming . . . I have to see him. Maybe the parents will let me meet him. Who are they? How can I reach them?"

"I can't tell you that."

"What?"

"I've already said too much."

"Then what was the point of any of this?"

"You could seek damages."

"Damages?"

Ashley looked away sheepishly. "From the clinic. For emotional distress. I'm sorry, but I really should be going."

"How can I be sure this is real?"

The doctor stood and slung an expensive-looking bag over her shoulder. She appeared conflicted. "I wouldn't put you through this if I didn't have evidence of the error."

"But you've given me nothing. How can I prove this? What should I do?"

Dismay flitted across the doctor's face. She winced, then frowned.

"There must be something more you can tell me," Priya pleaded.

Doctor Li pulled her wallet from her bag and placed a ten-dollar note on the table to pay for the tea. Then, slowly, as if as an afterthought, she retrieved an envelope that was folded in half and slid it across the table to Priya.

"I'm so sorry this has happened," she said. "I really am."

Priya reached out and touched the envelope, letting her fingers rest on it. She pulled it toward herself, her hand shaking.

"Wait," she said.

But when she looked up, the beautiful doctor was gone.

Twenty-Six

A LOAD OF LAUNDRY SPUN IN THE WASHING MACHINE AND
another tumbled through the dryer. The pots and pans were in
the dishwasher, and the portable heater radiated warmth onto a
clotheshorse draped in knits. Grace turned on the kitchen tap and
wondered how one little baby could seemingly be more work than a
whole boardinghouse full of schoolgirls. She filled a pot with water,
salted it, and placed it on the stove. As she turned up the hot plate
dial she heard a snap, a fizz, and a *crack!* Everything went dark. The
glow of the hot plate element faded to black and the radio made a
sad little noise, like it had been shot.

"Damn Victorian-era wiring," she said, turning the stovetop
knob back off.

She ran upstairs to check on Sam—still sleeping soundly in his
crib—then flipped open the fuse-box lid and shone the light of her
mobile phone at it.

"Is the whole house out?" Dan asked, emerging from the bathroom in a haze of steam.

"It's not the fuse box," Grace said.

"I'll call an electrician."

"No!" The word burst out of Grace's mouth. "I'm tired," she

added. "It's late, if you call now we'll have to sit up for God knows how long. Let's just eat the salad and go to bed."

They knew from experience in their creaking old house that after-hours electricians were capricious creatures who could take up to five hours to materialize, if at all. But that wasn't what worried Grace. The thought of letting a stranger into her home unnerved her.

"We'll deal with it in the morning," she said.

Dan looked ready to argue, and Grace knew he was reading her mind. This was who she had become—a woman too scared to call a tradesman in case he discovered their secret. But Dan didn't put up a fight. They ate by candlelight, brushed their teeth in the dark, and went to bed.

When Grace laid her head down her mind wouldn't stop firing. During the days her limbs were heavy and her mind was like a wet sponge—but the second she tried to sleep, her imagination started darting around like a sparrow trapped in a room. The prospect of an outsider seeing Sam had riled her. She knew the fear was irrational, but that was how she felt these days—in a constant state of paranoid readiness.

She managed to drift off but at two a.m. her eyes snapped open. Her face and chest were slick with sweat, the back of her pajama top soaked through.

She rose from their bed and walked to Sam's room. He was lying peacefully, with his little hands curled into fists. She knew if she gently prized his fingers open they would be full of lint. His face crumpled and he began to grizzle. "Sh-sh-sh." She gave the cradle a gentle rock. She hummed and rocked, and soon enough he settled. "That's my boy," Grace whispered. He was easily soothed. He got it from Dan, she told herself.

She leaned down and kissed her sleeping boy's forehead. The

thought of Sam being Dan's son and another woman's biological child did not injure her as much as the thought that her egg had been fertilized by another donor.

She didn't know why this was so, but she guessed it was because she already felt connected to him. His bones had drawn strength from her body. His blood was her blood. How did that make her less his mother than the woman who had provided the originating egg? That woman had given just one cell. Grace was responsible for all the rest. Each day Sam grew stronger because of Grace and Dan's love. What was one cell compared to all that?

She rocked in the chair, realizing as she made these arguments in her head that she was imagining them being read out before a judge.

Grace reluctantly called an electrician first thing the next morning, then hovered near the bottom of the stairs like an over-caffeinated royal guard as he replaced a circuit breaker.

After he left she picked up her car keys and told Dan she was going to the shops.

"I won't be long. I'll be back before you have to leave for work. Is there anything you want?"

"OJ?" he said hopefully. "And maybe some decent cheese."

At the supermarket she filled a basket with groceries. Bread, olives, juice, lamb chops, and a wedge of blue cheese for Dan. All misdirection.

Her last stop was the toiletries aisle. She selected a box of dark brown hair dye and held it next to a photo of Sam on her phone to see how closely the tones matched. His hair was blacker. She returned the brown to the shelf and selected a different brand that had a color called "ultra onyx." The model's hair was ebony. Grace tossed it into her shopping basket and made her way to the register.

When she got home Sam was asleep. Grace kissed Dan goodbye as he left for the office then put Sam into his stroller and wheeled it into the bathroom.

She had never dyed her hair before. Everybody always said they wanted a gold mane like hers, and around the age of sixteen her friends all started experimenting with different colors. Grace had been tempted to try a shocking shade of red but Fiona talked her out of it. "Blond hair like yours won't ever go back to its original color after you've dyed it. You'll have to grow it out. Can you wait three years to get it back to your original color?"

That didn't bother her now. She didn't ever want to be blond again.

"You're getting a new mother, Sammy," she said, tearing open the box of dye and pulling out a pair of black latex gloves and two small plastic bottles. She momentarily regretted not booking an appointment with a proper colorist. But she dreaded being asked why on earth she was dying her blond tresses dark. Besides, she wanted it done immediately.

She mixed the toner into the solution and squirted a dollop into her gloved palm. It looked like thick, pearlescent oil. Grace's eyes flicked up to the mirror and she took in her blond reflection one last time. With her clean hand she patted down the flyaway wisps. She took a deep breath and slid a streak of black goo through her hair.

When the bottle of dye was empty Grace looked like she was wearing a glistening black swimming cap. The solution was hot and made her scalp itch. She let it sit for thirty minutes then showered, thinking of the shower scene in *Psycho* as she watched the dirty water run down the drain. The solution clung stubbornly to her follicles and she had to rub hard to shift it. Sam, still in his stroller, stirred and began to cry. She turned off the tap and stepped out of the shower, wrapping herself in a towel and leaving dirty gray spots on it. She could still feel the dye residue in her hair.

"Sh-sh," she soothed as she tucked in the corner of her towel to hold it in place. She grabbed one of the old towels from under the sink and covered her half-clean head with it. "Sh-sh." She rubbed Sam's belly with one hand as she tucked her hair away with the other. Would he notice the new color? The dye reeked of chemicals. He wouldn't like that, she thought guiltily.

He squirmed and resisted as she lifted him from the stroller. He straightened his back, trying to twist free from her arms as he cried.

"Sh-sh, little one," she said. Gray water was trickling down her back and onto the tiles. "I'm sorry, little one, I have to put you down," she said. "I'll only be a minute. Just one little minute."

She didn't want the dye getting on him. She hugged Sam to her chest and padded quickly to his room. "Sh-sh, there, there," she cooed. Sam wailed as she lowered him into his crib. She could feel water dribbling down her back and knew it would be dirtying his bedroom carpet.

Sam wailed harder, opening his throat and baring his tonsils. "Sh. I'll be right back," she said, dashing again toward the bathroom, where she skidded dangerously on the wet tiles. She turned on the shower taps, cranking them up harder than normal so a heavy stream of water blasted from the jet. Grace scrubbed and scrubbed her head, releasing a seemingly endless stream of murky water. Despite the roar of the shower, she could hear Sam howling. She dug her nails into her scalp and raked them rigorously back and forth, needing to banish every last trace of chemical. Her hair looked so strange, hanging from her scalp like black squid tentacles.

When the water finally ran clear she turned off the tap, grabbed a fresh towel, and wrapped up her long hair. She put on her dressing gown and ran to Sam's room, where she scooped him up and held him to her chest. "There, there, little man," she said. She settled into the rocking chair to see if he would let her feed him. He latched on greedily and began suckling, clawing her breasts with his tiny nails. She felt another pulse of guilt at having let him go hungry while she washed her hair. She leaned back in the chair, taking the weight off her back. Her energy was sapped. She closed her eyes as Sam suckled, then swapped him to the other side. After he was fed, burped, and changed he was content and drifted off to nap for a few hours.

"What's this?" Dan asked when he arrived home to find a stew bubbling away on the stove.

"It's poor man's beef bourguignonne."

"Not this, *this*."

"Oh." She put her hand to her head, still covered by her towel turban.

"This little rascal gave you time for a shower, I see. What luxury." He leaned closer to the bassinet on the marble counter, where Sam kicked and cooed. "What luxury, Sammy." He took the scrubbing brush from her. "Sit down. Let me do the dishes. I've been in meetings all day. I've barely moved."

"Thank you."

"I bought gelato," he said.

"The good stuff?"

"Burned fig. It's in my bag."

She retrieved it, smiling. "My hero."

"How was he today?"

"He was perfect."

She unwound the towel from her head, black hair falling down to cover her shoulders.

Dan gave a start. "What have you done?" He touched it. "It's real?"

"It will grow out, but yes, for now, it's real. You don't like it?"

He brushed it with his hand sadly. "It's just . . . different."

"I'm tired of feeling like I have a big flashing neon sign on my head that makes people wonder why I don't look like my son."

She got up to look in the mirror that hung on the wall. Her entire face had changed. Her hair color looked flat. Unnatural. The individual strands were no longer silky but coarse. Against her golden hair her complexion had a summery apricot hue. The matte black washed it out, tinting it a jaundiced yellow. Though the sleepless nights certainly didn't help. Her eyes were receding into their sockets and her face had grown hollow. She now weighed several kilos less than she did before she got pregnant. Despite this, she felt a distinct hint of something she hadn't felt in months: relief. Repose. She touched the black ends of her hair; perhaps now she could relax, so she wouldn't look so suspiciously tormented all the time; and by extension, maybe she wouldn't feel that way.

The doorbell rang bright and early the next morning, an impatient *dingle-tingle-tingle* echoing throughout the hallway.

"Yoo-hoo! Gracie! It's me, Caroline."

Grace stayed perfectly still, like a savanna zebra sensing the presence of a big cat.

"Gra-ace!" Caroline rapped her knuckles on the door's frosted-glass panel. *Tap-tap-tapper-tap-tap-tap.* "Yoo-hoo!"

Sam was in his bassinet sucking on his thumb. Grace crept to the dining-room doorway so she could peer down the hall. Caroline's silhouette was framed by the white frosted glass. Her hair was blond and fluffy like a poodle's. She was holding something in her left hand as she banged on the door with her right. She wasn't going to give up. Fastidious, unwavering, and always prepared, Caroline was born to be a mother.

As the doorbell chimed again Sam started to grizzle.

"No, sh-sh, please, not now," Grace whispered. Sam ignored her, escalating to a full-blown cry.

"Grace, I can hear little Sammy! I'm not going away until you open this door."

Grace picked up Sam. If she let Caroline in now she would have to show her the baby. She couldn't leave him in his room crying while the self-appointed mother of the year was perched on her couch admonishing Grace's choice of nipple cream.

"For God's sake, Grace, if you're worried about looking like a disheveled new mother, I've seen it all before. I've got GMO-free ointment and some lanolin. Trust me. I'm here to help."

The knocking started again. Grace cursed quietly.

"Caroline!" she called out, trying to sound surprised. "I didn't hear you. Ah, just a minute."

A virus, she thought. I'll say Sam has a terrible, contagious virus and I want to keep him away from everyone. But what? Caroline, that walking syllabus of baby maladies, would want to know what Sam had and how he had contracted it. She'd probably have a list of a dozen remedies on hand. Grace picked up her phone, balancing Sam in one arm, and Googled common baby viruses. Meningitis? Measles?

Tap-tap-tapper-tap-tap-tap.

Grace slipped a pacifier between Sam's lips, took him upstairs, and wound up his musical bear. "Greensleeves" began to play from the furry stomach. She shut the door, smoothed down her hair and shirt, and then headed back downstairs to open the front door.

"Hiya—*oh*! Grace, your hair." Caroline's Avon-lady smile faltered.

"Hi, Caroline." Grace's hands went self-consciously to her blackened hair. "Um, come in."

Eyeing her friend, Caroline shuffled sideways into the narrow hallway. The lofty expression on her face said: *It's worse than I thought.* One arm was weighed down by a basket. The other cradled a Mason jar containing what looked to be a homemade unguent.

"Come into the dining room." Grace practically pushed her friend down the passageway.

"Is the little man of the house asleep? I just heard him."

"Yes. Finally. He's upstairs. I don't want to disturb him."

"Oh, Grace, let me just take a little peekaboo. We won't wake him. I'll be quieter than a church mouse."

"He's been really hard to settle—"

Grace had almost maneuvered Caroline into the dining room when Sam started to cry. Her heart sank, while Caroline's face lit up gleefully.

"There now, he wants to say hello," Caroline said, pushing the jar into Grace's arms and making her way upstairs. A word drifted into Grace's head, as it so often did when Caroline was around: *busybody.*

"Caroline—" Grace searched for something to say, but Caroline was pushing Sam's bedroom door open, placing her basket on the changing table.

Grace stepped past her to the crib and reached in to lift Sam, whose cries quieted to a whimper.

"Well, hello there," Caroline said, a shocked smile plastered on her face. Her manners and her curiosity were locked in a battle. Grace knew she would tell everyone about Sam. They would comment that none of them had met him. They would begin to make connections and wonder why he was being kept hidden. She should offer an explanation to stem the gossip, she thought. But what? Her tongue was paralyzed.

"Isn't he just the most perfect little thing?" Caroline said, regaining her composure. Sam was watching her with his big brown eyes, taking in her poodle hair and rabbity teeth. Caroline was looking back with matched curiosity.

Dan had been right all along, Grace thought. They needed to see a lawyer.

—

"I'm really glad we're doing this," Dan said.

He and Grace were in a waiting room on level twenty-seven of a skyscraper, their fingers knotted together. They could see for miles through the reception area's floor-to-ceiling windows. It made Grace dizzy and it felt prescient, like they were poised for a great fall.

A young woman took them through to a long boardroom with padded, paneled walls.

"Mr. and Mrs. Arden." A man came toward them with his hand held out. "Elliott Jones; I'm one of the partners here."

Dressed in a banker shirt of blue stripes with a white collar and cuffs, Elliott Jones exuded success. His impeccable grooming distracted from the fact that he was not naturally handsome. His face had a wolfish quality.

"Please take a seat," Elliott said, gesturing to the table, where a yellow legal pad lay waiting. "You were a bit vague on the phone. You're going to have to tell me exactly what your problem is."

Grace and Dan looked at each other.

"Nothing you say will leave this room. Promise."

"Perhaps we could show you," Dan said. He took his phone from his pocket and opened his photo gallery. It was a mosaic of tiles. There was Sam in his first sun hat. Sam having tummy time. Sam sleeping off a milk coma. He passed the phone full of images to Elliott. "This is our little IVF guy."

The lawyer smiled. "What a strapping lad. Let me guess. Custody issue? You used a donor egg and now the mother's making a claim?"

"No."

"Donor sperm? You didn't get the result you expected."

Grace and Dan shifted in their seats, embarrassed. "No. The embryo was created using our egg and sperm."

The lawyer leaned back in his chair and regarded the couple. "I'm guessing neither of you have relatives who look like Sam."

Grace twisted a strand of her lank black hair. "To be honest, Mr. Jones—"

"Elliott, please."

"To be honest, Elliott, we really don't know what happened. But our best guess is that there was some sort of mix-up. That maybe the clinic used the wrong egg or the wrong sperm."

"And you want to sue them?"

"No! The opposite. We want to make sure we can't lose him. We want to make sure nobody can take him away from us. Ever."

The lawyer leaped to his feet and started pacing the boardroom. Fissures of excitement rippled across his face. Grace could picture him sitting in expensive restaurants regaling his colleagues with the details of the predicament. Men like Elliott Jones, she sensed, lived for this sort of professional intrigue.

"We just want to shore up our parental rights," Dan said.

Elliott nodded as he paced. "Okay. Okay. Have you done a DNA test?"

"No."

"I'd say that's the first step so we know what we're dealing with."

"We're only guessing it was a mix-up. The doctor said it could be a recessive gene that's surfaced again," Grace said hopefully.

Elliott pursed his lips. "Perhaps." He tented his fingers. "Can I be honest with you? I've never heard of anything like this happening before. Ever. Can you sit tight for a day or two while I investigate the legalities?"

"There have been a few cases around the world," Dan said. "I looked into it. The outcomes were . . . mixed. Depending on the jurisdiction."

"You know, if there has been a mix-up you could sue the clinic for malpractice."

"What if they try to reconnect him with his parents?" Dan asked.

"And risk a public outcry? Exposure? Penalties? No, if there has been one guiding principle that I have relied on all my professional life it's to always back self-interest. They'll be eager to throw money at you and quiet you down. This is a big problem for them. They'll just want it to go away."

"I can't sue for damages when the so-called accident gave us Sam," Grace said. "He's the best thing that has ever happened to us."

"And what if a family appears claiming Sam is theirs?" Dan said. "Won't it look bad if we've sued?"

"I understand your concerns." Elliott nodded. "But the clinic should be held to account for this. They could do it again. Do you want to put other families through what you've been through?"

"Right now I'm just concerned with our family," Grace said, reaching for Dan's hand.

"If you sue the clinic, and we win, it doesn't do anything to protect us if there's a custody claim, does it?" Dan asked.

"No. But you have a better chance of fighting off any claims on the child if you have a legal team funded by a juicy settlement."

"We'll have to think about it," Dan said.

Grace nodded.

Elliott tapped his pen against his pad. "Leave it with me. I'll do some research and be in touch in the next couple of days. In the meantime, I'm going to have my secretary set up an appointment to have a DNA test. Now, I don't want you to worry, this is just for our information. If there was a mix-up we need to know exactly what error was made." As he shook their hands the links of his heavy gold watch shook.

"Thank you, Elliott," Dan said. "I'm glad we came."

"I am too," the lawyer replied. "It's best to be on the front foot with these sorts of things."

Grace and Dan had almost reached their car, which was parked at Dan's newspaper office in Pyrmont, when his phone rang.

He looked at it quizzically. "Elliott. Hello?" Grace watched as he listened, nodding. He hung up and said: "We need to go back."

"What? Why?"

"It's nothing to worry about, just something about paperwork we need to fill out." He pressed her hand.

When they returned to the office Elliott was waiting at reception with a young woman, who was holding some forms.

"Mr. and Mrs. Arden," she said. "Thank you for coming back. There was just one thing I needed from you, Mr. Arden. It will only take a moment."

"Sure," Dan said.

"Please come with me," the young woman said.

After Dan and the paralegal disappeared down the hall, Elliott looked at Grace. "Coffee?"

"A glass of water would be nice."

He smiled. "Of course. Through here."

Elliott led Grace to a small kitchenette, where he filled a glass with Perrier. He watched as she drank. "Grace," he said, tenting his fingers again, "I don't know quite how to ask this so I'm just going to come out with it. The story Dan told me in the boardroom . . . there's no way he could be mistaken about the baby's paternity?"

"Mistaken?" She looked at him blankly.

"Well, you gave birth to a little boy who doesn't look like you, or Dan. Such an outcome is not as uncommon as you think."

Grace wasn't picking up on the implication. "I don't—"

"I have a second guiding principle. It's that the simplest answer is often the correct one."

Realization hit Grace and she felt her face burn. "You think I slept with someone else?"

Elliott held up his hands. "I'm not accusing you. I just have to ask. Grace." He placed a hand on her arm. "No judgment. But you've got to be one hundred percent straight with me on this."

"No. No, there's no way." She pulled away. "I would never. And even if I had, there is no way I would have got pregnant. We did seven rounds of IVF and nothing." Her anger was swamped by embarrassment. Shame. "I've got medical records to prove it. Oh God. Is that what people will think? This is a nightmare."

"I'm sorry, Grace. I had to ask that. I believe you."

"How could you think I would drag my husband through this? That I would make up an IVF error to hide an affair?"

"I apologize. Truly. I'm on your side."

"Even we don't know exactly what happened. That's why we need your help."

"I understand." He laid a hand on her shoulder. "And I'm here to help. But we're in uncharted territory. It may be a long road ahead."

Twenty-Seven

ASHLEY WAS SHAKING AS SHE GOT INTO HER CAR AND DROVE away from Coogee. Her eyes were on the road, but in her mind she could see only Priya Laghari's face. Her large dark eyes had lit up when the news she had a son had sunk in, and just as quickly, that light had gone out as she realized the unique conundrum she was in. Ashley was certain she had done the right thing. But what of Grace and Dan? And little Sam? He was the one she had done this for. He deserved to know the truth. Out of everyone, he was the one whose rights most needed to be protected.

The blast of a horn brought her back to reality. Her car was lagging twenty kilometers below the speed limit and traffic had built up behind her. As a truck zoomed past her, the driver jeered and gestured abusively. Ashley's sweaty hands were slippery on the wheel. Another car roared past. *Honk-honk-honk,* it blared.

Rattled, she tried to reassure herself. She had done the ethical thing, but it gave her no comfort. And Roger. He would be livid when he discovered she had spilled the secret. He was wrong to conceal the mix-up, but she knew he wouldn't see it that way. All he would see was that she had gone behind his back. He would see it as a betrayal. Their relationship was over. The realization registered dully. His attitude toward the error was unforgivable and revealed him to be an unethical doctor and an uncaring man.

The Health Complaints Commissioner would have to get involved. If there was to be an investigation, her actions would most likely be examined. She braced herself against the steering wheel. Her body felt flushed and her skull full of pressure as if it were expanding outward. The world began to sway. She felt like she was suffocating.

Ashley pulled her car over to the side of the road and threw open her door, gasping for air. She put her head between her knees and tried to breathe, taking huge gulps of oxygen. She wished she could disappear. Her eyes stung with tears and her chest burned. There was a water bottle in her bag. She reached for it and drank deeply.

As the panic receded a curt text arrived from Roger: *Where are you?*

Ashley could feel the anger vibrating through the transmission, as if he knew what she had done. She had avoided him for days.

She wondered momentarily if she had miscalculated when she called Priya. But it hadn't been a calculation, she knew; it had been instinct. She had been carried along by righteous anger, fearful that Roger would seek to conceal the truth from the biological mother, and others would conspire to keep the truth of the little boy's origins from him.

Her phone rang. Roger again. She canceled the call and started the car engine.

Twenty-Eight

IF YOU COULD SAVE TEN STRANGERS' LIVES BY SACRIFICING *yourself, would you do it?*

Hypotheticals. It was a game Priya and Viv used to love playing when they were growing up.

Sometimes the question was about gross-out childishness. *Would you rather eat maggots or dog poo?* Sometimes it was a macabre moral conundrum. *What if you, me, and Mum ran into a hungry cannibal giant and you could only save one of us. Who would you sacrifice, Mum or me?*

Now, the game had come horrifyingly true. Priya could practically hear teenage Viv reciting the predicament she'd cooked up with a girlish thrill. *What if you'd wanted a baby all your life but you couldn't have one. Just as you've given up hope you learn your baby already exists. He's happy and healthy and living with another couple. The only way you can have your baby is if you take him from them. You don't know them. But they're good people. It's not their fault they have your baby and they love him. What would you do?*

"I wish she'd never told me," Priya said as she turned the envelope over in her hand.

"There's no hurry to make a decision." Viv put a plate of biscuits in front of her sister.

"Every minute I delay they're with him, growing more and more attached, making the situation worse."

"What does your instinct tell you?"

When playing hypotheticals, Priya was always the pragmatic one. She would ponder the problem, her bottom lip sticking out and her eyes moving from side to side as she tallied the consequences of the options before her. Ultimately she would choose the answer that would be easier on her. Viv tended toward the self-sacrificing answer. *(I'd let the giant eat me so that you and Mum could live.)* It was easy to be noble when there was little chance of running into a cannibal giant in Sydney's southwest.

"I can hardly think straight. I'm so angry at the clinic," Priya said. "My little boy is out there somewhere. I want to knock on every door in Sydney until I find him. But when I think about that door opening, and the couple, I just feel so bad for them. I'm so conflicted."

She slipped the piece of paper from the envelope. It was a printout of the surgery schedule on the day of the insemination. The couple that came in after Priya was the pair who had Sadavir. *Grace Arden. Spouse: Daniel Arden.*

"Don't think about them. What do *you* want?"

"I think, how can I take their child? But then, he's not just my son. He's your nephew and he's Avani, Shanti, and Shanaya's cousin. What if he turns ten and finds out he has a whole other family? One that looks like him, and has the same mannerisms, allergies, tastes, medical history. The same culture. Won't he want to know why we didn't want him?"

She had a flashback to primary-school recess when the other kids ate cakes and fruit buns, and screwed up their faces and pinched their noses as Priya and Viv unpacked roti bread. Their scorn had burned. She and her sister had shuffled closer together and finished their morning snack. She thought of Darsh holding her hand in the transfer room, and cheerily trying to rouse her from her post-separation rut. How could she deny this baby his family?

"I wouldn't even know what to do," Priya said.

"You would have to get a lawyer." Rajesh had been sitting quietly at the table.

"I . . . I don't think I could take their baby," Priya said. "I don't think I could live with myself."

"Could you live with yourself knowing that your son is out there somewhere and you did nothing?" Viv said. "He's family."

"Honestly," Rajesh said, leaning forward with a look of intense concentration on his face, "I think if you can get a DNA test to prove that baby is your biological son you've got a strong case. A very strong case."

"It's so hard to wrap my brain around it. Right now, I don't think I can do it. But then I think, what if in a year or two I realize I was foolish to let this go, and I try to get custody, and the judge rules against me because I waited a whole year. I feel like I have to make a decision now and it's just too much."

Every time she thought about it her heart started to pound and she felt like her brain was being overloaded.

"And what about these doctors who did this?" Viv said. "They sound incompetent. We don't know what care they take with the embryos. How many times have you been treated there?"

"Three."

"And you have no baby. Who knows what they're doing behind closed doors. Who monitors these places?"

Priya contemplated this. What if—as Rajesh had suggested—she was awarded custody. She would suddenly be responsible for a two-month-old boy. It was more than the human mind could grasp. She felt so unprepared. She would need a crib, a changing table, formula, nappies, a baby thermometer, and much, much more. She didn't know how to swaddle a baby. What if he got a fever? She had anticipated that if she adopted or chose a surrogate, she would have time to learn these things. This, she thought, is why you shouldn't play God.

"They are doctors and they're putting babies in the bodies of the wrong people," said Rajesh. "Even if you don't want to try to get custody, something needs to be done about the clinic."

⁓

That night, Priya lay awake for hours turning over possible outcomes in her head. Maybe, she thought, it wasn't an all-or-nothing situation. Perhaps Grace and Dan Arden would be willing to compromise. Let her meet him. And in exchange, she'd promise not to make a parental claim. The more she thought about it, the more she convinced herself this was a good idea. She could propose a civilized sort of good-faith agreement. Maybe in time she could babysit, and become a godmother figure, or something. Aunty Priya, who always sent a birthday card with a crisp ten-dollar bill in it and was invited to school plays and graduations.

She went to her desk, pulled out some writing paper and a pen. She thought about what she would want from them and what they might be comfortable offering. She didn't want to leave any room for misinterpretation. Most of all, she thought about what was best for the baby. *Sadavir.* When he grew up he would want answers, and together they could sit him down and explain what had happened. Why he looked like Aunty Priya but lived with Grace and Dan. Then she began to write. It took two hours, but around one a.m. she had a letter that she was happy with.

Dear Grace and Dan,

    To open with a cliché, this is the hardest letter I have ever had to write. In fact, I'm certain it is one of the hardest letters anyone has ever had to write, for I feel sure nobody in history has ever found themselves in the situation the three of us face right now.

    I was a patient at the Empona clinic in Alexandria at the same time you were. I had been undergoing treatment with my now ex-husband since 2015. My doctor, Cecelia Carmichael, collected six eggs after a stimulated ovulation. After I separated from my husband, the eggs were fertilized with donor sperm and the subsequent embryos were frozen.

    I returned to the clinic in September 2015 to be implanted with embryos fertilized by a donor I selected to give me the best genetic match to my child. I am of Indian descent and I was eager for my child to look like me. I felt it was important for the child too, so that he could feel connected to my family.

    Those two weeks were full of the hope that I might finally get the family I craved. I had had so many disappointments. I prayed. I meditated and I pictured myself with my baby. After two weeks, with shaking hands and a thumping heart, I took a test. It was negative. I would not get my baby.

    Little did I know my baby was growing—he just wasn't growing in me. It appears that a clinician made an error and a doctor implanted my embryo in your uterus, Grace. My

understanding is that you are presently raising a son who is the
product of my egg and the donor sperm I chose. He has my DNA
and he carries in him my genetic material, and the bloodline
of my family.

   Rest assured I mean no threat to you. When I learned of
this development I was at a loss for what to do. I only want the
chance to see the child grow and to know that he is healthy.
I would like to offer you my thanks, for the love and care you
have given our son.

She had put a lot of thought into that line. *Your son* didn't feel
right, but *my son* felt provocative. *Our son* was in keeping with the
spirit of her proposal.

   Perhaps, in time, a friendship will grow and the boy will
have the opportunity of knowing both the parents who raised
him and the mother who will always love him from afar. I hope
you will consider this suggestion as the best way to achieve a fair
outcome out of a strange and unforeseeable situation.

Sincerely,
Priya Laghari (Archer)

Below she wrote her phone number and her email address. Her
hands were trembling, but a sense of accomplishment was settling
the storm in her soul. It was a good resolution and a good letter.
How could they do anything but reply that they too would like to
make the best of this unfortunate situation?

Priya stood and walked to her window. In a neighboring yard
sat a sandpit filled with bright plastic toys. A rush of jealousy hit.

It seemed so unfair. She pressed her forehead to the cool glass. As she stared at the plastic tricycle and thought of the chubby legs that would power it, anger bloomed in her chest and she couldn't help but direct it toward these faceless people. The sense of injustice stung. Tears filled her eyes. She had to tell herself this was not their plan and that they were all victims of the clinic. It horrified her to think how they would feel when they learned the child wasn't their own.

Underneath it all, she felt an affectionate gratitude toward them. She had a son, and these two strangers had nurtured and cared for him. Although she grieved her failed pregnancies, she couldn't grieve this lost chance. Her son had survived, against all odds. He was brought into the world amid error and doubt, yet his will to live had prevailed. Such a special baby would surely grow up to be a remarkable man. She hoped desperately that she would come to be a part of his life.

Priya folded the letter and sealed it in an envelope. She had, of course, Googled the couple when she had learned their names. She knew that Grace worked at a girls' school and Dan was a journalist. She went to Dan's newspaper's website to find their postal address. On a whim she typed Dan's name into the search field. As she toggled through his articles she came across a piece he had written about the decline of strip malls. The opening line was: "In my neighborhood of Glebe . . ." Priya quickly tapped *D and G Arden* into the White Pages search engine and was surprised when an address popped up. Gottenham Street. Her baby was in Gottenham Street. She carefully copied the address onto the envelope, then pasted on a stamp.

She propped the envelope up on the windowsill, knowing she would hardly be able to sleep until it was sent. The nearest postbox was a kilometer away. She went to bed but ten minutes later she was up again. Her car was being serviced, so she ordered an Uber. She waited by the window until the car pulled into view.

"Just down to the postbox on Beach Street, please," she said, sliding into the back seat clutching the letter.

A few minutes later they were pulling up near the curb. The dark trees looked menacing under the streetlights.

"Can you wait, please?" Priya asked the driver. "I'll just be a minute." She hopped out of the vehicle and ran the few short steps to the letterbox. Without hesitation she grabbed hold of the cold metal handle, pulled it toward her, and shoved the letter into the chute. She breathed. It was done. *It was done.* A week ago she had felt more alone than she ever had in her life. Now she had taken the first step to becoming a piece of a new and modern family, with a surely grateful couple and a baby. *Sadavir. My Sadavir.* She knew she wouldn't be able to call him that. Whatever moniker the birth parents had chosen, she would respect, but she would always think of him by his intended name, the great-grandson of Dyuti's father, Sadavir, a foreman at a silk factory in Kerala who had done everything he could to give his children a better life.

She bounded back to the cab and slid into the back.

"You just wanted to post a letter?" the driver said.

"That's right." She was giddy, overwhelmed. She felt excited and proud. She had put Sadavir's needs first, as a mother should. "Could you take me back to where you collected me from, please."

The driver nodded. "Must have been an important letter."

"Very."

Her toes jiggled inside her shoes. She wanted an answer now.

"What was it? A check or something? You owe some people money?"

"No, nothing like that."

The car reached her flat a short time afterward. "You own this place?" the driver asked.

"I just rent."

"You're alone?" He was watching her in the rearview mirror.

"I'm separated."

"Must get lonely."

"Not really," she lied.

When he pulled on the handbrake Priya opened the door to leave.

"My family lives in Melbourne," he said. "I get lonely sometimes."

Priya gave a murmur of interest. She wanted to retreat into the privacy of her flat.

"Well, thanks," she said, climbing out.

"Hey," he stopped her. "Can I use your toilet? I haven't had a break in over seven hours."

"Oh, is that allowed?"

"It's allowed if you say it's allowed."

He undid his seat belt. "I'll be quick."

"Why don't you go to the McDonald's down the road?" Priya asked, feeling uncomfortable.

"We're already here. And they make you buy something if you ask for the key." He was sliding off his seat.

"I—I really would prefer it if you didn't."

He shut the door and came around to the front of the car as she stepped out.

"I really don't think—" she began.

He was advancing toward her. She turned and ran. The slap of her shoes on the concrete path echoed loudly across the deserted street. She didn't turn to look if he was behind her. She jammed her key in the security-door lock. It stuck, she jiggled it. Terror shot through her as she felt his hand laid heavily on her shoulder.

"I'll scream!" she shouted, turning. He jerked his hand away, as if her skin were red-hot. She yanked the door open and threw herself into the building, swung around and slammed the door behind her. He thumped slowly on the door. She could see the dark shadows of his two shoes. She backed away, as if he might burst through any moment. "I just want to use the bathroom." His voice was toneless. There was another thump.

She hurried up the stairs and deadlocked her flat, her ears cocked all the while, waiting for the noise of him banging on the door, smashing a window, but there was nothing. She stood in the dark, too scared to move. She peered down at the landing through her window. A bar of white light shone on the empty stoop. She snuck into the kitchen and looked out the window. The car was still parked, empty, out the front of her building.

Perhaps he was around the back, she thought. Or climbing up to her tiny balcony. She heard a crash and nearly jumped out of her skin. She found her mobile phone and punched in triple-zero, wincing at the loud dial tone echoing through the receiver.

The call connected. "What is your emergency?"

"Hello," she whispered, keeping the phone close to her mouth, her hands cupped around it. "Hello, there's a man outside my house."

"Ma'am, can you speak up, please?"

"I don't want him to hear me. I live in Fairfield on Merivale Road." She faltered. "No, wait, sorry, that was my old house. I'm in Coogee." She recited her address.

"Has the man threatened you?"

"He followed me to my flat. He was an Uber driver. When we got to my door he tried to come in. I ran. He grabbed at me but I got away. He's still out there somewhere. Please," Priya whispered, her shoulders hunching forward protectively. "Please hurry."

She hung up the phone and scanned the kitchen for a weapon. There was a cast-iron frying pan sitting in the drying rack. Behind it was the knife block. She grasped the pan's plastic handle and crouched low, with her back to the wall.

She thought of the weight of his hand on her shoulder, and the fact he was still lurking outside. At that moment, she wanted Nick. She wanted to press herself against his bulk and feel him reassure her. She dialed his number. It rang, but it went to voicemail. "Sorry I missed you. Leave a message." The mere sound of his voice made her feel less vulnerable.

"Nick." Her voice wobbled. "Nick, I . . . I don't know why I called, really. You see, there was this man . . . He followed me and . . . it doesn't matter. You're not there. I'd better just . . . I'm sorry to bother you."

She put the phone on the floor and hugged herself. There were cold patches of sweat on her T-shirt. She was too afraid to move.

When the doorbell rang twenty minutes later her heart pounded so hard it hurt.

A male voice spoke. "Police."

She tiptoed to the door with the frying pan at the ready. She could see two sets of shoe shadows beneath the door. "It's all right, Ms. Laghari," another male voice said. "The predator appears to have gone."

Ten minutes later she was sitting with the two policemen over a pot of tea giving a description of the driver. She traced her finger around the rim of her cup.

"I'm sorry for wasting your time," she said.

"It's always better to call in these situations," one of the officers said.

Priya was still jumpy, but she felt foolish all the same. He hadn't attacked her. She was just paranoid and not used to living alone. He had probably snuck around the back of her building and taken a leak, then driven home to his wife and kids, oblivious to her terror.

"You'd be surprised how often really dangerous creeps can be linked back to a string of strange reports. Every little bit helps," the constable said.

"Thank you for coming," she said. "I feel a whole lot better knowing you've been here and done a search."

⁓

After the police left, Priya tossed and turned and sweated, with the covers pulled up to her chin until the sky was a comforting blue and sunlight broke into the room. She wished it wasn't Sunday so that she could go to work and be surrounded by people.

She dressed, pulled on a jacket, and sank her hands into her pockets. Despite the warm day, it made her feel protected. She slipped on a cap and sunglasses and, in this approximation of urban armor, she stepped outside.

She needed caffeine. And sugar. And a bear hug from a close friend. She needed a deep sleep in a hotel bed with fluffy pillows and a roti breakfast just like her mother used to make. With sunny-side-up eggs, still a tiny bit runny in the center. At least she could do something about that last demand, and she set out on foot, glad of the sunshine.

Next to her favorite café was an overpriced gift boutique. Priya slowed as she passed the window, admiring the silver bottle openers from Italy. She noticed a pair of booties made of foal-colored leather with white sheepskin lining. They would be perfect for Sadavir. She had money enough now that she could make incidental purchases without having to run a mental audit of her bank account. And this was her son, after all. She knew it was dangerous to think of him as such, but, if this couple replied to her letter in the way she hoped they would, she would like to be able to give her son a gift.

She went into the store, picked up the booties and slid her fingers into the soft shoes, imagining the tiny feet that would fit inside. She put them on the counter. "Just these, please."

The young man at the register smiled obligingly and scanned the tag. They looked puny in his large hands. They seemed a paltry gift.

"Hang on a moment," Priya said. "I want to get something else."

She roamed around the shop's display stands. She laid a tiger-cub jumpsuit over her arm and chose a light-blue linen one-piece for summer. She selected a handmade wooden mobile and a pint-sized denim jacket. In all she spent $356 on baby clothes and toys. As the man behind the counter was wrapping the items, Priya's phone rang. She tucked it between her shoulder and ear as she handed over her credit card.

"Hello?"

"Priya! My God, I just heard your message. Are you okay?"

"Nick. Yes, I'm—"

"I'm so sorry I didn't get back to you last night. I was at Lee's place watching the game. My phone died. I slept on his couch. I feel awful. Where are you?"

"I'm in Coogee."

"I'm coming straight over. I'll be there in half an hour."

"Nick, it's okay, I'm fine." Her ordeal suddenly felt distant.

"I'm coming. No arguments. Text me your address."

Twenty-Nine

DAN STOOD AT THE GATE STARING AT TWO LETTERS. ONE was stamped with a logo the color of congealed blood—red with plenty of black in it. The other was a blue envelope addressed by hand.

The official envelope came from Griffith Pathology, and it held the results of the DNA test he, Grace, and Sam had taken. It had been a simple cheek swab.

"It's the same one they use when DNA-testing criminals," the nurse had chirped, while bagging and tagging the specimens.

He traced his fingers over the paper, trying to guess what was inside.

The results had come early. The pathologist had said eight to twelve working days, and it had only been seven. But he was glad it would shorten the wait. He couldn't take many more of the recurrent nightmares.

In the most recent one, the results revealed Sam was not Dan and Grace's son. *But he could be,* the typed letter teased. The folds of the page concealed a small piece of plastic that looked like a memory card for a digital camera. *Insert this in your son and download your own DNA,* the letter instructed.

In the dream, Dan could hear Sam crying. He searched the upstairs rooms and opened the cupboards, but they were all empty. He woke up before he could find him. He gazed up at Sam's bedroom window now, where Grace was feeding him.

"How's that boy of yours?"

Dan jumped as their neighbor sat up and raised her hand to ward off the sun. Edna Goss was on her knees behind the fence, making little divots in her garden bed with a trowel.

"Hello, Mrs. Goss. He's still . . . not out of the woods."

Illness was the excuse Grace had given to avoid taking the baby around to meet their neighbor.

"The poor little thing. Not to worry. I'm sure he'll come good. My Brian was very poorly when he was born. Now he's the director of his own company." Mrs. Goss struggled to her feet, pruning shears in hand, and began to clip away the vines that were choking her side of the fence.

Dan looked up at Sam's window again. He could feel the letter in his hand like a living thing.

"If you ever need someone to sit with the boy, just sing out."

"I will, Mrs. Goss. Thank you. I better go in."

He folded the blue envelope and tucked it into his back pocket, then made his way inside and up the stairs, with the white envelope held out solemnly before him, like a wartime telegram.

When he eased open the door he saw Grace seated in the rocking chair with Sam in her arms. The blue-and-white Turkish towel she'd wrapped around her wet hair had unfurled so that it hung over her shoulder. As she bent her face toward their baby, Dan was reminded of paintings he had seen of the Virgin Mary and baby Jesus, who was the only other child he could think of who was conceived in as unlikely conditions as Sam was.

"All okay?" Dan asked.

She looked up, tired but content. "He's behaving himself."

"Good little man. Mrs. Goss was asking after him."

"She must think we're deliberately hiding him from her."

"I said he was still ill."

"I feel a bit bad. She was so excited when I told her I was pregnant," Grace said. "Maybe I have been too paranoid. She's in her seventies, after all. Who is she going to tell? Perhaps I should take him down to meet her."

"No!" The word leaped out of Dan's mouth. "I mean, she seems to have accepted he's sick. Let's just leave it for now." He shifted on his feet.

"What's wrong?" Grace asked. "You look like you've seen a ghost."

Dan raised the envelope.

"Is that . . ."

"From Griffith Pathology."

She took a deep breath. "Have you opened it?"

"I wanted us to do it together."

Grace looked down at Sam, who was still feeding. "Oh God, I'm not ready for this."

"You think it will be bad news?"

"I haven't allowed myself to hope it could be anything but bad news."

"You don't think he could have my genes, or yours?"

"He's our son, Dan, I know it. We love him. But these numbers and cells and meaningless pieces of data could give someone the power to take him away from us."

He looked at the envelope, pale in his hand. "At least this way we'll know what we're up against."

Grace closed her eyes. "Okay."

Dan tore clumsily at the envelope, ripping part of the paper inside.

A string of numbers unfolded before his eyes.

"Well?" said Grace.

At the bottom of the column of figures was a businesslike percentile. It revealed a final, indisputable conclusion: Sam had no genetic relationship to either Grace or Dan. Dan dropped the letter.

"No?"

He shook his head. "Zero chance of parentage."

Grace pulled Sam closer to her. "So, it's true." They stayed silent for a moment until Grace said: "How did this happen?"

"I don't know."

"They're going to come for him, aren't they?"

"No." Dan went to her. He put a hand on her shoulder. "Nobody knows but us."

"But it's only a matter of time."

Grace's nightmares were different from Dan's, he knew. She had told him of her dreams: of brawny men in suits and dark glasses who would wrench Sam from her arms. She wept in her sleep and woke sobbing. It seemed like she was constantly on the tip of hysteria. One tiny nudge and she would topple over the edge.

"This doesn't change anything," he said gently but firmly.

Sam began to cry. Grace tried to push her nipple back into his mouth, but he shook his head, cranky. She tapped his bottom, testing the nappy.

"Do you want me to take him?"

"He'll be okay." She rocked slowly in the chair.

He needed time to think. If all hell was about to break loose, he needed to have a solution ready to offer up. He needed her calm. More important, Sam needed her calm.

Later, he went to the study, closed the door behind him, and pulled the blue envelope out of his pocket. He tore it open and read. *Dear Grace and Dan, To open with a cliché*... His eyes skipped over the body of the text. He crushed the page closed. "No."

He cautiously unscrunched the page.

In fact, I'm certain it is one of the hardest letters anyone has ever had to write, for I feel sure nobody in history has ever found themselves in the situation the three of us face right now.

The blue paper shook in his hands as his eyes skated over the words.

When he finished the letter he laid it flat on his desk and read it again, this time training the light on it as if it were a clue to a murder. He tried to look past the prose and separate out the facts. This was a journalist's stock-in-trade. Every day he was presented with information and claims that seemed to suggest one truth, but which, when he combed through them, offered little by the way of proof. The letter's claims were without substance. The writer didn't offer any evidence. She didn't make any threats.

"Okay," he said, frowning at the letter. "What is she asking?"

She wanted to meet the child. He blinked. What did she imagine—a backyard barbecue, with her and Grace in floral dresses, cuddles with Sam, and some sausages and coleslaw on paper plates? As the scene came to life in his mind's eye he wondered: Would her heart change when she met the little boy? Perhaps she was just trying to lure them out. Or confirm her suspicion. She had no way of knowing for sure that Sam was her child. Now that he thought about it, he wondered: How had she found out about them at all? How had she identified Grace and Dan Arden as the other party in the mix-up? And for that matter, how did she know the mix-up had resulted in a baby? None of it made sense.

He thought of all the unscrupulous tactics he had seen colleagues employ to land a yarn. The sports reporter who'd turned up on the doorstep of a Manly Sea Eagles player dressed as a fan shortly after the star rookie had undergone brain surgery. The political writer who had infiltrated the Young Liberals and recorded their private discussions.

There was nothing in this letter to suggest it was authentic. Nothing other than the extraordinary level of detail the writer seemed to know about their child.

If he answered it, he might be confirming what was only a guess on her part. He clutched the page in his hands and slowly, as if they were moving of their own accord, felt them tear the paper down the middle, then rip those pieces in half again, and again, until all he had was a lap full of blue confetti.

Thirty

PRIYA FELT A BUZZ IN HER POCKET. AS SHE HASTILY GRABBED her phone it slipped from her fingers and dropped with a clatter onto the kitchen tiles and skidded under the fridge. Every time her phone had vibrated in the past week she had immediately thought: *Could this be it, the answer to the blue letter?* She kneeled to retrieve it, relieved the screen hadn't smashed.

Hi Pri. How are you feeling? Quite a scare you had there. I can't stop thinking about it. Part of me feels guilty, I guess. If I had been there this never would have happened. I hope you're okay.

Priya stared at the message from her estranged husband. After he had come over the other day they had shared a bottle of wine at her kitchen table, catching up like distant cousins. She had been nervous when he'd said he was coming, but the apprehension disappeared when she saw his face.

The device buzzed again.

I'm so sorry about everything, Pri.

Priya contemplated the message. Then, for the second time that day, she walked downstairs to check her letterbox. It was empty. Her heart sank. She had been emotionally fortifying herself for the worst-case scenario: outrage, anger, abuse, or a threat peppered with legal jargon. She hadn't expected silence.

Maybe her letter had gone missing, she thought. They couldn't just ignore a revelation like that. She had been very gracious in her offer. After all, she was the one who had lost her son. She had hoped for some sympathy. Maybe an interest in meeting the genetic mother of their baby. Her anger flared. How dare they ignore her? If it wasn't for her they wouldn't even have a son. Should she write again?

Her phone buzzed one more time. Nick: *I won't harass you but I'm here if you need X.*

She bit her lip and dialed his number. He answered on the first ring.

"Priya?"

"Nick. There's something you should know."

⁓

Nick and Priya sat on a log at the edge of the dog park and watched Jacker chase ibis away from the rubbish bins. The sky was gray. Damp from the log was seeping through their pants.

"This is unbelievable," Nick said finally.

"I know. It feels like a dream."

"I can't believe another couple has our baby."

Priya's heart squeezed. "Nick." She closed her eyes. "Not our baby. My baby."

"What?" Nick said, shocked.

"The baby, he's not yours."

Nick's brow creased. "I don't understand. Empona made the mistake, right?"

She placed a hand on his arm and spoke gently. "After we broke up I went through two rounds with donor sperm."

Nick frowned, absorbing the information.

"The father is a man from Bangalore. I wanted someone who would give me a child that looked like me. I thought it would be less confusing for the baby."

He swallowed hard. "I can't believe this."

"Nick, what did you think, that I was going to use the sperm of a man who was with another woman?"

"I told you I never shacked up—"

"I didn't mean . . ." She held up her hand. "I was just trying to explain my frame of mind at the time. I don't want to fight. The point is, after we separated I still wanted a child. I wouldn't have gone through it with your sample without telling you."

"Yeah, but—"

Nick got up and walked toward the playground. He was wearing the same blue-and-white checkered shirt he'd had on the day she'd discovered the Bumble app in his phone. He seemed smaller now. He'd lost weight. Priya wondered if he was eating properly. Vestiges of loving concern filled her with the urge to cook him a big tray of roast potatoes. He kept walking and she grew worried he was going to leave.

He turned around and paced up and down the grassy verge. In the sky behind him were kites and drones, evidence of children below. A long moment passed before he spoke. "We've been together half our lives. How could you just do it with someone else like that?" His voice quavered. "After everything we've been through."

Priya looked him in the eye as she answered: "That's the question I used to ask myself every minute of every day after I saw those messages in your phone."

Nick's face fell. He paced some more. "I never shacked up with her." He threw his arm up.

"No." Priya stood. "You are not allowed to be mad. You broke us. I didn't want to do it alone. You forced me."

"I shouldn't have even told her we split." His tone was gentler now. "I was alone and she just appeared . . . I'm not making excuses, I just want you to show me you understand that I didn't just sub her in, like a reserve on the footy field. She . . . she was bonkers, if you want to know the truth."

"Let's not talk about her," Priya said.

He socked his fist into his palm. "So, these people, you've written to them?"

"Yes. I never heard back."

"How could they—how could they not respond?" He spoke haltingly, clenching and unclenching his fists.

She looked at him, at his clear blue eyes, which had for so long been home to her.

"I'm sorry too," she said.

He furrowed his brow. "For what?"

"It's a lot to dump on you. Not just the mix-up, but everything. Telling you I tried to have a baby with a donor. The divorce isn't even final yet. When I thought that you might have a family with her—if you did that, I'd—" She realized she wasn't angry anymore.

"Hey," he said, nudging her chin with his hand. "What a mess we made of things."

"Yeah." She laughed and wiped the tears from her eyes with her thumb before looking up at him. He smiled.

"I've missed you," he said.

Overcome, Priya could only nod. "Me too," she said.

"I think you should see a lawyer. I'll come with you if you'd like, or take Viv. But you should definitely get some advice."

"I thought of that. I can't say why I resisted. I guess the thought of taking a baby from a couple was too horrible to contemplate."

"What about the clinic?"

"I can't think about the clinic until I know what I want to do about Sadi . . . about the baby. The clinic might not know, and if they become aware, it might force my hand."

"But?"

"I think about him constantly. Part of me screams out for him. He's mine. But she carried him. I mean, the DNA will most likely say he's mine, but is he really mine? She nourished him from her bones and her blood. Her flesh. You know, they say you lose a tooth for every baby."

"I could never be as calm as you about this. That clinic, I'd want to burn it down."

After a moment she asked, "What do you think is best for him?"

He looked at her and smiled. "I can't imagine anyone being a better mother than you."

When the sky had grown dark and the dog owners had taken their faithful canines home, Nick had suggested they get some dinner and talk some more. "This is big, Priya," he said.

She was grateful, and part of her wanted to say yes, but there was something she had to do, alone. A plan had formed as she'd been talking to Nick. She told him she was going to see Viv.

"Say hello from me. I miss Viv and Rajesh, and the girls."

"I will and thanks, really," she said.

She climbed into her car and waved goodbye. She would go and see Viv, it wasn't a lie. But there was a small detour she needed to make first. Glebe was only a short drive from the Chippendale park where Priya had met Nick. Talking to him had dredged up feelings about their marriage, about the letter, and about Grace and Dan. She called up the White Pages on her phone and searched again. Then she drove to Gottenham Street. She had to see. She had to know.

~

She parked opposite the house she had addressed the letter to. A large streetlight gave her a clear view of it. The double-story house was made of blue stone, with a veranda and a row of rusting iron spears for a fence. The front yard was paved with brick except for a small circle occupied by a full-grown cherry tree that obscured the front of the house.

Priya watched, mesmerized.

After a few minutes the door opened and a man appeared. Priya panicked and slid down in her seat. He wheeled a bike down the front path. He had dark hair and a solid build, and a warm open face. He seemed like a nice man, Priya thought. It was a confronting observation. Then he paused and turned as if someone was calling to him. The screen door swung open, and there was a woman. She had Morticia Addams hair, and a baby held against her chest. The child's hair, a mess of black, matched his mother's. But the rest of their coloring was different. The man and the woman looked European. The baby did not.

Priya's breath caught in her throat as she realized she was looking at Sadavir. *My Sadavir.* Her heart sped up as she scanned his face. He had heartbreaker eyelashes. Perfect full lips. Wide curious eyes. Priya put her hand to her neck, where she felt the galloping pace of her pulse. He looked just like her when she was that age, with chubby cheeks and chunky legs.

Now she knew with certainty that they had her boy. The man—Dan—walked his bike back up the path to the door so he could kiss the baby goodbye. The wife smiled, watching on.

They had ignored her letter. They knew they had her son and they had knowingly kept him from her. Priya was stupefied. Even though they had Anglo names it somehow hadn't occurred to her that they were aware they had the wrong baby. Then, just as quickly, the mother and baby disappeared into the house and the man with the short dark beard threw his leg over his bike and rode to the end of the street and around the corner. Priya was left alone, trembling and short of breath, feeling like she had just been mugged.

⌐

It was a good twenty minutes before Priya calmed down. She had caught only a glimpse of the baby. A flash. But when she saw his face, something inside her shifted, and awoke. Up until this moment, he had been a theoretical baby. Someone born to another woman; someone who, on paper, and in vials of blood, may be hers but was unknown to her. But when she saw his curls, his lashes, the dimples in his cheeks, so like her sister's, he became real, and a raging river of righteous, angry love awoke in her veins. He looked a little like Avani. His ringlets were just like her own at that age. She had seen his face before in her own baby photos, except her ears had been pierced with gold studs in line with the practices of her culture. A culture he would be denied if she left him with his birth parents.

And then there was the mother. Grace. Her eyes appeared pale blue, even from a distance. She had very long black hair, but there was something not quite right about it. It was flat. Lifeless. The hair, it was off. The door swung open again and the woman appeared, alone this time. She walked to the gate, which she opened, then lifted a black garbage bag into the rubbish bin waiting on the nature strip. Priya realized something with a shock: around the woman's crown, and in the part, her black hair was starting to grow out, revealing pale, wheat-colored roots. Priya squinted, then started the car and did a U-turn and drove past the house very slowly as the woman walked back up the garden path. Priya scrutinized the woman and her light brows and realized she was naturally blond. She had dyed her hair black so as not to arouse suspicion. She didn't want anyone to notice how different she was from her baby. She didn't want anyone to guess that he wasn't hers. She had dyed her hair to conceal the truth so she could continue living with Sadavir. *My Sadavir.* Reality hit Priya like a bullet and she was filled with a howling, white-hot rage.

Thirty-One

ASHLEY WORKED QUICKLY, SLIDING PERFUME AND HAND cream off the dressing table in Roger's bedroom into her open bag. One of her jackets was lying across his armchair, so she stuffed that into her bag too.

She opened the ivory box containing Roger's cuff links and quickly sifted through the silver until she found the pearl studs her mother had given her when she graduated medical school. She checked her watch—half an hour until he'd be home—and rummaged through his drawers for items of her clothing.

She spotted her pendant sitting in a coil of chain on his bedside table. She picked it up by the clasp and the silver charm slipped silently off the end and fell behind the bedside table. Ashley bent down to get it.

"What are you doing?"

She jumped. Roger was standing at the door, watching her, as he loosened his tie. His eyes flicked to her large bag, now overflowing with clothes and cosmetics.

"What's going on?" he asked.

Ashley got up off her knees. "I'm clearing out some things," she said matter-of-factly as she smoothed down her skirt. Fluff from the carpet had stuck to her knees.

"Why?" His voice was ice.

"Roger, I don't think this is working out." She picked up the bag and lifted her chin. He didn't respond. "I don't think it's been working for some time."

"You're leaving for good?"

"I think it's best."

"Is this because of the mix-up?"

"No." She looked at the door, uneasy. "It's for a lot of reasons."

She had never officially moved in with Roger but spent most nights there, and his bathroom cupboard, drawers, and wardrobes had been under siege from her feminine lotions and silky items of clothing for months. Now, the perfumed brigade was in full retreat. There were drawers she had not checked, but she just wanted to be out of there. He watched silently.

"This is for you," she said, placing an envelope on the end of the bed.

"What's that?"

"My letter of resignation."

"So, it *is* about the mix-up."

She straightened her back. "I think your decision is wrong."

"What will you do?" His voice betrayed no emotion.

"Get another job."

"Not in reproductive medicine you won't. Not in Sydney. There's a noncompetition clause in your contract."

"Only for twelve months. I'm going to take some time off. Figure out what will make me happy."

Roger chuckled mirthlessly. "Good luck with that." He walked into the en suite and slammed the door.

⁓

Ashley hurried down the front steps of Roger's house. There was one more thing she had to do before she turned her back on Empona for good, and she had to do it now, before her security pass was decommissioned.

She drove toward the clinic, swerving in and out of lanes as her speedometer nudged the sixty-kilometer speed limit. She had thought she'd have at least another day or two to clear out her office before she confronted Roger. To gather her things. Her insurance. Never mind, she thought, as she parked and ran into the dark, silent building, armed with her phone camera.

The reception doors slid silently open and she made straight for the freezer. She opened the storage unit and snapped a photo of the Arden morula. She took several photos from different angles in case she missed anything, then she did the same for the Archer sample. When she returned them to their respective slots she took photos of them in situ, side by side. Then she went to her office and grabbed as much as she could, jamming documents and papers into the bag filled with her clothes and cosmetics.

Next she went to Doris's desk and took photos of everything she and Dale had uncovered—schedules, calendars, the roster from the day of the error and the days leading up to it and after it. She returned everything—it was vital it appear untouched—and was straightening Doris's desk when a tiny green light caught her eye. The lift doors were parting. At a quarter to eleven on a weeknight it could only be one person. Ashley darted for the fire-escape door. Her fingers were closing around the handle when she locked eyes with Roger as he stepped out of the lift and into the dim corridor.

His eyes narrowed. "What are you doing?"

She had seen his single-minded ambition. She knew now that what she had once considered his immovable professionalism was closer to Napoleonic brutality. He would protect his name, his business, his reputation above all else. Now he was looking at her like a bull that had seen red, a shark that had smelled blood.

They glared at each other through the glass door that separated them, Roger the hunter, Ashley the prey. His eyes fell on the bag full of paperwork in her hand. He touched his security pass to the sensor and the door began to open. Ashley darted into the stairwell. She knew she couldn't outrun the lift, and if he followed her down the stairs the chase would be short—her best chance was up.

She sprinted to the sixth floor, threw open the fire door, bolted to the lifts, and urgently slam-slam-slammed her thumb into the down button. The doors parted and she raced inside, furiously pressing the *G* button. She held her breath as the lift moved south. It didn't stop at five or four, but sailed safely to the ground.

As she entered the lobby she ripped off her heels, bounded across the marble floor and onto the street. The footpath tore the soles of her stockings as she ran for her car. She climbed inside and locked the doors, too scared to look back. Her breathing was shallow. The enormity of what was happening was seeping into her consciousness. A mix-up, a cover-up, an angry and powerful former lover, a phone full of evidence, and a baby in the wrong hands. Without taking her eyes from the road she fiddled with the heater knob, trying to find the setting that would clear the fog on the windscreen. She could hardly see as she started the ignition and pulled into traffic.

"Slow down," she told herself through gritted teeth. "Or you'll run off the road."

She pressed her foot against the accelerator, but realized she couldn't go home. If Roger wanted to find her, that's the first place he would look. All of her friends were connected to the clinic or the industry, in one way or another. There was only one place she would feel safe tonight, only one person she could count on. She changed lanes and headed west to her mother's house.

Thirty-Two

SAM'S FIRST WINTER PASSED WITH ALL THE FORCE OF AN OLD man blowing on his soup. The weather vane on Mrs. Goss's roof remained still, and people went out without overcoats, even late at night.

Inside their house, Grace was bathing her baby son and reveling in his smiles. Sam loved baths. Fiona, who frequently came over to spend time with her grandson, said it reminded babies of being in the womb. As the water lapped around him he splashed and laughed.

"Oh, look at you," Grace said, tickling his belly so his grin grew wider, exposing his gums.

A knock at the door interrupted the moment.

"Who could that be?" she asked with a nursery-song rhythm.

Grace lifted Sam from the tub and wrapped him in a towel. Holding him close, she went downstairs and peered down the hallway to the front door. She could see two silhouettes through the frosted glass. Her chest tightened. Grace had always wanted to replace the glass panel. It felt unsafe. But in their new, secretive life, it was proving useful. The shadows knocked again. Grace considered ignoring them, letting them think there was nobody home. She took Sam back upstairs and laid him on his changing table. Dan shuffled in in his pajamas, still bleary-eyed from the three a.m. feed. Grace and Dan tried to split the late-night feeds and were both surviving on thin, wiry sleep. When Sam woke, the whole house woke, and after Dan got up to give their baby the milk Grace had pumped earlier, she lay awake listening.

"Who was knocking?" he asked now, yawning.

"I don't know."

The syncopated *rat-tat-tat* came again.

"I suppose I'd better get it," she said.

"Try not to look so worried all the time. It could be the gas man come to read the meter."

She was greeted by two men, each wearing a suit and carrying a leather portfolio tucked under his arm.

"Mrs. Arden." The shorter of the pair offered a hand. "I'm Hugh Madigan and this is Paul Barr. We're from the McArthur and Lowe law firm. May we come in?"

They stared at Grace, waiting with what appeared to be complete confidence that she would say yes and move aside. One had over-gelled red curls and freckled skin. The other, taller, had tanned skin and deep frown lines. But to Grace they both looked the same. They were soldiers of her misfortune.

It took her a moment to find her voice. "What's this about?" she stammered, hanging behind the half-open door.

"We're here on behalf of the Empona fertility clinic."

"The clinic?" She felt a chill and instinctively drew back into the house a little. "Should I have a lawyer present?"

The men laughed indulgently. "This is just a friendly chat."

"Dan," she called over her shoulder. "My husband's just upstairs," she said, turning back to the men. "Could you excuse me for one moment, please." She held up her hand. *Stay.* "I'll be right back."

"They say they're lawyers from McArthur and Lowe," she told Dan.

"Huh."

"What?"

"That's the firm that acted for the clinic that was sued by the couple whose IVF-conceived boys had fragile X syndrome, even though they were screened for it."

"The case where they gave them the wrong test results?"

"That's it."

Dan's colleague Leo had broken that story in the *Herald*. A couple had discovered both of their sons had inherited the condition the wife's brother and uncle had. There had been a lab error, and the clinic was given the wrong results. They had settled out of court.

"What do they want?"

"They want to come in. All they said was they wanted to chat." She looked at him. "It's starting, isn't it?" Grace asked. "They're going to take him."

"No, no." He pressed her arm. "The clinic will not try to take Sam."

"You don't know that."

"I think we'd both better hear this," Dan said.

He put Sam into his crib and followed Grace downstairs. As she descended she could feel her fears rolling in like big black clouds. But she fought them back. For Sam. And once again she opened the door to the men.

"This is my husband."

Dan was tightening the belt of his robe around his waist. "You said you were lawyers?"

"Yes. For the Empona fertility clinic," the shorter man reiterated as handshakes were exchanged.

"What's this about?" Dan asked.

"I'd really prefer to have this conversation in private."

"In that case you'd better come in."

Grace moved aside and they stepped into the hallway. She led them to the dining room, sweeping Sam's bassinet away and tucking a large soft ball and his baby bouncer into the cupboard before the strangers entered.

Dan invited them to sit, which they did, stiff in their suits. "I'll just come out with it," said the taller visitor. "During a routine audit of procedures the clinic noticed some . . . anomalies in your treatment." He spoke slowly, gauging the couple's response.

"Anomalies?" said Dan cautiously. "What type of anomalies?"

"There was a clerical error."

Grace and Dan looked at each other, feigning innocence.

"Why wasn't it picked up earlier?" Dan asked.

The lawyer cleared his throat. "Tell me, were you both happy with your fertility treatment?" His words had the cadence of a preprepared speech.

They nodded, scared to speak.

"There were no . . . problems?"

"I'm so sorry, I didn't offer you anything," Grace said, standing suddenly. "Can I get you a drink? Tea? Coffee?"

"No, thank you," said the shorter lawyer, but the taller cut across him. "Coffee would be great, thank you. We both take it white with one."

"Dan, will you help me?"

"Excuse us," Dan said to the lawyers, who nodded, playing along.

Grace hurried through the kitchen into the laundry and hit the start button on the clothes dryer to muffle their voices. "What is this?"

Dan shrugged. "Perhaps they're going to make a preemptive settlement offer. Prevent a trial and a negligence payout."

"We need to call Elliott."

"Maybe they don't know what happened. Maybe they're just covering their bases."

But Dan wondered about the letter. Had the woman written to Empona too? The torn pieces of paper were jammed down the back of the top drawer of his desk. He hadn't wanted to be rid of them completely.

"Let's just hear them out," he whispered. "Whatever they have to say, we play dumb, tell them we need to think about it. Once they're gone, we'll call Elliott."

Grace nodded. "I'd better get them their drinks."

"I'll do it," Dan said.

"Lovely," Hugh Madigan said when Dan handed him a cup. He took one sip then put it down.

"So, these anomalies," Dan said. "Should we be worried?"

"No, no, no, it was purely an administrative issue. There's no risk to the health of your child. Your child is healthy? There's nothing . . . wrong?"

"He's perfect," Grace said quickly.

"How many other families have been affected?" Dan asked.

"Hopefully none," said the shorter lawyer.

"I'll be clear," the taller spoke over him again. "Our client, Empona, is willing to offer you a considerable sum for any damages you may have sustained as a result of anomalies in their processes while you were a patient there. There's no admission of guilt, but if you accept the offer, you will be required to sign a confidentiality agreement. I think you'll find they're prepared to be very generous."

"But if there's no admission of guilt and no complaint, why would the company want to pay us?" Grace asked.

"The clinic feels that the risk you were exposed to was unacceptable, and worthy of compensation," Hugh Madigan said clearly, carefully.

"So why the clause about keeping silent?"

"Mrs. Arden, our client believes that it is best for everyone if this matter remains a private one," the shorter one said.

"Better for whom?" said Dan.

The taller cleared his throat. "It's for the sake of Empona's other patients. The clinic feels it would be distressing for them to read that there had been a small hitch in some of the record keeping. If, say, it found its way into the newspaper you work for, Mr. Arden. The clinic knows how stressful fertility treatments are and they don't want to put further strain on their patients."

"Aren't they a caring bunch?" Dan muttered.

"No one will ever know?" Grace asked.

The lawyer slid the contract across the table and placed a heavy gold pen on top of it. "No one will ever know."

"Can we look this over?" Dan asked.

"Of course."

Hugh Madigan took a card from his wallet. "Here are my contact details. Give me a ring when you're ready." The men stood. "Thank you for your time. We'll see ourselves out."

Thirty-Three

PRIYA DESPERATELY NEEDED TO TALK TO HER SISTER, BUT when she arrived at Viv's, the house was in an uproar. The twins loved to run away from their mother in different directions, giggling and screaming. "I'm getting more exercise than I have in years," Viv said, as she tried to hold Shanti still so that she could pin on a nappy. As she reached for the Sudocrem, Shanaya kicked over a bottle of powder, sending it flying across the floor like wildfire and puffing a dry cloud into the air, making Viv cough.

Shanti, seeing her chance, was up off the floor in a flash and toddling toward the kitchen like she was motorized. "Shanti!" Viv called after her.

"I'll get her." Priya leaped to her feet. Shanti squealed with delighted terror as her aunt chased her into the kitchen. The toddler began running on the spot, then, overcome with excitement, peed all over the tiles.

"Oh, Shanti!" Priya said, grabbing a roll of paper towels.

"What?" Viv called from the other room. The second her concentration was lost, Shanaya jumped up too and followed her sister into the kitchen.

"Watch out!" Priya yelled. Too late—Shanaya slipped on the

puddle and went down hard, her head thumping against the ceramic floor. She was in such shock that she lay silently on her back for a moment, her delicate curls soaking up her sister's urine. Shanti screamed in fright, then exploded in a fit of tears.

"Shanaya!" Priya fell to her knees and scooped the wet girl up off the floor.

"What happened?" Viv appeared at the door, then put her arms around Shanti, thinking she was the one who was hurt. Shanaya began to cry.

"Sh," Priya soothed, rocking the girl. "She's okay. She just got a shock."

"Come here to me." Viv held her hands up for Shanaya, who walked through the puddle with her arms stretched out to her mother, trailing footprints across the floor.

"Did she hit her head?" Viv asked, smoothing the back of Shanaya's wet hair.

"She fell. There doesn't seem to be a lump. Are you okay there?" Priya asked, watching as Viv rocked Shanaya, whose sobs had quieted to deep shuddering breaths. "Do you think she needs to go to the hospital?"

"No," said Viv, standing up and taking a bag of frozen peas from the freezer before wrapping it in a tea towel and gently holding it to Shanaya's head. "They're tough little things."

"She does need another bath. She slipped in her sister's wee." Priya couldn't help but smile.

Viv started to chuckle. "She had a wee accident."

Laughter brewed in Priya's chest and soon both sisters were laughing on the wet floor, unable to stop.

The twins were bathed again and put to bed. Priya changed into some of her sister's fresh clothes, cleaned the kitchen, then put the kettle on, eager to talk. Viv's eyes were drooping and Priya realized how desperately tired Viv was and how much she needed sleep. She hugged her sister and said she would call her in the morning. Then she got into her car and, without really meaning to, found herself driving toward Chippendale.

The twins had momentarily distracted her from her rage, but now, as she drove through the empty streets, it was returning. Her evening of chaos and laughter was what the couple in Glebe had denied her. The black cloud of loneliness that pervaded her life was the result of their secrecy. She pulled over to the side of the road and sent a quick text. *Okay if I come over? Just for a chat.*

A reply came seconds later: *Sure.*

Nick sent another text with his address.

She arrived a few minutes later and made her way nervously up the path. Nick's new home had none of the hand-rendered hallmarks of their old house. It was a modern unit comprised of white surfaces and a courtyard full of ferns for Jacker. The thought of the mutt being confined to the sunless void made Priya unaccountably sad.

"It's not my style but it's a rental, so what can you do?" Nick shrugged after giving her a brief tour. He took her to the galley kitchen. "I wasn't expecting company. All I have is beer."

"Beer's great." Priya took the can he offered and rolled it in her hands. She was nervous and unsure why she had come. The beer slipped out of her grip and rolled across the tiles. Nick bent and caught it.

"I'm going to speak to a lawyer," she said.

"That's good." He smiled. "What changed your mind?"

She frowned. "At first I felt sorry for them. But they knew. They knew, Nick, and they tried to hide it. You should see him, he's so perfect. But he looks nothing like them. He looks like me. And the woman, she's dyed her hair. She's blond but she's put this terrible witchy black dye through it so that it's not as obvious that he's not her son. I can't leave my baby with people like that."

"Wait, you saw him?"

She froze. "Um, I—"

"Careful, Pri. What if they'd caught you snooping?"

"I wasn't snooping. I was just . . ."

He raised his eyebrows but his expression was not unkind.

"I wanted to know why they ignored my letter. I wanted to see what kind of people they are." She raked her hands through her hair. "Once I saw them, I woke up."

He placed a hand on her arm. "I'll come with you if you want, when you go to speak to the lawyer."

Priya didn't say anything.

"Speaking to a professional can help you get perspective." He paused. "My therapist has been really helping."

"You've been seeing a therapist?"

He nodded. "I know what I did was wrong. I was making excuses for a long time. But I realize now that I don't want to make the same mistake again. I can't accept that I can't change and I know it's up to me to do something about it."

"Nick, that's . . . I'm impressed."

"We have to take responsibility for our own choices," Nick said. "But that doesn't mean we have to do it alone."

Two days later, Priya was sitting on a chair opposite a large mahogany desk. The lawyer, Estelle Forlani, came highly recommended by Priya's boss, who had been through two complicated divorces.

"She's one of the best in the game. A real shark," he had said, handing Priya a card.

Estelle's fingers and earlobes were crowded with gems. Her hair was white and her eyebrows drawn on in ink. She was twice divorced herself, Priya's boss had told her, and each time she took her spouse to the cleaners.

"Tell me, Ms. Laghari," the formidable woman said, resting her cigarette on a gold ashtray, "what can we do for you?"

Priya sat up straight and in a firm, clear voice said: "I'd like to sue the Empona fertility clinic for malpractice. I'd like to take them for everything they've got. And I want to seek a court order demanding a DNA test of the child that was born to this couple." She pulled an envelope from her handbag and handed it to the lawyer. "If it shows there's a match with me, I want to sue them too. I want to sue them for custody of my son."

Thirty-Four

ASHLEY WIPED THE SWEAT FROM HER BROW WITH THE BACK of her arm. She felt like she was in a prison of her own making, but instead of bars and guards, it was glass that contained her and customers with tongs whom she had to watch out for.

She clasped her own tongs, her eye on the last brioche as stale airplane passengers in rumpled clothes shuffled forward in the bakery line. Ashley fanned herself with her airport map, inching closer to the bun. She stepped forward and lunged at it, smiling at the little victory as she deposited it on her tray.

In the nine hours since the ash cloud had grounded all flights, Kuala Lumpur airport had become unbearably crowded. Every few minutes a crackling, high-pitched announcement screeched from the PA system. There was no corner of the airport the noise didn't reach. Ashley knew because since she'd been trapped there, she'd explored every inch of the terminal.

Her phone rang. "It still hasn't cleared?" her mother asked.

"No," she said, paying for her brioche. "And they can't tell us when it will."

Ashley found herself a plastic chair in the dining area crammed with commuters, their faces shiny and unwashed, to eat her roll and allay her mother's fears.

"Come home," said the voice on the phone.

"I can't. I have to get away." She took a desolate bite of her bun, all pleasure in the triumph of securing it gone. "In nine years, I've never taken a breather. Not since high school finished."

She had gone straight into med school, competing for the best placements. Empona was go, go, go. What she was saying to her mother was true. She wasn't revealing the whole truth, but it wasn't a complete lie.

"I need some time to recalibrate. I need to go somewhere hot, with no phones."

"I don't understand, Ashley. Why won't you tell me what happened to make you quit? It's so unlike you."

Ashley didn't want to worry her mother. She would be fine. She just needed time to think. She needed to figure out what to do next. She had done possibly the first impulsive thing in her life: booked a one-way flight to Sri Lanka.

"I'm just burned out, that's all. And Empona wasn't taking proper care. Despite its elite reputation, that place was understaffed and overbooked. No wonder they . . ." She stopped herself. "I mean, how do they think they can retain staff in those sorts of conditions."

She had been poised to send all the photos and documents she had to the Health Complaints Commissioner when she stopped and reflected on what she'd done. Empona needed to be investigated, but she was concerned about the damage her revelation had already caused. She had been emotional. Reckless. She knew the truth had to come out, but she'd handled it the wrong way, and she was sorry. If she hadn't blurted the information to Priya Laghari, the Ardens might have had a chance of at least some sort of relationship with their boy. Now she had set in motion a chain of events that could mean they would lose their son completely. She had been rash, and she didn't want to make the same mistake again, so she was fleeing to clear her head. She was in possession of some powerful evidence and she didn't want to make another mistake.

"I've got to go, Mum. I'll call you if there are any updates."

She chewed the last of her bun and pulled the hood of her windbreaker over her head. The unnatural light hurt her eyes, but she couldn't escape the toxic guilt in the pit of her stomach.

Thirty-Five

IT WAS EERILY WARM FOR AUGUST. GRACE STEPPED ONTO THE porch, hoping for relief from the cloying air trapped inside the house, but the atmosphere outside was muggy. Rain was forecast. The clouds sat low, lurking heavily on the horizon, tinged yellow. Grace fished an elastic from her pocket and tied up her unwashed, gothic hair, feeling oppressed by the sulfurous sky pressing down on her home. The world was closing in on her.

She heard the chug of the postman's scooter. He was wearing aviators, like a cop, and gave her a nod as he reached into his sack. She stepped forward and took the thick envelope he held out for her. The top left corner bore the seal of the NSW Supreme Court.

She glanced furtively up and down the street, checking for nosy onlookers, then hurried back inside.

"Dan," she called, as she pulled a wad of paper from the envelope. "Come quickly."

"What is it?" He appeared in the hallway with Sam in his arms.

"More legal documents."

He looked at their son. "Those lawyers must be getting impatient."

"This isn't from Empona's lawyers." Grace showed him the legal crest.

He stared at it a moment. "Oh God."

"What?"

"It's a statement of claim."

"What does it mean?" She flipped open to the first page, which was filled with dense legalese.

Dan didn't answer. He was transfixed. The name was staring at him. *Priya Laghari*. It was her.

The letters swam before Grace's eyes. She could only see one word. *Custody*. The egg supplier wanted custody of their son. Phrases jumped out at Grace. The woman wanted Sam to live with her. She was seeking exclusive parental rights. It said Grace and Dan were "genetic strangers" to Sam, though of course it didn't say Sam, it called him "the child." The document called for restitution. She wanted him for her own.

Dan squeezed Grace's shoulder.

"This can't be real," she said. But she knew it was.

Grace's breathing slowed. Her heart felt too big for her chest. It was happening. They were coming for Sam.

⤳

"Elliott said to come in right away," Dan said, the phone still in his hand.

"Mum will be here in a few minutes," Grace replied, as she packed their legal documents into Dan's satchel.

"Should we tell her?" Dan asked.

"Why upset her?"

"Maybe it will be good for you to talk to her about it."

Grace shook her head. "Let's keep it to ourselves for as long as possible."

He nodded and smoothed his hand down Sam's back. "I'll take this one upstairs and see if he'll go down."

Fiona arrived bundled up in a scarf and matching gloves. "Those clouds are eerie," she said.

"Mum, it's not even that cold." Grace helped Fiona unwind the yards of colored wool from her neck.

"The last thing I want is to get a cold and pass it on to the baby," Fiona said. "Has something happened? You look upset. Why did you need me to come in such a hurry?"

"It's nothing." Grace turned away, pretending to busy herself with Dan's satchel.

"It doesn't look like nothing."

"Really, it's not worth getting upset over."

When Grace was little, there was no catastrophe her mother couldn't fix, but she feared Fiona would be undone by the threat that had come into their lives. As if reading her mind, Fiona said: "Grace. I am your mother. You don't need to protect me. That's my job."

Grace sighed. "Sit down, Mum. I don't really know how to say this." Her lip started to tremble.

Fiona put her hand on Grace's cheek. "Grace." She held her daughter's face. "Whatever it is, we'll figure it out." Grace closed her eyes, not wanting to inflict her pain on her mother. "Tell me, Gracie," Fiona said. "Let me help."

Grace drew a breath. "A woman is trying to take Sam from us."

There was a long pause before Fiona said: "What do you mean *take* Sam?"

"She wants custody of him."

Fiona furrowed her brow. "I don't understand."

"She says he's legally her son." The words sounded so melodramatic, so ridiculous, that for a moment Grace felt comforted—this couldn't really be happening.

"That doesn't make any sense. How could he possibly be her son?"

Grace felt on the brink of a hysterical chuckle. "Because DNA says she is. She's his mother, biologically. At least that's what she's claiming. But we think she could be right. Mum, Sam isn't related to us."

Fiona had grown pale. She put her hands to her temples. "I did wonder—"

"We've been talking to a lawyer."

"But this is preposterous. He's your son."

"Mum, look at him."

"Who cares about the color of his skin. You gave birth to him. That's the definition of a mother."

"That definition is from a time before doctors could take your eggs out and then put them back anywhere they liked. We did a test. He's not my son. Not genetically."

"And this woman wants to raise him as her own?"

"What if he *is* her own, in a biological sense?" Grace needed her mother to understand the seriousness of the situation. "She's demanding a DNA test."

Fiona looked confused and scared, but then clarity returned to her eyes and she seized Grace's hand. "Take him. Take him far away from here, where they can't reach you. Go live in Iowa. Or Bath. Or Egypt. Set up a life and live there with your son."

"Like fugitives?"

"Not like fugitives—"

"They'll come after us."

"You haven't committed a crime. It's your name on the birth certificate."

"Running will only make it worse."

"Worse than losing him?"

"We'd spend the rest of our lives looking over our shoulders."

"Who's to say who is and isn't Sam's mother? The other woman has never even laid eyes on him."

Grace often daydreamed of taking Sam somewhere vast and green, like Iceland. They could settle somewhere forbidding, get some goats, and cook on an open hearth. Or a remote cottage in England with a thatched roof and whitewashed walls, like something Roald Dahl would conjure up. They would adopt new names and new identities that they would slip over their old ones like masks.

"We can't do that, Mum," she said numbly.

"This is your *son*."

Grace looked away. "I think about it all the time. It wouldn't work. We could trek halfway across the world, to the most remote corner possible, only to have an email arrive in our inbox. A summons. Or a court order made in our absence. It's not possible to disappear anymore. Everything's automated, networked, and linked. Besides, what about you? You'd never see him."

"Well . . . there are greater things at stake." Fiona's voice wobbled.

In idle moments Grace found herself cataloging what they would need if they were to run away. Bank withdrawals and credit cards were traceable, so they would have to survive on cash. In Sydney they navigated life with a host of ergonomic baby apparatuses, all of which they would have to jettison. As long as she could breastfeed they wouldn't need much food, but that wouldn't last forever. She could strap Sam to her chest like a marsupial, carrying only what she needed. But they wouldn't be able to get by without nappies and wipes, rash cream, breast pads, formula, reliable medical help. She thought of all the money they had spent on a wireless thermometer to monitor his temperature while he slept, and she wanted to laugh at how naïve they had been.

Grace could teach English. Dan could freelance under a pseudonym. When she thought of the people she and Dan met when they traveled to places such as Bali and Goa, cut adrift from their own history, she realized they would fit right in. They all seemed to be people seeking a clean slate.

Grace shook herself from her reverie when she saw Fiona watching her with a funny look on her face.

"You could do it," she said.

Dan entered with Sam, freshly changed. He passed him to Fiona.

"There was no chance he was sleeping while Grandma Fiona was in the house," he said.

Fiona took him, her smile shot with sadness as she cuddled her grandson.

"We'd better go," Grace said, leaning down and kissing Sam. "We won't be long."

"Grace," Fiona said, "I want you to think about what I said."

Grace nodded.

She already had thought about it. Oh yes. She had thought about it a lot.

⁓

Elliott frowned as he scanned the statement of claim. Grace and Dan had read through it a dozen times. The baby was the result of an embryo, it said, made from an ovum belonging to Priya Laghari and a donor whom she selected and paid. The ovum had been inseminated by the Empona clinic at her request and her expense.

"This is our son, not some dispute over a fence on a property boundary," Dan said. "If all she cares about is money I'll pay her ten grand a year for the rest of her life to leave us alone."

Elliott read on: "'If the embryo had been implanted in his biological mother, as planned, the child Sadavir Sabad Laghari would grow up in his natural family, with a mother, aunt, and cousins to whom he has biological, familial, and cultural ties.'"

"Sadavir," Grace spat. "She doesn't even *know* him."

"The DNA results may prove otherwise," Elliott replied.

"It's bad, isn't it?" said Dan.

The lawyer grimaced. "It's not great. If this ends up as a full-blown custody battle it could get really ugly."

"But I gave birth to him," Grace said. "This is insane! You know this is insane, right?"

"There's no legal precedent for something like this in Australia," Elliott replied.

"Fuck," Dan said under his breath.

Grace grabbed his arm. "We need to take that offer from Empona so we've got the money to fight for custody of Sam."

"No. Turn down the Empona money. Sue them," Elliott said.

"But how can we afford to fight a big clinic?" said Dan. "They could drag it out for years. If we just take the settlement, we can be confident we'll be able to fight the custody battle."

"If they settle with you, they'll settle with her, and both of you will end up giving all the money to lawyers. Forget about the cost, we can work out a payment plan. Empona is liable."

"I can't believe this," said Dan, pressing his fingers into his eye sockets. "What other options do we have?"

"We don't really have any other options than to mount a defense against her claim."

"Can't we circumvent it somehow? Shut it down? Discredit it?"

Grace said. "Would the court even hear her case? What proof could she possibly have?"

"A custody battle can't be the only option," said Dan.

"You're not going to like this," Elliott said, "but you could agree to relinquish custody on the condition that you are granted visitation rights. That way you could still at least see Sam."

"What? No!" Grace leaped off her chair. "Are you suggesting we just hand him over without a fight?"

Elliott held up his hands defensively. "It's just one option. I want you to hear all your options."

"Well, consider that one struck from the list," she said. "We'll just have to go into that courtroom and plead our case. Hopefully the judge will see sense."

⁓

They stopped at the supermarket on the way home to pick up some ready meals and supplies for Sam. Grace was putting the regular box of nappies into her trolley when she saw a travel pack. *Easy to store and carry,* the label boasted, inspiring in Grace an image of herself walking up a steep hill with Sam strapped to her front and a pack on her back. She pictured herself changing Sam in a roadside hotel along a stretch of unpaved highway in Katherine, the dirt turning the white rubber soles of her shoes red. She imagined the sun on her pale skin as she breastfed him in the beer garden of a deserted pub while she picked chips from a plate.

Fiona's words echoed in her mind—*Take him far away from here, where they can't reach you*—and her mind began to race. She could put Sam in the car and just drive. They could head to Darwin. Take a circuitous route, up through the middle of the red flat land, maybe hole up on a cattle station for a few months. Feed him fresh milk.

Pay cash for everything. How much money could they liquidate if they needed to? she wondered. What could they sell? Once they got to the Cape they could hire a boat, pretend they were going on a cruise, disappear. Border Patrol were too busy trying to keep people out of the country; surely they wouldn't waste their time trying to keep Australians in.

They could sail into international waters. Chart a course to Asia. Keep going north. Carry Sam on their backs. Disappear into the Himalayas. An antipodean Von Trapp family in miniature.

But, she thought, standing in the fluorescent light of the supermarket aisle, what of everything she wanted for him? School, safety, friends, a yard to run around in, a puppy to love, Christmas with Grandma Fiona stirring brandy sauce made from her own grandmother's recipe. If they ran, where could he be normal? How would they provide for him?

The only option was to stay and fight, she thought, as she stared at the nappies. And despite this decision, she found herself picking up the travel pack and dropping it into the trolley, barely registering the thought in the back of her mind: It never hurts to be prepared.

Thirty-Six

THE LARGE GRANDFATHER CLOCK IN ESTELLE'S OFFICE TICKED loudly. The room had an Oxbridge air of oak and dusty leather, like a dean's private quarters. If the goal was to intimidate, it was working on the Laghari sisters. The lawyer gave a phlegmy cough, reached for her Marlboros, flicked the wheel on her lighter, and fired up a cigarette.

"The Ardens are yet to respond," she said, taking a deep, dramatic drag.

"What does that mean?" Viv asked.

Estelle blew a gust of smoke across the desk. "I'm more concerned about our case. We need evidence you are Sam's biological mother. What else do you have apart from that little piece of paper from the clinic?"

"What else do you need?" Priya asked. "This couple had a transfer right after me. I didn't have a baby. They did."

"That's not enough to sue for custody. Not successfully."

"Can't the courts order a DNA test?" Viv asked.

"He looks exactly like I did when I was little," said Priya.

Estelle pointed her cigarette at Priya. "I've never heard of a court ordering a DNA test on a couple's baby by request of a third party. You'd need something convincing to show there was a good reason for going through with it."

"If you could only see him . . ." Priya began. "I wrote to them explaining what had happened. They ignored me. Don't you think if they had nothing to hide they'd tell me?"

More smoke fumed from Estelle's nostrils. "You writing a letter to them adds nothing to your case."

Viv pulled Priya's phone out of her handbag and found the photo from Grace Arden's Facebook page. Grace had posted it two months earlier and since removed it, but Priya had had the good sense to save a screenshot of it before it disappeared.

"It's not a good shot," she said, showing it to Estelle. "But look, he looks just like Priya."

Estelle put her glasses on and squinted at the screen. "This doesn't prove anything. It's just a blurry tuft of hair and a hand."

"Exactly!" Priya said. "It's the only photo of the baby. Doesn't that strike you as strange? They're hiding him."

"And you say a doctor from the clinic told you about this?"

Priya nodded. "I didn't even know about the baby until she came to me."

"Okay. The first thing we have to do is track down that doctor. You've got to get her to agree to give evidence that there was a mix-up."

Priya nodded. "I don't know where she is. But I'll find her."

"Getting doctors to testify against other doctors is notoriously difficult," Estelle said.

"Can't we force her?" asked Viv. "I mean, not force her, but, you know, get a warrant or a subpoena. This is a serious matter."

"On what grounds?" Estelle asked. "So far you've given me half a schedule and a screenshot of someone else's Facebook account." She turned to Priya. "Go to her. Convince her to testify. I want to win this for you. We'll get you your son and then we'll go after the clinic. But we need proof."

Priya stayed up all night searching the internet for leads on Doctor Li. It appeared she had left Empona. Her details were no longer listed on its website, but there was no information about where she had gone. A lot had been written about Doctor Li before the mix-up. She'd been profiled and interviewed by everyone from medical journals to glossy women's magazines ("In 2016, the stork wears stilettos and drinks three cappuccinos a day," the *Australian Women's Weekly* gushed). But the publicity seemed to stop abruptly once the baby—Priya's baby—had been born. Ashley Li had a Facebook page but had never posted anything, and only had thirty-six friends.

Priya woke slumped over her desk with a crick in her neck and three missed calls from her office. She rang to explain she had gastro, then, dejected, she went downstairs to get her mail and discovered a hand-addressed envelope in her letterbox. She quickly ripped it open and removed a single sheet of paper.

Dear Priya,

You may have been wondering where this letter has been. It was more than six weeks ago that you first wrote to me and my wife, Grace. The letter was gracious and fair, and now I write to you, knowing I failed to match your rational approach. When I read your letter I panicked, forgive me. I couldn't believe it could be true, though in my heart I suspected it was. I never showed it to my wife. She had been through so much, I couldn't bear to do it to her. I didn't mean to conceal the truth from you forever. I just wanted to give her a little time to regain her strength. I thought about you every day. The guilt ate away at me. Each hour I'd say

to myself: Just one more day and I'll reach out to this woman.
This good and decent woman who has shown such honor under
pressure. I have finally found the strength to do it now and I
implore you, call off the lawsuit and let us sit down and discuss the
plan you originally proposed. Your plan was fair and, I believe,
in the best interest of our son. He is, I'm sure you'll agree, the
most important thing in this whole wretched mess.

I look forward to hearing from you.

Sincerely,
Daniel Arden

A string of contact details were listed, including a daytime business number. He had Priya's phone number, but she understood why he had chosen to write. It was less confrontational, while at the same time it commanded her attention. It allowed him to get out everything he wanted to say, uninterrupted by argument or interjection.

After reading Daniel Arden's missive a few more times Priya called Viv and read the letter to her. "What do you think?"

"Wow," said Viv. "You know what this is?"

"A desperate plea from a loving father?"

"Yes. But it's also evidence they knew about you and still tried to keep you from your son."

"I hadn't thought of it like that."

"This is it. This is what Estelle was asking for. The father has admitted they might not be the parents. Now you can ask a judge to order a DNA test."

Thirty-Seven

GRACE'S TROLLEY WHEELS SQUEAKED AS SHE CIRCLED THE supermarket's eclectic bargain table for a third time. Home potting kits rested against ceramic mixing bowls. Silicone muffin trays nudged foam bodyboards. All were marked close to half price. Her eye had been caught by a cluster of long rectangular boxes. *Light but sturdy,* said the label. *Safety guaranteed.*

Grace gripped the end of one of the boxes and pulled it free, testing the weight. It was surprisingly light. She scanned its other labels: *Swiss Made. For babies up to twenty-four months.* She opened the end of the box and tugged on a metal-and-plastic cylinder until it popped out. It was the leg of a collapsible travel crib. She stood for a moment, in the busy supermarket aisle, and thought of faraway snow-capped mountains, of villages where phone service was intermittent and Wi-Fi nonexistent. Then she tucked the box under her arm and made her way to the checkout.

Grace jammed the narrow travel crib into the back of the wardrobe in Sam's room, behind the winter coats and clothes Sam wasn't big enough for yet, amid the pile of supplies she had slowly accumulated.

She hadn't mentioned it to Dan, or really thought of it at all. The collection included an inflatable bath, a collapsible changing table and disposable changing mats, long-life baby food (even though Sam hadn't started solids), and baby sunscreen. She lifted a microfiber beanie small enough to fit snugly around a grapefruit and rubbed the fabric between her fingers. She couldn't even remember buying it.

"Grace!"

"Ow." Grace stood abruptly and bashed her head against the wardrobe shelf.

"Grace, what are you doing?"

She turned around to see Dan with Sam in his arms. Their son was sucking on his fist.

"Just looking for something," she said, closing the wardrobe door.

Dan didn't speak for a moment. "Dinner's ready," he said.

"Okay." She nodded. "I'll be down in a minute."

He didn't move. "Is something going on?"

She squared her shoulders. "No."

He nodded and left. Grace exhaled. They were due to see Elliott in the morning and fuses had been short. She made sure the crib and the travel items were concealed by their winter coats, then she went downstairs to join her family for dinner.

⁓

Sam barely slept. He was up at ten. At ten thirty. At midnight. At one. Each time he cried, Grace leaped out of bed and ran straight to him. When Sam started to roar again at three, Dan laid his palm flat on Grace's chest and said, "I'll go."

Her eyelids fluttered. "Okay," she replied, barely awake.

After a few minutes Sam settled, but when Dan didn't return

to the bedroom, Grace, rubbing her eyes, went to investigate the nursery.

Dan was on his knees, the wardrobe doors flung open.

"Grace, what's this?" he asked, holding up a bag of disposable changing mats like a piece of roadkill.

"What?"

Bewildered, Dan pulled another item out of the wardrobe: the travel nappies. And another, the collapsible crib. "What *is* all this stuff?" His face went red. "Travel-sized baby wipes? What are you playing at?"

"Nothing, nothing."

"An inflatable bath? Are you planning to try to run away from this?"

"No," she said, wounded. *Was she?*

"Don't lie to me, Grace."

She had never seen him this mad. "No, no. I don't know why I did it. I just sort of started. I would never—" She faltered.

"Since I didn't know about it, can I assume I wasn't part of this escape plan?"

"Dan, you're being insane. Of course I wasn't going to run off with Sam."

"Well, that's sure as hell what it looks like," he hissed. He was furious, shaking. He threw the pack of changing mats onto the floor.

"Do you really think I would leave you, and take your son?"

"I don't know, Grace. I mean, what am I supposed to think?"

"Dan, you're . . . you're being crazy."

"I'm not the one who made a doomsday bunker of baby gear."

"That's not what this is. Dan, please. It's just stuff. We have to see Elliott in a few hours," she said. "Let's not do this now."

The car ride into the city was silent. Grace had never seen Dan this angry. When they arrived at Elliott's office, the lawyer's face was grim.

"What is it?" Grace asked. She didn't think she could bear any more bad news.

"They're seeking an urgent hearing to order a DNA test."

"What?! But you said that was unlikely to happen."

"On what grounds?" Dan asked.

"They say an admission."

"What admission?" Grace said. "That doesn't make any sense."

Elliott rubbed his chin. His eyes darted to Dan, then back down to his desk. "It was a letter."

Dan went white. He placed his hand on Grace's knee but she didn't feel it.

"They're lying!" she cried. "They must have fabricated a letter. Can't we challenge it?"

Elliott shifted in his seat. "They say Dan wrote to Priya, responding to a letter she had written in which she explained what had happened. They say he admits he knows there was an error, and that a DNA test must be undertaken immediately."

"No," said Grace. "No, she never wrote to us. She *never* wrote to us."

Dan's skin was ashen. He said nothing.

"No," she said again, looking at her husband. "You couldn't have. You never told me there was a letter."

"Do you want me to give you two a moment?" Elliott asked.

"No! Dan, tell me there wasn't a letter." Grace's voice shook.

Dan's eyes filled with tears. "She wrote to me saying she just wanted to meet us . . . I thought I could convince her to call off the lawsuit."

"You hid a letter from the egg woman from me!"

Elliott was on his feet. "I'll give you some privacy." He disappeared out into the hall.

Dan turned to his wife. "I should have told you. I'm sorry. I'd take it back if I could. I didn't want to worry you."

"Well, I'm worried now. You were angry at me for putting aside a few . . . a few provisions when all the time you were secretly writing to *her*?"

"I'm sorry." He reached for her.

"Don't touch me." She jerked her arm away.

He reached for her again. "I'm not the bad guy. Grace, please. We're both a little crazy now but we have to stick together. If we don't, we'll lose him for sure. From now on we tell each other everything. Swear. It's you and me, in it to protect our boy."

She exhaled heavily, stood, and walked to the window.

"I'm so mad at you." She began to cry. "And I'm so tired. I don't know how much longer I can do this." She pressed her forehead against the cold glass.

He went to her and put his arms around her. "I know. I'm so sorry. I just wanted to protect you. I'm going insane here."

"I'm exhausted."

"I'm really sorry I didn't tell you about the letter, and that I thought you were going to flee with Sam. I'm not thinking straight."

"I know I should be mad still, but I just feel numb. I'm just so tired and numb."

"I know," he said.

"I don't want to lose our little boy."

"I know." He held her tight. "We're not going to let them take him from us."

PART THREE

Thirty-Eight

PRIYA HAD A FOREST OF PAPER LAID OUT BEFORE HER—HAND-written notes, bureaucratic forms, scrawled reminders. She wet her forefinger and leafed through a pile of references.

"Ask me another one," she said without raising her eyes.

"Okay." Nick looked to the ceiling for inspiration. "The baby got into the kitchen cupboard and ate a fistful of dishwashing powder. What do you do?"

Priya screwed up her face. "Would a baby do that?"

"Mel did it when she was three. Quick. He's turning blue. What do you do?"

"Right, um. Induce vomiting and call poison control. No! Call an ambulance. No—"

"Either of those would be fine," Nick said. "You're going to breeze through this."

"What did your mother do?"

"She threw me and Mel into the station wagon and drove to the hospital."

"I guess that was her maternal instinct working."

"Try not to worry. The interview isn't going to be a parenting pop quiz. They'll just ask about your work and your support networks. They need to know this is a safe home for a child. Which it is."

Priya pursed her lips, unsure. "Thank you for all of your help with this."

"Of course."

"Seeing your life's achievements reduced to a few pieces of paper is a sobering experience," she said. "One of the forms Estelle gave me had this big section for volunteer works and charitable acts. You know, to demonstrate my worthiness. And I had nothing. If I was hiring someone for the position of 'mother' based on this résumé, I wouldn't even call me in for an interview."

"You donate to the Cancer Council," Nick said.

"A fifty-dollar automatic withdrawal each month. That's hardly a reason to alert the Nobel Prize committee."

"You're a good person, Priya. You love your family. You work hard. You have integrity. That's why so many people wrote you such glowing reports."

Viv had written a letter of recommendation: *A loving and devoted aunt.* As had her boss: *Responsible and hardworking.* Rajesh, Darsh, and two of her girlfriends had also contributed. Still, Priya feared the dossier she would be presenting as part of the pre-custody hearing interview was flimsy.

"I'm worried about what I'm up against with the other couple. What if they, I don't know, spend their holidays vaccinating orphans or knitting blankets for the homeless. What if they have references written by MPs and CEOs. They both have good jobs. I bet they know a lot of important people."

"The interview isn't about competing with them."

"No, but the court case is. How am I going to persuade the judge my son is better off with me than with the woman who gave birth to him?"

They silently pondered this problem until Nick picked up Priya's empty mug. "More tea?"

"That'd be a good start." She leaped to her feet and took the cup from him. "Peppermint?"

"You sit. I'll get it."

He brushed past her and went into the kitchen and ran the tap. The pipes groaned and Priya shuddered. Her Coogee apartment was so shabby and old. She'd have to avoid running the tap when the social worker came for the interview. Nick returned, wiping his hands on a tea towel. "I think the washer in your sink tap needs replacing," he said.

"I know. I've been meaning to call the agent. But with all this," she said, gesturing at the paperwork, "I just haven't had the time to address leaking taps."

"Beachside living isn't all sunbathing and ice cream, eh? I reckon I've got some washers in my truck. I could do it." He moved to the door.

"You don't have to do that."

"It will take two minutes. One less thing for you to worry about."

He was halfway down the stairs before she could answer. Priya went to the kitchen and took out two cups. By the time she was drowning their tea bags in scalding water, Nick was slotting the tap head back into place, whistling cheerily. "All done." He wiped his hands again and accepted the tea she held out.

"That was fast. Thank you."

"All part of the service," said Nick. "Cheers." They knocked their mugs together. "It's nice to feel like I'm being useful."

Priya couldn't help but smile. She hardly ever had visitors to her flat, and she hadn't realized how desperately lonely she had been. Nick's presence was like a tonic, restoring her. Their time apart had changed them. They were kinder to each other. He was more considerate and she was more appreciative. He'd had his hair cut in a style shorter than he usually wore. It accentuated the corners of his brow and cheekbones, and made him appear more mature, as did the slivers of gray that had grown in around his temples and occasionally caught the light. Priya wondered if he really had grown during their months apart, or if it was only an illusion she wanted to see because she missed him.

"You've been more help than you can know," she said shyly.

"Really?" His blue eyes settled on hers.

"Really. This whole thing has been really draining." She held his gaze. "Can I show you something?"

"Of course."

She went into her bedroom and returned with some baby clothes.

"I bought him some presents when I first learned about him. I take them out every day and I lay them on my lap, or I fold them, ready for him to wear, and I imagine what it would be like if he were here." She closed her hand over the small cotton foot of one of the jumpsuits and imagined the little toes it was designed to keep warm.

"Pri." Nick hugged her. She let him hold her for a moment, relishing his sturdy warmth, then she pulled away and plucked a tissue from the box on her coffee table.

"I cry constantly," she said, blotting her face. "Just the other day I had to leave the office because I was so angry and frustrated that this could happen. I couldn't sit at my desk a minute longer." She felt a sob rise up but she held it back, swiping at her tears. "I went to Hyde Park. It was sunny. There was a woman there with a baby in a sling. She was a tiny thing, she couldn't have been more than a few weeks old, and she was sucking on her mother's finger, dozing, while the woman read."

She blinked rapidly.

"They looked so happy, so peaceful, and I thought, imagine

someone tearing those two apart. What kind of monster could do such a thing?"

"You're having doubts?" Nick asked. "You think that's what you're doing to the couple in Glebe?"

"No." Priya shook her head. Her tears were banished now and her voice hardened with determination. "No, that's the thing. As horrible as I felt, I knew with more certainty than ever that I had to do it. Because the woman with my son isn't like the mother in the park. She knows her baby doesn't belong to her and she doesn't care.

"When I wrote to them saying I wanted to get to know the baby but wouldn't fight for custody it was because I was thinking about what was best for him. I was worried about taking him from a loving home. But they ignored me. They weren't worried about what they were denying him. This woman thinks her desire for a child is greater than his right to know his real family and everything that comes with that. His history, and his heritage. And I won't abandon my son to someone like that, Nick, I won't do it."

"Priya." He gripped her arms, his face bright, eyes wide. "Ever since you told me about your baby I've been racking my brain, trying to come up with a way to help you, and then it occurred to me." He took her hands. "Let's stay married. Not go through with the divorce. It's not too late."

"What? Nick—that's crazy."

"Why is it crazy?"

"I appreciate your help with this but . . ."

"Listen, if you want custody of your son, it will help if there are two parents. The court will hear you'll have someone to support you. That you won't be doing it alone."

Priya licked her lips, suddenly hopeful as she realized this was true. She and Estelle had been building a case that would convince the court Sadavir belonged with her, among his tribe, but they couldn't argue their way around the fact that if she was granted custody they would be removing him from a two-parent home in Glebe to live in a one-bedroom walk-up with a single mother on a single income.

Nick continued: "We broke up so quickly . . . I know it was my fault and maybe this is something I can do for you that could make a real difference. And maybe you could learn to trust me again."

"Nick, I don't know."

"Think about it. It makes sense."

"And what if I do get custody? Are you ready to raise a stranger's baby with me?"

"Yes," he said with certainty. "Absolutely. I've put a lot of thought into this. This boy is your son and you are my wife. Even though we haven't seen each other for a little while."

"Ah—" Priya was speechless. "What if I don't get custody? Do you want us to live together as a married couple again if the baby is taken out of the equation?"

"Of course," he said earnestly. "If that's what you want."

She paced, frowning. "You can't use this horrible mistake as a way to paper over the broken trust."

"That's not what this is."

"I—I don't know." Her hand went to her chest. She felt the flutter of her heart banging against her breastbone. "I need some air," she said.

She slid open the glass door and stepped onto the balcony. Half-finished canvases leaned against the rails. She brushed her fringe away from her eyes and looked toward the horizon. Nick followed her out into the darkness. Beyond the buildings and treetops Priya could see the ocean glittering in the moonlight, and she wished for a moment that she could dive into it and swim away. India flashed through her mind, that faraway place she had never seen yet felt an intrinsic connection to. She wanted to go there someday. She wanted to take her son. She braced herself against the metal railing.

"Priya," Nick said. "Imagine the social worker asks you who will help you raise this baby. You say, 'My husband, Nick, we've been together more than fifteen years.'"

"Nick, I appreciate what you're offering, but this is huge. We've barely seen each other over the past fifteen months and now you want to pick up our marriage again like nothing happened."

"You know me better than anyone, the good and the bad." He spread his arms, as if presenting himself for judgment. "And I admit it's convenient that what I can do to help you also helps me, but the truth is, wanting to be with you again isn't sneaky or underhanded. I love you, Priya. I've always loved you." He grabbed her hand. "If a court is going to decide what's best for the baby, you've got a better chance of winning if you've got a partner to help raise him, and I want to do that. Not just for your sake and not just for my sake, but for all of us. All three of us. I want us to be a family."

Priya walked to the other end of the balcony, grateful for the ocean breeze. She recognized the logic in what he was saying, but her sensible self repeated a warning: he had broken her trust. He had gone to the Exeter to meet Rose. He had set up the meeting under their marital roof. And yet, she reasoned, after they broke up he hadn't done anything she had expected. He hadn't shacked up with Megan. And he wasn't dating anyone else. The only person he was seeing was a therapist. Darsh had confirmed it.

"Would you want us to be a couple again right away, like we were?"

"Whatever you want. Whatever you're comfortable with. I'm thinking about you and the baby."

She nodded. The baby. *Sadavir*. Dyuti's grandson. Viv's nephew and Darsh's second cousin. Priya silently stepped back into the comforting light of her flat.

"I have to think about this."

"Of course."

"It's such a big move."

He put his mug on the bench beside her, his arm brushing her body and making the hairs on her own stand up. She could smell him. Soap and aftershave. They filled her with comforting memories.

"I'll let you get some sleep," he said, stooping to kiss her chastely on the cheek.

She walked him to the door. "Thanks again for all of your help."

"I'll wait to hear from you."

"Okay." She nodded, and they embraced again.

She shut the door and went into the kitchen to rinse out their mugs. Lying on the drying rack was Nick's wrench. She snatched it up and ran out the door.

"Nick. Nick!"

He stopped and turned, his face aglow with hope. She looked at the wrench she was holding up like a torch. She opened her mouth and the word *okay* burst out.

"Okay?" He bounded up the steps to her, taking them two at a time. "You're sure? We're going to try again?" His hands were resting lightly on her hips.

She nodded. "We'll take it slow. But yes, I think we should try again."

She pressed herself against him, still a little shocked and a fraction reticent, as he put his arms around her. In the stillness, she felt like she could say what was on her mind. Her insides were charged with conflicting emotions.

"I'm scared you're going to grow bored with me again," she whispered.

He pulled away so he could look at her. "I was never bored," he said. "I felt like I'd failed you. You were so upset about not getting pregnant. I felt responsible. I needed you more. Not less."

He nuzzled her neck. His words scoured away all of Priya's anger. She needed to be held, and then, feeling the masculine solidity of his body, she needed more. Lust seized her. She drew his shirt free and pulled him back inside her flat. Understanding what she wanted, Nick unfastened her dress and tugged it down.

She remembered how, when he touched her, everything seemed all right. The text messages seemed inconsequential. Months of despair evaporated. Her love had always been guarded. But how much she missed him was tangible. It was the loss of the little everyday things that had stung: watching him build Sunday bacon breakfast sandwiches; opening a sack to show her a new treasure from a building site; keeping her warm with his body heat on winter mornings when the wind rattled the windows of their bedroom in the home he built for her. She missed that home.

"I love you," he said. "I'll do better."

"Me too," she replied.

They shuffled into the bedroom and tumbled onto Priya's bed. And finally, after knowing him for fifteen years, being married to him for seven and separated for one, Priya Laghari surrendered to Nick Archer.

Thirty-Nine

COLORS BLURRED BEFORE GRACE'S WEARY EYES. GRAY, NAVY, and indigo all became one. She reached into her wardrobe for a wool-blend twill skirt then withdrew her hand. Her life was spiraling so completely out of control that the few decisions she still had power over took on a new, weighty significance.

The sound of her babbling baby floated up the stairs, followed by Fiona's coos and coaxing as she attempted to feed Sam stewed apples. They had been experimenting with solids, without much success. They could get a spoonful of puree into Sam's mouth, but it would stay there only for a few seconds before he dribbled it back out again in a slow, sludgy stream. Dan had dedicated himself to creating several original baby food recipes before Grace heated up a big saucepan of apples in the hope that something sweeter would do the trick. She was just thinking that if Fiona had no luck with the apples she would try custard when the terrible reality of what was at stake seized her. She steadied herself against the wardrobe door and flicked through her hangers again, in search of a suitable outfit to wear to court.

She heard the clatter of plastic on stone—presumably the Peter Rabbit bowl being knocked from her mother's hands—followed by her mother's cry: "Oh, Sammy." On any other day the thought of her mischievous son would have made her smile. But today it upset and scared her. She stretched skyward until her back cracked and then focused once again on the task at hand. She had to do this for Sam.

Grace parted two coats and the solution appeared, pressed flat by the weight of her winter wear: a periwinkle-blue silk dress she had worn at the christening for Rochelle's third child, Daisy. The cinched waist and calf-length skirt would strike exactly the right chord with a judge raised in the era of single-income households. Grace slipped into the satiny garment. She added flat shoes and a cropped jacket and then appraised the effect in the mirror. Perfect. She looked like the valedictorian of Martha Stewart's college for mothers. But it gave her no pleasure. It was like picking out her burial outfit.

"Ready?" Dan came into the bedroom.

"Yes. Oh, I just had a thought," Grace said, turning back to their wardrobe. "Here." She held out a tie that closely matched the blue of her dress. "Put that on."

"Good thinking." He yanked off the red-striped Pierre Cardin he'd chosen that morning. "We want to look united. Team Arden." The taut, willful positivity of their IVF days had returned to his voice.

"Let me fix that." Grace straightened the new tie. Her worried eyes were on the knot when Dan took her trembling hands in his.

"We're going to win this," Dan said. "He's our son and he's going to stay here with us where he belongs."

"How do you know that?" Grace asked, desperate to believe.

"Because he has to. He just has to."

Beth had a car spot near her chambers, so she collected Grace and Dan in her black Land Rover and dropped them at the Family Court building on Goulburn Street, where the custody hearing was set down for five days.

"It looks like a crematorium," said Grace.

Elliott was waiting in the lobby with his phone pressed to his ear. He looked as sharp as a blade in gray. Grace felt a small jolt of confidence and even managed a hopeful smile when he slid his phone into his pocket and greeted her and Dan before taking them into a windowless interview room.

"They're probably going to try again for the DNA test, so be prepared. We want to avoid that at all costs but it's really up to the judge." He looked grave.

"You don't sound confident," said Grace.

Elliott grimaced. "I'd say it's a fifty-fifty chance you'll have to go through with it."

"Let's hope not. We already know how that ends."

"I feel so powerless," Dan said.

"You're doing great," Elliott replied. "I like the tie and dress combo. Nice touch."

"Every little bit helps, right?" said Grace.

Elliott put a hand on Grace's arm and squeezed. "Are you ready?"

She and Dan nodded and stepped into the lobby just as a couple rushed in through the entrance behind a woman in a pantsuit with a silver cap of hair. Grace nearly collided with a petite Australian-Indian woman, whose shoulder bag flew up and smacked into Grace's side. As the woman opened her mouth to apologize they locked eyes and her voice failed. Grace felt as if her breath were being sucked out of her.

"Dan," Grace squeaked, reaching for her husband's arm. "It's her."

A tall man in an ill-fitting blazer snaked his arm around the woman and swept her away before Grace could say anything else.

"Talk about hit and run," said Dan.

"It was bound to happen eventually," said Elliott. "Come on. We don't want to keep Judge Cameron waiting."

~

The courtroom had none of the pomp or grandeur Grace was expecting. It was a small, modern room with white paneled walls and a carpet made from tessellated red and maroon rectangles.

"I expected it to be more foreboding," Dan said.

Grace took a seat and gazed across at the enemy camp where Priya was seated with her lawyer, studiously avoiding eye contact. Priya turned and spoke to another couple behind her, then tucked a lock of hair behind her ear, flashing blue metallic nail polish. Grace felt a twist of dislike. *How tacky.* And yet, the small woman had a quality that cured Grace's hate. The howling hostility in her heart was arrested. Her mood shifted and her anger was replaced by a disconcerting curiosity. Grace shifted in her seat, disturbed. Trying to be discreet, she glanced up quickly at Priya again.

At the same time Priya snuck a look at Grace and their eyes met. Grace turned away, smarting like she'd been slapped. Her rival's face was familiar. It was the eyes, and her nose and its relationship to the features around it. She'd gazed at it a million times, in Sam. An unexpected emotional alchemy was occurring. Grace's hatred mutated into empathy. She felt the woman's loss and pain. The full force of the tragedy of what had happened revealed itself to her, then smothered her. She grieved anew for her own lost biological baby, her own unfulfilled Petri with blond pigtails, and Sam, who, one way or another, would be denied a loving parent and a part of himself.

"She looks like him," she whispered to Dan. He nodded somberly. "Who's that man with her?" she asked. "He can't be the father."

Priya's companion was a solid man in an oversized jacket and R.M.Williams boots. Dan shrugged. "One of her lawyers?"

"No, look how close they are. It must be a boyfriend. Did the statement of claim say anything about her living with a man?" And just like that, the rage that had been tamed by Priya's familiar features returned. "Who is this stranger who thinks he has the right to take our son?"

Three loud taps rang out and a hush fell over the room. A door opened.

"Here we go," said Dan, rising to his feet.

Judge Diane Cameron entered the room, bowed, and settled in her seat. As she regarded the assembly, her clerk read out the case details.

"Priya Laghari versus Grace and Daniel Arden."

Grace steeled herself. Every second was agony. There was some administrative nattering and the lawyers introduced themselves before the judge cleared her throat.

"There is one matter I want to address before we get started," Judge Cameron said, sliding the arms of her glasses into her tuft of blond curls. "It is critical the child at the center of this dispute never comes across any reports that might suggest to him that his existence is a mistake. To ensure that never happens, he will be referred to from this point on as Baby S. This will also put us on more neutral footing as I believe there is some dispute as to what he should be named." Judge Cameron looked around the courtroom. She saw Grace and Dan, miserable and puffy-eyed, and Priya, determined to press forward. "Ms. Forlani," Judge Cameron said, "are you ready to begin?"

Priya's lawyer got to her feet. "Your Honor, before we begin our opening statements I'd like to be heard on the matter of the DNA test request. The letter we provided to the court written by Dan Arden indicates the couple at the very least had doubts about the child's biological makeup. We think that is grounds enough to test the child. It's noninvasive and the results would significantly alter the case."

Dan squeezed Grace's hand.

"Hmm." Judge Cameron tapped her index finger against her lip. "I find everything about this case extremely unsettling. And I don't think much of this evidence. Where is the clinic in all of this? Why has there been no investigation?"

"That is part of the reason we need the DNA test," Estelle said. "My client can't take legal action against the clinic until she can prove an error was made."

"I see." Judge Cameron looked at the Ardens. "And I suppose, Mr. Jones, your clients don't wish to make any allegations against the clinic?"

"No, Your Honor," Elliott said. "My clients were perfectly happy with the service provided by the Empona fertility clinic." He added as an afterthought: "They love their son. Very much."

"I suspected as much. Ms. Forlani, if I were to order a paternity test, how long will it take?"

"Five business days."

"Your Honor," Elliott interjected, "we strongly object to testing this baby's DNA. My clients are his parents. Their names are on the birth certificate. All the plaintiff has is a couple of pieces of unverified paper. The printout of the clinic's schedule that she claims is evidence of a mistake shows nothing and the letter doesn't prove a thing. Ordering a DNA test on the basis of one letter and one table that could have been whipped up on Microsoft Word is extremely unorthodox."

"Yes, well, I'm sorry, Mr. Jones, but everything about this case is extremely unorthodox . . . and extremely serious," the judge said. She paused to pinch the bridge of her nose, a pained expression on her face. "I do think we need to delve into this deeper, and a DNA test seems the best starting point. Based on the letter written by Daniel Arden and the visible difference between the child and his birth parents, I think there's evidence to support the *possibility* that an error has been made by the clinic. Baby S will undergo a DNA test to determine who his biological parents are. Once we have the answer I can consider the matter of custody."

"Thank you, Your Honor," Ms. Forlani said. Grace closed her eyes. Dan swore under his breath.

"I'll order that Baby S be taken for a swab test that will be compared against both Mr. and Mrs. Arden and Ms. Laghari. I'll adjourn the hearing until next Wednesday, which should give the lab ample time to analyze the sample. When we return we will know who Baby S's biological parents are."

Forty

WHEN THEY RETURNED TO COURT THE FOLLOWING
Wednesday Priya kept her head down and her hands clasped tightly,
as if she were holding the new knowledge in her hands, like a glowing,
precious gem. The tests had come back. The baby was hers. Sadavir
was her son. Their kinship was encoded in his cells and, along with
it, familial traits and tastes were woven into his being. Her intol-
erance for coriander. Her widow's peak. It was exciting to imagine
that maybe he would have a talent for painting or a love of color
that they could share. One day she might find him, as a teenager,
frowning over a sketchbook as he attempted to render an arm in a
foreshortened perspective for a school assignment. Priya, watching
over, would be able to gently guide his hand and show him how he
could use cross-hatching to create shadows.

Perhaps he would be very particular about the color of shirts
she bought for him and insist on a specific shade of green for his
bedsheets. She would take him into her office and show him her
color charts and paints, and his eyes would light up like pinwheels.

She squeezed her fists in silent exaltation. At last. *At last.* Her
baby, her boy. It was proven he was hers. She tried not to let her
excitement show on her face. Grace Arden was only a few meters

away and she would soon learn what Priya and Estelle knew: the boy in her nursery was a biological stranger. This was a massive blow to the Ardens' case.

Priya watched Grace take off her sunglasses and slip them into her shoulder bag, then rub each eye with her thumb knuckle. Exhaustion was painted across her face in purple and gray. She had bags under her eyes and sallow skin. Up close her adversary looked different from Priya's memory of the black-haired woman she'd seen on the Glebe porch. Her mind had contorted that person into a fairy-tale hag with sharp yellow teeth who steals children. In the flesh, Grace looked normal, aside from her weariness. Her black hair had been retouched and cut. Its shiny ends rested neatly on her shoulders. On her lapel she wore a teal ribbon for ovarian cancer support. Did this hint at some other tragic chapter, Priya wondered, or was Grace trying to score points with the judge? She rubbed her arms and felt a shiver of unease. Her stomach was full of crickets.

When Judge Cameron entered and Estelle revealed the results of the test, Grace let out a single, solitary sob, then smothered her mouth with a handkerchief and let her head collapse onto her husband's shoulder.

The judge nodded sympathetically in the direction of the Ardens, and her associate produced a box of tissues. Priya too felt powerful emotions. She was so close to getting to hold her baby in her arms. But it was by no means assured. She wasn't free yet to hope.

"Are you okay?" Priya felt her sister's hand on her shoulder. Dan and Grace were whispering with their lawyer. Dan's eyes shone, wet. Large tears were rolling down Grace's cheeks. Priya reached for her glass of water. Her mouth was dry.

Estelle stood. "Your Honor, there is one more thing before we deliver our opening arguments. Ms. Laghari asks that until the case is resolved, the baby be given over into the custody of a court-appointed guardian to avoid the risk of the family absconding with him."

"What? No!" Dan jumped out of his seat.

"Your Honor," his lawyer bellowed at the same time.

Priya's head snapped up. They had discussed this the week before, but she had been so focused on the DNA test that the request to remove the baby early had completely slipped her mind.

The judge ignored Dan's interruption. "Mr. Jones?"

"You can't remove a child from his parents simply because of an as yet unresolved dispute," the lawyer said hotly. "You would be punishing my clients for no good reason. Not to mention it would hardly be in the best interests of the child. He's only a few months old. He needs to be with his parents."

"It is a reasonable concern." Estelle's gravelly voice was slow and authoritative. "There is a risk the family will try to flee."

"What risk? On what grounds?" the opposing lawyer demanded.

"Mrs. Arden recently underwent testing for postnatal depression and scored an eight on the Edinburgh scale," Estelle said.

"In English please, Ms. Forlani," said the judge.

"It places her in the high-risk category for postpartum depressive thoughts. It's in the documents." Estelle lifted a thick ring binder that contained the evidence in the case.

"Are we in the business of removing children from loving mothers simply because a test finds they are at risk of *potentially* developing a common mental illness?" Elliott Jones said. "If so, the courts are about to become very busy rehoming an awful lot of babies."

Judge Cameron frowned. "I agree with you, Mr. Jones. But it may well be that Baby S needs to get used to being without the people he has come to know as his parents."

Grace let out another choking sob. Judge Cameron turned to

Grace and Dan. "Mr. and Mrs. Arden," she said gently, "where is Baby S now?"

"He's at home being cared for by his grandmother, Your Honor," Dan said.

"Grace has a very close relationship with her mother," Elliott said. "She also has a good job and many supportive friends. At her school she spearheaded a program to feed the homeless."

Judge Cameron murmured.

"It's a question of risk," Estelle said. "The prospect of losing the baby will exacerbate the potential for depressive thoughts. Who knows what an unstable mother might do? People have fled the country over less."

Priya could see Grace's cheeks burning with shame and rage. Dan pulled her closer to him, his expression stoic.

"Enough, Ms. Forlani," Judge Cameron said. "Mrs. Arden is not on trial here, and her potential future actions certainly aren't. She is a gainfully employed woman with ties to the community, a supportive family, and an impeccable record. Removing such a young child from parental care will distress him and his parents. I see no reason to increase the level of anxiety everyone is feeling about these proceedings. Baby S will remain with Mr. and Mrs. Arden until the custody hearing is complete. Now, we will take a fifteen-minute recess and then you, Ms. Forlani, may open your case."

⁓

Priya watched Grace leave the courtroom, the rawness of the mother's grief chipping away at her determination. Outwardly, she would remain steadfast. But sympathy for the Ardens had crept into her heart. She reached for Nick's hand and held it tight.

When Judge Cameron returned to the court Priya sat up straight, trying to focus.

"Are we ready to begin?" the judge asked.

Estelle stood, her expression confident as she prowled back and forth across the front of the courtroom. She started with some rhetorical flourishes before plunging into the guts of the matter. "In 2015 Priya Laghari engaged the Empona fertility clinic to help her fulfill a lifelong dream of becoming a mother. Like many women, it is a wish she had cherished from a young age.

"Flash-forward three years . . ." Estelle went on, teasing out the details of Priya's life like a seasoned storyteller: how her marriage had faltered, how her desire for a child was so strong she sought a donor.

"If a mother leaves her child with a friend while she goes away for a weekend, the child does not become the offspring of that temporary carer. That might seem a ridiculous concept, but it is, in essence, what the Ardens are contending. This child, Priya Laghari's child, was in the care of the Ardens for a short time. Five months, to be exact, from his birth to now. That does not make him theirs.

"Grace Arden, we know, works at a boardinghouse, where she cares professionally for many children while their parents work overseas or on remote farms. She cares for them nine months a year, yet she knows that does not make them hers. The only difference between those children and Baby S is that Baby S's rightful mother did not agree to hand her child over to the care of Grace Arden. It happened by accident, through no fault of Ms. Laghari's.

"We can employ all the rhetoric in the world," Estelle went on. "In the end it comes down to one simple fact: Priya Laghari is this boy's rightful mother, by blood and by design. I say design because it was through her actions that the father of Baby S provided the sperm necessary to fertilize her egg. It was through her actions that an egg—*her* egg—was extracted so that it might be so fertilized. The combination of this chosen father's sperm and her egg did create a viable embryo, and it was through Priya Laghari's actions that this embryo was placed in a womb so that it could safely grow into the baby he is now. The only thing in Baby S's life that Ms. Laghari did not plan for was the gross incompetence that led to her son being placed in the wrong womb. And of course she had no way of knowing that the woman who would carry and give birth to her child would conspire to hide him from the world."

Estelle Forlani argued that the months that Grace and Dan spent bonding with Baby S were only allowed to occur because they didn't alert the clinic as soon as they suspected a mistake had been made. "They cannot lie to the world and then cry foul when the people hurt by the lie attempt to reverse its effects.

"If Baby S is removed from their custody it will be painful for them, there is no doubt of that. But if they had not tried to conceal him in the first place their pain would be far less.

"It's not too late to rectify this error," Estelle said. "No harm will come to the child by removing him from the Ardens now. Indeed, when he is a grown man, he will not remember the few months he spent living with two people who have no biological connection to him." Estelle paused for dramatic effect. "He will never even know they exist."

There was a booming echo of a closing door. Grace had fled the court.

"Well," Viv said when they broke for lunch, "that seemed to go as well as could be expected." They were huddled around a metal café table on a footpath of a busy city road.

"You were very convincing," Nick told Estelle. "At first when you started talking about looking after other people's kids I thought it was a long bow. But you're right, it is just the same. He's stayed with them for a bit. That doesn't change who he is. What do you think, Pri?"

Priya's voice was quiet. "I just want it to be over."

She had been buoyed by Estelle's performance, but fear still weighed heavily on her heart.

"I think it will be really hard for them to make a stronger argument than that," Nick said.

"Don't pop the champagne yet," Estelle said, lighting a cigarette in spite of the No Smoking sign. "It's still their name on the birth certificate." Her phone rang. "Excuse me. That's the office. My associate is trying to track down the doctor who exposed the mistake." She accepted the call. "Yes? You haven't? No, it's not too late. Keep trying. We don't want to leave anything to chance."

"Isn't the error proven by the DNA test?" asked Viv.

"Yes, but what's not clear is how much the Ardens knew. If this doctor told you, perhaps she told them. We have a chance to show the type of people they are. Are they sneaky? Are they deceitful? Are there other things that might make them unsuitable parents? If so, I'd like it on record before the court."

"Is that really necessary?" Priya asked. "We're already putting them through so much, do we have to attack them as well?"

Estelle flicked the ash from her cigarette onto the ground. "We do if you want to win this case."

After lunch it was the Ardens' lawyer's turn to present his argument. Before he began he buttoned his jacket and ran his palm down his tie. None of the lawyers were wearing black robes and wigs, as TV dramas had taught Priya to expect.

"Your Honor, Ms. Forlani has tried to confuse the issue by stating that Priya Laghari is this child's mother, and this is simply a matter of a switched-at-birth-style mix-up. She has ignored the role Grace Arden played in the creation of this boy's life and tried to reduce the question of maternity to a matter of genes. To do so is to overlook a crucial thing," said Elliott Jones. "Birth cannot occur without pregnancy. Carrying a child in your womb, nurturing him from a two-cell embryo to a baby with lungs and eyelashes and toes, is an essential part of mothering him. To fall back on genetic links disregards this important, precious task."

Priya reluctantly found herself in agreement and a fog of confusion settled over her. This case, she realized, wasn't about an immutable truth. It was about definitions, collectively agreed upon and codified. It was about humans messing with the laws of nature and obscuring certainty.

The lawyer continued. "Ms. Laghari had trouble conceiving with her husband, that's why she went to Empona. We do not know that if this embryo had been transferred into her uterus it would have developed into the healthy baby now at the center of this custody dispute. Grace Arden, who was forty-four at the time she conceived, was deemed high risk, but she put herself in danger in order to bring this pregnancy to term. She ensured the fetus was monitored and nourished and kept safe. Every day and every night for nine months she devoted herself to the baby, and when he arrived in the world, after a grueling twelve-hour labor and twenty-six stitches, she redoubled her efforts, and was up with him day and night. That is not the same thing as 'caring for a child' the way Ms. Forlani characterized her work at the boardinghouse. What Mrs. Arden did was create life. Without her, this baby would not exist. How then can Ms. Forlani say she is not his mother?"

Elliott went on to address Estelle's other points. When the Ardens were handed their bright-eyed baby, they didn't know it had been a mix-up, he said. Dan's lineage included ancestors from Syria, Lebanon, and Malta. They had believed the doctor who told them Sam's complexion was the result of that ancient bloodline rising to the surface of the gene pool. How could they not? The baby was born from Grace's own womb. Who else's would he be?

"Why should these good, loving people"—he gestured at the Ardens—"be punished for the clinic's mistake?"

"In cases of mix-ups at hospitals, newborns are quickly returned to their rightful parents. But we also know of times when the error isn't discovered until after the parents and child have had a chance to bond, and so offspring have elected to stay with the nonbiological parents. What, then, is the limit on the growing affection between parent and child? The Ardens have loved and cared for Baby S for five months now, in addition to the nine months they spent nurturing him in utero. How short does a period of parenting have to be for it to be dismissed as irrelevant? Ms. Laghari here, why, she's never even seen Baby S. She wasn't even sure she was his biological mother until it was confirmed by a lab. Her bond is purely theoretical."

Estelle got to her feet. "The relationship developed in utero is not mutual," she responded. "The Ardens may have felt love for Baby S during the gestation, but there can be no question that he returned that love, as he was a fetus."

"Your Honor, what do we know of the mind of a baby?" Elliott asked.

"If our chief concern here is the baby's welfare, the bonding up to this point is moot," said Estelle. "He won't even remember them."

"There is no way you can know that for sure," Elliott replied.

And Priya, agreeing, began to regret that she'd allowed herself to hope.

Forty-One

"ARE YOU READY? ARE YOU FEELING OKAY?" THEY WERE BACK in the airless interview room and Elliott was looking at Grace, seeking her assurance. "You can do this," he said, rubbing her arm. She could see the tiny red veins in Elliott's eyeballs from the late nights he was working.

"I want to know more about that man," she said to Elliott and Dan. "The tall one. He's not the donor, so why should he be in our child's life? If the crux of their argument is biology, he's no more the father of the child than Dan is."

"We'll focus on him tomorrow. Today is about you."

"Neither father has a biological connection to Sam, but Dan is his birth father. Doesn't that count for something? A point in our favor?"

"We'll address the fatherhood issue later, Grace. Today I want you one hundred percent focused on your role as Sam's mother. Do you want to go over the questions again?"

"No, I'm okay." She smoothed her skirt.

The lines they'd agreed on were on a constant loop in her head. She'd been up late, practicing them until she forced herself to take a sleeping tablet so that when she took the stand she wouldn't appear as crazed as she felt.

⌒

The Family Court witness box was only three steps off the floor, but to Grace it was an endless climb to the gallows. She gripped the polished wood rail and took her seat to plead her case. Beth gave a discreet wave from the body of the court. She had taken the day off to be a friendly face for Grace to focus on. Fiona had also offered to come, but Grace had said no. "I need you to stay with Sam," she had said, clutching her mother's hands. "Make sure he feels loved." There was no one else she could trust.

"How are you today, Grace?" Elliott asked, his eyes crinkled by a kind smile.

She nodded bravely, just like they had practiced. "I'm okay. Considering."

"You gave birth five months ago. Tell me, how has life changed since you became a mother?"

Grace swallowed the lump in her throat. "It has been the happiest time of my life."

She spoke of the day she first laid eyes on Sam and how the love she already felt for him had expanded. She was careful with her language. When she looked down at her baby the euphoric love she felt was like nothing she had ever known.

"The bond was instant," Grace said. "And Sam, he is such a content, sweet little boy."

"Tell me about him," said Elliott.

"He loves to suck his own toes," Grace told the court. "He's always trying to get them up into his mouth. And he's very verbal. He makes little sighing sounds like he's fed up." She couldn't help but smile. "A sort of 'a-humph.'" She looked at her husband. "Dan and I call it the Harried Businessman. We say he sounds like he's worn out after a busy day of being a baby."

A-humph, she heard in her head. *A-humph,* she silently replied.

The room was still. Beth was mouthing something to Grace. It looked like "I love you," but it was hard to tell. Priya was crying; her whole face shone wet. Grace felt a kick of annoyance in her gut. How dare that woman feel sadness, or pity, or anything at all, really, given she was the one putting them all through this.

What did Priya know of Sam's short life? She didn't even know his father. She claimed history and biology were the only things that mattered, yet half of Sam's remained shrouded in secrecy, hidden by the Empona clinic's privacy policies. Grace had bled for that child. She had carried him for nine months and torn herself in two so that he could live, and she'd do it again if it meant she could keep him.

But she didn't voice any of these things. The cost could be too great. Instead she spouted inspirational quotes about mother-hood. Blessed, fulfilled, willing to do anything for him was how she described her frame of mind. She felt like a pageant contestant parroting answers about world peace. *Poise, poise, poise,* said the voice in her head. *Show them you're unflappable; the calm, collected, ideal person to raise this boy.*

"He likes stewed apples," she said. "They're the only solid he'll eat. And easy-rock radio, since before he was born. When he was inside me, the radio would come on and he'd stir as if to say, 'What's that?'" She remembered how happy it had made her.

"I gave him life," she said. "*Me.* I love him." She could feel the anger rising in her. She tried to push it down, but it reared up, uncontrollable. She was wrung out. On edge. "How can she love him?" Grace looked at Priya. "She doesn't even know him."

"Your Honor!" Estelle interjected.

"Mrs. Arden," said Judge Cameron. "Please."

"Nothing further, Your Honor," Elliott said, retreating to the bar table.

The court was silent as the judge's associate hurried to fill Grace's water glass, and then Estelle Forlani slowly approached the witness stand.

"Mrs. Arden, you said you loved your son before you knew him."

"That's right."

"I wonder if you could tell me, who was it that you loved? Was it a child who would be both a combination of you and your husband, but also their own surprising person?"

"I . . ."

"Perhaps someone with your lovely blue eyes, and your husband's smile? A nose that is a mirror image of your own mother's?"

Grace looked to Elliott for help. He leaped to his feet.

"This case isn't about who loves the child and who doesn't love the child. It's about who his rightful parents are."

Estelle was unfazed. "That is what I'm trying to establish," she said.

"Mr. Jones, Ms. Forlani is entitled to question your client."

Elliott threw his hands up, annoyed. His Adam's apple was straining against his starched collar and his neck was mottled and red. "Your Honor, during this entire hearing Estelle Forlani has treated my client like a suspect she needs to break. Grace Arden is not a criminal. She's a victim," he said hotly.

"It was a legitimate question," Estelle barked.

"She is deliberately goading my client!"

Grace rubbed her eyes, exhausted. The constant crying had left her skin itchy and sore.

"Okay." Judge Cameron raised her voice above the din. "We're all on edge. I'm going to adjourn for a short break, and when we return I hope to see more decorum from the legal counsel."

⁓

Grace was eventually excused from the witness stand and experts were ushered in. As Estelle Forlani harangued the court, Dan and Grace huddled together.

"The important thing is who is Baby S's rightful mother. Not just for his birth but for his whole life," Estelle said.

Grace recalled all the nights she lay in bed, on her back, her orb-like stomach swollen with expectation. The worst of it wasn't just that she had to give him up, it was that he would forget her; that was the central plank of the silver-haired lawyer's argument, and she couldn't stop hammering it home.

"There's nothing connecting them but the Ardens' desire to fulfill their own goals of parenthood," she said.

"All right, Ms. Forlani," Judge Cameron barked. "You've made that point forcefully enough. As Mr. Jones has said, the Ardens are not on trial here."

Estelle's statement tore right through Grace. She thought of Sam's little face. He was everything to her, but if they lost the case, she would be nothing to him.

Forty-Two

BY THE MORNING OF THE FINAL DAY, PRIYA FELT LIKE SHE
had run a marathon. Nick cooked up crispy bacon breakfast sandwiches while Priya was seized by a cleaning frenzy.

"This flat," she said as she wiped dust from the TV cabinet,
"is filthy."

"Perhaps your nesting instinct is kicking in," Nick said, handing
her a plate of food.

"I can't believe we're nearly at the end."

"You know, Rajesh was saying he pulled out one of the twins'
cradles last night and cleaned it up. We could drive over there
tomorrow afternoon and pick it up."

"No, not yet. It would be bad luck to start preparing before
we know the outcome." Priya took a desultory bite from her bacon
sandwich. Nick put a gentle hand on her arm.

"Hopefully you've reached your quota of bad luck for one lifetime," he said.

⁓

Estelle delivered devastating arguments she had drafted and re-
drafted, calibrating the language for maximum efficiency. She

brought in child-behavioral specialists to talk about separation anxiety in infants. Geneticists to speak on the issue of nature versus nurture. Psychologists cherry-picked for their views on the detrimental effects displacement could have. Bespectacled men and women with strongly held opinions and many letters after their names.

One spoke about the inviolable bond of family.

Another said the child would never be truly happy if he grew up in a home that was not his own.

Elliott, of course, wanted to grill Priya thoroughly. How would she juggle work and raising a child alone? What role would Nick play in the baby's life? What would she feed him?

"Formula, at first," she said, her voice uncertain.

"Formula. A substitute for the breast milk Grace Arden has been providing."

Estelle interrupted: "Formula is a perfectly suitable substitute. What else does he think she would feed the baby? What an idiotic question."

Elliott continued. "Ms. Laghari, is it true you initially didn't want custody of Baby S?"

Priya stiffened. "No, that's not true."

"But you wrote to the Ardens when you learned of the mix-up and said you didn't want to claim Baby S as your own."

"I wanted him," Priya said haltingly. "But I was more concerned with what was best for him. I thought taking him away from the people who had been caring for him would be bad for him."

"And that's something you no longer care about?"

Priya flinched. "No! I mean, I think he would be better off with me."

"Is that so?" Elliott rocked on his heels, his stare clamped on Priya. "What changed your mind?"

Priya shifted in her chair. She didn't want to reveal that she'd driven to the Ardens' house and spied on them.

"I was in shock," Priya said. "When I first learned of what had happened I could hardly believe it."

"And you didn't seek any professional advice? You didn't ask for guidance and support with making this monumental decision?"

"I was overwhelmed."

Elliott gave her a mean little smile. "Ah, well, yes. Having a child can be overwhelming. You completely collapsed at the mere thought of it."

"Your Honor!" Estelle was out of her chair like a shot.

Elliott changed tack. "If you're granted custody, you will be supported in raising Baby S by your partner, Nick. That's right, isn't it?"

"Yes, he's a very responsible man."

"But Nick isn't the baby's father, is he?"

"Not biologically, no."

"Not biologically?" Elliott raised his eyebrows, theatrically turned to the Ardens, then returned to face Priya. "No?"

Priya flushed red. "No."

"But you say your relationship is solid?"

"Yes. Very."

"Because you were married, or are married?"

"We separated but we are back together."

"And, despite your long marriage, your solid relationship and so forth, you broke things off with your husband and proceeded with IVF using a donor. That's correct, isn't it?"

"I wanted to have a baby. I wanted to be a mother," Priya answered, her voice rising.

"Please, just yes or no, Ms. Laghari."

"Yes."

"Huh." Elliott paced up and down the front of the courtroom. A sense of trepidation crept up Priya's spine.

"You're very cavalier about starting and severing relationships, aren't you, Ms. Laghari?" He shot Priya a withering glare.

"Don't answer that!" Estelle ordered.

"Mr. Jones." Judge Cameron's voice held a warning. "I'll remind you of what I told Ms. Forlani yesterday about badgering people."

"Sorry, Your Honor, I'll withdraw that." He turned back to the witness stand. "Ms. Laghari, did you undergo IVF treatment with a donor sperm mere months after embarking upon the process with the man you now say is a dependable partner?"

"Yes, but we'd had trouble—" Priya tried to blurt out her answer, but Elliott cut her off with a palm held up like a stop sign.

"That will be all. Thank you, Ms. Laghari."

⁓

The Ardens' lawyer was summing up. Priya watched him as he peacocked, striding up and down in front of the judge, projecting his voice as if performing on a stage. "How can you make a distinction between genetic bonds and gestational bonds?" he asked. "How can you say one is more important to the life of a child than another?

"There was no guarantee that if the same egg had been implanted in Ms. Laghari it would have flourished. Perhaps it was the very fact that the embryo was in Grace Arden's uterus that made it become a fetus that became a baby that became Baby S. By that logic, Grace was just as responsible for Sam's existence as was the provider of the egg."

After he had finished, it was Estelle's turn.

"This is about dislocation," she said. "The idea of genetic bonds and gestational bonds may seem conceptual and slippery, but there are some very tangible elements at play in this case. Culture. History. Family. How can you dismiss this child's right to his heritage because of the emotions of two people who have no familial link to him?"

At the end of the day Judge Cameron thanked both the lawyers and the families.

"I will make a decision as quickly as possible. You will be notified before noon on Friday."

And then it was over. There was nothing anybody could do but wait.

Forty-Three

IT WAS SEVEN O'CLOCK ON FRIDAY MORNING WHEN PHONES in Coogee and Glebe ripped the air with hysterical *priiings*. Priya and Nick were seated at Priya's dining table when the phone stilled the scrape of cutlery on plates.

Grace was lying on her side speaking with Dan in a whisper lest they wake Sam, who now spent his nights nestled between them. They had abandoned his crib since the hearing began, not wanting to be separated from him a moment more than necessary. The phone's peal made Sam whimper. Grace froze.

"I know, little man," Dan soothed. He rolled off the bed and answered with a tense "Yes?"

Judge Cameron would make a ruling at nine, said the dour voice.

"We'll know at nine," said Nick in the kitchen across town.

⁓

The venerable judge looked pale as she shuffled onto the bench. When her associate tried to fill her water glass she shooed him away. "Let's just get on." The air was charged as she raised her voice to the assembled families.

"I know you're all nervous, so I'll try to get through this as quickly as possible. This . . . this has been a very difficult case.

"The bond between mother and child is indelible. I have three children of my own." She stopped, looking pained. "It is only recently that the complex question of who can be considered the mother of a child has existed. Prior to the introduction of assisted reproductive technology, it could only be the woman who conceived and gave birth to the child that could claim that right. However, times have changed. Technological advancements that have allowed wondrous things to happen have brought with them a tangle of tricky ethical and philosophical questions.

"It is hard to imagine a question more difficult than the one we face today. Before us, we have the case of one baby and two mothers, each with a connection and potential claim to the child. Each with a fierce, true love for the boy. So, how do we decide?

"There is neither legislation nor case law in Australia to help us navigate this thorny issue.

"A case that came before the California Supreme Court grappled with a similar conundrum. In that matter, a surrogate who had given birth to a child from a donated embryo decided she did not want to hand the baby over. A custody battle ensued and the judge was forced to decide whether genetic relationship or the act of giving birth conferred mothering rights. The court ultimately found the party that intended to bring about the birth of a child was the rightful parent; that she whose actions and wishes initiated the conception is the natural mother under California law. But that is no help to us here, where there was an intention to procreate by both parties, and indeed more than an intention, a very deep desire such that they each undertook invasive and costly procedures to do so.

"It is ironic that the very clinic the hopeful parents thought was the answer to their prayers was the source of this tragic mistake.

"It is no less a tragedy that due to a medical error, the sincere intention of two women to procreate resulted in the birth of only one child between them, with each having a role to play in his creation." She was reading quickly, aware of the desperate anxiety in the hearts of all assembled before her.

"It is no exaggeration to say that this was the hardest, most complex decision of my long judicial career. There are no winners here. I do not believe that Ms. Laghari takes pleasure in her bid to deny Mr. and Mrs. Arden the child they so obviously love. Likewise, the Ardens are motivated solely by the desire to keep the child they bore—and not because they want to withhold him from a woman with a primal biological connection. Though some of the arguments and lines of questioning have been abrasive, I see before me nothing but good people full of love. Ultimately, the best I can hope for is to try to protect the rights and interests of the child.

"For the fourteen months Baby S was in the care of the Ardens, nine were in utero when the error could not be known. While it is true the Ardens did not alert the medical authorities or seek to rectify the mistake as soon as practicable, they were not malicious. I think it would be a rare person who would fail to sympathize with the very cruel circumstances they find themselves in. What I am about to say therefore is not intended as punishment."

Grace gripped Dan's arm. Priya drew a breath.

"The error separated Baby S not just from his biological mother but from cousins, an aunt, an uncle, and his culture. If he lives to be one hundred—as modern science suggests he may well do—the five months he spent with the Ardens will be a small fraction of his time on earth. It seems the only course open to the court is to ensure he spends the remaining years surrounded by his biological family, and those to whom he has genetic and cultural ties.

"I find that in the long term, Baby S will be best served if he is to grow up in the home of Ms. Laghari.

"I have read the Ardens' truncated medical history that was provided to the court, and as this is, I understand, the end of their chances of bearing their own children, the loss they will feel will be a very grave and very deep one. Many people have given evidence here to their fine characters. I hope those same people will rally around them now when they will need them more than ever."

Judge Cameron took off her glasses and rested them on the bench.

"When I examined the law closely, I found the difficulty arose only from not wanting to deprive this decent couple of the baby they love so tenderly and so wholly. The child belongs with his biological mother. He belongs with his intended family.

"I will make orders as to the conditions of the transfer of custody, and then I will adjourn the court to allow all parties to get on with the tasks that fall to each of them."

Forty-Four

IT COULDN'T BE TRUE. GRACE'S HANDS GRIPPED HER CHAIR as she willed herself to wake up from this nightmare, warm in her bed, her baby snug by her side.

Appeal was the word on her lips. "Appeal!"

She got to her feet, legs unsteady, and staggered toward the door. She had one thought: get to Sam. In her mind she was already sweeping him up in her arms and bundling him into the car, pulling onto the freeway, her seat belt unbuckled, her hair whipping in the wind. She was turning onto the main road, slipping unseen into the traffic, disappearing among the fast flow of cars. She was entering the freeway and pressing her foot on the accelerator, stopping only to fill her tank with petrol and empty her account of cash before speeding north. She grabbed the handle of the courtroom door. Her arms would hardly obey. Her breathing was shallow.

A voice shouted across the courtroom. "No!" She recognized it as her own.

"Grace." Elliott was behind her. "I think you should sit. You look pale."

"Grace!" It was Dan. "Grace, are you okay?" She felt wild. She turned and her eyes settled on Priya, who was clutching her sister.

Their faces were red, the shock of the victory rendering them speechless, but their smiles were big and their cheeks bulged like polished apples.

"No," came Grace's own disembodied voice again. Someone was restraining her, holding her back. She felt like she was having a heart attack.

"Grace, sit down, you've had a shock." The voice was her husband's. But she couldn't see him. The room swayed. Her field of vision narrowed.

"I need to see him. I have to get home," she gasped. Her grip slipped from the courtroom door handle. Her hands were sweaty, as was her forehead. The temperature in the room was soaring. People were closing in around her. A rush of heat scorched her chest, her face.

She pulled her sleeve over her hand and tried the door again. The lock's click heralded freedom. She stumbled into the corridor. She could see the light of the door to the street. Her link to Sam was stronger than Priya's could ever be, Grace thought. If Sam lived with Priya for a hundred years, that woman would still never know what it was like to feel him flutter to life in her womb. Grace tried to walk but her legs failed her. Her heartbeat was flickering, like an overheated lightbulb about to burn out, ready to snap into blackness.

Now what would her life become? She was a mother without a child. A song without sound—just words on a page. Flat. Dull. Her ribs were crushing her lungs. She gasped for breath. Darkness descended, and then there was nothing.

⁓

Everything was white and smelled of disinfectant. Metal bars rose from either side of Grace's bed. The sheet pinning her flat was thick and rough. She could see Dan. Her husband's head was hanging forward. He glanced up at her and relief washed over his face.

"Grace!"

She tried to speak but her throat was dry.

"You fainted," he said, stroking her forehead. "The doctors say you had a panic attack." The memory hit her like a freight truck. She sat up. Dan rushed into her arms, enfolding her in a hug. She clung to him, tears coming quickly.

"So it wasn't a dream?"

"No. No." His voice was small. "It wasn't." His fingers dug into her back. Her tears soaked into his shirt.

She took a deep breath. "Have they taken him?"

"Not yet. He's outside with Fiona."

She felt a tug and looked down to see a drip in her arm, her blond hairs flattened under the sticky tape. Heart-monitor pads were glued to her chest. She ripped the sticky tabs from her skin and pulled the needle from her arm. "I have to see him."

"Take my arm," Dan said, lowering the metal bar.

Grace reached for Dan and sadly rubbed the collar of his shirt between her thumb and forefinger. "I hope I didn't give you a scare."

He patted her hand. "They're just out here."

Grace found her mother on the bench, jiggling Sam to stop him from crying. His face was tearstained.

"Oh, my poor boy," Grace said as Fiona passed him over. He began to calm down as she drew circles on his back with her palm. "Mum's here," she said. "Sh. Mum's here."

A uniformed officer stood on either side of Fiona alongside the court liaison officer. All three looked uncomfortable, shuffling aside to accommodate Grace and Dan but with no intention of leaving. Grace cocooned Sam in her arms. "I'm sorry, little one," she said. "I'm sorry we couldn't keep you. I'm sorry. I'm-sorry-I'm-sorry-I'm-sorry."

Dan put his arms around his wife, the baby sheltered between them.

"We love you, little man," he whispered. Sam yawned and rested his cheek against Grace. "We will always love you."

⁓

Grace remained in the corridor holding Sam until the liaison officer prized him from her hands. She slid down onto the linoleum floor and sobbed unreservedly while Dan held her, until two nurses hooked their arms under her and tenderly lifted her to her hospital bed. One covered her face with a plastic mask then punctured her arm with a needle that made the world soft and cartoonlike. Later they gave her tablets to help her sleep, which she did, waking only long enough to take more pills. She was instructed to stay in the hospital.

"The doctor asked if you wanted something. For the pain," Dan said the next time she woke.

"Ha." She laughed, a hollow croak. "There isn't enough medicine in the world."

When she was discharged they went not to Glebe but to a house in Pearl Beach that Beth had rented for them. "I thought it might be hard to face the house straightaway," she had said. "Stay here until you feel ready."

"We don't deserve you," Dan replied.

They opened the fridge to find it full of casseroles, curries, and pasta packed in Tupperware, each from a different friend, each labeled with a handwritten note of love.

Grace accepted Beth's offer to clear out the nursery for them. When they returned home the white room was bare, but for a large bunch of flowers and a book on loss. For the first few nights Grace would leave their bed in the middle of the night to sleep on the floor in Sam's room under a blue blanket embroidered with an *S*. Dan would wake up alone and find her cried out on the carpet, her nose red and puffy.

"I'm sorry," she would say when he helped her up. "I don't mean to make this harder for you."

"We have to help each other," he said.

Grace had five months of maternity leave remaining and she decided to take it all. Dan returned to the office after a month.

The grief hit him hardest around six p.m., which was when he would usually come home to his wife and son. This was when Grace was at her most useful. Making dinner became her daily mission. If she did nothing else it was okay, as long as she made Dan dinner. The simple, achievable task gave each day purpose.

The weeks stretched on, boundless and blank. Visitors came but were forgotten the moment they left. Weeks waned but the pain did not.

Grace tried to read to pass the time, but she couldn't focus. She tried to run, but she had no stamina.

"How will we go on, Dan?" Grace asked, as she slotted another gift of lasagna into the freezer one unremarkable day.

"Perhaps we could get that dog we were talking about?" Dan said.

"I don't think I'm ready."

"We can go somewhere," Dan said. "Somewhere completely different."

"That's not a bad idea," said Grace weakly.

"Asia? Or Eastern Europe."

"Yes, I like that. I want to be as far away as possible," Grace said. "Somewhere nothing can remind me of him."

Forty-Five

"IT'S HERE." NICK DRAGGED THE CARDBOARD BOX INTO THE cramped Coogee lounge room. "I'll set it up in the bedroom until we get the keys to the house."

"Thanks. When did I think I was going to shop for cribs and strollers with a new baby to care for?" Priya was seated on her couch with her son in one arm and a bottle in the other hand, trying to gently press the teat between his lips. Bags of hand-me-down baby clothes crowded around the two of them like nosy relatives. Priya's feet were propped up on the box the new car seat had come in.

"I understand why you didn't want to fill the house with baby things until after the hearing. Imagine having to return them if the judge had gone the other way," Nick said, scoring the tape that sealed the box with his Stanley knife. Neither spoke for a moment. Specters of Grace and Dan Arden packing away all of their baby's things hung in the air.

"Anyway, we've done all right." Nick started pulling crib pieces from the flat pack.

Viv had loaned Priya a truckload of stuff, but now Priya wanted to give her baby his own things. It was irrational, but she knew everything in the Arden house would have been new, and she didn't want any less for him now that he lived with her. Already she feared she was falling short.

"He won't feed," Priya said, as her son again twisted away from the bottle.

"He's adjusting."

"I want everything to be perfect for him. I keep thinking, what if he's sad? What if he misses Grace and Dan? What if I inflicted that on him?"

"Pri." Nick sat on the couch beside her. "You can't think like that."

"When he won't eat, I think, is it my fault?"

"You're just tired." The bottle teat slipped into Sam's mouth and soon he began to suckle hungrily. "There now, does that look like the face of a miserable baby?"

"No," she said, stroking his cheek with her thumb. "He's a prince."

"It's natural to take time to acclimatize. You'll see. When we've moved into the new house you'll feel much more like yourself. Maybe we could have a little party. Introduce everyone to him. Like a naming day."

"I like that idea." She smiled. "I was thinking I would keep his name. He's been Sam all his life. I don't want to change him. Not after all the other change he's been through."

"You don't think it will upset you to use the name the other couple gave him?"

"No. I had an uncle Samad. It means 'eternal.' Sadavir can be his middle name."

"Sam Sadavir Laghari," Nick said, caressing the baby's cheek. "What adventures you'll have."

Forty-Six

ASHLEY LI LEANED FORWARD AND ADJUSTED HER SKIRT, thinking she had to be the only person on earth who returned from a shoestring tour of Asia having put on weight. She had not had time to shop for a new outfit, so her waistband was cutting uncomfortably into her side.

"And you left your last job because . . . ?"

"Umm." She still hadn't come up with a satisfactory answer to that question: something that wouldn't cast her in a bad light, but was also truthful. *I walked out on my much older lover after he covered up a major medical error, which I also had a hand in* wouldn't do.

"It was time to move on," she said.

The interviewer grunted. "It's perplexing. Empona is so revered. And you're not without a profile yourself." He raised his eyebrows, wanting Ashley to elaborate.

Ashley's fingers curled tightly around the leather portfolio on her lap. "I'm looking for new challenges," she said, not untruthfully.

Doctor Forsyth's clinic was the last on her list of prospects. He was a round-faced man of roughly fifty, and his questioning was far more pointed than she had been prepared for. He was looking down at her résumé, frowning, until he clicked his tongue and passed it back to her.

"I'm sorry, Doctor Li, I'm looking for a very specific skill set and you're just not the right candidate."

She smiled. "Doctor Forsyth, I have addressed every single point on the advertised selection criteria. If anything, I'm overqualified." Her voice acquired a tremble. She hadn't worked in months, and she had been told she wasn't right for every other job she had interviewed for that week. She swallowed. "If the issue is money I can be flexible."

"That may be true. But a team is like a machine. Every single piece has a purpose, and I'm afraid you're not fit for our purpose."

"But if you'll just—"

He stood. "Thank you for coming in, Doctor Li."

"Well," she said. "If anything should come up that I would be a right fit for . . ."

"I have your details." He did not return her smile.

"Thank you."

As she turned and walked toward the door her eyes alighted on a framed certificate from Monash Medical School, class of 1990. It was the same institution Roger had attended, in the same graduating year.

⁓

"I've reached the end of the line," Ashley told her mother as they strolled along the Bronte foreshore. "Roger has blacklisted me. He knows or wields influence over every fertility specialist in Sydney."

"How can that man still be practicing after what the clinic did?" Wendy Li asked.

"The commissioner investigated it. He was fined. I heard on the grapevine Empona has instituted a barcoding system for every patient, and every single movement now has to be double-checked."

"And he wasn't sanctioned?"

"It was human error. No lives were lost. He didn't breach any rules. The industry is self-governing." Ashley kicked a stone that was lying in her path.

Thanks to the evidence she provided, a ruling had found that Ashley played no role in the mistake; rather, the embryologist who failed to properly clean the catheter was at fault. However, the investigator had also noted the embryologist had done everything required and the blunder was chalked up to a learning experience. It was an unfortunate, unforeseeable error, the report concluded. Roger had managed to minimize the damage to his reputation by having the finding supressed. He claimed it was necessary to protect the baby involved from prying journalists.

"He settled with the families," Ashley told her mother. "It was all dealt with very quickly. I think he wanted to avoid a trial. I don't know the exact payouts, but they were huge. The mother will never have to worry about her baby's financial future. The Ardens got even more."

"That's fair enough."

"I think about them every day. I liked them. Particularly Grace." A shiver of guilt passed through Ashley's body. "Perhaps I deserve to be blacklisted."

"That's not true." Wendy pressed her daughter's arm. "You did nothing wrong. Things will die down. You have plenty of money to see you through. Why don't you take some time off? Learn Mandarin properly. Or French cooking."

"I took a break. I need to work."

"Roger Osmond's influence doesn't extend beyond Sydney."

"He was trained in Melbourne."

"So go to Brisbane."

Ashley gazed out at the ocean. She and Roger had stayed in Brisbane for a conference during her last year at Empona. It was pretty. It had Sydney's sunny disposition without its big city aggression. But it didn't feel right.

"Perhaps I need to get away completely. Start over somewhere I can do something useful with my skills, where the reward isn't measured in dollars."

She had seen so many things during her travels. In India, her friend Lata had lectured her over daal about the impending gender-imbalance crisis caused by the corrupt use of sex-selection technology in a country where a boy is more desirable. In South Korea she'd heard stories of baby boxes, which had been set up so desperate women had somewhere safe to put unwanted infants. Since Ashley chose her destinations based on where her old university friends were living, she tended to experience each country through the lens of the newly born.

In the Philippines she had met up with her friend Samara De Silva, who was on a sabbatical at a university hospital training young doctors in assisted-reproduction advancements.

"This country has a huge problem with abandoned children, and here I am engineering babies for those who otherwise might adopt," Samara had said. "It's so frustrating, but it makes money for the hospital, which is desperately needed."

They had walked to the viewing bay where babies who were just hours old slept behind a window while their mothers recuperated. The nurses had swaddled them in a triangular style so that the blanket ended in two points. Ashley put a hand to the glass. There was something heartwarming about the provincial swaddling style. The past year had been a long and lonely battle with her demons and now here she was, in the middle of the Philippines, looking at newborns wrapped up like unbaked samosas, smiling.

"Aren't they adorable little things?" Samara said.

Afterward they ate kaldereta from one of the dozens of open-faced food places that operated in an alleyway along the western flank of the hospital.

"I really love it here," Samara said. "Even though what I'm doing is nonessential, I feel like I'm helping them exploit a profitable service that will ultimately be good for the hospital. And God knows they need it."

Barefoot children ran up and down the alley. Occasionally one stopped and held out a palm for money. Samara produced a seemingly endless stream of coins for the outstretched hands. "How long have you been traveling around the Philippines?"

"Just a week, but I've been on the move for about nine months now," Ashley said.

"Reclaiming your misspent youth?"

"Actually, I'm getting a little restless. Bored, I guess."

"You know, this is a beautiful part of the world. Troubled, of course, but it's sunny every day and they could really use someone with your expertise."

Ashley, nodding, had said: "I should look into it."

And she had meant to. But she didn't. Until now. Now she would. She had to.

Forty-Seven

"IS THAT IT?"

The waiter had placed a slice of fish in front of Dan. The underside was a pearly white, but on top the silver skin looked slimy, and the fin, which was still attached, threatened to start flapping around any moment. "I know they said fresh, but I was expecting some sort of food preparation," he said.

"That's their speciality here," Grace replied, lifting a neat square of blushing salmon with her chopsticks. "I'm sure it will be delicious."

Dan cautiously sliced off a small corner of flesh—the knife glided through like butter—dabbed it in the sauce, and put it in his mouth.

"Well?" Grace asked.

"Oh, it's amazing." Dan sighed.

"Mine too, but I don't get any pleasure from it," she said, glum.

"What do you say afterward we go out in search of some Japanese dessert? Are you game for some black sesame ice cream?"

Grace nodded and reached across the table for his hand, grateful, despite everything, to have found such a marvelous man.

They had first traveled to Japan and tried to lose themselves in onsens and sushi bars. Next, Grace booked a hotel room in Reykjavík, Iceland, a city that smelled like fresh-cut pine and snow. They swam in the Blue Lagoon and drank frosty beer while submerged in milky water under a dome of blue sky, and Grace could almost imagine a time when she would not be miserable. Almost.

Then they went to Germany, and then on to Slovenia. They admired Lake Bled and skirted the Alps. Word came that Elliott's application for leave to appeal had been refused. Heartbroken, they detoured through Belgium, searching for respite. Grace made a study of chocolate fudge truffles, though they tasted like ash in her mouth. The beer might as well have been bilge water. Both she and Dan grew thin, despite their efforts at indulgence.

When Grace saw kids running barefoot through the busy streets of Naples she thought again about fostering a little one who needed a stable home. The vague notion both excited and scared her.

She felt like she was waiting, but for what she couldn't say. A resolution? She knew there could be no happy ending. Sometimes her grief filled her with a dark dread and made it seem like there was nothing left to look forward to. There was something about flying that triggered it, the sense of expectation a voyage brought with it that was somehow hollow because they couldn't outrun their loss. It traveled with them. In them.

As she contemplated her options while waiting for the lights to change at a smoggy Napoli intersection, she felt a tug on her shirt. It was a little boy holding up an empty, gnawed McDonald's cup, begging for change. Grace dropped in a five-euro note and knew what she wanted to do next.

"Dan," she said, "let's go home."

Forty-Eight

SAMARA PUT IN A GOOD WORD FOR ASHLEY, WHO SOON FOUND herself on staff at the University Foundation Hospital in Angeles City. It was a strange town. The sun perpetually shone, but the air was hazy. And despite the manifold churches and the religious icons that filled shop windows, the rosary beads that dangled from car mirrors, and the tropical flowers that made every street corner and shop appear to have been festooned with leis, there was an air of seediness in the dirt-poor town.

The hospital, however, was efficient and clean. Much of the equipment was ancient, but it was well maintained by fastidious staff. From time to time a diplomat or businessman would come in with his wife for fertility treatment, but mostly Ashley delivered babies. At dusk she rode her bike home to her house in a gated community, past boxy buildings and exposed wires. The work was easy, but the challenge of finding her way in a foreign country invigorated her.

She and Samara would often meet for lunch, eschewing the American fast-food chains that dominated the main road, instead eating sisig and adobo with perfectly caramelized pork, and icy halo-halo on stools in the sun outside the alley stalls.

"You don't miss your Sydney life?"

Ashley shrugged. "I miss my mum. But we Skype. It's nice working at this end of the pregnancy, when you get to see the babies, instead of just cells in a dish."

The days went quickly. Whenever Ashley felt low she went up to the viewing area and looked at the babies in their samosa swaddles. She was daydreaming there one rare quiet afternoon when a nurse burst through the stairwell door. "I found you!" she said, her cheeks flushed. "Thank God."

"What's happened?" Ashley asked.

"Come quickly. It's urgent."

Ashley followed the young woman back down the stairs to the neonatal intensive-care unit on level three.

"They're in here," the registrar said, her shoes clipping the linoleum.

Side by side in plastic cribs were two babies with legs like spindles and arms as fragile as twigs. They had no names, no date of birth, and they were desperately malnourished.

Samara was helping one of the specialists, Doctor Marie Chavez. "They can't be more than a day old," Doctor Chavez was saying.

"They don't even look full term," said Samara.

"I'd estimate a gestational age of thirty-two weeks," said Doctor Chavez. "They're small, but they look healthy. Doctor Li, could you please assist? I want a vitamin K shot for each. Doctor De Silva, on top of the normal newborn screens, I want to check blood glucose levels and screen for sepsis, hep B, hep C, and HIV."

"Where's their mother?" Ashley asked.

"They were abandoned."

"How awful. Do we have a next of kin?"

"No, we don't know anything about them," Samara said. "The

police found them in a dumpster wrapped in newspaper. An officer heard a mewling coming from the bin. He thought it was a cat."

Ashley went to one of the babies and administered one milligram of vitamin K. His skin was soft and tattooed with smudged black letters where the newsprint had adhered to his skin.

"Poor little mites," Ashley said, injecting the second baby, who screwed up his face but didn't cry.

"They seem to be responding well," Doctor Chavez said.

Ashley lowered her head so she was level with their little bodies. "What are the police doing about finding their family?"

"They'll investigate, but unless someone comes forward there's not much hope."

"This isn't the first time this has happened," Samara said.

"What will happen to them?"

"The Department of Social Welfare and Development usually takes care of cases like this," Doctor Chavez said.

"State-run care is notoriously overburdened," Samara said sadly.

"There must be a relative who can claim them," Ashley said.

"We'll reach out to the churches."

"Could we get the local paper to run a story?"

Doctor Chavez laid a hand on Ashley's shoulder. "You could try that, but don't get your hopes up. I'm afraid the odds are against these two little ones."

Forty-Nine

GRACE'S CLOTHES HUNG OFF HER. SHE WAS WEARING JEANS from her university years while purging her wardrobe of all the dresses and shirts she wore when she was nursing. She pulled a flannel shirt from the bottom wardrobe drawer and rubbed it against her cheek. Clinging to the cotton fibers was the faint aroma of baby powder, No Tears shampoo, and milk. In other words, Sam. The pain was so acute she gave an involuntary whimper, then she threw the shirt into the packing box that was open at her feet.

Her hair was blond again. The roots that had grown through were tawny, but with a bit of care from her hairdresser the color was restored. She taped up the box of old clothes and carried it downstairs to the car boot. Dan was riding up the street with his backpack slung low on his back. He dismounted and wheeled the bike up the path.

"Looks like a successful morning," Grace said.

"I got eight books," he replied, kissing her.

"I'm glad you're writing a book. I think it will be good for you."

"You're right. A man needs a purpose in life. Did you see the email? We've had another offer on the house. Doug thinks we should hold out."

"No, I didn't see that," Grace said. Dan showed her the offer on his phone. The sale of their Gottenham Street house was part of the purge. But the property market was softening. "Maybe we should accept it. It's the best offer we've had in months," she said. "And it's not like we need the money."

Grace and Dan had accepted a settlement from Empona. It was nowhere near enough for Grace, but it was far more than she wanted. It struck them that there was something grotesque in the suggestion that any amount of money could ever compensate for their loss. She wanted to throw the money in their face. She also wanted to strip them of every last cent.

"I'll go back to work eventually," she said. "And your book is sure to be a bestseller. I just want to be done with this place."

They had already purchased a large blue-and-white weatherboard house with three airy bedrooms and an open-plan living space near Coogee beach. It had fresh paint, fresh carpet, fresh everything. When Grace stood in the middle of the empty living room she could see the ocean.

Dan nodded at the box. "You're packing already."

"It's just some old clothes for Vinnies."

He tapped his backpack. "I'm going to get started on some reading."

Grace returned to the bedroom and ripped more garments from their hangers and stuffed them in plastic bags. In went the yellow dress she had worn on the first fine day she took Sam out in his stroller. In went the red jumper with the knitted baubles that fascinated him and that he loved to grab at with his tiny hands. In went

Dan's Midnight Oil T-shirt that he'd been wearing when she went into labor. He didn't share her need to rid himself of everything Sam had ever touched, but she jammed it deep down among her knits and skirts anyway.

She bundled up the bag and tossed it over her shoulder to put in the car boot. She was three steps from reaching the front door when the doorbell rang.

It was Edna Goss. Desperate to help, she had insisted on tidying Grace and Dan's front garden for the open inspections.

"I was just doing some weeding when the postman came past," she said. "I guess he thought I lived here because he handed this straight to me."

She gave Grace an envelope from the Department of Human Services' Adoption Coordinator. Grace tore it open hungrily, then her face fell. Their latest application had been denied.

Fifty

"THEY'RE LUCKY, REALLY," SAMARA SAID. "THE SANTA MARIA orphanage is a far better outcome than the dumpster they were rescued from."

She and Ashley stood over the twins' humidicribs. It was late and the NICU was quiet except for the hum of machines and the snores of a mother dozing in a chair beside her baby.

"But they deserve someone who will love them. So many people want babies. Can't we do something to help find them a family?" Ashley asked.

She now spent every spare moment in the NICU watching over the twins. She willed them to grow strong, hoping they could sense that someone cared about them.

"You know that adopting through the state can be incredibly slow. The staff are swamped, and without the proper paperwork it can be very difficult to arrange adoptions. How do you get a birth certificate for a baby found hidden in a bin? And that's just the beginning. How do you prove they are eligible for adoption? You need a parental signature, or a death certificate."

"But we tried everything to find their family," Ashley said. "It's so frustrating."

Samara shuffled closer to Ashley and dropped her voice to a whisper. "There might be something you can do."

"Tell me; I'll do anything."

"There's a lawyer down in Manila who's making a little headway expediting the process, and is starting to get a reputation in certain circles. He seems to know who to speak to and what to say."

"How do I find him?"

"I don't remember his full name but I can get it."

At the end of her shift, Ashley went back up to the nursery and gazed at the babies.

"Do you want to come out for a beer?" Samara asked, as she hooked a silk scarf around her neck.

"Thanks, but I have work to do," Ashley lied. The most her night could promise was the glow of the television and a Kingfisher beer, but she wanted to be alone.

She rode her bike home, waved at the sentry guard, and unlocked the padlock on her gate. The fence surrounding her house was a concrete fortress crowned with looped razor wire. A cage within a cage. She let herself in and locked it behind her. The house was dark. She unbuckled her shoes, padded across the tiled lounge room, and retrieved a beer from the fridge.

When she woke up a few hours later she had a text from one of the nurses. It was a photo of the twins, each drinking from a bottle that looked like novelty oversized props in their small hands. *They're drinking by themselves!* was the caption. *They'll be ready to be discharged soon.*

She texted Samara. *Any luck finding that lawyer? We need to move quickly.*

Early the next morning Ashley unchained her bike and rode out to the orphanage. Iron bars confined the white complex like a prison. Rust bled dirty red stains onto the walls. The yard was desolate. Greenery was sparse.

"We can't send them there," Ashley said when she was back in the NICU. "We have to be able to do better for them." Samara took a card from her pocket and handed it to Ashley. "It might take time. And money. But he's your best shot."

As soon as Ashley got home that evening she dialed the number on the card and asked for Mr. Ramirez.

"How can I help?" boomed a voice with a reassuring timbre.

"Hello, Mr. Ramirez. My name is Ashley Li and I'm a doctor based about an hour north of Manila," Ashley began. She felt like she was lining up a job interview. She needed to convince this man to help her. She explained her situation and what she was hoping to do for the two little boys.

"And you say they were found in a dumpster?" the lawyer asked.

"That's right."

"So, no birth certificates?"

"No certificates of any kind," she said. There was an agonizing pause.

"Never mind," Ramirez said. "That's the sort of obstacle I try to overcome. It sounds like these two little ones deserve some loving intervention."

"Yes." Ashley laughed, relieved. "Yes, they do."

They were healthy, she explained, and growing stronger every day. They were alert and playful. She smiled as she pictured them, side by side, in the traditional Angeles City Hospital samosa swaddle. Still, nobody had come forward to claim them. "We tried everything to find a relative," she said.

"Doctor Li, I think we can find a way around this. The first step, which you can initiate at your end, is to have the state declare them abandoned. Now, have you got a pen? I'm going to tell you what you'll need to do . . ."

The final call Ashley made that night was to Australia. She dialed a number she had copied from a website, feeling suddenly nervous, but excited too. The long-distance call rang, then connected.

"Hello," Ashley said. "I'm trying to get in contact with Grace Arden."

Epilogue

IT HAD THUNDERED ALL NIGHT, BUT NOW THE SKY WAS clear. Raindrops beaded windshields, and the neighborhood shone, newly rinsed. Pink worms had risen to the surface of garden beds to writhe in the dirt. The day had been eagerly awaited, but now that it was here, Grace was feeling wistful. It had come too soon.

Sitting on the kitchen countertop were two matching Spider-Man lunch boxes, each containing a ham and cheese sandwich, cut diagonally, along with an apple and a box of sultanas. Water had been decanted into identical drink bottles (also Spider-Man themed) and two bran and blueberry muffins sat beside them, as a treat.

Above her head Grace could hear the *thump-thumpety-thump-thump* of stiff Clarks school shoes running up and down the first-floor passage.

"Dan," she called. "How are we going? It's eight thirty."

"Nearly there."

Soon after came the familiar stampede down the stairs.

"Look at you," she said, beaming at the boys at the bottom of the stairs in their new, oversized uniforms. Everything sat slightly askew.

Dan joined her. "Hold still." He snapped some photos of the boys. "One more. Now a silly one. Good." He hugged them and kissed them goodbye.

Outside the boys jumped in the puddles. "Hey-hey, watch those new shoes," Grace called. "Come on, into the car."

Four legs and four arms tumbled into the back of the family wagon. The boys chatted happily as Grace pulled onto the road and drove toward the small primary school with the blue gates and a path painted with smiling sunflowers.

"You know, I used to be a teacher."

"We know, Mum," Xavier said. His school cap sat low over his brow. He pushed it up so he could see out the window. They passed other children climbing into cars with new backpacks on their backs, on their way to class for the first time.

"What do you think will be the best part of school?" Grace asked.

"I like the alphabet song."

"I like duck-duck-goose."

"And what about the garden? I liked the garden," Grace said. On orientation day they had picked peas and popped them from their pods into a big green bucket.

"Duck-duck-goose."

"Alphabet song!"

Xavier began to sing. "A-B-C-D!"

Joseph followed his brother's example. "E-F-G!"

"H-I-J-K," Grace joined in. "L-M-N-O-Peeee!" The *pee* always cracked the boys up. Grace waited until the cackling stopped and then prompted them: "Q-R-S."

"T-U-V." The chorus continued along its bouncy, singsong way. As she completed a left turn Grace glanced up at her rearview mirror to watch the boys sing together.

When they finished they went back to the beginning. Faster this time, racing each other. Competitiveness, Grace already knew, would be a feature of their shared future. The song was barely over a second when their jaws swung open, poised, as they eyeballed each other—*Shall we?*—and then the alphabet song began again. Double speed this time and punctuated with giggles.

Listening to them, Grace wondered if it was time to go back to work. The boys were doing wonderfully and her psychologist had been gently suggesting she was ready. She wouldn't take on a role at a boardinghouse, or anything that would mean time away from her family. But perhaps she could teach again. She had loved teaching the boys the alphabet song and how to write their names. The first successful attempt was exhibited on the fridge: *Joseph Arden* and *Xavier Arden* spelled out in wonky purple crayon. Grace had never been prouder.

She found a parking space and eased the car into it.

"We're here," she announced. The boys squealed.

They had been so excited about this day—wearing their uniforms around the house—but when they reached the blue school gate their courage disappeared.

"Come on, come on, they'll start without you." Grace nudged them along. "Are we ready?" She took each of the twins by the hand and walked them to the gate. "Now be good boys," she said, kneeling. She picked a piece of lint off Joseph's collar, stalling, surprised by how hard it was to let them go. "Let me just—" She bent and tightened each of their laces.

She was mustering the courage for the final goodbye when she heard something that took her breath away. Her heart stilled. She cocked her ears. It sounded like . . . a woman's voice . . . familiar. She heard it again: "Sam!"

As Grace stood and slowly turned, the hairs on her arms stood up. Before he came into focus she knew it was him. His shiny black curls had come in thick. His big eyes were unforgettable, and now he was running up the sunflower path waving at the kindergarten kids who were arriving for the first time. At this young stage of life, the differences in ages were marked and this little boy, Grace knew, was exactly seven years and nine months old. She was aware that she was staring at him but she couldn't look away. He stopped at the end of the path, where she stood, her boys melting into the folds of her skirt.

"Mummy," the curly-haired boy said, and Grace's heart began to pound. "Mummy!" He turned around. A woman and a little girl who looked to also be starting kindergarten followed the boy up the path. Sam was pointing at Grace. "That lady's got hair like Rapunzel." He turned and ran to his mother and tugged her arm.

"Yes," Priya breathed, barely audible. "Isn't she pretty."

The two women faced each other. Priya's dark hair had also grown long since the trial.

"He's usually very shy," Priya said, with an unsure smile. Grace tried to speak, but she couldn't find the words.

"This is Isa, my daughter," Priya said, then she bent down to the twins. "And who do we have here?"

Grace placed a hand on each boy's shoulder. "This is Xavier, and this is Joseph."

"Aren't they handsome," Priya said. Joseph covered his face with Grace's skirt. "Is it your first day of school?" Priya asked. Xavier nodded.

"I'm in Year Two," Priya's son announced.

Grace crouched. "Hello there, Sam." Tears filled her eyes. For the sake of her boys she held them back, swallowing, and tried to sound normal. "It's very nice to meet you." Shy now, Sam slowly placed his hand in Grace's. For a moment she was confused, and then she realized it was a handshake.

"It's his new trick," Priya said. Laughter bubbled up in Sam as he held Grace's hand and shook. Grace laughed too, tears stinging her eyes. A memory echoed in her head. *A-humph!* Her businessman. He was loved, he was well. For that she could only be thankful.

"You're very tall," said Xavier.

"I'm in Year Two," Sam said again.

"He's doing very well," Priya said gently.

Grace discreetly swiped the tears from her eyes with her knuckle.

"The boys are very excited about the school garden," Grace told Sam. "Do you like the garden?"

Sam nodded. "We've got a new hen," he said. "Her name is Pumpkin."

"Pumpkin?" Grace said. "That's a funny name for a chicken."

"It's because she's orange and round." Sam puffed out his cheeks like a blowfish. The twins cackled with glee and the sound lightened Grace's heart.

"Want to see?" Sam asked.

Xavier and Joseph nodded eagerly.

"I'll show you," Sam said, his bashfulness gone.

He took each twin by the hand and they ran toward the garden, with its tomato vines and blossoming sweet peas, leaving their mothers behind them, watching on. As the sun warmed the schoolyard and the squeals of children filled the air, each woman was able to take a breath and watch, sharing a brief, shining moment of pride.

Acknowledgments

THANKS FIRST AND FOREMOST TO MY WRITING PARTNER, BEN Phillips, who loved this book before it existed and helped bring it to life. Thank you also to Jacinta White and Anna Fox, who were, as ever, generous early readers who provided invaluable advice, insight, and feedback.

I owe an enormous debt of gratitude to my agent, Jeanne Ryckmans, for her enthusiasm and dedication, along with everyone at Cameron's Management, especially James Ward. Thank you to everyone at Allen and Unwin who worked to shape my lump-of-clay manuscript into a polished book, especially my editor Tessa Feggans and copy editor Claire de Medici and, of course, my publisher Annette Barlow. Thank you, Annette, for believing in this story, but more important, thank you for taking time out of your busy schedule in 2012 to have a coffee with an aspiring writer and offer some much-needed advice. I am so glad you have been the one to bring this story into the world. Thank you too to Monique Cowper and Stefanie Costi, who were able to offer feedback on IVF and family law—any mistakes are mine alone—and Nicole Hickson for her sharp eye.

I have the good fortune of being surrounded by dedicated, creative minds in my day job at the *Australian Women's Weekly* and must make special mention of my editor Samantha Trenoweth, who is endlessly patient, supportive, and wise. Sarah Akikusa, Anna Whitelaw, Bianca Hall, Erin Birch, Amber Manto, Andy Cameron, Melinda Oliver, and Emma Owen have been there as I've attempted to build a career as an author over many years, as has my family, particularly my sister Viv, brothers Joe and Bede, Gabe, and our matriarch, Barbara Blair, and for that I would like to say: Your love and faith are appreciated more than words can express. And finally, thank you to my mother, Margy Blair.